W9-BAU-375

3/15

IMPASSE

Also by Royce Scott Buckingham

IMPASSE

Royce Scott Buckingham

Thomas Dunne Books
St. Martin's Press ⚏ New York

This is a work of fiction. All of the characters, organizations, and events portrayed in this novel are either products of the author's imagination or are used fictitiously.

THOMAS DUNNE BOOKS.
An imprint of St. Martin's Press.

www.thomasdunnebooks.com
www.stmartins.com

Library of Congress Cataloging-in-Publication Data

Buckingham, Royce
    Impasse : a novel / Royce Scott Buckingham.—First edition.
        pages ; cm
    ISBN 978-1-250-01154-1 (hardcover)
    ISBN 978-1-250-02106-9 (e-book)
  1. Wilderness areas—Alaska—Fiction. 2. Wilderness survival—Fiction.
3. Revenge—Fiction. I. Title.
    PS3602.U2644I47 2015
    813'.6—dc23

                                                    2014037067

St. Martin's Press books may be purchased for educational, business, or promotional use. For information on bulk purchases, please contact the Macmillan Corporate and Premium Sales Department at 1-800-221-7945, extension 5442, or write to specialmarkets@macmillan.com.

First Edition: March 2015

10 9 8 7 6 5 4 3 2 1

This book is dedicated to those among us who are not terribly fond of lawyers.

ACKNOWLEDGMENTS

I'd like to thank my editor, Brendan Deneen,
primarily for being a cool guy.

IMPASSE

PROLOGUE

"No body, no case," Stuart Stark's fellow attorneys at the Bristol County, Massachusetts, DA's Office had warned him. He'd tried the Butz murder anyway. But as he lay dying in a ramshackle cabin in the middle of the Alaska interior wondering if he could fit the business end of the borrowed Browning .30-06 in his mouth and still reach the trigger, he wished he had listened to them.

When Marti Taylor remarried to become the second Mrs. Raymond Butz, her decision had been bad for a number of reasons besides the obvious downgrade in surname. One of those reasons was Ray's anger problem. Marti struggled with a scrapbooking addiction, and on March seventeenth at five thirty in the evening, after a Visa bill containing three hundred dollars in charges from the Scrap-a-Doodle store arrived in the mail at their subsidized low-income apartment in northern New Bedford, Ray had strangled her to death with a ligature—probably his belt; he worked construction and didn't own a tie. It was a clean killing that left no blood at the home, the presumptive murder site. The blood came later, on Bolt Construction's private fishing boat, the *Iron Maiden*, where Butz worked as a deckhand when construction was slow, and where he cut his wife into pieces with a blue Ryobi reciprocating saw. Marti and the Ryobi then went over the side, never to be seen again.

Over the three years taken to investigate the case, Butz was interviewed a total of six times. The first five times he was not in custody when questioned, and so his Miranda rights were neither required nor given. He provided bits of incriminating information each time. On the final occasion, he was arrested, Mirandized, and he quickly exercised his right to have an attorney present, effectively ending the interview. Thirteen days later, in the local jail while awaiting trial, he gave his cell mate a full description of what he'd done, not realizing that such information could be used by his questionable confidant as currency to secure a plea bargain in his own drug offense. Between Butz's six interviews and blathering in jail, Raymond fully admitted the crime and twenty separate corroborating details. Enough for up-and-coming Assistant District Attorney Stuart Stark to convict him at the highest profile trial in New Bedford history since Lizzie Borden.

The news crews were camped out at the courthouse—a true-crime author was including the case in a book—and *America's Unsolved* followed Stu around with cameras during the trial, putting his confidence and legal prowess on display for the entire world, or at least the true-crime and reality TV–watching world.

After the verdict, Stu played modest, crediting his sharp lead detective, Randy "Rusty" Baker, for obtaining the confessions. It was always good for a prosecutor to give the investigating officers credit—they earned it, and it earned Stu Rusty's undying friendship. Stu told his adoring public that he was satisfied with the outcome, but that it was unseemly for an assistant DA to publicly celebrate the condemnation of a man. Then he returned to his office, closed the door, and called his greatest cheerleader—his wife, Katherine—who celebrated for him.

"I can't wait to tell everyone I'm married to the most famous lawyer in Massachusetts!" She whooped into the phone.

Nine months later Butz walked out a free man.

It was "unfortunate," in the opinion of the Court of Appeals, a quirk in the law, they said, but dictated by precedent.

The corpus delicti rule in a no-body homicide required proof that (1) the person was dead, and (2) that a criminal act caused the death. Simple enough. But the cause of death had to be established by other evidence *before* the suspect's own statements could be admitted. Otherwise, a crazy person could confess to crimes that might never have happened, the Court said. The prosecution had to prove there *was* a murder before anyone could confess to it.

Regrettably, in this particular no-body homicide, a missing woman was not enough to establish murder as the cause of death. The fact that Butz wore a belt didn't prove anything without his confession to his cell mate that he'd used it to choke the life out of his compulsively scrapbooking spouse. The missing Ryobi? The absence of evidence was less compelling than the useless presence of the belt. And the blood that might have indicated a death by criminal means? On the deck of a fishing boat regularly awash with fish guts, the forensics produced little more than conflicting results and a lot of hydrogen peroxide.

Without Butz's full confession, there was simply no evidence to establish that Marti had been murdered. The Court had no choice, the justices lamented, but to suppress everything Butz had said. They sent the case back for retrial, disallowing the confession, knowing full well that, without it, refiling the case against Raymond Butz would be impossible.

"Unfortunate," the Court declared in its unanimous written opinion.

The opinion was unfortunate enough that the young assistant DA and star of *America's Unsolved,* who had boldly volunteered to handle the case and become a media sensation, was fired. The elected DA of Bristol County, Robert Malloy, couldn't weather being blamed for having a confessed murderer walk free on his watch, not in an election year. Instead of being his boss's presumptive successor, Stuart Stark became the most famous lawyer in Massachusetts ever to lose a case and his job in the same week.

And so, after placing his law enforcement badge in Malloy's in-box, Stu returned to his office, closed his door, kicked his government-issue metal desk once as hard as he could, swore quietly to himself, and limped away from criminal law forever.

CHAPTER 1

Stu circled the block to find street parking. He could usually get a spot by the curb in front of the firm, and he finally squeezed his aging Ford Taurus between a beat-to-hell Chevy Silverado and the orange Prius with a white skull on its hood, owned by the tattoo artist down the block. He slid coins into the meter for the maximum two-hour period. He would hustle downstairs to feed it again three more times that day at ten, during lunch, and at two in the afternoon. Parking enforcement knocked off at three thirty. It worked out to a monthly amount that was less than a parking garage, even if he included the inevitable ten-dollar ticket he received on occasion.

The two-man firm's office was a low-rent second-floor space in the five-story Bluestone Building in Clark's Cove. A relic of New Bedford's textile industry past, the Bluestone was almost devoid of tenants. It also wasn't as close to the courthouse as he would have liked. Nor was it blue or stone or particularly attractive. But after shelling out good money for their online research service and a full-time secretary, they couldn't afford much more. They had, however, invested several thousand dollars they couldn't afford in the huge BUCHANAN, STARK & ASSOCIATES sign, which lorded over the postage stamp patch of grass out front. Stu fertilized the lawn himself early every fall and mowed it each week. There were no true associates in the firm, but they did partner with other local attorneys when cases were outside their expertise, and they had a recent graduate working ten hours per week doing cheap research for them while she studied for the bar exam.

BUCHANAN, STARK & ASSOCIATES

Stu took a moment to hate the gaudy sign. His partner was Clayton Buchanan, the handsome face of the tiny firm who jokingly called himself the Drizzle Maker. It was a modest nickname; Clay was as gregarious as Stuart was cautious. As a result, Clay brought in the work, and Stu did it. Stu had become the quiet workhorse, something Katherine lamented. Wooing clients was a game for the bold, the risk-takers. Not him. Not anymore. Clay, on the other hand, could backslap a local politician, swap profane limericks with a dockworker, and pick up a virgin in a church pew. Clay had once gotten them a client by taking a smoke break with a guy, despite the fact that Clay didn't smoke. He'd grabbed a dirty butt from the cat-litter-filled ashtray atop the public garbage can, stuffed it in his mouth without hesitation, and joined the man in the Plexiglas shelter. After ten minutes of empathy puffs, he walked away with 33 percent of a solid L&I claim. In this, and other creative ways, Clay found clients, while Stu buried himself in cases and codes. It was satisfactory to Stu. And besides, Clay hated doing work.

Stu hiked up the worn concrete rear stairwell to the second floor—the landlord no longer maintained the elevator in the foyer. He still marveled at how he'd fallen in with Clay, who was not from New England originally. They'd gone to the same law school, the University of Oregon; that was the root of their association. Stu had impulsively gone west because his college sweetheart had told him he had "no sense of adventure" when she broke up with him just before going to Europe her junior year. He still wasn't sure why Clay had landed at U of O.

So they were both Fighting Ducks. But Stu had been in the class a year ahead of Clay, and they hadn't spoken more than a few words to each other in the two years they'd overlapped. Stu had noticed Clay's arrival at Oregon. Everyone had. The guy had shown up a neatly dressed kid with an undergraduate record cobbled together from several obscure colleges, and he strutted into the law school's huge main hallway looking far too comfortable for a recent undergrad stepping into the pressure cooker, already joking with the back-row guys, and with his hand on the hip of Sophia Baron, a shockingly pretty second-year gal from Portland, Oregon, who Stu hadn't even had the courage to speak to his entire first year.

The only class Stu and Clay had taken together was Civil Procedure II in Stu's third year, Clay's second. Clay sat mostly in the back, but one day he'd plopped himself down next to Stu with nothing but a pencil and a single sheet of paper, whereupon they'd had their most memorable, and longest, exchange of law school. The professor was already lecturing when Clay sat down, leaned over, and whispered to Stu in an overly familiar manner, as though they were already in on a secret together.

"You've got the best seat if someone comes in and shoots the place up. Is that why you picked it?"

"Excuse me?"

"The brick half-wall will protect you. All you need to do is drop down behind it. Anyone bursting in here would come through that right-hand door. Your exit is down here at the end of the row on the left. If it happens, you're golden. My seat's next best."

That was the extent of the conversation. Stu had turned his attention back to the lecture. By the end of the period he had scribbled seven pages of notes. He glanced over at Clay's paper. The only writing was a diagram of the room with arrows pointing to the two exits and Xs through a dozen seats nearest the right-hand door.

The Bluestone's rear stairwell was dim and echoed, and Stu's footfalls were fifteen pounds heavier than they'd been when he'd left the DA's office with his tail between his legs. The stairway rail was loose and rattled as he used it to pull himself up the steps.

I need to work out more.

He thought the same thing every day, but he never did work out more. He wasn't *un*healthy, and his wife liked him "fine" the way he was. Katherine had said so just that morning as she wished him a happy fortieth birthday.

"Forty." He said it aloud to see what it sounded like. It sounded old, and as he trudged up the back stairs of the low-rent office building in a cheap brown suit, it echoed through the stairwell like the voice of a ghostly harbinger of ominous tidings.

After law school Stu had sought his first job at the Bristol County District Attorney's Office. His grades were good—top 10 percent—and his criminal coursework and internships had prepared him for precisely such work. He wrote his résumé to fit the position exactly, and he'd prepared night and day for the nerve-rattling mock trial they'd put him through at the end of the four-day interview and callback process, practicing his arguments in the mirror, the shower, the car, and one final time outside the courthouse before he went in. The entire office full of experienced assistant district attorneys sat in a jury box staring at him while two senior attorneys put him through his paces, objecting during his faux direct examination of the fake witnesses, and moving to dismiss his entire case at the close of his case in chief. Worst of all, Malloy, the elected prosecutor, acted as judge.

He'd made a titanic effort and, somewhat to his surprise, he'd won the job over nineteen other impressive men and women. Soon he was standing in front of juries trying misdemeanors—driving under the influence and minor domestic assaults mostly—and it didn't take him long to earn a solid reputation as a well-prepared and confident trial attorney.

A year later Clay arrived like a couch-surfing fraternity pal. Only, Stuart had hardly known him then. He showed up in the lobby, unannounced, wearing a sweatshirt and asking the receptionist for "Stu, a good friend of mine from law school."

"Hey, Stu," he said when Stuart stuck his head out through the security door to see who was asking for him. "Good to see you! Aren't you going to invite me in?"

Clay said he was in New England for a few days. He'd remembered Stu from law school and had heard he was practicing in the area. "And what a coincidence," Clay explained, because he was looking to work in a DA's office too, and he was just starting to send out résumés. Could he speak to Stu's boss while he was in town? Clay talked fast, and somehow they'd ended up in Malloy's office, yucking it up with him about Oregon football and NCAA sanctions. Before he knew it, Stu was explaining to Clay about the mock trial, which Malloy had said they could throw together for the next day. It was a surprise, and with one day to prepare, Stu was certain it would be a disaster, but Clay insisted that he could interview immediately.

"Stuart can help me," he joked. "And loan me a suit."

Clay took Stu out for Thai food that night and paid even though he had student loans. He joked that it was his "thirty-dollar bribe."

Stu offered advice. "You'll want to research the areas of search and seiz—"

Clay leaned forward over his green curry. "Cut the crap, Stu. What are the answers?"

When Stu hesitated, Clay pressed him.

"You said yourself it's impossible to prepare in one day, and I know you wouldn't leave a classmate standing there with his dick hanging out, would you?"

Stu wasn't sure exactly what Clay meant, but he certainly didn't want it to happen.

The objections were standard—hearsay, relevance, and a demand for an offer of proof—all basic evidentiary rules easily dealt with if a guy knew they were coming, and Stu knew exactly which ones were coming. The motion to dismiss was trickier—failure to establish jurisdiction. This was handled more subtly, through a request that the judge take judicial notice of the location of the road upon which the fictitious officer had stopped the fictitious car. Most new lawyers wouldn't think of it. Nor would Clay, had Stu not warned him, but he did.

With one day's prep and Stu's help, Clay got the same offer for which Stu had prepared his entire law school career. The fact that Clay's grades were mediocre didn't matter. His transcript didn't even arrive until after the paperwork was signed with personnel and he was already screwing one of the secretaries. It didn't matter that he'd only taken one criminal course, or that he had no internships involving crime. He'd simply buddied up to the boss and then impressed the entire office with his ability to think on his feet—with a little help from Stu, or, more accurately, a little cheating. It was a well-spent thirty dollars.

Six years later, when the Butz disaster happened, Stu had nowhere to go. About that time, Clay unexpectedly turned in his resignation. "I just need a change," he said. "Five years under the fucking microscope is enough for me." With a good bit of prodding and cajoling, Clay convinced Stu not to give up on life or law and to start over in private practice with him. Katherine lamented Stu's demotion as much or more than he did. His rise in the DA's office had been steady, and the social status they were beginning to attain about town was considerable. They were invited to political events and charity auctions, where Katherine remembered everyone's name and distributed polite hugs like candy. Everyone had agreed that he would have the top spot one day, and Katherine had talked him up the most.

Instead he'd slunk off in shame, hung out his shingle, and had his name engraved on Clay's ridiculous lawn sign. He'd only had the energy to demand one deal-breaker stipulation: the firm would do no criminal defense work. None. Zero. Period. And with that they'd begun their struggle in private practice without government medical benefits, pensions, or paid vacations.

Stu blinked and realized he'd been standing on the cement landing outside his office for several minutes. Just standing. Thinking. Remembering. Wondering what might have been, while in front of him stood the worn, ill-fitting, painted-over door to what was. He reached out and jiggled the handle until it opened.

"Can we get that fixed?" he asked their all-in-one receptionist, secretary, and paralegal, Pauline. She was a plain woman from across the New

Bedford-Fairhaven Bridge in Fairhaven and dressed in a loud fuchsia dress. Her body was lumpy, and the edges of her shapeless face were defined only by the white base makeup she caked on like a mime's mask; otherwise, her face would have melted directly into her neck. She'd been married since high school. Three kids. Good at her job. She knew how to do some legal research. More important, she had previously worked at the courthouse. Ergo, she knew the judge's clerks and their labyrinthine system of document formatting and filing.

"I think there's a screwdriver in the miscellaneous drawer," Pauline replied, tilting her head toward a bank of aging cabinets without looking up.

"Can't you call Sitzman?"

"We get one hundred dollars off our rent if we don't call the landlord for thirty days, and we're on day twenty-four."

Stu put down his car keys, loosened his tie, and headed for the cabinet. He fished around inside and came up with the screwdriver, an extra from his own home that he'd donated to the cause.

"Clay's in his office," Pauline mentioned as Stu passed her on his way back to the broken door.

Stu glanced at the clock: ten minutes after eight. Clay was never in his office before nine. "What's the occasion?"

"I don't know." She paused dramatically. "Maybe it's the letter we received from Shubert, Garvin and Ross."

The Molson case! Stu thought. Their best chance yet at breaking out of their scrape-and-hustle private practice funk. Two weeks earlier Stu had sent a demand letter outlining the reasons that Shubert, Garvin and Ross should settle for an amount that might just fix their broken elevator and door. *If things go right, it could buy us an entirely new elevator, and perhaps a new building to go around it.*

He'd been checking the mail every day for a response and, apparently, Clay was sitting in his office casually mulling it over with his morning coffee.

"Good news?"

Pauline gave him a coy shrug.

CHAPTER 2

The Molson case was a hot potato that had bounced around town, with at least two other more prominent firms passing on it. The client, Sylvia Molson, had been crossing in front of a Mazda Miata stopped at an intersection when the defendant, Yuri Blastos, struck the Miata from the rear with his hulking Nissan Armada, a vehicle so big it was named after a fleet of ships. It catapulted the diminutive sports car onto Sylvia, snapping her neck at the second vertebra. He'd been drinking, and fault was easy to establish. The defendant, however, was judgment proof—he had no money. He was also uninsured. Sylvia, a yoga instructor and mother of two, was suddenly in a wheelchair for the rest of her life. Her own auto insurance paid her the limits of her policy for an uninsured motorist, but it would not be nearly enough for her care.

But Sylvia was a chipper, optimistic woman. She'd wheeled into Buchanan, Stark & Associates and been undeterred by the broken elevator; she yelled up the back stairwell until Pauline had come down to find her stuck at the bottom of the steps. Stu had carried her up the stairs himself, then hurried off to review the case while Clay signed her on as a client.

Stu wasn't optimistic that he would find something two other teams of lawyers had missed, especially because Buchanan, Stark hadn't dealt with many personal injury cases. Their biggest had been a severed finger. Lost digits were assigned different values under the law—a thumb being the amputated digit jackpot—and all they'd gotten was a measly pinky.

The police reports said that Blastos had consumed eight beers over three hours and had blown a .11 on the breathalyzer machine, well over the .08 legal limit. He hadn't slowed at the intersection, judging from the absence of skid marks prior to the point of impact. He was at fault, no doubt.

Blastos worked as an inspector for Septi-Spect, a small company that inspected septic systems. Septi-Spect was, in turn, owned by Jennings Plumbing, an international company. Jennings had deep pockets—they could pay for a catastrophic injury. But the state police report did not attribute any fault to Jennings. Blastos was driving his own car at the time of the collision, not an inspection vehicle. He was not on his way to or from an inspection site. According to the report, he was neither working as an employee at the time nor acting on the company's behalf. In fact, he'd gotten off work three hours earlier, and the company had a strict policy against drinking when their drivers were working. They were 100 percent not responsible for any accident caused by off-duty drinking. No doubt. Complete dead end. Multiple prior lawyers had said so.

But Stu hadn't given up, or, more accurate, he hadn't had enough other work to keep himself otherwise occupied. He made a motion to obtain Blastos's cell phone records, even though it was well established that his company phone was hanging on a hook at the office at the time of the crash, where he put it every day when he left work.

But Stu didn't request the man's *company* phone records. He requested his *private* cell phone records. Stu didn't even know if there was a private cell phone. It turned out there was. And there was one call on the day of the collision. It came in at 5:15 p.m., thirty-two seconds before Sylvia Molson lost the use of all her limbs. When Stu received the cell records, he called the number. The dispatcher at Septi-Spect answered.

Bingo!

Although Septi-Spect had a long-standing written policy against drinking and driving, it did *not* yet have a policy against talking and driving. They'd meant to update their guidelines, they said, but hadn't gotten around to it. In other words, they were aware of the problem and did nothing about it until it was too late for Sylvia Molson. To make matters worse, they had a custom of calling their drivers en route to sites in order to alert them to inspection appointment changes. They were making just such a call to Blastos to tell him about an appointment change the next morning.

Bingo again!

It still wasn't enough. There was the alcohol problem. Did the Septi-Spect cell phone call cause the wreck or did the alcohol? If it was the alcohol, then Blastos owed, and he had no money. If it was the cell phone, Jennings, Inc. and their millions in assets could be tapped for the cost of Sylvia's injuries.

This was where joint and several liability came in, a legal principle that law nerds, like Stu, found fascinating. Stu named both Blastos and Jennings, Inc. in the lawsuit. If the jury found Jennings partially liable, say even 1 percent, Blastos and Jennings would be responsible for the entire verdict jointly. Normally, Blastos would have to pay 99 percent and Jennings 1 percent. However, the joint and several rule was designed to make the plaintiff whole. If Blastos couldn't pay his 99 percent—and he certainly couldn't—then Jennings was responsible for paying the entire amount to Sylvia. Jennings, in turn, was permitted to go after Blastos for indemnification. But so long as Sylvia got paid, they could damn well take it out of his turd-inspecting wages for the next few centuries, as far as Stu was concerned.

This was Stu's theory of the case, and his demand letter laid it out in painstaking detail so that Jennings would know exactly what they were up against when considering whether to settle. He included a vivid quote from Sylvia describing the enduring image of a small blue sports car taking flight and blocking out the sun.

"Bad news, pal," Clay said, propping his feet on the desk as Stu walked into his office. "I'm going to have to fire you."

Clay wore an aging navy suit, yet he made it look good, filling out his fitted white shirt with a healthy chest. He also had hair that never seemed to need combing, but simply fell into place. Stu's own shirts were a boxy traditional cut, which helped to hide holiday weight gains. And he could comb his hair for an hour without ever getting it to fall right; although, at his age, he supposed he should just be thankful he didn't have a horseshoe of thin hair framing a shiny bald spot.

"You can't fire me," Stu replied. "We're partners. We'd have to dissolve."

"Like a body in acid."

"Morbid, but yeah. Now, show me the letter."

Clay held it up, teasing. "You sure you want to know?"

"Yes."

"I'll give you a hint. They think your theory of liability is novel."

Stu gritted his teeth, annoyed. "So now they'll move for summary judgment and try to dismiss our case? Fine. Bring it on. But if we get past the motion, we'll have sufficient leverage to settle. Their exposure could be more than our demand letter requested. Sylvia is going to need care for the rest of her life."

Clay laughed. "You and your legal speak. It's so cute. We all know they don't want a crippled plaintiff in front of a jury."

"Quadriplegic. Please practice *not* saying *crippled*."

"I don't think I'll need to practice." Clay finally handed over the letter.

Stu ripped it from his partner's hands like a kid reclaiming a stolen love letter. In the middle of the neatly printed page of thick linen paper from Shubert, Garvin & Ross et al. resided an awful run-on sentence, typical of lawyers. Stu skipped to the bottom. Below the horrific sentence was a single number. A big number.

"Oh my," Stu said quietly.

"Oh yes," Clay replied. "It appears your novel theory has scared the proverbial shit out of them."

Stu read the counter offer again, while Clay extracted from his desk a bottle of Booker's bourbon—126 proof and sixty bucks a bottle. Clay poured Stu a glass and one for himself. The one for himself was symbolic—he was on the wagon. After downing his own tumbler of Booker's served neat, Stu read the letter once more, carefully. The sentence was still awful, but it didn't modify the number.

"Just one sentence and a number?" Stu said.

"Just *that* number."

"Wow. Sylvia is going to be pleased."

"Fuck Sylvia and her motorized golf cart. I'm pleased!"

"I am too. This is a good result."

Clay smiled. "A good result? It seems to me that thirty-three percent of nine million is somewhere around three million, if I'm not mistaken. That's better than good. That's fucking awesome."

Stu frowned.

Clay's smile disappeared. "Why are you frowning? Don't frown. I hate it when you frown."

"It's not that simple."

"Obviously, I don't have an extensive background in mathematics, but if you grab a calculator, I think you'll find that I'm right on this one."

Stu was accustomed to explaining the law to Clay, who often neglected its finer points. It was a daily ritual, good news or bad. But Stu was not adept at softening blows, which was one of the reasons Clay handled the clients. Stu hardly noticed the devastating effect his words were having on his partner.

"Remember that attorney with the bushy hair in Fall River? Roger Rodan?"

"No. Why?"

"Last year Rodan challenged another lawyer's contingent fee as excessive on appeal, and he won. Now, by law, even a contingent fee must reflect either the work done or the risk involved. In our case, we wrote one demand letter. And we didn't invest more than nominal cash to pursue it. Very little work. No risk. Ergo, no basis for a three-million-dollar fee. If we had borrowed money to do extensive discovery or we had written briefs and gone to motion, that would be a different story. But we didn't. And the courts especially frown on a windfall fee when the plaintiff needs the money for their care, versus, say, when a punitive award is given. And Sylvia definitely needs the money for her care."

"What are you saying? We don't get our thirty-three?"

"Not if Sylvia contests it. No. The court would reverse it and give us what they consider 'reasonable' under the law."

"She won't contest it. She'll be delighted with six million."

"Others might ask the question. Her family. Her friends. And if she, or someone on her behalf, did contest our fee, it would likely result in disciplinary action by the bar under the unreasonable fee provision of ethics rule two-point-one. We'd risk formal reprimand or even a license suspension."

"I can take that risk."

"I can't."

"You mean you won't."

"Right, I won't."

"What if we reject this offer? Can you win the motion that justifies a higher fee?"

"Sylvia would have to reject the offer."

"Yeah, yeah, I know. But she loves you. Better yet, she doesn't understand a fucking word of your legal jargon. She'll do whatever we advise."

"And I'd advise her to take this. It's a good offer. It meets her needs and minimizes her legal fees."

"Our fees! It minimizes *our* fees!"

Stu finally heard the panic in his partner's voice and tried to offer some consolation. "I think we might be able to justify charging four hundred thousand dollars. It's a stretch, but . . ."

"Two hundred for each of us?"

"Yeah. Minus taxes. Minus overhead."

"Minus my right arm and my left testicle. You're making this sound better all the time."

"You want the truth, don't you?"

"Sure. Keep going, sunshine."

"Listen, it's almost two years' salary for a week's work. Our rent is suddenly no longer an issue, at least for a year or two. I can get the stupid elevator fixed, or at least the door, for God's sake. Pauline will stop bitching for a raise, because we can finally give it to her. You can probably even pay off that BMW you should never have bought. We ought to be happy with that. Look at me: I'm happy. I'm smiling and taking slugs of your ridiculous whiskey." Stu fought to maintain his grin as he sipped the fiery tonic, contorting his face in a way that should have amused his partner.

But Clay's dark eyes narrowed, the playful light in them extinguished. "It's just that my half of three million would change my life," he mumbled. "Two hundred doesn't. I'll wake up tomorrow the same goddamned guy I am today, only with the rent paid through next December."

Stu hadn't contemplated a life change. He might have won at trial and gotten more, a lot more, but it was a safe, clean, substantial payday that he'd created from nothing, and they were doing the right thing.

"Well," Stu said, "here's to paying the rent."

Stu raised his tumbler. Clay didn't meet his toast. He ignored the glass in favor of staring out the window, as though watching his dream drift away with the passing clouds. Then he turned to stare past the tumbler at Stu himself. It was a curious stare, like that of a bird deciding whether a grain on the ground might be a seed, or merely sand, before plucking it up to eat. "It seems we're at a bit of an impasse," he said.

Stu braced himself for further argument.

But then Clay sighed. His mood seemed to pass, and he clinked his own tumbler against Stu's. "All right. It saddens me to say this, but if you won't let me get rich this way, I'll just have to find another."

Stu was relieved that Clay had processed the defeat and acclimated. Adaptation was his partner's best trait, and it served him well; he could not be kept down for long. He did, however, drain his symbolic glass of 126-proof whiskey in one gulp.

CHAPTER 3

When Stu arrived home, Katherine was wrapping up a workout with five other sweaty women from the South Dartmouth Athletic Club, the gym she'd insisted they join for a lifetime initiation fee of ten thousand dollars, plus regular dues that rivaled a car payment. She'd argued that if Stu met one client there, the club would pay for itself. The trouble was he didn't go, he didn't meet anyone, and, thus, it didn't pay for itself. Instead Katherine went, Katherine met people, and they paid for it each month.

The living room was a sea of brightly colored Lycra. All wives of professionals. Some were rich, and the others thought they were, except for Katherine, who considered life in their not-quite-two-thousand-square-foot home at the east end of William Street in South Dartmouth akin to abject poverty. The others all lived on the waterside of Rockland—on Flagship Drive or Mosher Street or the ocean-view end of William, overlooking Clark's Cove.

Margery Hanstedt was busily perspiring on their leather couch in a pink unitard, but Katherine wasn't likely to say anything; Margery owned three restaurants. She was married with kids, but was also a ferocious flirt and wore makeup to the gym to advertise it. Holly Plynth was married to a doctor. Jenny Plantz-Werschect *was* a doctor. Stu recognized the fourth woman in the blue shorts and should have remembered her name, but couldn't—an increasingly common problem as he approached forty. He wondered momentarily if his memory lapses were due to his age or the fact that the identities of people wandering in and out of his life simply didn't matter much anymore. Unless the person was a relative or a client, they were just another face in the parade of humanity that came and went. There was no romantic intrigue to be had—he was married—and, without children, he had no connection to parents. He tried not to make eye contact with Blue Shorts so he wouldn't have to guess her name or reintroduce himself.

Katherine smiled when he entered, a bigger smile than she spent on him when he found her alone. She was more generous with affection when others were present. A bit backward, now that Stu thought about it.

"Stu! We just finished a session of extreme power-cross. Jill is from the SAC, but she does home training." Katherine gestured toward a harsh-looking woman in a sports bra cinched so tight it squished her chest as flat as the trio of angry abs below it. She looked serious and expensive—she almost certainly charged extra to do house calls. "Jill, this is my husband, Stu." Katherine lowered her voice. "He doesn't work out."

"I bike," Stu said defensively.

"Stationary bike," Katherine clarified, as though it didn't count. "In front of the TV."

"I watch sports while I ride." In the presence of six exercising women it sounded better than admitting he watched *Weird Worlds* on the Syfy channel and only flipped to football when Katherine walked in.

"He could lose a few," Katherine said so they could all hear. It was the opposite of what she'd said to him privately that morning.

Also backward, Stu noted.

Jill looked him up and down, evaluating him like a shopper debating a loaf of bread from the day-old bin. "I could rip you up in a month," she said. Then she tilted her head for a better view of his backside. "Maybe two."

"Sounds great," Stu said, thinking that being "ripped up" sounded excruciating.

Margery flipped her sweaty hair, spraying more droplets onto the couch. "You work with Clay Buchanan, don't you?" she said, casually bringing up his handsome—and single—partner.

"He's the first name on the sign."

Katherine frowned. "I told Stu to fight to have our name first, but he doesn't have a taste for confrontation anymore."

"Funny trait for a lawyer," Jenny remarked. Jenny was known for making anti-lawyer remarks. It was rude, but a lot of doctors hated attorneys. Stu didn't blame them. Lawyers sued doctors.

"Well, tell Clay hello for me," Margery said, sticking out her sweaty pink chest.

"Will do," Stu said, wondering if he was supposed to also relay the message she was sending with her fuchsia-colored boobs. "I'll be seeing him later this evening."

"On a Friday night?"

"Stu's turning forty," Katherine whispered loud enough for everyone to hear.

"No party," Stu announced. "You all heard me. I'm not dying. No black balloons. No novelty candles that I can't blow out with my aging lungs. No rented wheelchair."

Katherine rolled her eyes toward her friends. "And no fun."

The women shared a laugh at his expense, and he hated them and their brightly colored clothes for a moment. Then he walked into the kitchen and forgot about them; there was leftover pizza.

Stu microwaved a slab of Canadian bacon and pineapple, his favorite. It was a small, temporary slice of happiness. He should have felt elated about Molson; as soon as Clay obtained Sylvia's agreement to the settlement, it would officially be a big win for him. But he didn't feel elated; he felt fucking depressed. Clay was right about nothing changing after the case was won. One of the settlement terms would be a non-disclosure agreement; nobody in town could know what he'd done for his client or that he'd bested three other lawyers. Ergo, no public boost to his reputation. And the money didn't really change anything. Clay was right about that, too. It just made paying bills more comfortable. Today he'd turned forty years old, and he was the same goddamned guy he was yesterday.

For a moment he was miserable enough to allow himself to think the dark thoughts. They could cheat Sylvia and collect a huge fee, and he could leak the settlement terms. Odds were he'd get away with both—Clay was also right about that. But he'd always been the good kid, the Cub Scout, the responsible student, the nice young man with whom parents were comfortable sending their daughter to prom, all the happy sappy stuff. At the DA's Office he'd taken an oath to uphold the public trust, and years of making decisions that affected people's lives forever while under the glare of public scrutiny had cemented those indigenous ethics in him. He was a rule-follower. He didn't push the envelope. Never had. Never would.

Same goddamned guy.

He snarled and flipped the butter knife, catching the handle deftly with one hand after two full rotations directly over Katherine's slab granite countertop.

Ha! Take that, caution! he thought. Still, he snuck a look around to make sure his wife hadn't seen him.

He'd have to tell her about the Molson case, he thought. Not tonight, though. Like Clay, Katherine had hoped they'd finally made a big score, and Stu hated to let her down. She was also likely to pout and withhold sex. Besides, he had an unwanted surprise birthday party he needed to pretend to enjoy.

CHAPTER 4

Once Stu was gone, Katherine glanced from friend to friend, embarrassed. "It's still on for seven o'clock," she whispered.

"Is he depressed about turning forty?" Holly asked, her trademark nosiness carefully disguised as sympathy.

"Stu is working on a big case," Katherine explained. "Molson could be the one." She hummed the last word as though she were giggling with college girlfriends and Molson was a boy she'd just met.

"Suing anyone I know?" Jenny grumbled.

"It's not a medical malpractice," Katherine assured her. "He doesn't do that sort of work. And I'm not at liberty to discuss it, but it could be a potential life-changer."

"Would you move across Rockland?" Margery asked.

"I hadn't given it much thought," she lied. It was exactly what she'd been thinking, but Margery was still a bit of a bitch for asking. "He's still putting the case together. He's very thorough."

They all nodded. Stu's work ethic and intellect were well known—Katherine had made sure of it, dropping comments over the years about his top 10 percent class ranking in law school and ninety-fifth percentile LSAT scores. Margery had once commented that grades were a great measure of a man's "potential." It annoyed Katherine; forty was too old for "potential." Everyone else's husband was already a success, and the whole lot of them already lived by the water.

Katherine sighed as the women gathered up their things. Stu was loyal, like a hound, and cute in a nerdish way. They'd married when he was a newly minted prosecutor. She'd been a couple years out of college, struggling along in a crappy apartment with her degree in visual design from the UMass Dartmouth campus, and she saw his potential—potential that should have blossomed by now. At twenty-nine he'd already been handling front-page felony cases and was on track for a career in politics. He'd built a reputation as steady and confident back then. Not necessarily dynamic, but she could be social enough for the both of them. And he'd been a relatively easy catch, because he thought she was beautiful.

He'd actually used the *B* word. No one else, man or boy, had ever called her beautiful. Her prom dates and awkward young suitors used words like *cute* or *nice-looking* or *attractive*, all horrible watered-down versions of the *B* word. And Stu continued to find her beautiful at thirty-six, which was important. He still said so often, and she could tell by the way he sat up in bed to watch her undress at night that he meant it.

He'd better, she thought; she cardio-blasted her midthirties body for an hour every afternoon, added weights on odd days, and took one vital day off each week to let her muscles rebuild and rejuvenate. She also worked hard to keep her wardrobe both current and unique. Exercise and fashion were something many women let slide in their thirties, especially mothers. She hadn't been a stunner in her youth—she knew that. She'd been bookish then and always small-breasted. But now was her time. She was quickly passing up women who'd once been beautiful but were succumbing to age, saggy tits, childbearing hips, and simple complacency. And while it always felt good to have her own husband say she was hot, it felt even better knowing objectively that she was finally moving up in that category against her peers. If she continued to work at it, she thought, she'd soon be the hottest middle-aged woman at the SAC.

Stu didn't just give her compliments. He gave her space to network and develop a respectable collection of important friends for them. And he honored her decision to pursue her photography instead of wasting her time working at some dead-end job. He'd also given up pestering her about children once she'd made it clear motherhood wasn't for her. And, even after thirteen years, when they made love, he still politely thanked her afterward.

He was a perfectly good man, but none of it hid the fact that he was a beaten man too. She'd worked hard to mold him, promote him, and motivate him, but it was clear he would never again be an alpha male, certainly not after the Butz fiasco. And it was gut-wrenching to watch all her hard work go down the toilet.

She walked her sweaty friends to their Volvos and Mercedes, and saw them off with fist bumps and the traditional round of mutual compliments regarding how hard they'd worked out and how good they all looked. Holly wasn't actually in great shape—a little meaty, and her thighs brushed together when she walked—but Katherine said she looked great anyway.

She envied them. They were comfortable and cocky, with vacation condos in Boston or apartments in Manhattan, kids off at boarding schools, and bulging 401Ks, while she and Stu were still clawing out an existence at the inland end of William Street. But when her husband finally won a big case, *this* big case, some of those pieces would fall into place for her, too.

CHAPTER 5

The William Street house was a "fixer." With the prices in the South Dart-mouth neighborhood inflated by its status-inducing proximity to the ocean and its distance from the crime of north New Bedford, a beat-up mid-1800s place had been the entry-level home. Its wooden floors were un-even, none of its old three-panel doors shut properly, and the cobweb-filled unfinished basement still flooded when it rained; their plastic bins of high school yearbooks and family photos were stacked on pallets to keep them off the wet floor.

Katherine crept down the narrow basement steps. She hated going down, but there hadn't been enough room in their smallish kitchen re-frigerator to hide the birthday party food. In her brown suede wedge heels she carefully stepped over a puddle toward their spare tag sale fridge. Then she filled her outstretched arms with plates of hors d'oeuvres, the way she had when she was slogging through college with her miserable job at the Silver Spoon restaurant. She kicked the fridge door shut with her foot, and when she turned around with her arms loaded, Clay Buchanan was standing on the third step up, blocking her way.

He wore a tight smile and a button-down shirt tucked into equally tight jeans. The top and second buttons of his shirt were undone, revealing a hairless chest. Katherine found his lack of fur strange; at his age he should have at least a little patch. Perhaps he waxed it. His jeans carefully defined every contour of his lower half. Katherine thought she would appear vulgar if he caught her staring, so she didn't let her eyes linger. The snug ensemble might have been tacky on a man with the standard middle-aged tummy, but Clay was trim, muscular, and wore it well. He seemed to know it too.

"Ah, there you are," he said pleasantly.

"Here I am."

"I need to ask a favor of you."

"If it involves food, I'm your man."

"You're definitely not a man, nor does this involve food. It involves a potential client. Dugan."

Reginald Dugan. Katherine recalled the large land developer. Big guy. Lots of money. She'd met him while volunteering at the Veterans KIA charity auction, a good place to mingle with movers and shakers, and he was definitely a mover. No college education, but he'd elbowed his way to wealth and power. The story was that his family had lived in the New Bedford area for generations. He'd taken over their ailing Bristol County farm and somehow turned it into a multimillion-dollar development, which was quickly annexed by the city council, upon which his cousin sat. It wasn't as tidy as that, but those were the basics Katherine heard while she was on the treadmill at the SAC.

Clay had heard a more recent rumor—that Dugan was dissatisfied with his current attorneys—and Clay had called Katherine that very morning to insist she invite the man to her next event. It made no difference to Clay that a birthday party was an inappropriately personal gathering for a stranger.

"I mentioned the party to him," Katherine said coolly, "against my better judgment."

"Well, he's here," Clay said, wiggling his thick eyebrows, "against your better judgment."

Katherine was surprised but tried not to show it.

"Favor done then," she said curtly. "You're welcome."

"No. Not done. I've already taken a run at him tonight, but he needs more persuasion. A different sort than I can provide."

"What sort?"

"He likes beer and beautiful women. And he's already got a beer."

Katherine's heartbeat quickened. She glanced down at her form-fitting cocktail dress, self-conscious and proud at the same time. It pushed her modest breasts into reasonably pert mounds and showed off her firm legs. When she looked back, Clay was grinning, his dark eyes boring into her. Her husband's handsome partner was the last person she'd expected to call her beautiful. Her neck felt warm. *This is what those thousands of reverse crunches and glute kickbacks are for,* she told herself. But it was a compliment with a catch.

"You want me to flirt with Reggie Dugan?"

"I learned something today," Clay said. "Had a bit of a revelation, really. Success isn't going to drop into our laps, not real success. People who trap themselves with rules and propriety are rats in a maze. They work late into the night for scraps, they walk on an endless wheel, and they earn themselves a ratty little life. I don't want that for us anymore. We need to up our ante to play with the big boys. And Dugan is a big boy—easily worth two hundred grand in fees. Annually."

"And you want me to flirt with him," she confirmed, annoyed. "He's fifty and fat."

"Forty-eight. Not a lot older than your husband . . . and he's a big strong contractor guy, not fat."

"Contractors have dirty fingernails," Katherine said with a tone of finality. "Not my type."

"So if I get him to clean his fingernails, you would flirt with him?"

"I didn't say that. Look, my arms are getting tired holding all this. I need to go upstairs."

"No, you don't. You used to wait tables, didn't you? And you exercise every day. Your bis and tris are seriously cut. I know you can hold up a few baby carrots and snap peas a bit longer while we discuss this."

Another compliment. He'd noticed that she kept her thirty-six-year-old body in top shape.

"It's no longer a discussion," she said. "I won't flirt with the grungy construction guy. And you're being an asshole."

Clay chuckled, and then shook his head as though disappointed in her. "My, my, Kate. What does Stuart do with you when you won't behave?"

She cocked her head, bewildered. "Nothing."

He nodded. "That's what I figured."

Clay stepped down from the stairs to face her and moved close, *inside* her personal space. His eyes never left hers. They were narrow and buried beneath low brows, dark brown, almost black. Katherine backed up against the old fridge, but he inched even closer, near enough that she could smell him—a clean male scent with a hint of something lavender, a body wash, perhaps. Her eyes flickered to the door at the top of the stairs. He'd closed it behind him. They were completely cut off from the party. He spoke slowly and deliberately, the cadence of his voice almost soothing.

"Kate, you *are* going to go up there and talk to him. You *are* going to smile. And you *are* going to make him want to be around you and around our firm. This isn't just for me. It's for your own good too."

"I don't like the way—"

He reached up suddenly and grabbed her by the hair. He grasped it in the rear, behind her neck where it was thickest, and he pulled her head back firmly. Her words caught in her throat, unsaid, and the carefully prepared food on her arms teetered.

"And I don't like the way you're defying me, Kate." His tone did not change. "Stuart might put up with it, but not me."

She couldn't push him away with her arms loaded—she didn't dare; it had taken an hour to prep the veggie tray alone. And when she tried to speak, he tugged her hair again, not hard enough to dump the plates, but hard enough to silence her.

He was still talking at a low volume with an even rhythm, and smiling sympathetically as though delivering a lesson to a child.

"This isn't a game, Kate. This is life, our livelihood. Mine, Stuart's, yours. This isn't about your reputation or your sense of honor, which I'm guessing you surrendered to some college bad boy who broke your cherry and your heart before you met Steady Stu. We're not kids anymore. You're not a little nerd guarding your virginity. This is about success. If you're going to stay home and play the society wife, you're going to need to grow up a bit and contribute with the tools you have at your disposal. You don't get a home overlooking the water by being a nice girl."

Katherine's heart beat madly, but she wasn't sure what the emotion was. Confusion? Anger, perhaps? Stu would never do this to her. He wouldn't dare. Even her father had never disciplined her; he'd concentrated on her delinquent older brother. *Katie will be fine,* she'd overheard him say when she was ten. *I don't need to spend my time on her.*

"I'm going to let go now, Kate," Clay was saying gently. "I'm not asking for much. Stu and I will do the heavy lifting. We just need a small effort from you. But if you'd like to tell me that you don't want to help us earn hundreds of thousands of dollars, just say so."

His body was against hers now, his hand still tangled in her hair, his chest flattening her smallish breasts between them, his pelvis pressed into her.

Is he turned on?

He was right about Dugan, she realized. He was right about the college bad boy too. She *was* a little nerd girl. And she *did* want a house with a view. The trays of food needed to be served, her husband's partner smelled terrific, and he was an asshole with amazing eyes that never looked away.

When he let go, she calmly handed him one of the trays to carry upstairs. When he took it, she slapped him. He blinked, but didn't move. Instead he simply stood, waiting for her to refuse him. But in the end she couldn't.

CHAPTER 6

Stu hated adult birthday parties, especially his own. Ever since he'd turned thirty he hadn't felt that having a birthday merited any sort of celebration—he certainly hadn't done anything to deserve one. He'd merely gotten older—again. It just made him feel tired. But Katherine loved any excuse to host a function, and other people seemed to like them. So, although he'd put up a token protest, he accepted that turning forty was his destiny, and when people began ringing the doorbell, he acted surprised and reluctantly pleased about the festivities for Katherine's benefit. It made her smile, and for that he was always willing to put a lid on his inner Grinch.

The food was not yet out; Katherine liked to present it with a flourish after a substantial number of guests had arrived so that she could collect her well-deserved *ooh*s and *aah*s. But expensive beers were already bobbing in an ice bath, and three bottles of wine were open on the dining room table—a chardonnay, a cab, and a merlot called Aged to Perfection with an aluminum walker on the label.

Very funny, Stu thought.

A white lace tablecloth, which he'd bought Katherine for her birthday, covered the table. She'd picked it out; he'd just purchased and wrapped it. He wasn't good at guessing what his wife wanted for her birthday, and she was happy to provide a list because she certainly didn't trust his judgment. It was an efficient arrangement, and she never opened a dud gift.

Stu plunged his hand into the ice water to retrieve a cold beer, and when he turned to grab one of Katherine's imported ceramic steins, he found his part-time legal associate standing before him pouring herself a glass of the bloodred merlot. He stared, surprised.

She looked up and smiled. "Happy Birthday, Stu."

At thirty-seven, Audra "Audry" Goodwin was old for a new lawyer, less than a year out of law school and still needing to take the bar exam. She had a daughter who was away at college. No husband—she'd never had one—and she openly described herself as a former teen mom who had "ducked out of life for a decade" before she finally decided to get her shit together again. Then she'd buried herself in school and work for another seven years. Audry wore practical shoulder-length hair and an equally practical knee-length flowered dress. Her amber eyes were large and round to begin with, like a cat's, and freakishly oversized when she donned her reading glasses. But it was not her outward appearance that Stu noticed around the office; it was her energy. Judge Pennington had once commented that he wished he "had as much enthusiasm for *anything* as Ms. Goodwin has for *everything*." Her thirst for knowledge was boundless, not just in law, but in music and sports, science, political trivia, yard care. Hell, anything that came up, she was interested in it. It was as though she'd hoarded her zest for life while she finished school and raised her daughter, and she was only now unleashing it. Boosted by such positive spirit, the words *Happy Birthday* didn't sound so bad coming from her.

"Thanks, Audry. I'm so glad you could come."

"Wouldn't miss it." Then she pointed down. "You're making a puddle, by the way."

Stu's sweating beer bottle was dripping onto his shoes. He scrambled to find a napkin, hoping that Katherine wouldn't see him dribbling water on her dining room's fir floor; the wood was original with the house, and they'd had it refinished professionally when they'd moved in.

"No worries," Audry said. "Your floor finish looks recent, and if you've got the industry-standard three coats of a good water-based polyurethane finish on the wood, it'll repel a few drips of water just fine."

"I, uh . . . yeah, I know. I just don't want people to think I wet myself in my old age."

Audry laughed freely, and they stood together at the table and chatted. She knocked back her wine like a college student and filled her glass again. Halfway into his beer Stu felt better, and Audry didn't let the conversation lag for even a moment.

The gaggle of Katherine's SAC women stood in a tight formation in the living room, whispering amongst themselves. Their husbands were nowhere to be seen; Stu's birthday party was apparently not their obligation. Soon Margery Hanstedt broke from the group and drifted over to procure herself some wine.

"Hello, Stu," she said. "Is this a cab?"

Stu nodded and pointed to the label, which said *cabernet*. She coughed out a polite *How silly of me*–style laugh and began to pour a glass for herself.

"Hi, I'm Audry," Audry said, smiling.

"Hi." Margery kept pouring.

"This is Margery Hanstedt," Stu said when Margery didn't offer.

"I'm a neighbor," Margery added. "We're down at the other end of William Street . . ."

"By the water," Audry finished for her.

"Yes."

"Hanstedt? That sounds familiar. That's the name of the family who owns the Finicky Fish, right?"

"And the Arbor and Stationbreak."

"Oh god, I loooove Stationbreak. The Italian–Asian fusion menu is awesome."

"We like to think so." Margery turned to Stu. "Stu, you said Clay was coming tonight, but I haven't seen him."

"He's here somewhere," Stu said.

Margery's wineglass was finally full, all the way to the brim instead of the traditional halfway mark. "Well, don't bother telling him I said hello. Since I'm here, I can tell him myself."

"Got it."

Audry waved as Margery pulled away. "Nice to meet you."

"You too," Margery said over her shoulder.

As soon as she was gone, Audry grabbed Stu's arm. "Oh my god, she didn't say 'Happy Birthday'!"

"What?"

"Happy Birthday. She didn't say it. How could she not have said it?"

Stu looked around. The SAC women had reconvened. Reggie Dugan, a big local developer, was filling a nearby love seat and considering them with a beer in each hand. Pastor Richards—another connection Katherine felt was valuable—was speaking politely with Brad Bear, the head of the photography studio where Katherine shot on Wednesdays. Stu didn't attend church, and it made him feel strange whenever Pastor Richards smiled at him, as though God were silently saying, *I see you*. . . .

"None of these people are my friends," Stu realized aloud.

Audry gave him a puzzled look. "Really?"

"Yep. Not one."

She looked around, considering the crowd. "That's sad," she said. "Clay's here, isn't he?"

"Yeah, but he disappeared. Who knows what he's off doing."

"Well, we can't have you feeling this way on your birthday." She hoisted her drink. "Tell you what: I'll be your friend. We'll just be a couple of guys sharing beers and talking about bitchy women. What say you, friend?"

"You're drinking wine."

Audry gasped. "Like a bitchy woman. God, you're right! What kind of drinking buddy am I?"

She laughed and reached for a beer, plopping her wineglass on the table and sending a red splash of Aged to Perfection over the edge and onto the white lace tablecloth. The wine hit and spattered like a Rorschach pattern. It looked to Stu like a wheelchair or maybe a cluster of dark balloons.

Audry's upbeat smile turned to a rueful grimace. "Uh-oh. This table-cloth definitely does *not* have three coats of varnish on it."

Katherine chose that moment to enter carrying the food trays. There was no time to hide the crime; Stu and Audry could do nothing but part to make way for her. Stu didn't know what to say, and so he said nothing, and the trays descended toward the wine stain. But just as he thought Audry was busted, Katherine sat the tray over the top of the spill and covered it without saying a word.

Stu waited for the hammer to fall. When his wife merely rearranged the trays, he wondered if she was so angry that she couldn't speak. It was impossible that she'd missed it.

"I spilled that while pouring Audry a glass," Stu lied, unable to endure the silence.

"Excuse me?" Katherine said.

She was distracted and hadn't heard him, Stu realized. "The wine. I'm sorry."

"It doesn't matter." She absently patted his arm and then wandered off to greet the guests who'd arrived since she'd disappeared to retrieve the food.

"That's amazing," Stu said.

Audry sipped her beer. "What?"

"She gave me a free pass on the wine spill."

"You mean *me*. Thanks, by the way."

"She never does that. That deserved the passive-aggressive treatment at least."

"It's your birthday. What a great wife. Here's to her." Audry raised her beer.

Stu clacked his own against hers, and they drank together as Katherine crossed the room to welcome Reggie Dugan.

Just then Stu felt a firm slap on his butt.

"Clay," he said without turning around. "I wondered where you'd gotten off to."

"I was previewing the food," Clay said. "Your woman is a culinary genius, by the way. Hello, Audra."

Stu noticed that he used Audry's formal name.

"Hello, Clay," she replied. It was brief, polite.

"Happy goddamned Birthday, buddy. Guess I should have said that at the office this morning."

"We were focused on other things. Besides, I don't like birthdays."

"Nonsense! How can you not like birthdays? Especially this one. I got you something special to celebrate the end of your fourth decade, you know."

"I did *not* know that."

"Well, now you do, old man."

Stu winced.

Audry interrupted. "Clay, there's a nice woman over there who owns restaurants and wants to speak with you." She pointed at Margery.

"About what?"

"I dunno. Culinary shit?"

Clay gave the situation a look, sizing Margery up, and then nodded. "Excuse me for a moment." And he was off.

Having finished an entire beer, and no longer having the alcohol tolerance he'd cultivated back in college, Stu felt loose. Otherwise he wouldn't have said anything. But he did. "You sent him away," he whispered to Audry. "Why?"

"You don't need 'old man' comments. You're not even old."

"Forty is getting up there. It's halfway, right?"

"That's nothing. I've dated men a lot older than you."

Stu's eyebrow arched, but he didn't feel it was appropriate to comment on her love life; she was an employee, after all. "It sounded like there was more to it than that. What's up?"

Audry thought for a moment. "Nothing I can put my finger on. His karma is just off, and he seems to sense that I sense it."

"That's a little vague for me. I don't really do karma sensing. No offense."

"I think he's damaged."

"How so?"

"He's a good-looking, successful lawyer, but he's thirty-five and single with no ex and no prospects."

"He doesn't think he's successful."

"The economy sucks right now, and there's a glut of attorneys. Look at me; I don't even have a real job. No offense. Any lawyer who can pay their rent is a success."

"That's what I told him just this morning!" Stu laughed. It felt good to laugh. "Great minds think alike."

"And so do we, apparently." Audry tipped back the last of her beer and immediately retrieved her half-full wineglass. "I'd better go mingle before your wife thinks I'm flirting with you."

Stu's pulse quickened. *Is that what we're doing?* No. Audry had explicitly said she was cutting it off before it got to that point, and she was very direct. She was just being nice to him, he realized, and he would be careful not to cross the line or initiate minor physical contact when they parted, such as touching hands or patting her shoulder. Lively, attentive conversation was the most action a married guy should hope for from a single woman, he decided. *And a forty-year-old should be thankful for even that much.*

"Okay," he conceded. "Thanks for sharing a beer, buddy."

"No worries," she said, smiling. "Happy Birthday." And then, before he could avoid it, she hugged him.

From there the party progressed pretty much as Stu had expected—lots of polite handshaking and meaningless chatter, culminating in his ritual humiliation by Katherine's friends, wherein they all gathered around to sing "Happy Birthday" to him off-key. He smiled and thanked them all for coming. He didn't want to spoil anyone else's good time, especially Katherine's; she worked hard to put on events. Something was strange, however. She was usually "on" for parties, but tonight she seemed preoccupied. He wondered what was bugging her.

"Can I have everyone's attention?"

Stu looked up. Everyone looked up.

What's this?

It was Clay.

"I have a little announcement," Stu's partner said, projecting his voice across the room as he stepped up onto their coffee table, a wedding gift from Katherine's maid of honor.

Thank God he doesn't drink anymore, Stu thought. *Who knows what he'd be on top of.*

Clay had stopped drinking years earlier after a series of incidents, one involving talking himself out of a DUI from an officer with whom he'd worked when he was a prosecutor. The officer had been disciplined for cutting him a break, but Clay, who'd been three sheets to the wind, had gotten off without even taking a breathalyzer test, receiving only a one-hundred-and-fifty-dollar traffic ticket for an open container of alcohol in his BMW. Stu glanced at Katherine; standing on furniture was as serious an offense as dumping wine on white lace. She was biting her lip, and probably her tongue, but she didn't say anything.

Again—strange.

Clay waved his arms and pointed at Stuart. "Ladies and gentlemen, I give you Stu!" Clapping ensued and continued until Clay held his hands up for silence. "Our friend Stu has reached the ripe old age of forty, but he doesn't look a day over, well, forty. How does he do it? Well, I'll tell you how. He's careful. He follows the rules and takes the safe route every time. Am I right?"

Heads nodded in agreement as Clay worked the crowd. Stu didn't know where this was headed, but he didn't like it already.

Clay continued. "Stu's the guy who walks all the way to the crosswalk, even when no cars are coming. He's the man who won't go in the pool when the lifeguard's not on duty. When he uses a gas station bathroom and it says 'customers only,' he feels obligated to buy a pack of gum. He's the sucker who buys the extended warranty just in case. Let's face it, he's a bit of a pussy."

Stu suffered through giggles and murmurs of agreement.

"So, Stu . . . ," Clay said, turning his smug gaze upon him. "Now that you're forty, there's something that I need to give you. Indeed, I'm going to give you something you've needed for a long time. I'm going to give you an adventure."

"A trip to Disneyland!" someone shouted from the crowd.

"No, no. Nothing so pansy-assed as fifty-five-mile-per-hour upside-down roller coasters or as tame as mobs of screaming children. No, sir. We're going to Alaska!"

A puzzled silence fell over the room, and over Stu.

"Alaska?" Stu said finally. "On a cruise, or, like, with a fishing guide?"

"No guides, my friend. No all-inclusive meal plan. Just you, me, and the last frontier. Nothing but a single solitary cabin."

"Out in the wilderness?"

"Wouldn't be much of an adventure if the cabin were in downtown Fairbanks. Our friend Reggie Dugan is helping arrange it. I've got the airline tickets in my desk. One week in the wild. Knowing you, you'll want to make a detailed list of things to pack."

"But I have to get my calendar from the office and schedule the—"

"No, you don't. I'm going to get you *out* of that office."

Stu looked around, openmouthed. Katherine's eyebrows were raised practically to the top of her head, and her lips were pursed tightly. Dugan stood right behind her, watching the show with a self-satisfied grin. Others murmured excitedly. Besides his wife, they all seemed to think that taking Stu far away and dumping him in the middle of nowhere was the greatest thing ever.

"So are we talking next summer then?" Stu asked, trying to appear game.

"We leave in three days," Clay said. "You're welcome."

CHAPTER 7

When Clay offered to help Katherine carry out the garbage at the end of the evening, she knew it was time to face him. The industrial-size green plastic trash can was tucked behind a worn wooden fence beside the garage, where the two of them would be concealed.

After the incident in the basement, she'd set out to avoid him during the party—at first. Oddly enough, he'd left her alone too; and, after the intensity of their encounter, she wondered why. He was patient, it seemed, waiting to see what she would do, biding his time. She began to feel as though he were ignoring her, so she had purposefully brushed against his hand once at the punch bowl to see if he would flash her a knowing look. He'd only turned away as though he'd forgotten that he'd sent her on a mission.

But he hasn't forgotten.

No words were spoken on their journey to the garbage, but he was marching her to a secluded location, and when they got there, it would be time to report in. She wondered how he would react to her news.

Katherine opened the garbage can, and Clay slid the bulging plastic trash bag inside. When the lid thumped closed, she stood facing him, waiting for him to ask. But he just waited too.

"I did it," she said finally, exhaling. She hadn't realized she'd been holding her breath. She watched for his reaction, but he said nothing. He simply motioned for her to continue.

"I talked to him. Just small talk, like you said."

"Did it go well?"

"I'm pretty sure he liked me, if that's what you mean."

"How do you know?"

"Because he felt me up. . . ." She let the revelation hang in the air. She meant to shock him. It *should* have been shocking, but Clay only nodded.

"Just a pat or an actual feel?" he asked matter-of-factly.

She rolled her eyes and took a deep breath. "Hand on hip at first, then he slid it around to my rump. He left it there while we talked. It was very awkward. Thanks a lot."

"Did you reel him in?"

"We didn't talk business."

"Fair enough. I appreciate the effort, Kate. I really do. That wasn't so hard, was it?"

"Says you."

"You probably just closed the deal for us."

"What?"

"On his way out he told me he wants a meeting. Congratulations."

Katherine was surprised. She'd done it, and, like Clay said, it hadn't been that hard. When she'd asked Dugan to follow her to the upstairs hallway, away from the party, she'd been intimidated; not only was he large in stature, he was bold, confident, and no-nonsense. But she was a good talker—that part came easy. It felt natural, even. She'd smiled. He'd laughed. Then his hand had found her thigh. He was smooth; she didn't even notice it move to her rear until he gave it a gentle squeeze. He'd left it there for no more than a minute. *Two hundred thousand dollars per minute,* she thought. She had to hold back a giggle that was equal parts relief and excitement. She and Clay turned to walk back to the house.

"He *is* big," she said.

"Powerful," Clay replied. He cocked his head and looked at her. "Did it turn you on?"

"Of course not," Katherine said automatically.

"Of course not," he agreed, then he smiled and strode off toward his BMW.

Moments later Katherine slipped inside the house. The other guests had left, and Stu was still banging around in the kitchen, cleaning up. She hurried upstairs and dragged her makeup stool into their walk-in closet, then closed the door behind her. She sat and listened for a moment with her cocktail dress bunched up around her waist before pulling her panties down to her ankles.

As aroused as she was, it took her less than a minute to satisfy herself.

Stu finished up in the kitchen. Doing dishes wasn't his favorite chore—he didn't like getting his hands dirty—but if he left them for Katherine, she would fuss over them for the rest of the night, and there would be less chance of getting some birthday sex. He put the last pan away, wiped his hands, and headed for the stairs.

He still enjoyed sex with his wife immensely. They had a routine that worked for each of them. It was efficient and convenient, and it satisfied both her and him every time. And she kept her body in such magnificent shape. Her flat tummy and narrow muscled buttocks were as much as a middle-aged husband could ask for. Just the thought of them still stirred him. He eased open their bedroom door and stepped inside. He heard a muffled sigh. It sounded like Katherine was inside the walk-in closet. He'd hoped to catch a glimpse of her undressing—always exciting. But the closet door was closed. He kicked his shoes into the corner and pulled off his socks, shirt, and pants. He'd already brushed his teeth in the guest bathroom downstairs—one less thing to interrupt the mood.

As soon as Katherine walked out, however, he knew it wasn't going to happen. Not only did she look surprised and annoyed to find him standing there in his white briefs, but she was wearing baggy pajamas and looked spent. He couldn't blame her; she'd just put on a big party for him. Besides, she'd seemed a bit distracted all evening. He wouldn't pester her, he decided. She hated being pushed when it came to sex.

He smiled instead. "Thank you for the wonderful party."

"Oh yes, of course." She walked to him and gave him a peck on the cheek, and then skirted him to get to the bed.

He called after her. "You seem tired."

"I'm sorry," she mumbled, confirming that there would be no action.

"No problem. I am too," he lied. "I'm getting old, you know."

"I know," she said.

He winced. He'd hoped she would disagree. He glanced at the man in their bedroom mirror. A significant roll of white flesh hung over the elastic band of his underwear, not a grotesque amount, but enough. His shoulders were narrow, and a few gray hairs peppered his otherwise dark chest. Black hair was now growing over his shoulders too, and it crept down his stomach in a narrow line. Clay had called such hair a "treasure trail" once when he'd dated an Italian woman, but on a paunchy male it looked more like the seam on a basketball.

"Do you think I need an adventure?" he said to the mirror.

"I think your partner is an asshole," Katherine answered from the bed.

Stu turned, surprised. "Why do you say that?"

Katherine didn't answer for a moment. Then she rolled over away from him, turning to the far wall. "He didn't bother to ask me if you could leave for a week, for one thing. A little notice would have been nice. I have a calendar too. You'll miss the closing ceremonies for the farmer's market, my gallery showing, and the mayor's banquet. We bought a table."

"Sorry. This is unexpected, even for Clay."

"You don't have to go."

"I don't want to go."

"Then don't."

She was right, Stu thought. He could make some excuse and decline. He stared at his wife's back and considered it. "Will you think I'm a pussy if I don't?" he asked.

Katherine made a snorting noise somewhere between a sigh and a laugh.

"It's just not you, hon." She pulled one pillow between her knees and draped her arms over a second so that she was armored in memory foam. "Get the light, would you?"

Stu turned out the light and groped his way into the bed, where he gave her a kiss on the back of the head. "I love you," he said.

"Happy Birthday," she mumbled.

CHAPTER 8

Stu stood in front of the boot wall at the Great Beyond, the warehouse-style outdoor sporting goods store the size of a city block on the outskirts of New Bedford. The towering display was designed to look like a climbing wall, and each sample boot sat on a narrow rock shelf that jutted from it. A smiling nineteen-year-old clerk in a khaki uniform stood at his shoulder, eager to help and more excited about Stuart's trip than Stuart was himself.

"I'm going hiking," Stu said. "It's been a few years, and I don't have any sense for what type of boot I need." In truth, it had been a few decades.

The clerk bobbed his head. "No worries, bro. How far is your trek?"

"I dunno. Five miles, maybe?"

"What kind of terrain?"

"Alaskan wilderness."

"Five miles in Alaska? That sounds more like a walk between homes up there than a hike."

"I just need something basic. It's only for this one trip."

"If it's really five miles, you can go with the Tenderfoot. It's eighty-five dollars. A solid low-end choice. Good all-around boot."

Stu pulled down a different but promising-looking pair. Brown. Simple.

"No," said the clerk. "That's the Urban Explorer. It's more of a groomed trail shoe."

"Groomed trail?"

"Gravel paths. Packed dirt. Concrete. I think you want something more in an adventure style."

Adventure. "That sounds right. What's the difference?"

"Weight. Waterproofing. Breathability. Durability. Traction. Ultimately, blisters."

"Okay, okay. What do you recommend?"

"Do you pronate?"

"I have no idea what you just said."

The kid pushed him on the shoulder, and Stu staggered backward. "Hey!"

"Chillax, man. I just want to see your stance." He looked down at Stu's feet.

Stu tried to maintain his stance, whatever that was. "Well, what do you see?"

"Trail Quest Extremes would be good for you." He pointed to a rainbow-colored pair of boots with reflective lettering that promised "Eco-Gel Comfort."

Stuart turned over the price tag, and his eyes widened. His clerk nestled up to his shoulder to whisper in his ear like his conscience.

"Are you a guy who likes to be prepared, or do you wanna take a chance and go with the cheap ones?"

Thirty minutes later Stu hiked across the massive parking lot of the Great Beyond wearing two-hundred-and-fifty-dollar TQ Extremes. He also carried a sack stuffed full of Hi-Tec brand gear the clerk had recommended, including fifteen-dollar socks, water-resistant pants, and a frameless backpack, and a five-hundred-page book titled *Edwin's Comprehensive Guide to Wilderness Survival.*

———

"Six hundred dollars?" Katherine cocked an eyebrow.

"I thought it best to be prepared," Stu explained.

"I hope Clay knows what he's doing, because I know you certainly don't."

"He dated an outdoorsy gal at Oregon. They went camping and stuff."

"Screwing a girl in a tent isn't the same as taking on the Klondike."

"There's a cabin. The floatplane drops us off at the lake, and we hike in a few miles. We suffer for a week. We hike out. The plane picks us up again. No worries." Stu tacked on the snippet of the young clerk's vernacular to lend credibility to his faux outdoorsy confidence, but it didn't sound quite right coming out of his mouth, and Katherine was unimpressed. He tried a different angle. "Clay's new target client, Reggie Dugan, goes there all the time. He arranged it for us. He was at the party; Clay must have invited him. Land developer. You remember him?"

Katherine stiffened. "I think so. Big man, right?"

"Well, he's a man's man for sure, and a big game hunter. He keeps food and supplies in a hunting cabin for his visits. And he's a builder, so the place should be nice. I'm guessing it's a little open-beam number with a propane stove and a few mounted heads."

"Lovely."

"Clay says we have to catch fish and shoot cute furry animals to cook, or we eat beans."

"There's a gun? You've never shot a gun in your life."

"Can't be that hard. Point and pull the trigger."

"You should probably leave that to Clay."

"Why do you say that?"

"He seems more the type."

"Type of what?"

"No offense. It's just . . . 'Stuart the Great Hunter'? I don't think so."

"I could kill . . . something."

And then Katherine laughed. It was worse than if she'd outright said he wasn't man enough. It didn't make him feel annoyed or angry. Just sad. And old.

"I'm going to bring you something dead that I kill. You'll see." Then he smiled. He was relieved when she smiled back.

Katherine gave him a smooch on the forehead. "Some frozen salmon fillets would be fine."

Logan International Airport was what Clay called "a cluster," which Stu understood to be a polite shortening of the term *cluster fuck*. Crowds of travelers hurried to wait in lines at counters and security checkpoints. Stu and Clay had finally checked in and were on their way to security. Stuart had been forced to check two huge bags and pay extra for each.

Clay smirked. "I think you overpacked." He carried only one bag—a backpack that was a standard size and weight. Stu couldn't understand how he'd done it. Clay rubbed it in. "We're gonna need a sled for all your stuff."

Stu frowned. "There won't be a lot of snow this time of year, will there?"

"Alaska pretty much invented snow, pal. But it shouldn't be bad where we're going for a couple more weeks. When you turn fifty, we can go back and do the Iditarod if you like."

"Let's just get through this."

Clay held up their tickets. "Alaska Airlines to Seattle, then on to Fairbanks. A hired car will take us from there to the private airstrip. Our pilot will have rifles for us."

"Wow. Sounds first class."

"Dugan is rich. This is what happens when you run with the big dogs."

"Maybe this trip won't be so bad after all."

A wolf whistle came from Clay's pants, and he stepped out of the security line to fish around in his pocket, eventually producing his cell phone.

"Excuse me for a moment, partner."

Stu watched as Clay paced back and forth a polite distance away from him and the other travelers. It was hard to determine the nature of the call. Clay looked both pleased and upset at the same time—a difficult expression to read. Finally he hung up and came marching back to the line.

"Dry cleaning done?" Stu joked.

"Dugan wants a meeting. He'd like to talk about jumping ship from Lambert and McClure."

"Dugan? Really?" Stu knew Clay had been wooing the developer, and he knew the stakes.

"Yep. We're his first call, thanks to your and your wife's hospitality."

"Next week is good. We should see him as soon as possible, before he visits other firms."

"I agree. But next week is not as soon as possible. He'll schedule other firms in the interim. He's a man who makes decisions and takes action."

"We don't want to do it over the phone. That's not a good idea. The phone is very impersonal."

"We need this, Stu."

"I agree it's a good opportunity."

"Cut the crap. This is the biggest recurring client we've ever had interested in us. And I've been working him for months."

Stu felt his heart flutter. "You want to cancel the trip? Because I'm okay with that."

Clay paced again, debating. "No. In fact, hell no. You need this."

"I *don't* need this. Besides, I can need it next year. We'll reschedule."

Clay shook his head. "No. You go. I'll stay and take care of Dugan."

"What?"

"The directions are all in this packet, and your pilot will get you where you need to be. Done."

"No, no. *Not* done. We should meet with Dugan together. He had a firm of ten lawyers. We're only two. Without me, we're only one."

"I can handle it. You know I can. I'm the one who's been working this. I'll dazzle him, and when you get back, you'll calculate the rates and do all of the paperwork and boring shit."

"Thanks."

"That's what you're good at. This is what I'm good at. Look, this is exciting. You're getting the best of both worlds here. You go, you clear your head, you become a new man. When you get back, we kick our practice into a higher gear. It's all good. Besides, I'll be able to tell him that you're out blasting crap at his cabin. That will give him a boner for our office for sure."

Stu's head swam. The idea of heading into the woods alone was significantly different than going with Clay. It felt like a bad decision, rash and rushed. The sort of decision he didn't make. Ever.

"Come on," Clay said. "Don't be a pussy."

"This isn't the ninth grade. You can't shame me into going." But he did feel shame. Caution's birthplace was fear; he was scared. There was no other way to analyze it. Katherine would nod knowingly and say the she'd known he wouldn't go through with it. His own woman would think him less a man than Clay or Dugan. Dugan himself would think he was a coward. And Clay would probably make a joke about it at the meeting.

To Stu's surprise, however, Clay's expression softened. "Sorry," he said. "If you want me to go with you on the trip, I'll schedule Dugan for next week. I just have to call him back."

"No," Stu said suddenly. "I'm going. You stay. Get the deal done."

"You're sure?"

"Yeah. I'm sure. In fact, hell yeah. You're right. I've never done anything like this." *A week in a cabin,* he thought. *How hard can it be?* A professional pilot and not too much snow. Couldn't be worse than law school or the bar exam, and he'd survived those lower planes of hell. Besides, he had Edwin's five-hundred-page guide to everything the wilderness could throw at him. He hoisted his carry-on to his shoulder with a manly grunt. "Actually, I'm psyched. I'm going to split wood and shoot shit and not take showers, and it's going to kick ass."

CHAPTER 9

The turnaround in Seattle was quick, and Stu had to take a mini-train to a satellite terminal to catch his Alaska Airlines flight to Anchorage. His last connection would be a regional carrier to Fairbanks. He fretted over whether his luggage would make the transfer, and the annoyingly chipper counter agent couldn't reassure him. She would only say that the ground crew would "do their best," which sounded suspiciously like the phrase's less polite cousin "no promises."

He'd been skimming the *Edwin's* survival guide. It made everything seem easy enough. A lean-to was apparently a mere matter of leaning a couple of poles in the crooks of branches and stacking sticks on them. Simple. Starting a fire was, likewise, an easy step-by-step process, it said. And if he needed to hike anywhere, he had one goddamned expensive pair of boots to do it in.

A few disturbingly short hours later Stu stood in the Fairbanks International Airport terminal. He retrieved his two bags without any of his imagined troubles and put them on a cart with a loose wheel, then wobbled off looking for his ride. He wasn't sure what to look for, so he kept an eye out for a man with a black sedan or a sign that said STARK on it. There was a phone number he could call from his cell phone if he didn't spot it right away. He stood at the curb for a minute or two with no luck. Not only did he fail to spot his sedan, he failed to see *any* black sedans or signs held overhead. There were plenty of dirty pickups and old SUVs, however. Finally he went for his phone and dialed. It rang. A man answered at the other end.

"Hello?"

"Hi. This is Stuart Stark. I've just touched down, and I'm supposed to have a car waiting."

"Just a sec."

While Stu was on the phone, a grizzled man leaned out of a beat-up Ford F-250 4x4 with a winch bolted to the front. "Hey, bud!" he called out.

Stu stepped back from the curb to get out of his way.

The man honked. "Hey, bud!"

Stu waved him off.

The man on the phone came back on. "You standing at passenger loading?"

"Sorry," Stu said. "Some idiot in a Ford POS is yelling at me."

"Funny," the man said. "I think that idiot is me."

Stuart turned. The grizzled man held up a cell phone and wiggled it.

Nice. Stuart waved back and dragged his hamstrung cart toward the truck.

"Sorry," Stuart said.

"That's two sorries in two sentences. Not a great start. And what's a POS?"

"I'd rather not say."

"I'd rather you did."

"Umm, it means 'piece of shit.' Sorry."

The man laughed. "That's okay. You can make up for it with your tip. I'll grab your bags."

The man snatched up the duffel and flung it over the side of the truck into the bed with an ominous *crunch*. When he went for the backpack, Stuart leaped in front of him and grabbed it protectively.

"I can get this one."

"Suit yourself. Hop in."

Stu rode with the pack on his lap. It was heavy, and as soon as they hit the rougher roads, it began to crush his testicles at every pothole.

"I'm going to a private airstrip east of town," Stu announced. "Yukon Air Tours."

"I know it. Bush pilot. You going to fish or hunt?"

"Presumably," Stu said.

"You get up here much?"

Stu thought it best not to seem too green or naive. He hadn't asked the price of the fare and wondered if it might change depending upon his answer. "No, but I'm a personal friend of Reginald Dugan, who employs a pilot at Yukon on an annual basis," he said importantly.

The man eyed Stu. "Reggie. I've heard of him."

"Really? It must be a small community."

"Smaller than you think. And bigger."

"Is that cab-driver philosophy?"

"Naw. It's census statistics. The state's forty-seventh in population and first in size. We're low-density here. Did you know we bought all this from the Russkies for two cents per acre?"

"Seward's Folly."

"Aha! So you're an educated man. Or else you like trivia."

"I was a history major."

"Really? What kind of job does that get a guy?"

"None. I had to go to school all over again after I got my undergraduate degree."

"For what?"

"Law."

"Oh. . . ."

That was all the man said. Stu didn't expect more, not aloud anyway. The unsaid conclusion of the sentence was usually, *So you're probably a bit of an asshole, huh?* He didn't blame people who thought so. A lot of law-yers were.

"How far out of town is the airstrip?"

"Thirty miles, give or take."

"Do you enjoy living up here?"

"Yeah. People say it's what America used to be. I like that, so I say it too."

The remainder of the thirty miles was mostly quiet with scattered small talk. Stuart never asked the man's name, and the guy didn't offer. The river town melted away quickly, replaced by long miles of scattered driveways with homes in the distance. When they finally turned at a dirt road and completed the last ball-smashing half-mile of the journey, any fare that meant stopping seemed perfectly reasonable. When the trip came to a mer-ciful end, Stu tipped 20 percent and hurried out to retrieve his duffel bag himself. The man leaned out of the window.

"Good luck to you."

"Thanks. Do you have a card or anything so I can call you when my week in paradise is up?"

The man fished around in his pocket and came up with a bowling cou-pon, upon which he wrote a phone number. "That's my direct line," he said, handing over the piece of paper. He patted his cell phone. "Anytime you need a POS, just give me a call." With that, he winked and drove away, leaving Stu standing in the middle of a dirt driveway.

YUKON AIR TOURS was carved into a rough-cut sign of solid wood. The sign hung overhead, dangling from chains on the gate he'd driven through when he'd arrived with his nameless driver. Not fancy, but quaint in its way. The business itself appeared to be located in a one-story ranch-style home. *Not so first class.* Stu slung a bag over each shoulder and staggered to the front door under their weight, where he rapped with a heavy knocker in the shape of a salmon against the metal receiving plate. The metallic boom echoed inside and rang sharply outside. The weather was what Stu's father used to call "crisp." The bite of fall was tangible, but the tempera-ture was not yet uncomfortably cold.

No one came to the door. Stu rapped again, annoyed; he'd called ahead to provide his approximate arrival time. But when the clang of the steel salmon died away, a woodsy silence fell over the forested property again. Stu looked around. He shared the porch with a life-size pair of carved wood bear cubs in playful poses at either end of a handmade wooden bench.

Sure, easy for you to frolic, Stu thought. Wood bears didn't have demanding clients likely to call to complain that they were goofing around in the forest all week and neglecting their cases.

Stu put his bags down, squeezed past the bears, and was beginning to peek through windows when he heard the unmistakable sound of a chainsaw firing up. It was loud and nearby, in back of the house if his ears were correct. He walked around. The house sat on a slope that fell away until it met a lake about one hundred yards downhill. Between the two were several dozen trees. The chainsaw roared steadily now, and Stu spotted its operator. The man stood facing one of the trees with the gas-powered tool cocked to his shoulder while he studied his victim, a simple pine with no branches below ten feet.

Stu started down the hill toward him. Shouting would have done no good, considering the awful din the saw made. The man seemed to be taking a long time to decide where to make the first cut. The walk was pleasant, though. In fact, the smell of forest and sight of the lake might have been soothing, had it not been for the noise. Stu ambled along, trying to enjoy it. Halfway down, however, he noticed the first face.

He jumped. The bearded man stared at him from a nearby tree. Not from behind the tree, but from the tree itself. Indeed, the shadowy face *was* the tree. The man's face had been carved directly into the wood, his wild, bushy hair flowing up the bark, while his long beard ran down the trunk almost to the ground. It was a reasonable likeness of a wrinkled elderly male, but something in the expression was just a bit off—the open mouth that was a black hole without teeth, or perhaps the empty eyes that were dark brown orbs with no whites. He looked, Stu thought, like a crazy soulless transient.

Old Man Winter on a bad day. Or the Unabomber.

Stu glanced about. There were more, dozens more, all of them variations of the same grotesque face, with deep gashes forming their wrinkles and unruly hair. The misshapen visages glared at him from trees all around. Some tried to smile, but with their dark mouths they could only manage leering grins. Stu suddenly wanted to be away from the old men, but there was no way out of the forest of faces except through it.

Downhill, the chainsaw roared and bit into wood, its pitch dropping an octave as it spat sawdust. Oddly, a strange man wielding a chainsaw seemed less creepy than the gawking trees, and so Stu hurried through them toward the lake.

The man was wearing leather gloves and large sound-dampening headphones. Stu gave him a wide berth in case he was startled and wheeled around with the whirring saw. As soon as Stu stepped into his line of sight, the man killed the engine.

"Oh! Hiya!" he said loudly, overcompensating for the headphones.

"Hiya," Stu parroted.

Chainsaw Man removed his headphones. "You must be Stark."

"Yep."

"I'm Ivan." He grabbed Stu's hand and pumped it vigorously, swinging the chainsaw with his other arm. "I was just working the wood here while I was waiting for you to show up."

"You did all these faces?"

"Ay-yuh. Like 'em?"

"They're lifelike and inhuman at the same time."

"I know. Great, huh? I sell them, if you want me to cut one loose for ya. Most people want a bear cub, though. Don't know why. I sell those, too, by the way. You ready for liftoff?"

Stu nodded. "Are you on the staff of Yukon Tours?"

"Ay-yuh." He laughed. "I *am* the staff. Right this way, dude." Ivan started toward the house.

"How far is the private airstrip?"

Ivan pointed back over his shoulder at the lake. "Floatplane."

Stu sighed. *The lake. Of course.*

Up at the house, they gathered Stu's bags, then Ivan started back toward the lake.

"Isn't there any prep work?" Stu asked. "Filing a flight plan?"

"Nope. We get in, we take off. I used to have a checklist, if that's what you mean. But I got it all memorized now, and she's gassed up and ready to go."

"I think I'm supposed to get a gun," Stu added.

"Ay-yuh. Right."

Ivan invited Stu into the house, which looked more like a dorm room. Empty pizza boxes and beer cans littered the kitchen table, and a computer with a naked-lady screensaver sat on a small desk in the living room. Ivan threw open a closet door near the back door, and the smell of marijuana rolled out. It was an unmistakable scent Stu associated more with the Bristol County sheriff's evidence room than college parties. At least five rifles leaned against the wall inside. Two handguns had been tossed haphazardly on the upper shelf. Ivan selected one of the rifles and rummaged through boxes on the shelf for the correct caliber of ammunition. When he turned back to Stu, he took a long sad look at the gun, seemingly reluctant to hand it over.

"You sure you don't just want some bear spray?" Ivan asked.

"I'm supposed to hunt. I don't think I can hunt with a can of spray." *Not too bright, this one,* Stu thought.

"True." Still, he hesitated.

"Don't worry. I'll bring it back in a week. Odds are, I won't even fire it."

"A-course." Ivan smiled and handed it over. "Browning thirty-aught-six. Keep it pointed at the ground or at the sky and you'll be all right. Unless a bear comes at ya. Then point it at the bear."

They loaded Stu's gear into the plane, a yellow Piper Super Cub with a fading black lighting bolt down the side, a cracked passenger window, and a dent in its left wingtip. A dark exhaust stain fanned out from the nose cone, and green mold had a foothold in the seams of the pontoons. Given the craft's obvious age, Stu hoped it was well maintained. He walked around the dock, examining it. He didn't know what he was looking for, but it made him feel better to do a rudimentary examination. He imagined that the small plane had once looked like a bright buttercup perched atop its white pontoons, but age and the elements had turned it into a dingy old school bus for two. *The short bus.* The fuselage was not much wider than the seats, which were stacked one behind the other.

It seemed that the first test of his manhood would be to board the tiny, rickety-looking thing, and when he couldn't procrastinate any longer, Stu took a deep breath, ducked his head, and squeezed in behind Ivan. He didn't notice that Ivan himself smelled strongly of weed until they were closed in the small space together.

Great.

"The overhead wings are overhead," Ivan explained as he checked instruments and started the engine. "So you get a good view, because they're not in the way when you look down."

Wow, this guy's an engineering genius. "I hear some pilots make amateur modification to their planes. Is yours modified at all?"

"Nah. Well, I did cut out the baggage compartment to give it more space toward the back a bit. And it's got the bigger twenty-four-gallon gas tanks. But that's it. Oh, and I threw on an extra ten-gallon outboard I got off a wrecked cub. And the battery mount is forward a touch to help with takeoff in tight spots. Do you know planes?"

"No."

"Then why do you ask?"

"Just the curious type."

"You seem like the nervous type to me. No need to get all jumpy. Just relax and enjoy the ride, bud. This is what I do. You're a lawyer, huh? Once you know your stuff, you just walk into the courtroom and go at it, right?" Ivan didn't wait for an answer, but simply taxied noisily out onto the lake and turned the Cub to start their takeoff run.

It was probably true that Ivan knew as much about planes as Stu did about law. Problem was, Stu had crashed. And burned. It could happen to the best of them, and Ivan clearly wasn't the best of anything. Stu's co-workers had called his titanic failure bad luck, but it was overconfidence. He'd taken too much risk. He'd asked for the unwinnable case. *Anyone would have lost,* he'd told himself a thousand times.

But I was the one who did.

"I won't be nervous if you keep it simple," Stu yelled over the engine.

"I don't need any treetop sightseeing, and don't bother buzzing herds of reindeer."

"Caribou, dude."

"Whatever. No need to bother them."

Ivan shrugged. "Sure thing. You're the client."

Stu allowed himself a smirk. *That's a switch.*

Ivan punched it. "Here we go!"

CHAPTER 10

The Cub buzzed along above the treetops. Fairbanks and the outlying homes associated with the riverside city quickly dwindled as they flew north, and the wilderness took over. Swaths of trees followed snaking streambeds near town, but soon merged into a solid green expanse dotted by occasional circles of bright blue water. From the Cub, the ground looked like brilliant sapphires sewn into a green tapestry. Ivan chattered incessantly from the pilot's seat, talk-shouting over the engine.

"Did you know there are over three million lakes in Alaska?"

"Wow. I did not know that," Stu yelled back. *How do we find the right one?* he wondered.

The view was indeed spectacular, and the land was as vast and beautiful as advertised, but it was difficult for him to get used to the fact that the Piper Super Cub's motor sounded like an oversize lawn mower engine.

"It's amazing how well these little planes fly, considering how flimsy they are," Stu said.

"Not flimsy, dude. Light. The best bush pilots can land a Cub in only twenty feet on an uphill slope, and take off in just about as little."

"I read that airplane fatalities are twenty times more common here than the rate nationwide."

"Yep," Ivan agreed.

That was all Stu's pilot had to say on the matter. There was no argument or justification. He seemed almost proud of the grim statistic, as though mangling oneself in a heap of metal on a cold glacier was as romantic an end as a man could meet, the inevitable result of the age-old battle pitting man against the elements coupled with the more modern struggle of man against machine.

Or just man against reason, Stu thought. "Are we still heading north?" he asked.

"A little east now."

"How far to go?"

"An hour."

"We're way out here, huh?"

"I've been farther."

"This cabin, is it on the lake?"

Ivan hesitated. "Close to the lake. I'll drop you on the near side. It's a short hike."

An hour later a small mountain loomed, and Ivan yanked the Cub up and over it, treating Stu to an unwelcome moment of vertigo and then a sweeping view of the small lake on the other side. Once they'd cleared the peak, the Cub dropped suddenly and zeroed in on the water. Ivan took it down at a steep angle that made Stu grab ahold of the seat, and then leveled out and slowed for their water landing. Stu had only ridden on commercial jets, and so traveling less than the speed of a car during the landing was an odd sensation. The pontoons skipped, then caught in the water with a slight jerk, and the Cub quickly drifted to a stop. Ivan rotated the nose toward shore, and they putted into the shallows.

"Hop out here."

"In the water?"

"It's rocky, dude. I don't want to beat up the pontoons. Wade in. Hold your bags overhead. I'll be here a few minutes while you get packed up. I gotta do my halftime inspection."

Ivan did a halfhearted round of checks outside the plane, but mostly waited while Stu loaded a bag atop each shoulder and slung the .30-06 over his back. Then Stu lowered himself from the pontoon into the lake. The water crept up to his testicles, which had only recently recovered from the beating they'd taken in the truck. They'd had a hard day.

"Cold!"

Ivan stared at Stu with a genuinely sympathetic look.

"See you in a week," Stu called. "Already looking forward to it."

Ivan frowned. "Good luck."

And then Ivan was back in the cockpit and puttering out onto the lake for takeoff. The shore wasn't far, but by the time Stu struggled over the slippery stones on the lakebed to dry land, the Cub was disappearing over the mountain peak.

No turning back now.

The lake sat in a natural bowl. Stu began searching for a path up the slope, because up was the only direction to go. The thing about finding the path up the mountain, however, was that there *was* no path up the mountain. The sheer cliff of crumbling dirt directly in front of him was not an option. Beside the cliff, a rockslide had created a field of boulders he might be able to scramble over. Not promising either, considering he was carrying two heavy bags. Farther along, a steep area crowded with underbrush seemed the best choice. So long as there wasn't poison oak or ivy or horrible thistles, he could push his way through in a half an hour or so, he thought. He hitched his bags onto his shoulders and started up.

Two hours later he stood at the top of the ridge, gasping for breath and overlooking the lake. The view was spectacular, almost better than from the plane because he'd earned it. The air was the cleanest he'd ever breathed, and the waning sun cast long, amazing shadows of the fir and pine trees down the opposite slope. The quiet was broken only by the occasional distant titter of a squirrel or the chortling of some variety of warbler. Stu scanned the entire ridge, turning his head a full 180 degrees to take it all in, and he took a deep breath, filling his nostrils with pristine air. He felt more alive than he had in years. It was everything Clay had promised, with one exception. There was no cabin.

"What the hell?"

CHAPTER 11

It must be tucked in the trees, Stu thought. *No problem.*

He circled for an hour, taking short forays from the stony ridge into the forest, checking the direction of the sun each time he emerged. The distant and strangely pale circle of light remained stubbornly and directly across the lake from him, descending steadily due west. *I'm on the east side. This is the right spot. No doubt.* But Ivan wasn't the swiftest fish in the school. He could have made a mistake. Again Stu scanned the slope across the lake for a clearing. Perhaps Ivan the pot-smoking, wood-carving idiot pilot had dropped him on the wrong side. Then a more horrifying thought occurred to him. *What if he dropped me on the wrong lake?*

Up the hill to the ridge. Look for the clearing. Can't miss it.

Stu had repeated the words over and over. Only there was no clearing on the east ridge, unless bare jagged rocks counted as a clearing. Nor was there a visible clearing on the west side of the lake. Based upon his initial climb, he calculated that a trip to the other side would take at least two hours. But the sun hung low in the western sky.

I don't have two hours.

Stu felt his heart rate rise as the sun sank. Darkness was coming, and he was without shelter. He dug in his pack, yanking out thermal socks and spare long underwear with an orange waistband to get to *Edwin's Comprehensive Guide to Wilderness Survival.*

The lean-to had looked so simple to build in the diagrams—find two trees about seven feet apart with forked branches four to five feet high on the trunk. He glanced about. Nothing nearby fit the bill. That was the first problem. He read on. If he did find likely candidates, he would then need to place a pole in their respective forks. *Where the hell am I supposed to get a pole?* He could have stripped a fallen branch if he had a hatchet. He didn't. He had a large knife, but he couldn't cut thick limbs with it. *Retrieve a branch and carve some notches,* it instructed. *Find another branch. Find many branches to cut and lean across the pole.* It all presumed a hatchet. *Locate some more branches, grass, moss, and so forth,* Edwin's casually suggested, as though all these materials could be found neatly labeled in bulk outdoor bins. There was no moss in sight, and the rocky slope had no grass. He supposed he could cut some of the thorny brush for cover, but it was not dense enough to effectively repel water. The estimated time of construction, according to *Edwin's,* was an hour, assuming the right tools and readily available materials. He had neither. And the sun wasn't waiting for him.

Screw you, Edwin!

Stu slammed the book closed. He had to get going or he'd be working in the dark. He could start a fire, and he had a flashlight. If he gathered all the materials first, he could construct the lean-to by firelight. Not very comforting.

Then something caught his eye. It wasn't on the far side of the lake nor on his own eastern slope, but south. It was a small patch of tan where the trees parted, like a small hole in a green blanket. He didn't have binoculars, and he strained to see. The dot looked out of place.

Unnatural.

Stu stepped up onto the rock against which he'd leaned the .30-06, to gain a better vantage. It didn't help; he could see no better from on top.

When he looked down, the barrel of the gun was pointing straight up at him. It was unnerving to have instant death immediately at hand. Police officers carried guns, of course. And when they'd come to the DA's office wearing their sidearms, the idea that another human being could decide to make him dead at any moment had always made him uncomfortable. The magnitude and finality of the decision did not match the ease with which it could be made—a moment of bad judgment, anger, or even just a touch of insanity and . . . *blam!*

He slid off the rock, careful to avoid bumping the gun and potentially blowing his own head off. Then he paused. *The scope.* He scooped up the rifle, pointed it toward the dot, and peered through the elongated hourglass-shaped black metal tube mounted on top. It took him a moment to find the right distance to hold his eye from the glass, but when he did, a small clearing popped into focus ten times closer than when viewed with his naked eye.

There was something. *Wooden.* Possibly the corner of a structure peeking out from the trees. He'd read in *Edwin's* that desperate men sometimes saw what they wanted to see, like an oasis in the desert, and so he was wary. But staring longer didn't help; it just made his eyes go buggy. He lowered the gun.

His choice was simple. He could either use his hour of sunlight preparing a lean-to, or use the hour to hike to the possibly imaginary structure. If he built a shelter, it would be modest. If he walked to the clearing and found that it contained only a downed tree or a rail fence, he'd have no shelter at all. Once he descended the hill, he wouldn't have a view of the clearing again until he stepped into it. It would be either a pleasant or decidedly unpleasant surprise.

His impulse was to take the safe route and build the lean-to in order to ensure himself some shelter in case of rain, or worse, snow. He couldn't read the sky. It was gray in one direction, clear in another, and clouds were moving at notable speed in yet another. In its very first chapter, *Edwin's* had warned against guessing and taking chances.

Lean-to it is.

He began to scout around for branches. A curious squirrel tittered above him. He couldn't see it, but he could hear it up in the trees somewhere. *Easy for you to say,* Stu thought. *You probably have a place to sleep tonight.* He recalled that *Edwin's* had listed squirrels as an easy source of food in a pinch. They were crepuscular, meaning they were active during the morning and afternoon and could be caught in the light of day. They hid at night when nocturnal creatures came out. *Nocturnal.* There was something horrible about that word. The darkness. The unknown. Unseen predators. There was a reason squirrels hid at night. Stu recalled a story he'd read about a woman who'd been dragged from her tent by a Kodiak bear.

Stu dropped the branches he'd gathered and began madly stuffing his clothes and supplies back into his pack. He didn't bother refolding anything; the sun was no longer visible over the ridge, and it was a long walk to the clearing.

An hour later Stu broke from the shadowy trees on the south slope with his heart pounding. Exhausted and terrified, he prayed that Dugan's luxurious hunting cabin would be nestled in the corner of the darkened clearing.

It wasn't.

Instead a small dilapidated shack little larger than a toolshed stood against the trees. *Stood* was generous; it was older than he was, and if it had not been leaning heavily against a sturdy fir, it would have long since collapsed. If he needed moss for a lean-to, however, there was plenty. The sagging roof was a green blanket of the stuff.

It's shelter, Stu thought. *Sort of.*

He wasn't sure whether to laugh or cry. But the sun was gone, and the glow from the western horizon that had guided him the last hundred yards to the clearing was waning fast. He hurried to the shack and tried the door, which was newer than the logs that made up the body of the place. It opened out. Stu recalled that doors in bear country were made to open outward so that they could not be forced in. A sobering thought. It was sticky, but a hard yank produced a crack and a cloud of dust that made him cough and stagger backward—the air stank of stagnation and something else foul he couldn't put his finger on. But he had no choice. He put an arm over his nose to attack the door again, and further struggles drew it wide enough to shine his flashlight inside.

Movement.

Stu whipped the flashlight to follow the motion. Dark shapes scurried in the shadows.

Rats?

He hadn't given vermin any thought. In fact, if a fat brown one wasn't crouched squarely in the beam of his flashlight, he'd have guessed they were strictly urban pests.

At least three of them.

Under normal circumstances, he wouldn't have set foot inside. Unfortunately, the circumstances were decidedly *not* normal. Given the choice between bears and rats, he lowered his pack and duffel to the ground and slipped through the crack in the door, flashlight at the ready.

He couldn't very well stab the rodents to death with his knife—too close, too personal. And he didn't have an ax or a heavy branch. But there was no way he was going to sleep in the cabin with three rats.

The thirty-aught-six, he thought.

As targets they presented little challenge. The trio of vermin neither hid nor fled, but simply moved to defensive positions and bared their teeth as though ready to duke it out with him over occupancy.

Stu shook his head. "Sorry, but I'm in no mood to take any shit from the three blind mice," he said, and he drew a bead on the nearest one.

It perched overhead atop a ceiling beam directly over the wooden platform that appeared to be the cabin's bed. The gun's scope was trained at one hundred yards, according to Ivan, and no good at close range, so he nestled his forehead beside it and sighted down the barrel. Then he slowly squeezed the trigger.

The gun boomed, and Stu's world went white for a moment. Then he saw stars. At first he thought the bullet had ricocheted and hit him in the head. But he also realized that, if he was thinking about it, he probably wasn't dead.

Probably.

When his sight returned, he saw that he still held the flashlight, but the gun was lying on the floor. He touched his forehead. It was sore, and his hand came away covered with wet sticky fluid. He was bleeding. It took another moment to piece it together. He'd been holding the .30-06 too loosely, he decided, and the recoil had jerked it out of his hands. The gun had kicked, and the scope had smacked him in the head. But there was too much blood. He turned the flashlight to the beam overhead. There was a red notch in the wood where the rat had been. The rest of the rodent was splattered across the ceiling. He gagged. The blood wasn't his.

Thirty minutes later he emerged with the beaten carcasses of the other two rats. It had taken some time to grope through the dark with the flashlight for a branch to club them, but he couldn't bring himself to shoot the other two and sleep in a bloody slaughterhouse. He wiped the rat guts from his head with a shirt and threw it outside. Then he stretched out his sleeping bag. His coat became his pillow. There was a rock-lined fire pit in one corner and a sheet metal hood built to funnel its smoke toward a hole in the ceiling. But starting a fire didn't appeal to him. His matches and other fire-starting tools were deep in his pack, which was now jumbled because he'd had to empty it and restuff it in a hurry. Nor did he have kindling, and he wasn't about to go out in the dark again to find some.

There were signs of some human use in the cabin—an old burnt log in the fire pit and the replaced front door—but not frequent use. Stu knew he should unpack his gear and get organized. But the door was shut, the rats were gone, and he was much less likely to be eaten by a bear than if he were in an Edwinian lean-to, so it seemed best to simply go to sleep. When he was a child, his mother had told him that if he was having a bad day, going to bed was like hitting the reset button.

And that's exactly what I need at this point.

Stu pulled off his damp pants, socks, and underwear, and hung them over his pack. Then he fished out the orange-banded long underwear, which made him look like he was wearing an orange hula hoop, and stuffed himself into the sleeping bag, thankful that the aggressively laid-back sales kid at the Great Beyond had talked him up to the Arctic Fox model.

He settled in, bitter and confused. The cabin was in the wrong location, it was the wrong size, and it certainly wasn't what he'd expected from Dugan. The wood bed frame was hard without a mattress, and he could smell rat blood. He didn't bother to clean it; he found that he was physically spent from his hikes up and down the mountain, and emotionally drained. And when the rain began to pour through the ceiling, he didn't even bother to get up, but simply cursed Clay, Dugan, Ivan, and anyone else he could think of, and curled himself into a ball in one corner beyond the spatter, like a cowering pretzel.

CHAPTER 12

Stu uncurled from his fitful sleep as a shaft of light crept in through the bullet hole in the roof and settled on his face. He found himself staring at the log wall inches from his nose. Something was crawling there.

A walking yellow and black thumb drive? No, that made no sense. He blinked. *Oh, a wasp the size of a thumb drive.*

As he watched, two more emerged from a nearby hole. Yellow jackets. Stu snapped into a sitting position, fully awake. He'd been half awake for an hour, drifting in and out, too uncomfortable to sleep, too tired to rise. Sitting upright, he could no longer fool himself that he was trying to sleep in a puddle on the hard cot. Now that the sun was up, however, he might be able to get a fire going, he thought.

That bastard Edwin can at least help me with that.

He rose to change clothes again, goose bumps standing out on his pale flesh. He had no idea how cold it was, except that he could see his breath. He finished donning a moisture-wicking T-shirt and a wool sweater, and then he pulled out *Edwin's Comprehensive Guide.*

Chapter 1 discussed climate. It said breath became visible at fifty degrees or less, depending upon humidity. The weather had been rain, not snow, the night before, and his hands weren't growing numb, which meant it probably wasn't freezing. Closer to fifty. *Thank God.*

With his coat on, he tried to shake the chill by moving about to inspect the cabin and rummaging through his pack to organize his gear. The cabin inspection took all of two minutes. *I'll have to clean it,* he decided immediately. There was no counter space upon which to prepare food, the yellow jackets were a lurking menace, and the rat slaughter demanded a thorough scrub. There was no stove. More distressing, there was no canned food tucked away on shelves or in a cabinet. In fact, there were no shelves or cabinets at all. Stu tapped on the walls to see if there might be a hollow space. No dice. He even got down on the floor and looked under the cot. There was nothing—no cans of beans or freeze-dried soup or even Spam. He began to get a sick feeling in his gut that was either hunger or dread, or both.

I'll have to hunt.

The cabin was also smaller than he'd thought the night before, which didn't seem possible. Seven by seven. *Forty-nine square feet, with the cot taking up fifteen of it and the fire pit five more.* The cot would have to double as the food prep area, Stu decided, and he wished he hadn't sprayed rodent guts all over it. His pack and duffel sat atop a cut log just inside the door, which kept them off the damp dirt floor. The cot still harbored small puddles of water courtesy of the hole he'd blasted in the ceiling. He wiped it off as best he could with his hand so he could sort his clothes. He already needed to hang his sleeping bag out to dry. With that thought in mind, he turned to the door. There was no more putting it off; it was time to face the day.

The wood groaned, and the flood of light made him wince. He poked his head out and glanced about for bears, then shoved the door fully open and stepped through. The first breath of air was sharp and clean in his lungs. The sun still hid behind the ridge to the east. Its generous light spilled over the mountain and into the valley, but it remained stingy with its heat.

"Friggin' brrr!"

Stu's human voice sounded foreign in the quiet clearing. *I don't belong here.* It also deflated the morning's bubble of surrealism. He could have mistaken his dim minutes inside the cabin for a bad dream, but once he breathed the chilled air and talked aloud in the silent glade, there was no denying reality. And when the lush green backdrop of immaculate forest didn't melt into the taupe and starched lace of his familiar bedroom walls on William Street, his Memory Foam pillow didn't materialize beneath his head, and Katherine wasn't pushing him off her side of the bed, there was no denying that he was thousands of miles from home in a completely ludicrous situation.

He hung his sleeping bag on a limb to dry and sat nearby on a log to read. *Edwin's* chapter 1 also had a short list of survival necessities. It first advised that a person should have appropriate clothing. *Check. Thank you, Great Beyond, and one-percent-cash-back Visa card.* He was supposed to secure shelter next, according to the list. *One rotting cabin. Check.* At least, it would be secured as soon as he did some roof repair and cleared out the wasps. A clean supply of water was the next priority. Stu looked down the hill. *One huge pristine lake. Check.* Then Stu's stomach turned.

Food.

He'd been avoiding thinking about it, but this was the killer. He had no food. The cabin had no food. *Edwin's* had suggestions. Wild vegetables. Edible flowers and trees. Hunting, trapping, or scavenging dead animals. *Dead animals?* Stu turned slowly.

The decaying body of one of the rats he'd clubbed lay nearby. Its lips were pulled back to expose its long teeth, and the resulting expression was an angry shut-eyed grimace. *Fuck you for killing me,* it seemed to be saying. *Especially if you're not going to eat me.* Stu quickly decided that he wasn't that desperate yet. He'd only missed breakfast so far. Besides, the flies were already at the body, along with one of his wasp friends.

There was a lesson, however; any food he left out for more than a few moments would be eaten by other hungry animals. The second rat corpse was already missing. It had been thrown beside the first one. His bloody shirt was gone too. Stu shuddered to think what he'd attracted by leaving it there. *A mistake. Edwin's* pointed out that "mistakes" in the wilderness accounted for more deaths than severe conditions. It also annoyingly reminded him that he should only kill what he intended to eat. *I wonder if rats wrote that section,* Stu thought.

He gathered wood for a fire. Another piece of advice from *Edwin's*. Filling the rock pit in the cabin took only a few branches, which he found lying around on the ground or snapped from nearby trees. He broke them to length by leaning them against the wall and stomping on them. He couldn't stack them very high in the pit or they crept too near the top of the rock and too close to the log wall. There was space for one large dense log, but he had no ax. In Cub Scouts he'd learned to start fires—small tinder on the bottom, larger kindling in a pyramid on top, logs later. Easy enough. Some underbrush seemed a good bet for the tinder, and he lined the bottom of the rock pit with it.

The Great Beyond fire kit contained a small box of matches along with the traditional and notoriously difficult-to-use metal match, designed to be used with a knife as a flint and steel. Stu went straight for the matches. Once he had a fire started, he could keep it going by adding wood. Simple. After that necessity was provided, he could try to learn the new skill. He went through five matches, however, without success. The shrubs caught, but the small branches didn't. As he reached for a sixth, he decided to count the remainder. Ten. Not nearly enough for a week at his rate of failure. He gritted his teeth, swallowed his Cub Scout pride, and consulted *Edwin's*.

Avoid damp or green wood was the first hint in the little gray box in the margin. Stu slapped his forehead. Half his wood was directly from trees, and the other half had been rained on the night before, and who knew how many other nights.

Stupid.

He took another trip outside to find drier branches, and was soon crouched at the pit and at it again. This time the wood caught, sending a promising white wisp up the sheet metal hood. *Better.* Stu stacked some of his damp wood on the dry layer.

Now this stuff will catch, he thought. And it did.

The smoke drove him from the cabin, and he stumbled to the ground beside his rat victim, gasping and wheezing. The space inside was so small that he'd noticed the black cloud gathering on the ceiling only moments before it descended to try to kill him. The wasps hadn't liked it either, and they'd come stampeding out right behind him, looking for something to sting. He'd avoided all but one by throwing his hood over his face and pulling his hands up into his sleeves until they gave up and wandered off.

The crude chimney hadn't worked, he realized, as he unwrapped his face and climbed to a kneeling position. And the small hole he'd shot in the ceiling certainly hadn't provided enough ventilation. Stu stared up at the roof as the wasp sting on his cheek started to swell. He didn't think he was allergic, and hoped to God he wasn't; there was no way he could get a shot of whatever stopped people from dying when they got stung. The chimney atop the cabin was a shorn plastic tube with a coffee can thrown over it upside down. The smoke coming from it was barely a trickle. It was blocked, obviously. Stu glanced down at the dead rat. Its grimace looked more like a grin now.

"Laugh all you want. I have to go up there to fix my bullet hole anyway."

His fire was still burning, still producing gouts of black smoke, which rolled out the door. He'd left it open to air out, but guessed that there was still another hour's worth of wood burning in the pit.

I definitely got a fire going.

He'd thought about dashing in to feel around for his packs, but dying from carbon monoxide poisoning would be stacking stupid on top of stupid, as he used to say about criminal defendants who skipped their court appearances hoping their problems would go away.

And Edwin's *probably has a chapter warning against running into a smoke-filled room.*

The tree against which the cabin leaned had no lower branches to climb, but Stu was able to wedge himself between the stump and the wall. He placed his feet on the top half of the rounded logs, pressed his back against the tree, and inched his way up until he could grab the edge of the low roof, where he hung like a plucked chicken.

"Shit."

He kicked his legs to swing back and forth, and finally pressed them against the tree to boost himself up onto his belly atop the cabin roof. He inched his way up and found the bullet hole first. It wasn't difficult to locate; a steady stream of smoke the width of a dime streamed up from it.

Got you. He wedged a flat piece of bark beneath the upper shingle and tapped it into place with a stick he'd tucked in his pants for the climb. *Done.* Stu nodded, satisfied. It felt good to accomplish something after a night and morning of screwups and debacles.

He crawled up to the makeshift chimney. The can sat tilted on top. He removed it. Beneath, the pipe was filled with small woody debris. *A nest.* A smooth brown object was nestled in the center. *And breakfast!* Stu reached in and removed the smallish egg. He couldn't hold it in his hand and crawl, so he slid it into his mouth. The stick served to clear out the PVC pipe. Twigs and mud had been packed into the pipe ingeniously. *Instinctively,* Stu thought, and he began to plunge them out, careful to keep his face away from the opening to avoid the inevitable rush of smoke that would burst through.

Soon a thick abrupt stream of smoke poured out. Stu replaced the coffee can and sat back on the mossy shingles. He hadn't worked with his hands since he and Katherine had fixed up their home on William Street four years earlier. They'd poured a lot of sweat, and memories, into the place; he still recalled carrying her across the threshold when the floor was cracked mustard-yellow linoleum. It was a good place for them, practical, manageable, and scheduled to be paid off well before he retired. He'd forgotten the satisfaction of fixing things. Nothing he did in the law seemed to fix anything. He simply absorbed other people's problems like a conflict sponge. It felt good to set a shingle and repair a chimney.

Stu turned to look out over the valley, the lake, and the endless blue sky, his new domain. Perhaps doing guy stuff in the wilderness for a week wasn't so bad.

I fixed a goddamned roof and found some food, he thought. *And without any help from a book!*

He heard a creaking sound, and then the deeper groan of straining wood. He froze but it didn't matter. A loud *crack* was followed closely by a sudden feeling of weightlessness as the roof collapsed, and he watched the endless blue sky recede as he fell.

CHAPTER 13

Stu spat gooey egg whites and yolk out onto the dirt floor amongst broken shingles and green clumps of moss. There were injuries—a cut on his arm where he'd grazed the wooden cot, a lump on his head, and nasty soft-tissue bruises he'd certainly discover later. No concussion symptoms, it seemed—no loss of consciousness, no ringing ears or seeing stars, he knew who he was, and he was painfully aware of *where* he was. That was good. But when he sat up, his ankle screamed in pain.

Oh God, don't be broken, he thought.

Stu dragged himself up onto the cot, where he prodded his rapidly swelling flesh, and grimaced. He was annoyed to look over and see his fire innocently blazing away, its smoke drifting happily up through the new and improved hole in the roof.

His backpack had a Great Beyond deluxe emergency kit in a large outer pocket, hopefully with some gauze to stabilize his ankle, whether broken or sprained. And his cut would need to be cleaned. Untreated, an infec-

tion could start. Stu limped two steps to his pack and hauled it back over
to the cot.

The kit contained a cloth wrap, and *Edwin's* advised him to use it to
immobilize and compress the ankle. It hurt, but soon he had his lower
leg wrapped like a mummy's.

The emergency kit also contained three plastic tubes, the contents of
which was not apparent at first glance. *Perhaps an antibiotic ointment.* Stu
removed one. It was labeled GREAT BEYOND GOOP. The first ingredient listed
was dried soybeans. They were "water activated," it said. He read the fine
print; the package boasted enough calories and nutrients to keep a man
alive in the wild for one day for each tube.

Food!

He was not yet starving, but he was injured and he'd missed breakfast. Waiting for a lunch that might not arrive seemed unnecessary. *Better to get something in me,* he thought. The directions said that the contents
formed a paste when mixed correctly. Easy. His pack had a one-liter water bladder built into it. He poured a bit into a collapsible plastic cup and
squeezed in a tube of Goop.

It looked like russet-colored toothpaste and tasted like what he imagined baby food might taste like; that is, if the baby food was plasticized
and pumped full of preservatives. Stu wondered if the brownish Goop
would be better fried into a Goop fritter. *Everything tastes better fried, right?*
He forced down the paste and chased it with a hearty swig of water. Then
he checked the time on his receptionless cell phone. He was surprised to
find that less than an hour had passed. The sun was still just peeking over
the ridge to the east.

Time feels different out here. Slower.

He didn't feel like walking anywhere, so he let the treacherous fire
smolder, and sat on the cot, reorganizing his pack and duffel. His clothes
were jumbled and smelled like smoke. He pulled them out, shook them,
and refolded them. It was quick work; he did the laundry at home, while
Katherine mowed the lawn and paid bills. Stu did the dishes too. She didn't
want the chores to feel like they were assigned by gender. She was proud

that way, and she'd made it clear before their wedding that their union would be an equal partnership. She'd even written her own customized vows. She certainly wasn't going to obey him, she'd laughed.

It didn't seem like a good idea to hang the clothes to air out. He already had his sleeping bag hanging, and if the weather changed suddenly, he didn't want to have to scramble around on his injured leg trying to retrieve his underwear. One corner of the cabin was still protected from the large hole in the roof, and he stored the duffel there. He emptied the backpack, which contained the majority of his gear and supplies.

It didn't look like much when it was all laid out. The absence of the items he'd thought Dugan's cabin would provide was obvious and distressing. Many of them were on *Edwin's* "must-have" list. He had no food beyond the Goop. No cooking gear. And he couldn't cook in his collapsible plastic cup. No container for water except his one-liter bladder, which meant frequent trips down the mountain to the lake.

He was going to have to hunt. Or fish. That much was clear. He laid the .30-06 and a box of ammo down with the supplies. Plenty of bullets for a week of killing. Heck, he'd already bagged a rat. There was also a roll of fishing line and three hooks. Promising. No fry pan, but he could carve a spit to cook small game or trout over the fire. He had fished as a kid on the ocean once. Not so much on lakes.

How different can it be? Stu thought.

Edwin's highly recommended that he stay hydrated, so he sipped at the water regularly, which, in turn, meant a trip to the lake was the first priority. He'd take the gun, he thought, in case he saw game on the way, and he'd find a long branch to whittle and use as a fishing pole when he got there. *A regular white-collar Huck Finn.* The Great Beyond pack had a detachable mini-pack, into which he inserted the water bladder, the fishing line, and the hooks.

The walk down to the lake should have been pleasant. Stu imagined that people from metropolitan areas paid big money to enjoy such peace and solitude. But mostly, his foot hurt. He concluded that it wasn't broken before he left the small clearing, but by the time he had shuffled halfway down the hill, it was complaining with every step, sending vengeful little jolts of pain up his leg as punishment for putting it to work so soon after its traumatic encounter with the cabin's dirt floor. The need to carefully watch where he placed every footfall on the steep slope made it hard to scan for game. He saw squirrels as he approached the water, but he did not yet have an appetite for rodent meat. Besides, after seeing the devastation wrought on the rat by the .30-06, Stu didn't think there would be much meat left on a squirrel if he shot one.

Better to try for a fish, he told himself. He just needed to find some worms. *No problem.*

He turned over rocks for ten minutes, but nothing squirmed beneath them except tiny black beetles, so he moved to another area and pushed over a downed log, hoping to find some worms in the rotting earth. Nothing. He didn't have a shovel, so he dug with a stick, which was painstaking work. The earth turned reluctantly, and again he found no worms.

Perhaps a different type of insect.

There were huge flies, but they proved savvy and vengeful. Whenever Stu tried to swat them out of the air with a pine bough, they eluded its needled limbs and went for the exposed skin of his neck and face, which was still swelling from the wasp sting.

After several painful bites, he gave up and stuck his hook through the largest of the small beetles. It broke in half. The next three also broke in half. He finally had to start experimenting with locations for inserting the point into the squirming bugs, which felt a bit like animal torture. Five beetles later, though, he had one suspended like a tiny entomological science exhibit in the middle of the oversize hook. Stu held it up, staring doubtfully.

Perhaps the fish aren't too observant, he thought.

When he tied the hook on and pulled to test the fishing line, he found that it was difficult to get the tiny knots to hold. The line was smooth and slick, and the knots slipped loose under the slightest pressure. He tied it several times before he gripped the hook at the wrong angle. The needle-sharp hook punctured his thumb, sliding neatly beneath the skin just past the barb. Stu bit his lip and held back a yelp as he stared at the hook in his flesh.

I caught myself, he thought stupidly.

Fortunately, it did not penetrate deeply, and the shaft was near the surface. But the barbed hook wasn't coming back out the way it went in. He removed his knife and, after several moments' debate, pressed the blade against the skin atop the shaft. His flesh popped open, releasing the hook and leaving a small bloody trench. Adding insult to actual injury, his beetle snapped in half again.

Eventually he constructed a solid granny knot twice as large as the eye of the hook, and rigged up another beetle. Then he went to work on the pole. A downed four-foot branch nearby would serve nicely, he decided. He set it against a rock and pressed his foot on each limb to snap it off. It hurt to balance on his injured left foot, so he switched to standing on his right and tried using the left to break the branches instead. But the sudden jarring of the first snap sent an unbearable jolt of pain through his ankle, and he decided that there was no reason a fishing pole couldn't have a few branches. He tied the line around the end and laid twenty feet of neatly coiled slack behind him. Then he stepped to the lake's edge.

His first cast made clear the reason fishing poles didn't have branches. Without sufficient weight, the line didn't fly out into the lake but instead lurched forward only a few feet and tangled itself amongst the limbs.

"Dammit!"

His profanity echoed across the water, bouncing back to mock him. He shook his fan-shaped fishing pole in frustration, causing the line to foul even more severely, and by the time he stopped shaking the pole to work on the tangle, the line looked like an asymmetrical spider web strung between the limbs.

The untangling took patience, and he was running low, but he eventually had the line coiled neatly again. He needed a weight to cast, and settled on a small pinecone. More beetles had to be split, broken, decapitated, and otherwise mutilated, but he finally landed one out in the water far enough from shore that a fish might venture from the depths to at least investigate. Then he laid the gun across his lap and sat down to wait.

There was a comfortable grassy spot on the bank where he could sit and prop up his foot, which was beginning to feel tight in his two-hundred-

and-fifty-dollar boot. With a light wind, the cold Alaska water was rippled glass. It reflected the encircling mountains, showing Stu a distorted and inverted parallel world. The day was warming, and a sapphire sky had draped itself overhead like a bright canopy pinned to the jutting peaks and stretched from ridge to ridge. He'd never seen such a deep color.

Blue skies.

It had been the color of his future in the DA's office, once upon a time. His senior assistant position in the major crimes unit had been a whirlwind. More cases than he'd had time to juggle—ten per week. But somehow he'd done it, lining them up for court dates and backing down bluffing defense attorneys who threatened to overload him with trials. Most cases pled out—95 percent, according to the office manager's stats. He threw others together for trial in a few days, prepping on weekends while Katherine grumbled, although she hung on every word as he argued each case to her for practice. And when trial day came, it was game on. He flipped a switch and became a performer, a salesman, a preacher, and a professor all rolled into one, giving opening statements and closings that were somehow both carefully crafted and spontaneous. He grilled defense witnesses in between with questions carefully designed to trap them in lies, and he drew ugly facts from reluctant victims like a healer drawing poison from a wound. During multiday trials, he'd stay up until one a.m. poring over his notes from the day, and he'd rise at five the next morning to revise his witness questions in accordance with the previous day's revelations.

And there were always revelations.

A pastor accused of molestation had once cursed him from the stand in the name of God, and was convicted. A robbery victim was caught lying about a computer the defendant had stolen from him at gunpoint, because he'd shoplifted it from a store in the first place. Stu had convicted that defendant too, surprisingly. In another case, a juror was thrown out for drinking on the job. Evidence got lost once in the middle of a trial—a pound of pot from the evidence cart. Newly discovered videotapes proved people absolutely guilty or suddenly innocent. Cops forgot details or changed their stories. Rape victims stuck up for their abusers. And people were devastated or vindicated based upon ten-second breath-holding verdict pronouncements. It had been his crazy, exciting, uncertain life full of risks and rewards, and it was difficult now to remember what it felt like to be that person. He wondered if professional athletes who were injured and never stepped onto the field again felt the same.

Stu frowned and threw a pebble out into the lake, watching the splash he'd made settle into ripples and then fade away. Why he'd been reduced to chasing down deadbeat clients to collect fees for their tedious, routine landlord-tenant disputes was still a bit of a fog. Sure, he objectively knew *how* it had happened to him, but he still didn't understand *why*.

The fishing pole branch twitched. Stu froze. It had been ten minutes or maybe thirty; without a watch, it was hard to tell. After a moment of surprise, he scrambled to grab the pole and jerked upward, hard. There was resistance, and then the line came loose. He pulled it in with his hands, and it came easily. Too easily. When the hook swung dripping out of the water, it was empty. The beetle was gone. No indication of whether it had been a bite. The hook might have just snagged on the bottom, he had to admit to himself. He held the hook and stared at it, wondering. Should he stay and try his luck indefinitely? Should he move on? New bait? He sighed. The worst part was not the idea that he might have lost a fish; it was not knowing whether he'd ever had one at all.

It was early, but he was hungrier than he was when he skipped breakfast at home. The tube of disgusting soy paste hadn't filled him up—it only promised to keep him alive at one day per tube. He'd give fishing another hour, he decided, then try something else. *Edwin's* had other suggestions for food.

Fishing had just sounded so easy. It should have been relaxing and fun, too. It always was on the TV fishing shows. He'd grown up one hundred miles inland in Hartford, and his accountant father had only taken him fishing once, when he was seven. An ocean charter. The crew had rigged the lines, and he'd merely sat in the chair. He caught one, a sea bass—a dark spiny monstrosity from the cold depths that he was scared to touch. They bludgeoned it in front of him, laughing while it gasped for breath, and then they "cleaned" it, slicing it open and spilling its blood and guts all over the deck, a lot like Stu imagined Marti Butz must have gasped for breath while being strangled, and how she had her entrails spilled out on the deck of the *Iron Maiden*. He'd wanted nothing to do with eviscerating living things as a boy after that, and didn't like it any more as a grown man.

Saddled with that image for the remainder of the hour, he was almost grateful when there were no more bites, or even phantom bites.

He drank deeply from the lake until he couldn't drink any more. The water was ice-cold and crystal clear. Then he loaded up his one-liter and began his trip back up the mountain.

He had no watch. Clay had forbidden it. He could check the time on his cell phone when he returned to the cabin. It was back in the bottom of his bag. He'd had to turn it off to save the battery. No use leaving it on without reception. Judging from the sun, it was still before noon.

The walk up was painful, harder than the walk down. He limped, picking his way through the trees and underbrush. It was a trudging chore, and he stared into the hill, purposefully placing every step. Halfway, he stopped to rest and looked back at the lake through the foliage. The view of the calm water nestled in the bowl of the mountains was breathtaking. It was a bit like looking back at his youth; his perspective was better now, and he appreciated the beauty of where he'd been, but he was moving away from it, the path ahead was uphill, and it hurt to keep walking. The wilderness wasn't helping him relax or rejuvenate, he decided. It just reinforced that he was getting old.

Forty sucks, Stu thought.

Forty had not arrived suddenly. The date on the calendar had, but the feeling of swimming through unflavored oatmeal had been building through the last years of his thirties. It wasn't the sharp, severe depression he'd experienced after Butz, but a dull, longer-lasting version of the same thing. Struggle. Failure.

And a throbbing foot.

Clay had helped him through Butz. Katherine had too. He had both of them to thank for his current life, though it was not the one he'd chosen or one he embraced. He wasn't the type to develop a drug problem or burden others with his issues. Instead he'd checked out. He buried himself in his work. No more fund-raisers. No more hand-shaking or meeting important people. *America's Unsolved* had returned like ghouls to broadcast the death of his career to every friend and complete stranger with a cable subscription—rising star to fallen star in one season of reality television. They seemed delighted; couldn't have scripted it any better. For a time even a trip to Market Basket was painful. He imagined everyone eyeing him with either disgust or pity.

The guy who let the murderer walk.

He'd hoped that as long as he kept his head down and worked hard, it would pass. But it didn't pass. His head stayed down. He handled cases that didn't take him to court where his former colleagues would see him and have to shake his hand awkwardly. He wrote wills and trusts. Contracts. No litigation.

He sent Katherine to her parties alone, begging off sick or busy with files he brought home. She'd pestered him at first; then she'd given up. She couldn't argue with hard work. Arguing with a lawyer was difficult and tedious on any topic, but trying to tell a man not to focus on his job was a difficult position to take while also wanting him to be ambitious. But he wasn't ambitious. He was treading water, hunkered down and defensive and doing nothing to change his tarnished image. She didn't like it. Nor did she complain, particularly. She just kept trying to push him.

Not push, you idiot, support.

She'd tried to help him, and his self-imposed malaise made it impossible. He hadn't wanted to burden anyone, but he'd burdened his wife, he realized, as he stared out across the pristine lake. He hadn't quite thought of it that way before, and the clarity with which it struck him here in the wild was astounding. He suddenly felt guilty for it—crushingly guilty. His disinterest in life was something he had to fix when he got home, he decided, and not in the way a man fixed a sink or the lawn mower. He needed to find the spark in himself that Katherine married him for. Not so that she would love him more, but so that she wouldn't have to keep digging through his bullshit pouting to recover it herself.

Stu nodded. Fixing intangible things was something he could do. He fixed complex contracts. He fixed invisible boundary line disputes. He fixed controversies between neighbors who absolutely hated one another. *I can damn well fix myself.* With that resolved, he turned to continue up the hill.

The five-foot-tall animal stood motionless about twenty yards from him, partially visible through the brush, but only an instant from disappearing if it so chose. For now it only watched him. Stu froze too. *A deer?* That was his first thought. But a set of great, arching, rust-colored antlers curved skyward like leafless branches another three feet high above its head. If it was a deer, it was the most spectacular or malformed rack of antlers a deer had ever grown. *A small moose?* Its blunted snout and hanging bib were mooselike, but that wasn't quite right either. The horns were narrow and tall, not thick and wide. *Caribou!* he realized finally, though he'd thought they lived in the open plains and ran in herds. Stu glanced about nervously, but he didn't seem to be surrounded by an angry pack of the big beasts. *I'm the hunter,* he reminded himself. With his lame foot he didn't feel like a hunter. In fact, if the thing charged, he wasn't sure he'd be able to hobble out of the way before it gored him with its formidable set of miniature spears.

Stu unslung the Browning from his back, keeping his movements slow and smooth. The caribou watched him, curious but not bothered. Stu hesitated. The Europeans called them reindeer. It made Stu think of Santa Claus. *I'm about to shoot Prancer.* He held the gun loosely against his shoulder, but tightly with his hands, not wanting to make the same mistake he made with the rat. He sure as hell wouldn't let go this time.

He drew a bead on the animal, which was easy at this modest range, once he had his eye the right distance from the scope, but he didn't know whether to shoot the animal in the head or the torso. His recollection was that people usually shot big game in the body. Probably so they didn't spoil the trophy head. But he just wanted the meat. He trained the rifle on the head, and the animal's eyes suddenly filled the scope lens. It stared at him through the glass with shiny black orbs, like a big trusting dog. Its nonchalant stare reminded Stu that he didn't have a lot of experience killing things. Bugs as a kid. More recently a rat. But never a big mammal. When their dog needed to be put down, he hadn't even gone to the vet with his parents.

The caribou was munching foliage now. It even dipped its head and disappeared from the scope for a moment. Then reappeared. Very comfortable for something in a gun sight.

What if the thing comes to this spot every day? Stu wondered.

Perhaps this was its vacation spot. If they could coexist for the week, he might make friends with it. When he was a kid, he'd seen a movie where a farm boy went out hunting, but instead of shooting a moose tangled in barbed wire, he'd set it free. Later the moose had saved the boy's life.

Stupid!

Stu scolded himself. What was the caribou going to do? Climb up on his roof and nail in a few shingles while he warmed himself by the fire with a cup of cocoa? He settled the sight on the caribou's head again, directly between its big innocent eyes.

I don't have a license for this, he realized.

He wondered what the rules were. Caribou weren't endangered, as far as he knew. There was probably an exception for starvation, but he wasn't technically starving yet, and it was more meat than he would need for one person. The responsible hunter only killed what he was going to eat, he remembered. Stu wiped his brow. How to prepare the meat once he bagged the caribou was another problem. *Edwin's* had a chapter on slaughtering large game. *Field dressing,* they called it, maybe because *slaughtering* sounded so awful. He hadn't read that chapter yet, but the diagrams made it look difficult and gory. And how would he carry an animal that big up to the cabin? He had no idea how much it weighed. More than a large man, certainly. More than two men, from the look of it.

The caribou's eyes disappeared from the scope. He lowered the gun. It was beginning to wander off. Stu had stood so still for so long that it seemed to have grown bored. He raised the gun again quickly, held his breath, and pulled the trigger. Nothing happened. He examined the gun. The hammer was in the safety position.

"Dammit!"

Stu drew the hammer back and held the gun up again. The caribou's flank was just visible through the trees; at least, it looked like a flank through the scope. He fired. The gun boomed and kicked, as it had before. This time he held on, and it slammed into his shoulder instead of his eye. The report echoed through the peaceful valley like an amplified version of his profanity, a more violent expression of his frustration.

Stu groaned and rubbed his shoulder. The caribou was no longer visible. He limped into the thicket where it had stood. No body. It was gone. He'd missed. No, it was worse than that—he'd hesitated.

The ground was soft under his feet. Stu looked down. His boot was mired in pile of damp steaming pellets. The caribou hadn't been bored. It hadn't been relaxing in its favorite shrub hideaway where it would return each day. And it certainly hadn't been connecting with him. It had been taking a dump.

CHAPTER 14

Stu awoke to throbbing pain. He reached down and found his ankle swollen to the size of an orange. The trip down to the lake and back up the hill the previous day had done wicked things to it. His skin was purple, and there was no way he'd be able to wear his two-hundred-and-fifty-dollar TQ Extremes. The fact that he'd had no ice pack when the injury occurred hadn't helped.

Stu rolled over and looked up through the ragged skylight. For the second day in a row his discomfort had awakened him before the sun had had its chance. It hadn't rained during the night, thank God, so he was dry.

Food.

The thought was singular and compelling. It immediately displaced the pain in his leg as his number-one concern. The gnawing in his belly was profound, so bad that he almost *wanted* a tube of disgusting paste. Almost. He'd eaten two already. The third needed to wait until he was dying, he decided.

Dying.

For the first time he thought seriously about the possibility that he could die. He'd kidded himself about the cliché ways in which he might perish in the wilderness—death by bear or plane wreck were the two most popular. But he hadn't considered that he simply might not be able to provide for himself. Stu stared at the wasp hole in the log wall for a time. The concept of his week had changed. *Survive for four more days.* The plane would be back then, with that idiot Ivan asking him if he'd had a good time.

He rose and faced the day with his clubfoot and a tender cheek. At least the swelling from the wasp sting had gone down. Had he been allergic, he'd be dead already. Had his coat and sleeping bag not been high quality, he'd be near frozen at night. Though there'd been no rain in the night, there had been cold. The dramatic drop in temperature was unmistakable. Not only could he see his breath, but his hands quickly grew numb. He donned gloves to start his fire in the pit. *It could snow,* he thought. And for some reason this thought scared him more than any other, short of a bear. His matches were at an end, and so the fire needed to stay lit, or else he'd have to learn to use the flint and steel.

He gathered wood and his wits for the first hour of the day, keeping an eye out for the edible grasses that *Edwin's* suggested he could eat. He tried a couple, but without a cooking pot in which to boil them, they were woody, bitter, and difficult to swallow. Nor did they seem to fill him. He ate just enough to make him want some real food.

Edwin's also touted the food value of various bugs that were easy to catch—worms, grubs, maggots, slugs. He couldn't find worms, of course. *If I could find some goddamned worms, I'd be eating a tasty fish.* He wasn't sure what a grub looked like, and *Edwin's* seemed to assume that everyone knew, because it didn't have a photo. Maggots were too disgusting to contemplate, considering he'd have to raid the rotting rat carcass to get them. Which left slugs.

He'd seen several sizeable black slugs on the shady side of the cabin, and they weren't exactly built to elude him. An easy answer to his little food problem, according to *Edwin's*.

It didn't take long to locate a fat one, which he plucked from the rotting wood with two fingers. It was a sleek animal, almost a half foot in length, jet black and shiny, with a delicately textured mantle and deeply grooved tail. Two smooth antennalike protrusions with bulbous end caps forked from its head. *A beautiful animal, really*, he told himself. And big. *A mouthful.* He talked himself into thinking that it would taste like oysters or, if cooked to firmness, maybe clams. Without a pan in which to fry them, he decided to go with the oyster image. *Just let it slide down your throat.* He wondered if he could also imagine a bit of cocktail sauce.

There didn't seem an obvious way to kill the thing, so he decided to eat it as is. *Better not to think about it too much anyway.* With that, he popped the slug into his mouth. But the squirming gastropod quickly produced a variety of mucus that made it very *unlike* oysters. The meaty body slid down his throat just fine, but it left a sticky film in his mouth. Stu's face twisted, his lip curling in disgust—he could feel the slug writhing in his stomach. Oysters didn't do that. He took two steps and wretched into the bitter-tasting grass, vomiting up the slug and the few pathetic half-chewed greens he'd consumed. The five-inch black thing still lived, its horrid taste and texture all of the defense mechanism it would ever need against hungry humans. It slithered off through the bile- and puke-laden grass, none the worse for wear, while Stu staggered back to the cabin, spitting mucus and cursing under his breath. The realization that he had fewer nutrients in him than before he'd tried to eat the damned thing was incredibly disheartening. Then he reached into his mouth and pinched himself.

"Aww, thit," he mumbled. He couldn't feel his lips.

With that, Stu gave up on scavenging for food, and as soon as he thought his stomach could handle it, he ate the last tube of Goop. At least he couldn't taste it, because his tongue was also numb.

The remainder of the morning was spent limping around the cabin gathering firewood and ten-foot-long branches to lean across the roof. The walk to the lake was too far for his swollen ankle, especially without a boot that would fit over it. He cut one of his spare tennis shoes open with his knife and stretched it over his fat foot so he could walk on the rough forest floor without cutting himself on rocks or thorns.

He drank regularly—*Edwin's* advised it—and his water was soon gone. Just thinking about a trip all the way to the lake was torturous, but he'd seen a small drainage near the spot where the caribou had made its grand show of disrespect for his lack of hunting prowess. It was only halfway. He took the small pack with its water insert and hobbled down the hill.

He was failing, he thought as he walked. And if he didn't pull his head out soon, it would be the biggest failure of his life since . . . *Butz*. The name intruded on his thoughts. Butz was bigger. If he died in the wilderness, only those close to him and maybe a few people who read news blurbs from Fairbanks would know. Strangers. When Butz happened, everybody knew. *America's Unsolved* made sure the entire nation knew. One national news reporter had asked him how he felt about letting a killer walk free. She was smug, shoved the microphone at him, and couldn't have been more than twenty-two years old. Given his politically sensitive position as a government employee, he couldn't even tell the pantsuited cub reporter what an incredible bitch she was. The appellate court had done their part too, publishing their opinion about the case so that the entire profession knew. The case was used as persuasive authority by lawyers all over the country. Even Stu's death couldn't top that sort of notoriety. Especially a quiet death in the woods.

Stu couldn't stop the memories, the second guesses, the regrets. He'd analyzed Butz one million times in his head, and every time the result was the same. He lost. A very efficient private attorney had taken Butz's appeal. Stu had puzzled over that, too. The unknown lawyer used a Providence PO box for correspondence, but listed no office address. Peter Tippet was his name. Stu figured that Tippet took the case for the publicity—Butz certainly had no money to pay for private counsel—but Tippet had gone about his business quietly and without talking to the press. His only public appearance had been the day of the oral argument before the appellate court. He was brief, direct, and he stuck to the narrow legal argument presented by the corpus delicti doctrine. No esoteric crap about rights or the constitution. No fanfare. Afterward he marched out, head down, and disappeared back into the hustle and bustle of Providence. When the decision came out, he didn't crow about it. In fact, Stu didn't hear a word from him ever again. It was possible he practiced some mundane civil law and only took on the occasional pro bono criminal case, but Stu thought it unlikely. Tippet's briefs and presentation hit just the right matter-of-fact note for an unsympathetic client. All law and procedure. Not one word about the ugly facts or the concept of fairness for murderers. Yep, he was an experienced crime guy.

Stu arrived at the drainage, a seasonal-looking puddle either fed by an underground aquifer or simply a low spot of oversaturated soil. There were animal tracks in the mud—small paw impressions, a trail of three-pronged bird prints that looked like someone had held down a punctuation key on nature's keyboard, and a set of hoofprints. *My caribou.* He dipped his bladder in the three-inch-deep runoff. It drained the puddle, but as he sat watching, the depression quickly refilled itself.

The remainder of the morning was spent dragging himself back up the hill and sitting with his foot elevated on the cot. The cold and light poured in through the branches he'd propped over the roof. His small fire crackled in the pit, but it couldn't banish the chill.

Colder.

The temperature drop was sudden and astounding. Just a day earlier he'd been walking around outside in only a shirt. Now he was huddled in his Great Beyond jacket beside the fire inside the cabin and, though the sun had been up for hours, he still couldn't seem to get warm. His father would have called it a cold snap. But it was more than that, Stu knew. Winter was coming. Alaskan winter. The state was famous for them.

Four days.

CHAPTER 15

I was just surviving, Stu thought as he lay waiting for the plane, *as much at home as here in the wilderness.* The rock upon which he had hoisted himself and his injured leg jutted from the water near the spot where Ivan had dropped him at the beginning of the week. Even if he passed out, the pilot couldn't miss him.

He was leaving defeated. No way to sugarcoat it. He hadn't taken on the Klondike, he hadn't kicked ass, and though he was sort of a new man, it wasn't the sort anyone had hoped for. *I'm an even bigger pussy than everyone thought I was.* In fact, he was physically a shell of the man he'd been when he arrived. After four more days of eating grass and two skewer-roasted squirrels he'd blown in half with the .30-06, he'd sloughed off ten to fifteen pounds. He'd vomited at times, and diarrhea had begun draining him of fluids two days earlier. He still limped when he tried to walk. And he smelled like stale soggy Fritos corn chips; it had been too cold for him to wash himself in the lake. Worst of all, he was starting to have delusions. The day before, he'd imagined helicopter sounds and stumbled out of the cabin to find a woodpecker knocking at a nearby tree. Twice. That very morning, he'd scooped dirt into his collapsible plastic cup to make coffee and only missed drinking it because the cup had melted when he held it over the fire.

His bags sat behind him on the shore, packed and ready to go. He'd been lucid enough to drag everything down immediately after the coffee incident so that there was no chance he'd miss his ride out. He was going to live, thankfully.

He'd had a lot of time to think about living while he shivered and starved in the tiny shack, and he was surprised at how few reasons he could come up with that he truly needed to do so. But *Edwin's* said that finding something to live for was among the top five common factors in survival success stories. Stu had come to dislike *Edwin,* and despised the preachy text a shade more for forcing him to try to inspire himself when he felt like dog shit. But he did try.

The idea of surviving to return to work so he could fight about other people's problems was profoundly uninspiring. And struggling to retirement so he could stop participating in everyday society felt more like an anti-goal. Nor did he have any kids who needed him. A shame, really. *I'll survive for Katherine,* he'd decided finally sometime around noon on day three. She had steadfastly supported him, rain or shine. She deserved his effort, and so he'd made one. He'd eaten burnt squirrel, for God's sake. *I'll make a better effort at home, too.* But he couldn't have survived much longer in this miserable territory, he thought. *If this is the way America used to be, then thank God bygone America is bygone.* He wasn't the type of guy that settled the Old West. Not a cowboy.

I survived law school in Oregon, he thought as he watched the sky and listened for the lawn mower buzz of the Piper Cub's engine. Not everyone could do that. There were dropouts, of course. Five in his class in the first year alone. One sad kid just out of undergrad had actually committed suicide. Stu tried to recall how he'd done it. Pills? A rope? A gun? Couldn't remember. He thought of Sophia Baron. She'd quit.

Of the women Clay had burned through during law school, Sophia was the most memorable, a sparkling diamond in the landslide of law nerds who crowded the square 1970s geometric brick monstrosity that was McKenzie Hall. She was more like an airbrushed model for the graduate school's brochure than a real student wearing sweatpants and a glazed look from studying too late. Indeed, she'd been photographed for the cover. She'd also hobbled around after Clay for a semester in four-inch heels that no other female law student would be caught dead wearing on a weekday. But Clay moved too fast. He'd quickly morphed into an environmentally aware, laid-back dude in tie-dye when he realized that post-hippie-era Eugene celebrated the earthy-outdoorsy culture, and he'd left her behind in her ridiculous shoes. He adapted. She didn't. After they broke up, she'd wandered around for a few days, clicking through the halls looking lost and missing classes. She finally had the dazed law student look, but its origin wasn't the suffocating academics. People began to talk. Then, in the second semester of her second year, she'd dropped out, which was odd, because most law students who had already sweated through the grueling weed-out first year were willing to put their legal career ahead of their relationships, and most everything else. In fact, the two married couples in Stu's class who had divorced during school wound up hating each other, but all four individuals sure as hell stayed to complete the Juris Doctor. He wondered what ever happened to Sophia.

And then he was back on the rock. His mind had wandered again, and the sun had climbed high in the empty sky. *Empty.*

Stu's butt hurt. He had to drag himself off the rock and step onto shore to stretch his legs. He'd judiciously avoided running down his cell phone battery, keeping it off most of the time. He checked the time. It was almost noon. Ivan was late. *Idiot.* The idea of suing Yukon Tours had occurred to him. Or Dugan. Someone. He'd almost died. He wondered how much he could get for a week of pain and suffering, plus medical bills for his ankle, which was almost certainly healing wrong.

The fact that three or four hours had passed almost without him noticing worried Stu. He was light-headed, not thinking straight. He chewed some grass. He wouldn't be suing anyone until he got some real food in him for a week or two. He tried to stay on his feet, but it felt too good to sit down, and when he did, he lost track of time.

One o'clock came and went. Then it was three. Stu wondered if he should walk around the lake to make sure Ivan wasn't looking for him in the thicker stand of trees to the south. He'd walked half mile when he decided it was crazy. The plane had to land *on* the lake. He couldn't have missed it. Besides, he'd forgotten all his gear back at the rock.

"Shit!" Stu flung his curse upward toward the God he'd tentatively decided did not exist in his twenties. "Shit, shit, shit!" Nothing changed. His foot kept hurting. His empty stomach continued to churn like a dying blender. The plane still didn't come.

Shouting sapped his remaining energy. His voice fell to a mumble. "Katherine, I've failed you."

He hadn't calculated the days wrong. Even when he'd been in his right mind, he'd pegged today as pickup time. He'd checked it a dozen times, even turning his cell phone on to consult his calendar. *Ivan must have gotten it wrong,* he thought. *He'll be here tomorrow.* The thought of enduring another day was almost unbearable.

What if Ivan crashed? Alaska had twenty times more crashes per capita than any other state, after all. *Edwin's* said it was dehydration that would kill him. He could linger another week or two without food, but he needed to keep some water down and retain it. Between the vomit and diarrhea, he was ejecting fluids as fast as he could collect them. Stu groaned, sitting heavily on the soft, damp shore, and he might have died there if the thought of being eaten by a bear hadn't horrified him.

It was nightfall by the time Stu climbed back up to the cabin. The fire was out. He'd brought his backpack and the gun. The duffel bag was stashed beside the shore so that he wouldn't have to haul it back down again in the morning. He was unable to get a fire started with the flint and steel, and so he huddled in his bag, occasionally rolling over to throw up into one corner—he'd given up trying to go outside to do it. He could no longer distinguish the smell of the cabin from that of his deteriorating body or the taste of vomit in his mouth and throat. He still had the dignity to crawl outside to void his watery bowels. Sleep came and went. During his waking times, he occasionally thought he was having an Alaskan night-mare and that he might wake in his own bed. Other times, he dozed and dreamed of Katherine and, strangely, Audry. They wore cheerleader uni-forms, but it wasn't sexual. He himself wore a suit and carried the .30-06. Butz was there, sitting on the witness stand. Stu trained the rifle on him, and a small cork popped out. And the jury laughed.

Stu awoke to something tickling his face. Wet and cold. He started awake, wondering if he was still lying by the shore and a wolf was nosing him to see if he was dead and rotten or alive and delicious. But the touch was lighter. Not a snout. Snow. Large flakes were settling on him. A small pile of the stuff had accumulated on the cot and there was a dusting on the floor. Enough had floated in through the limb-crossed hole in the ceiling that there would certainly be much more outside.

No, no, no!

He wasn't cold. The Great Beyond bag did its job well. But he couldn't live in the bag. He pulled himself out. It was agony. His limbs ached, and as soon as he sat up, he dry heaved. He was alarmed to find that he didn't even have any bile to spit up. He wasn't wet. No fever. But he had to scramble across the dirt floor to get outside and drop his pants. There was little to dispense from the other end either.

The lake. I have to get down to the lake.

He took the gun. Ivan would be sad if he left it behind. His pack stayed on the cot. It was heavy, and there was nothing inside that money wouldn't replace. The cell phone came. A habit, he supposed. It wouldn't help him hail the plane. He pulled on one boot and one torn tennis shoe and exited. The clearing was quiet. He said a meanspirited, profanity-laced fare-well to the leaning cabin, wishing it an imminent collapse, then started his last trek down the mountain and around the lake.

That idiot Ivan. Seven days, six nights. Vacation rental companies counted each night of occupancy, which was six, not all seven calendar days. Clearly, obviously, Ivan had screwed up the count. It was the only reasonable ex-planation. *Except for a crash.* No, a crash was not reasonable. Even at twenty times the average of other states, the odds were against that. Besides, Clay and Dugan knew where he was. If he wasn't back on time—and he already wasn't—they'd come looking for him. It might take another couple of days.

Stu moaned at the thought of two more days and slogged down the hill through three inches of snow. He was surprised to find the caribou waiting for him halfway, in its customary spot beside his water spring, happily defecating. He stopped and sat. It was a good place for a rest anyway.

"You're lucky it's my last day," Stu said. Although he was fairly sure he didn't have the energy to butcher the large animal even if he brought it down. He'd had enough trouble figuring out how to cut up a squirrel, which had very little meat. The caribou's antlers towered over its head like some Ice Age radar array, a far cry from the fuzzy nubs Stu had always seen on Santa's reindeer in pictures and cartoons. "Nice rack, by the way, Dasher." The caribou finished its dump and wandered off. No human-animal connection. No bonding. "Yeah, you'd better run. Or walk. Or dash away. Or whatever the hell it is that you do."

The one-sided banter was strangely relaxing, but *Edwin's* warned against getting too comfortable when one was sick or starving in the wild. Any spot he stopped at could be his final resting place. Stu tried to think of Katherine waiting for him at the airport, worried. Then he rose and moved on.

CHAPTER 16

The plane didn't come. Stu lay on the rock again, fighting to stay alert. He pinched his skin, talked to himself, and checked the clock on his phone every few minutes. *Screw the battery.* And still, nothing came over the ridge but a lone hawk, and even if he squinted, he couldn't pretend it was a plane. It took all evening to drag himself up the mountain again. He stopped to rest and to drain his bowels every hundred yards, too proud to soil his pants, and when he reached the hard wooden cot, he collapsed like a marathoner who'd overrun his training. In the night he was either uncomfortable or unconscious.

He couldn't hike back down to the lake the next morning. His tortured body was too weak, so he simply hauled himself outside and leaned against the cabin, which leaned against the pine. He imagined that he looked like a small domino leaning against a large one. And he listened for the plane. He planned to fire the rifle as a signal if he heard an engine, and to use the flare from the Great Beyond emergency kit. But the sky remained quiet. It was cloudy and cold, and his hands were numb, but he didn't have the energy to drag himself back inside for gloves, so he mostly kept them shoved into his pockets. This time the day didn't warm up. Soon he couldn't feel the toes on his tennis-shoed foot either. And everything that he *could* feel hurt. He wasn't vomiting so much anymore, but stomach cramps doubled him over at intervals. Nor was he thirsty, but he was aware he needed to drink, and he forced himself to do so, sipping a small mouthful every minute or two. He was out of water by ten o'clock in the morning. By noon he was out of cell phone battery. The one thing he had plenty of, he noted, was bullets.

And then it began to snow again, big wet flakes. Stu wondered if the indigenous people had a name for this particular type. He sure did, and it wasn't a nice one. They fell on him for maybe an hour—he could no longer keep track of the time—before he crawled back inside. He would still hear a plane from the cot, he reasoned. But it was token logic. He didn't expect to hear anything now. He just wanted to be comfortable, or as comfortable as possible.

But as Stu stretched himself on the cot that might be his final resting place, he couldn't get comfortable. It was a grim realization: he would die slowly and in pain, watching white snow trickle through the torn ceiling, past the red stain of rat blood he'd painted it with.

How did I get here? A simple question with an easy answer. It had all started with Butz. He'd had a sinking feeling the first time he'd read the Court of Appeals decision that had walked his murderer, and his life had been the second half of a bell curve graph ever since. This was merely the inevitable ending for which he'd volunteered seven years ago. "No body, no case," Stu's fellow attorneys at the Bristol County DA's Office had warned him. He hadn't listened. But as he lay dying in the ramshackle cabin in the middle of the Alaska interior, he wished he had.

CHAPTER 17

(ONE WEEK EARLIER)

Katherine hadn't spent much time at the firm's office, but Clay's e-mail summoning her had been insistent. She arrived to find the formerly half-empty Bluestone Building abuzz with activity. The back door was locked, but the front was open for a change, and several men and women in suits were arriving. She entered through the main entrance to find the previously locked and dusty lobby scrubbed and furnished with a three-foot-high vase full of fresh flowers. A large new plaque on the wall pronounced Buchanan, Stark & Associates the proud occupants of the fourth *and* fifth floors, instead of just the second. A stunning young receptionist behind an antique table hailed her while she stared about. The girl was smartly dressed in a dark pencil skirt and a conservatively ruffled white blouse—the uniform of real law firms. No fuchsia in sight.

"May I help you?"

Katherine was befuddled. "Yes, I'm here to see Mr. Buchanan. Usually, I'm forced to hike up the back stairs, but it seems they're locked."

"I'll phone up for him. Name?"

"Katherine. He should be expecting me. What is all of this?"

"Please forgive the chaos. We just settled a big case and we're remodeling our local offices."

Katherine cocked an eyebrow. "A big case? Really? Sounds exciting. I'll have to ask your boss about it."

Pencil skirt girl buzzed the phone. "He'll be right down, Katherine. Can I get you some bottled water or tea while you wait?"

"No, thank you. I'll just loiter in the entryway until he decides to let me in." She smiled curtly and wandered back into the foyer, studying the newly polished marble and admiring the fresh bouquet. The space smelled like baking soda and potpourri.

Katherine was surprised when the elevator clanged its arrival. The clunky old thing hadn't worked since they'd started the firm. Its doors shuddered opened, and Clay strode out wearing a new perfectly tailored suit.

"Kate! Thanks for coming."

"Fixing the old place up?"

"Big meeting today."

"Big win, too, I hear from the receptionist I've never seen before. What's going on?"

"Stuart didn't tell you?"

Katherine gave him a blank look.

"Molson," Clay said. "We settled it on his birthday."

"No. He didn't tell me."

"Hmmm." Clay cocked his head, thinking, then he took Katherine by the hand and marched her to the elevator. He ushered her inside, then joined her and closed the door. The elevator car was small, and they had to stand shoulder to shoulder. The familiar scent of lavender on him made her nostrils flare. Standing so close, she noticed that he was at least three inches taller than Stu. He didn't look at her, and instead stared politely at the floor numbers. He hit number five and the button lit up.

"Not the second floor?"

"We're on the fifth today. I would have thought an observant girl like you would have noticed the new sign in the lobby." He gave her a self-satisfied grin.

"Touché. So tell me about Molson."

"Isn't that for your spouse to do? He must have a reason for keeping it from you."

"He probably wants to make sure it's a done deal before he tells me. He likes to be certain all the *i*'s are dotted and *t*'s crossed. He's like that. But I'm not. I'm the curious type."

"I see. He's protecting you. Doesn't want to get you all worked up if nothing's going to happen." Clay's eyes darted to her and then back up at the floor numbers again.

"But something *is* going to happen, isn't it?"

"Yes."

"Then don't tease."

"Okay." Clay gave her a quick summary of the facts and procedural posture of the case. She already knew them by heart; Stu debated them with himself in the shower, and so she'd heard the arguments over and over. Now that the case was done, the only thing she didn't know was *the number*. Stu had said the number might be big if they went to trial and won. But they hadn't gone to trial. They'd settled. Settlements could fetch nothing more than "go away" money, or they could make dreams come true. And from the looks of the remodeled office . . .

Katherine's pulse quickened.

"Three million," Clay said.

Katherine's heart leaped into her throat. As soon as she was sure she'd heard right, she started doing the math. "That means our third is one million dollars?"

"No," Clay said.

"No?"

"Three million *is* our third. One-point-five each."

"Oh my God! It was nine million?"

"Precisely. I phoned Sylvia today, and she is delighted with her six."

The old elevator creaked to a stop on the fifth floor, and they exited. Katherine felt like she was floating.

The new office space was spare but sharp, a minimalist style with slim computer terminals instead of paperwork scattered across desks. There were four people in suits that Katherine didn't recognize tapping away at keyboards with their office doors closed.

"Who are all these people?"

"These are the previously mythical associates of Buchanan, Stark & Associates."

"You hired more attorneys?"

"Temporarily. For today. And not necessarily attorneys, but they sure look the part, don't they? Step into our conference room, please, Ms. Stark."

She entered. He followed, right at her shoulder. A large conference table dominated the room, and twelve chairs surrounded it. The previous conference room was an empty break room with a sink; it had seated five, uncomfortably. Clay took the head of the table. Katherine sat on the side and left an empty seat between them. Given the good news, she had a mad urge to leap across the table and hug his trim, lavender-smelling body, but it was best to keep some distance, she thought.

"You look like you have questions," he said, and Katherine realized she was staring at him without saying anything.

"There's so much going on here, I don't know where to start."

"That's exactly how I feel," Clay replied, smiling. "In fact, it's a bit overwhelming, but winners plan for success."

"Stu hasn't mentioned any of this."

"He's been resistant. He doesn't adjust well to change, you know."

Katherine giggled. "You've got that right."

"Then you see the genius of my scheme, the reason I sent him to Alaska. He truly does need it. And it's better if all this is in place before he gets back from his trip. Besides, much of it is just for show. We've got a big meeting today."

"Dugan?"

"Yep. And we need to impress. Bigger is better with men like him. He'll want to see a show."

"If you land his business on the heels of the Molson settlement . . ." Katherine didn't finish her sentence. Her head was spinning as though she'd had one too many glasses of Aged to Perfection.

"It's all part of the plan. Success begets success. Imagine you have one-point-five million dollars, but you have to pay your bills with it. Nice. Comfortable. But you're not rich. Now imagine you have one-point-five million dollars, and your bills are being paid by a second source—monthly fees from Dugan's corporation, for instance. Now your million-five is spending money. Get it?"

She *did* get it. This was Stu's first million. And at forty it wasn't too late. If Stu had been there she'd have kissed him right in the middle of the office. He wasn't. But his handsome partner made for a very interesting proxy, she thought. She let her imagination play as Clay sat smiling at her in his fitted suit, allowing her to enjoy the moment.

"I still can't believe it," she said at length. "Three million? Stu said it was possible, but I had no idea it could happen this fast." In fact, Stu had warned her that it would take years of work with no guarantees. It was just like Stu to understate the upside of something, she thought. He made only safe predictions. He also reveled in toil and had a perverse need to earn every penny he made; it came from his parents, who were children of Depression-era farmers. He was uncomfortable with money that didn't have the stink of sweat on it. For her, however, it was a relief to laugh after all the years of struggle, and she did so freely for the first time in as long as she could remember.

"Clay, I take back all of the bad things I've always said about you."

Clay's eyes found hers. He leaned toward her, pushing the chair that sat between them out of the way. She sucked in a breath when he put a hand on her knee, but she didn't protest. He spoke softly but was perfectly audible in the empty room. His tone might have been playful or menacing; it was hard to tell.

"Oh really? Have you been saying bad things, Kate?"

She couldn't hold his gaze, and blinked. "Just that you're such a cowboy."

"That I am. But a lot of people consider cowboys heroes." He sat back. "And let's not forget your husband. He's been a most excellent sidekick."

Stu as a sidekick was an amusing image. Katherine pictured Clay sitting tall in the saddle, wearing a ten-gallon hat, with the big outlaw Dugan being led behind him with his hands tied to a rope, and Stuart walking alongside in a bowler, like some fussy banker. Stu wasn't dynamic, fair enough, but he did do all the work. And so, although the comment was funny, it was a touch insulting, too.

"He's the brains of the operation," Clay added quickly, not letting the slight stand for more than a moment.

"So you're comfortable having your brains in Alaska for the big meeting."

"I don't need brains for this. I just need you."

"How so?"

"You represent a 'partner presence.'"

"I can't replace Stu."

"You won't. You'll just meet and greet our prospective client. I'll call him Mr. Dugan, but you call him Reggie. He'll ask for coffee, black. You'll get it for him."

She considered objecting—she wasn't a serving wench—but then she remembered Clay's hand in her hair. At the party her own pride had almost kept her from scoring the meeting with Dugan. She'd been hesitant, like Stu, and careful. But Clay wasn't. He'd been bold. He'd grabbed her and set her on a different path, the path to success. *And he'd been right.*

Clay was watching her. "I understand your hesitation," he said. "But Reggie's old-fashioned, and you have to play people the way they lie. Our goal isn't to change our clients; it's to understand them and make them want us. We're working here. You can be a feminist on your own time."

Katherine was amazed. It was as though Clay were reading her thoughts, only he wouldn't let her hold herself back. She wondered if she had been holding back for years. She'd been unyielding in building an image of herself as a progressive, independent woman, and Stu had blindly supported her one-dimensional approach. Now, suddenly, Clay was encouraging her to employ other facets of her womanhood, not as a concession, but as a stratagem. Clay knew how to adapt. Did she? She'd never considered that she could be a modern woman with Stu but put on a retro face for another man and, thereby, play them both.

"Okay," she agreed. "Today I serve. Where's Pauline? She can point me to the coffee."

Clay shook his head.

"You didn't . . ."

"Pauline doesn't face change well either." His hand was still on Katherine's knee. His grip was firm but seemed meant to reassure her. "It's a new day, Kate."

He left his hand in place until she looked away, and then let it slide off.

"What's this about a 'local office'?" Katherine said, changing the subject.

"We opened a branch in Providence just today."

"Providence? Are you kidding?"

"Don't be impressed. It's just a phone book ad with a Providence number. It rings through to the receptionist here. If we get a client on the hook, we rent an office space over there for an hour for an initial consultation. Then we tell them that they are so important, we're referring them to the home office here."

"Who's going to do all that new work?" *Stu will*, she thought.

Clay anticipated her concern. "The more work we get, the more of it we farm out to 'associates.' We'll bill them at two hundred an hour and pay them one hundred. They become another income stream. There are plenty of young lawyers out there looking for work. That uppity bitch Audra is dying for more hours."

Katherine couldn't help herself. She giggled. "She *is* an uppity bitch. I think she spilled wine on the tablecloth Stu bought me for my birthday."

"Well, now she can help buy you a new one."

"You know, I could tell Stu was covering for her."

Clay lowered his voice. "Do you think they're fucking?" he said with mock solemnity.

Katherine laughed out loud. The idea of Stu carrying on an affair in his white briefs without her knowledge was as comical and preposterous as a dark-suited attorney saying the word *fucking* in the middle of a law office. She shook her head. "Puh-leez. Our Stu?"

Clay grinned along with her. "You never know about a man facing a midlife crisis. Is he getting enough at home, Kate?"

The conversation had taken a decidedly raw turn, but Katherine was having fun, and she was about to launch a playful retort—something about being more woman than Stu could handle—when Clay put a finger to her lips to shush her.

Just then Audry herself pushed open the conference room door. The aspiring attorney wore a blue suit for the occasion. Sharp, but definitely off the rack, and probably a size eight, Katherine judged. *Maybe even a ten.*

"Dugan is here," Audry said. "Do you want any other 'associates' to sit in?"

"No, Audra," Clay said. "You'll do fine. Just behave."

"Yes, sir."

"And could you get me a cup of tea?"

"Sure. And would you like milk, sugar, or a dollop of piss-off in that?" She didn't wait for an answer. "I'll go get our budding client."

Clay winked at Katherine as Audry departed, and he mouthed the word *uppity*.

Katherine had to suppress another giggle. Dugan was coming.

CHAPTER 18

Audry led Reginald Dugan into the conference room. At six-foot-four he towered over Buchanan, Stark's petite associate and filled the hallway.

He nodded at Katherine, his broad chest alone wider than her shoulders. "Mrs. Stark, good to see you again."

She nodded back. "Mr. Dugan."

"You have coffee here?"

"Absolutely. Would you like me to get you some?"

"Absolutely," he repeated, smiling.

When Katherine returned with the steaming cup, Clay and Dugan were huddled around the table talking business while Audry took notes. Dugan looked up.

"Thanks, darlin'. Say, can I ask you a couple questions before you go?"

She glanced at Clay. He nodded his permission.

"Sure," she said.

"I'm a straightforward guy," Dugan began. "And I'm thinking of hiring your husband's firm. Clay here has given me the hard sell, and Audra seems smart as a whip. But I'd like to get a couple things straight from the mare's mouth." He shifted his large frame in the chair, facing her. "Why do you think a man like me ought to ditch my big overpriced law firm for a small operation like this?"

Katherine gathered herself. *I'm on.*

"Because we're not overpriced, for one," she began. "And we're successful. Look around. We're growing; a new satellite office in Providence is coming online within the week."

"Providence, eh?"

"Yes. And maybe you didn't know that Stuart graduated in the top ten percent of his class, just like those big firm lawyers. He works hard. And we don't have children, so this job is his baby."

A moment of silence followed, but Dugan did not yet seem convinced. He spoke again, his tone more serious. "Pardon me for bringing it up, but the DA fired Stuart a few years back. Shouldn't I be concerned about that?"

The big man wasn't delicate, and he certainly didn't pull any punches. "Stuart was a rising star," Katherine said. "He was obviously next in line for Malloy's job."

Dugan nodded. "And men on top don't like to be challenged."

"Of course not."

"How about Clay here? What's he like?"

Katherine thought for a moment. The situation felt too formal, too academic, like she was reciting résumés. The dirty-fingernailed developer didn't look comfortable. He didn't feel at home in their office the same way he didn't feel comfortable with the firm he was firing.

"You have to make your own call on Clay," she said. "I don't know him the way I know my husband. He could be a huge prick."

Dugan laughed out loud. "You're feisty. Boy, do I like that! Just as long as he's *my* huge prick. That's exactly what I pay my lawyers to be."

Katherine smiled back, relieved. It had been a gamble, but she was good at making people relax. Dugan needed to feel like he was among friends, not dazzled by professionalism. Buchanan, Stark wouldn't win a résumé battle against the big firms anyway.

"Is that all you needed to know?" she said.

"Yep," he said. "Thanks, babe. You've been a great help."

"I aim to please."

Clay gave her a clandestine nod, and Katherine stepped out of the room to let them talk again. She felt elated. She'd made Dugan comfortable. And it had been a decade since she'd been called a babe.

They concluded their meeting a few minutes later, and Dugan stepped out to use the bathroom. Clay sent Audry back to one of the new offices.

Katherine peeked into the conference room. "How did I do, boss?" she joked with a smug grin.

Clay looked up. "I could have sworn I told you to call him Reggie," he said, unsmiling.

Katherine winced. "He called me Mrs. Stark. I replied in kind. It just felt right."

Clay gave her a blank look, and her stomach did a flip-flop. She'd screwed up. She knew it. He knew it. And he knew she knew it.

"It was just a little thing," she tried. "And he laughed when I called you a prick."

"Yeah, we'll talk about *that* later too. Look, I know you're accustomed to improvising your life, but I have a specific strategy that happens to be working for us, so I think it might be best if you follow my lead. Do you have an issue with that?"

She'd been having some fun, but fun wasn't the goal, she realized, and Clay was quite serious. More important, his strategy *was* working. He'd given her very specific direction and she'd immediately ignored it. She shook her head. "No issue. Sorry. I'm yours to command."

"That's what I like to hear."

Dugan reappeared in the hall. He and Clay were shaking hands, but Katherine couldn't tell if the deal had been struck or not. Without a written contract, it probably still hung in the balance.

"Thanks for the meeting," Dugan said. "I'd love to see the rest of your office, but I've got to go out to inspect some model homes we're building."

Clay brightened. "That's great. You know, Katherine is looking for a new place. Have you got anything with a bay view?"

"One. It's a bit pricey, though. We had to do a teardown of the existing home first. This one's brand-new with high-end materials."

"Perfect," Clay said, foregoing any discussion of the price. "I know she'd love to see it."

Katherine held up a finger to object, but Clay's narrow eyes flashed to her, and her finger melted back into her palm under their burning gaze.

"It's okay, Kate," Clay said. "I'm sure Reggie doesn't mind giving you a private showing." He held her eyes with his. "This is one of those things I'm willing to take the lead on, if you're feeling shy."

"Never be afraid to ask for what you want," Dugan rumbled in his deep voice. "I'd be happy to take you out there. I'm going now, if that's good for you."

When Katherine hesitated, Clay nodded at her.

"Okay," she said. She took a deep breath and threw on a playful smile. "I'm game."

Katherine dropped her aging Toyota Corolla at home and walked back down the driveway to Dugan's waiting Dodge Ram pickup for the trip south. The Ram was new—fifty thousand dollars, at least, Katherine guessed. It sat so high off the ground that she had to tiptoe in her heels and pull up her skirt just to reach the running board with her right foot. Dugan opened the door for her to help her in, one of his massive hands wrapping around hers. *Very gentlemanly.* His other hand found her butt again. *Less gentlemanly.* He hoisted her up onto the heated leather passenger seat.

The Ram's ride was smooth, more luxurious than any car she and Stu had ever owned, though the heated seat made her buns feel like they were being slow-cooked. The premium sound system played at a low volume so they could talk, and a navigation panel boasted voice activation and audio directions, which Reggie said he didn't use because it sounded like an annoying customer service woman trying to get him to calm down. His Bluetooth headset remained activated, but he'd tucked it in the door pouch so that she had his full attention.

Perhaps the most ostentatious option was the beverage cooler in the center console. Katherine would have preferred that it had a bottle of wine stuffed in it—a white zin for the middle of the day—but she didn't refuse the can of Miller High Life that Reggie offered. It felt good to calm down with a cheap beer and his blue-collar companionship after Clay's intensity. And drinking alcohol while riding in a car felt rebellious—something Stu would never do.

"This place is across the bridge. You okay with that?"

"Sure. Why not?"

"The drive into town would be longer."

"I don't go downtown too often. The farther from New Bedford, the better." He probably meant the drive would be longer for Stu, but she didn't want to talk about Stu. "Did you work on this home yourself?"

"Of course. I like to get my hands dirty. Makes me feel . . ."

Like a man, Katherine thought. He was thick, muscular, and tall. Mostly thick. Not in a bad way. Her eyes ran from his corded neck down over his chest. It was deep and wide. He had a bit of a stomach, but it was the healthy belly of a man with big appetites, not the gut of an inactive loser. His belt was cinched beneath it, and below that . . .

Vulgar to stare, she thought.

But she was *supposed* to be flirting. Hell, the man fondled her ass at every opportunity. Besides, she was curious—he was a big guy. She risked a long look. Reggie's bulge was not the standard crease that all males' jeans formed whenever they sat; it was a taut dome of denim the size of an orange, straining to accommodate what it held.

Katherine considered allowing him to see her stare, but there was a well-defined flirting hierarchy to consider—*friendly, flirty, naughty, dirty, nasty, raunchy, and slutty.* She was still only at stage two. Not naughty yet. She looked away before he noticed.

"Useful," Reggie finished. "I get to feel useful. I use the same contractors for all the projects I finance. They like my money, and I like to pound a few nails."

"I'll bet you do." She watched him grin at that. It was satisfying; she'd shut off her playfulness when she'd gotten married, but it was easier than she thought to turn her hip swing back on. And the results were almost instantaneous. When she'd aged into her mid-thirties, she'd thought the opposite sex had forgotten her—the young guys who populated the SAC didn't give her a second look anymore. But Dugan was definitely looking. The men hadn't forgotten—only the boys.

They crossed Apponagansett Bay and turned down Smith Neck Road. He hadn't told her the address yet.

"So, Reggie, is the location supposed to be a surprise?"

"You wanna know?"

"No. I like surprises. Just take me there."

"Yes, ma'am."

It was a short trip. The Ram hummed, Reggie Dugan's deep voice narrated the neighborhoods, and Katherine sipped from her sweating can of beer. She felt an instant buzz that was hard to separate from the excitement of the Molson settlement, the fun of flirting, and the pressure of her mission to coax Dugan into committing. Clay would be very disappointed in her if she failed. *Better not blow it,* she thought.

They pulled into the driveway.

"End of the line. Everybody out," Reggie announced.

"All two of us?"

Dugan held up the key to the house. "You want to go in alone?" He pressed it into her palm. It was silver, like treasure, but jagged and cool to the touch. When she closed her hand around it, the teeth bit into her flesh.

Katherine hesitated. It was a test. He was making her tell him whether she wanted him to come inside with her. "If I'm going to buy it, I might have questions."

"Guess I'll have to come with you then." He threw open his door and swung his big body out.

The footpath to the front entrance was heavy natural stone, expensive. The Bolt Construction sign declaring it ANOTHER HIGH-QUALITY BOLT PROJECT was still stuck in the as-yet unlandscaped dirt. Dugan narrated the exterior features as they approached.

"Double-pane argon windows. Fifty-year roof. Fiber cement siding. All the best."

But Katherine wasn't listening. She ignored the front door and strode to the corner of the home to peek around back, where she stopped in her tracks and gasped. Behind the house, Buzzards Bay pressed up against a thirty-foot ribbon of light-colored sand that snuggled up to the property like a lover. It wasn't as good as her SAC friends' homes; it was *better*. She took a deep breath as she felt, rather than saw, her two-hundred-and-fifty-pound escort nestle up behind her to share the moment.

"This house is on the beach," Katherine said, allowing him to press against her. "Right *on* the beach!"

"Yep," Dugan said, smiling over her shoulder like a boy showing off his hot car to a date.

"I hate to ask . . ."

"Right around a million. Still want me to take you in?"

Two days earlier she would have felt silly accepting a private showing of a million-dollar home. Reggie would have seen her eyes flicker away with the embarrassment of not being able to afford it. But today she had a million-five on the way and, if she played it right, two hundred grand per year more coming. Today she felt like a little girl with the keys to the candy store being dangled in front of her. Instead of glancing away, she turned to look straight up at Reginald Dugan. He really wasn't a bad-looking man.

"Absolutely," she said.

Ten minutes later Katherine was seated on the edge of the model home's five-thousand-dollar leather couch. The view of Buzzards Bay from the living room was jaw-dropping, and she couldn't help but peek out of the corner of her eye at the full 180 degrees of waves thrusting themselves ashore with a persistent rhythm.

She took a deep breath, filling her nostrils with salty air, and felt more alive than she had in years. It was everything Clay had promised, with one exception: Dugan stood waiting before her with his pants around his ankles.

CHAPTER 19

Katherine lay on her back on the living room carpet with her knees pulled up to her chest, one set of toes pointing up at the chandelier and the others toward the skylight on the far side of the room. She pumped her hips and squeezed her butt as tight as she could in an urgent rhythm.

"Almost there, almost there . . . ," she grunted.

Panting and grunting wasn't ladylike, but she didn't care, and the only other person in the room certainly didn't. Besides, she was almost finished and she couldn't hold out much longer.

"Done!" Jill announced finally, and Katherine went limp, dropping her shaking legs to the carpet, exhausted. Jill consulted her watch. "Thirty minutes in the books, and you look fucking fabulous."

Katherine took a few slow, deep, warm-down breaths. "Thanks. I don't think I've ever felt better in my life." She rose, caught the towel that Jill tossed at her, and noted that it was the second time in two days that someone had said the word *fucking* to her. It was raw and jarring. And she liked it. She wiped sweat from her dripping hair.

"I'll get my checkbook. One hundred, right?"

Jill looked apologetic. "Sorry. We can always arrange the group work-out, which splits the cost."

"Money's not a problem," Katherine said, pausing to savor the words. For the first time in her life she meant it. "Holly always slows things down, and Margery talks through the entire session. This is good. I was totally focused today."

"I'll say. You're an ass-kicker."

Katherine smiled. "I am now."

"What's changed?"

The doorbell rang.

Katherine hurried off to answer the door. On the way she paused at the entryway mirror. She was still sweaty, but the crystalline beads of per-spiration only highlighted her bulging arms and glowing face. She *did* look fucking fabulous. She didn't bother straightening her hair, but simply strode to the door sweaty and threw it open.

Clay leaned against her porch rail. He wore a leather dress jacket cinched at the waist over jeans. His eyes ran over her spandex-wrapped body, and she allowed it. He finished with her feet and worked his way back up un-til he was looking her in the eyes.

"Busy?" he said, frowning.

"You don't call?"

"I should ask you the same." He walked past her into the living room. "Can I come in?"

"Uh, make yourself at home," she said as she closed the door and trot-ted after him.

He stopped abruptly and whirled. She nearly ran into him and tried to step back, but he caught her by the wrist. "I was expecting some word about your little trip to the model home yesterday. I arranged it special for you, but apparently my efforts were forgotten."

"I didn't realize it was such a chore for you."

"I don't think you understand. I got you in the back door. They're not going to show that property publicly. When they put it up for sale, there will be multiple bidders, people of privilege who don't go through the normal channels. You can be one of them. And, if you play your cards right, you could be the only one."

"It was nice," she said, squirming to try to free her wrist.

He squeezed harder until she stopped resisting, but his expression didn't change. "Do you want it?" His dark eyes were calm, and they never left hers.

"I like it," she said finally.

"I know. Your pulse is pounding at just the suggestion of it." He tapped his finger on her wrist and grinned.

Her heart *was* beating hard, although she wasn't sure it was due to the house on the water.

"I think you should let go now," Katherine whispered.

"Why is that?"

"Hello?" Jill said, poking her head into the living room.

Clay released Katherine's wrist.

"Clay, this is Jill from the club," Katherine said, stepping away from him. "Jill, this is Clay." When Jill stared, Katherine patted Clay's shoulder to show that nothing was amiss.

"Oh," Jill said. "You're Stu's partner."

Clay smiled. "And his good friend, yes." He stepped to Jill and extended a hand. "Clay Buchanan. And judging from your lats, you must be Katherine's personal trainer. Those are a neglected muscle among ordinary women, you know."

"Don't waste your charm on her," Katherine interrupted. "She's already got a partner."

"You can waste a little," Jill said, and she gave him a coy smile.

Katherine frowned. Jill's body was rock hard, more well developed than her own. But she had a horsey face, and Katherine imagined that Jill welcomed any male attention she could get, however gratuitous.

"Unless you two need me to leave," Jill offered, sensing Katherine's disapproval.

"Oh no, stay; I've got iced tea," Katherine shot back, trying not to seem nervous. But she spoke too quickly, seeming nervous as hell. She *was* nervous, she realized, and her own visceral jealous reaction to Clay's casual flirtation with Jill surprised her.

Jill could see she was a third wheel. She hoisted her athletic bag to her shoulder and headed for the front door. "Thanks, but I actually should get going. Nice to meet you, Clay."

"And you," he said.

Katherine took the opportunity to walk Jill to the foyer, out of earshot. "Sorry, he thinks he's God sometimes."

"He's right, you know."

"About what?"

"Not many women have well-developed lats."

Or cut bis and tris, Katherine thought, annoyed.

When she returned to the living room, Clay was turning a crystal half globe over in his hand, making it snow on some very cold-looking miniature villagers.

"What are you doing here?"

"Can't a friend drop in?"

"Like I said, you could have called. Do you know how this looks?"

"It looks like I'm bringing you something." His hand snaked into his coat pocket, and he produced a piece of paper folded in the shape of an origami bird, like a magician making a dove appear.

Katherine awaited his explanation without comment.

"You're curious, yes?"

"I'm mildly irritated."

"Ask me what it is."

"No. Just tell me."

"Or don't. Your choice. Shall I go?"

She sighed. "Okay, what is it?"

"Weak effort."

"Please tell me what it is before you get away and I die of curiosity."

"Better. Though we'll have to deal with your sarcasm when we have a chance."

He handed her the paper bird, and she quickly unfolded it, ignoring the artistry with which it had been created. It was an oversize cashier's check. She read it once, and then a second time, slowly, to be sure she hadn't misread it. One hundred thousand dollars.

"You got the money?"

"Not yet. This is a small advance on the settlement from one of our fine local lending institutions. We should get the real thing in a few months, but there's no need to starve until then."

Katherine wandered to the couch and sat, staring at the figure. There were a lot of zeroes for one check.

"We're not starving," she said.

"Figure of speech. No offense."

"Stu wouldn't want to borrow against money we don't have yet."

Clay slid onto the coffee table facing her, his legs wedged between her knees. "Kate, have Stu's methods been working?"

No, she thought. *They have not.* He was right again. He was right about Jill's lats, he was right about Dugan, and he was right about success. Katherine's pulse began to pick up speed again. His eyes were very dark—cowboy eyes squinting at her from beneath a white hat. Or a dark hat. It was tough to tell. He was saying something.

"Do you want to make an offer?"

"Huh?"

"An offer. On the house."

She glanced at the huge check. "Things are moving a little fast."

"As they should. As they always should have, I've come to believe. Those who can move fast win the race. The question is, can you keep up?"

"I think so."

"The house will be offered to others potential buyers next week, but I'm willing to ask Dugan if you can bid now. I think a full-price offer will deliver it."

"Isn't it good to bargain them down a bit?"

"Only if you want them to look at someone else's offer."

"We don't have the money yet."

"You leverage it. Keep your cash. Let the bank buy it for you."

"More borrowing. And I have to talk to Stu before I buy a house."

"Nonsense. Put a contingency clause in the offer. Something about an inspection. If we can't get Stuey on board, you can nix the deal later."

"You're sure Reggie would do this for us?"

"You're the one who spent the afternoon with him. You tell me."

"He showed me the house. I was friendly, like you said. But we didn't talk business."

"Did you fuck him?"

Katherine's neck felt warm. Three days ago she'd slapped Clay for suggesting such a thing. Today she only looked away.

"No. Of course not."

"Good. Because a motivated man is most easily persuaded when his goal is just out of reach."

"What do you think I am, Clay?"

"A woman who became too accustomed to being careful." Then he smiled. It was an ambiguous smile, one that could mean a couple of different things.

Careful. Katherine rolled the word over in her mouth. The word *careful* was high praise coming from Stu, but sounded like criticism coming from Clay. She wondered if reaching out to put her hands on his knees would be careful. *No,* she decided. And so she did it.

The deep blue denim of Clay's new jeans was coarse, and she could feel the muscles of his lower thighs tighten beneath her touch. It warmed her in places other than her neck. Before she could change her mind, she ran her hands farther up his legs and lifted her eyes to smile at him.

"What the hell are you doing?" he said.

Katherine yanked her hands away as though his jeans had burned her fingertips. "Nothing. I just—"

"I'm your husband's partner, for God's sake. He's my good friend. You yourself said it looked bad having me drop by. Do you want to screw up everything we've been working for?"

"No." She drew back like a reprimanded child. "I just . . . I appreciate the life you've breathed into, uh, my life. I mean *our* life, Stu's and mine."

"A thank-you will do for now. Just stay on task, all right?"

"All right."

"Do you understand me?"

"Yes. I get it."

"I'm not sure you do." He waited.

Katherine was puzzled. "Thank you," she tried finally.

"That's a start," he said. "I'd better get going."

With that, Clay stood, zipped up his coat, and started toward the door.

Katherine watched the tail of his long jacket sway back and forth for three steps, but she didn't rise to follow. When he turned, she instinctively clutched the check in her lap as though worried he might take it back.

"Cash that," he said. "And buy yourself something nice. Don't stuff it away somewhere and wait until you're old and wrinkled to enjoy it."

"Okay."

He waited for her to escort him. She didn't. "I'm on my way then," he said.

Still she didn't budge, but simply sat holding the hundred-thousand-dollar check between her legs.

He stared. "Shall I show myself out?"

Katherine shrugged. Then she crossed her legs and conjured a grimace. "Sorry," she said. "I've been exercising and hydrating. I really have to pee."

He chuckled and then, mercifully, turned and let himself out.

Katherine slumped, as exhausted from their exchange as she was from her workout, and she cursed herself for misreading the situation. But the chemistry was unmistakable, and he was practically ordering her not to hold back. She'd felt more alive than she had in years. And aroused.

She wondered what aroused a man like Clay Buchanan—perhaps strategizing and manipulating people. He was complicated, even contradictory at times. Not like Reggie Dugan. Reggie was a simple, straightforward male specimen. A hard-bodied married woman aroused him. *Obviously.*

Now Katherine wondered if she'd misfired with him, too. If she had, and Clay found out, he would almost certainly reprimand her again, maybe even punish her.

It didn't occur to her that perhaps he already knew.

CHAPTER 20

Katherine drove along the beach on Smith Neck Road, humming to herself. It was hard to keep all the exciting developments to herself, so she'd made excuses to call her friends. All of them. She still had Holly's plate from the party. Jenny was on the volunteer committee at the museum where Katherine had an upcoming show. Margery's kids might be interested in a children's author she'd heard was doing a book signing. Of course, she mentioned the beach house to each of them in passing. With her newfound success, she mused, she was thinking of buying something on the water, but she couldn't tell them where just yet. Didn't want to get ahead of herself, she'd said. Then she shrugged it off, saying it was no big thing.

She pulled into the red-stamped concrete driveway for the third time in as many days. It was private and shaded by shrubs on either side. She turned off the old Toyota's laboring engine, and sat. She'd peeked through the windows like a burglar the previous two visits and walked the grounds, amazed that such a gorgeous property could be hers.

Managing Reggie had been a challenge, but she'd placated him without folding completely—she hadn't had full intercourse. She'd been honest with Clay on that score. If she'd bedded Dugan, he might have simply notched his contractor's belt and lost his motivation. As it stood, he only wanted her more; he was the sort of man that felt the need to finish the job.

Katherine stuffed her car keys into her jeans pocket and leaned the seat back, admiring the fifty-year roof and argon windows, details she'd been too excited to appreciate on her previous trips. Reggie was right: the details made a difference. *The devil is in them too,* Stu would have said with his patented doubtful frowny look. But Stu wasn't here. In all their years together, her husband hadn't been able to arrive at this place. Clay had set this up. Reggie had delivered it. The alpha males.

Katherine settled into her seat as she recalled the big man.

As assertive as he was, he'd been surprisingly gentle when he'd first embraced her on the deck overlooking the water, one hand in its customary position on her hip. And when she'd allowed it, he'd quickly escalated, and soon he had her pressed against the rail with his mouth buried in her neck and his big hands kneading her SAC-hardened ass.

As confident as advertised, he hadn't been afraid to ask for exactly what he wanted. But she'd declined the short trip to the master bedroom. It was too much. She needed to find a compromise, an accommodation. And so, after allowing his hands to explore her body for a time, she'd led him inside the model home and seated herself on the luxurious couch in the living room, while he took a standing position in front of her.

Business. That's all she was doing, she told herself. Younger girls in the SAC locker room called it doing "a favor," which made it sound no more significant than giving a buddy a ride to the airport. *I can do this,* she'd told herself as she unbuckled his belt, reached in, and lifted him out. Given the thickness of the big contractor's member, she couldn't help thinking of it as simply shaking up a warm beer can to make it foam over. *Seriously, no big deal.*

She'd peeked past Dugan at the sandy shoreline at the moment she'd finally put her mouth on him to finish the job. The house was a dream.

Her dream. More important, it was about to become a reality. *This is success,* Katherine had thought as he began to shudder. Everything she had worked for was about to arrive. . . .

Katherine smiled as she stared through the windshield at the model home from her reclining position in the driver's seat. She wanted it. And the memory of sitting in front of its huge picture window on the luxurious couch with a half-naked man was uniquely arousing. She wrestled down her jeans and pulled her underwear aside. With her left leg against the driver's door and her right propped up on the aging Toyota's center console, she had reasonable access to herself. She tried to picture Stu's face, but in her imagination her husband looked indecisive. Not assertive. Not confident. *Not sexy.* She relented and touched herself to the memory of Dugan for a time. It helped, but the big contractor was blunt, indelicate. Just when she thought she might lose her momentum, Clay's face popped into her head. She'd resisted calling up the image of her husband's partner, but it came just the same. Katherine shoved her foot against the dashboard and groaned. Suddenly, there was a loud *crack* as the plastic dash split under the pressure of her muscular leg.

Katherine went limp and giggled. "Oops. . . ."

Pleasuring herself was becoming a habit. She couldn't remember the last time she'd let her impulses drive her the way she had in the days since Clay had enlightened her. Maybe college.

The home was beautiful, she thought as she slid her panties back into place and tugged up her jeans. And the private driveway was a benefit she'd not previously considered. It was so private, in fact, that she almost screamed when the man rapped on her window.

Katherine shot bolt upright and found herself staring into the weathered face of a round-shouldered man with a crew cut. He looked familiar—not like someone she knew, but more like someone she'd seen in a photograph. Very plain. Dumpy. *Not a celebrity or politician.* Nor a social acquaintance, at least not from her circles. But very familiar, and becoming more so as she stared.

He had a tool—hedge clippers, from the look of it. And he wore coveralls. A landscaper, maybe. But why she would recognize some yard worker, she didn't know. He tapped on the window again as she fumbled with the snap of her pants, and her stomach turned over as she wondered how long he'd been standing there.

"Can I help you with anything, ma'am?" he was saying, his voice muffled through the window.

She shook her head and groped for her keys, but they were bound up in her front pocket, which had twisted when she'd pulled her jeans back up.

"You can get out and look around the place, if you like," the man continued. "I can't let you in, though. They don't give me a key."

She waved him off, raising her hips to dig into her pants pocket. Her rude gesture was as dismissive as she'd intended, and his expression grew dark. When she glanced up at him again, he looked like a brooding gorilla in a jumpsuit framed in her driver's-side window. *Like a mug shot.* And suddenly she realized who he was.

Oh God, she thought. *Raymond Butz!*

CHAPTER 21

"What the hell was he doing there?" Katherine was still shaking from her close encounter with Butz.

Clay picked up his phone and dialed reception. "Kaylee, cancel my eleven o'clock appointment." He removed his whiskey bottle from the desk and poured a single shot into a tumbler. "Here. Drink this, Kate."

He held out the tumbler pinched between two fingers. It was unusual for her to drink anything besides a social glass of wine during the day. And she never drank hard alcohol straight. But the glass hung precariously and looked as though, if she didn't take it, it would drop in her lap, so she accepted. She sipped, made an *icky* face, and then sipped again.

"What were you doing out there?" Clay said.

"I was just driving by."

"You saw him while driving by?" Clay asked doubtfully.

"I pulled into the driveway. I was just sitting my car."

"Doing what?"

"Just looking."

"I see." Clay gave her a patronizing nod.

"I was excited," Katherine admitted. "I love the house. I want to get a thorough feel for it."

"From the driveway?"

"Yes. I know it sounds silly."

"You weren't meeting Dugan for another tour, were you?"

"No."

"Good. Because I'd expect you to let me know if you did."

"I *am* letting you know. And I didn't."

"Before. Not after."

"Look, I came here because I was confronted by a murderer. I'm a little freaked out."

"He's not a murderer. He was acquitted."

"He was standing by my car. He was watching me."

"Watching you sit in your car?"

"Yes. It was creepy. Why was he even there?"

"He works for Bolt Construction. Always has. Probably there maintaining the place."

Katherine was taken aback. She recalled that Butz worked construction, but she hadn't realized it was for Bolt. "You knew?"

"That he would be there today? No. Of course not. But it doesn't shock me that he'd be working at one of his employer's project sites."

"You knew the man my husband prosecuted for homicide helped build the house that you sent me to look at? A house I'm considering buying? You knew he works for the client you're having me charm?"

"Butz works for Bolt, not Dugan. Dugan just uses Bolt as his contractor."

"I don't want that man around my house."

"It's not your house."

"I don't want that convict anywhere near me."

"He's not a convict. He went through the system and was exonerated."

"He was turned loose on a technicality."

"He rolled the dice and won. He's entitled to his life back."

"He killed his wife."

"Look, I know his case hurt Stu's career, but you have to move on, Kate. The life of a lawyer is about picking your battles. That case goes in the loss column. Let it go."

Katherine raised the tumbler to her lips again, but it was empty. Clay quickly refilled it before she could put it down, and she took another swig.

Clay leaned back. "You know what we hired guns say: 'your enemy one day is your ally the next.'"

Katherine gave a pained chuckle. "So one day a killer is ruining my life, the next he's building my home."

"Maybe. You never know what's coming next. You need to be a bit more flexible."

"Flexible?"

"Changing the world is hard. Changing yourself is easy." Clay spun in his new leather chair and put his feet up on his burled wood antique desk. "You want Thai for lunch?"

The whiskey had warmed her, and she was no longer shaking. Clay's confidence was reassuring. And sexy. "Are we having lunch?"

"I am. You're welcome to join me." He rose and traded his suit jacket for a tailored trench so new it still had sharp creases where it had been folded in its box. "Or not."

She did, and they drove to the Poor Siamese downtown. Going home alone didn't appeal to her. No matter what Clay's philosophy was about Butz, running into the man had creeped her out. She worried that he'd seen her talking to Stu in the courtroom during the trial and knew who she was. She'd attended sporadically but mostly sat in the back, and she wondered if Butz would remember her face from the crowd. After seeing her with her legs propped wide on the dashboard of her car at the beach house, he certainly wouldn't forget her now.

"Back here," said the owner of the Poor Siamese, a young guy named Jimmy who wore a white coat and greeted them at the door. He was not Thai, but his cook was. There was only one other customer in the place, and Katherine wondered how it survived; no crowd for lunch on a Wednesday was a sure sign that a restaurant was dying. Jimmy pumped Clay's hand as though they were old friends, and then turned to her.

"And you must be Mrs. Stark." He beamed.

"Yes. Nice to meet you." She gave him one of her professionally social smiles.

"Anything you need, you let me know personally, Mrs. Stark." He turned to Clay. "I have you set up in the red room, Mr. Buchanan. No one will bother you."

She and Clay were quickly ushered into a private room in the rear with a red curtain. She was surprised to see a man waiting for them, slurping tom yum soup from a small bowl.

Clay introduced her. "Frank, this is Katherine Stark. She's a professional photographer. But I promise she's not here to take pictures. She's Stu's wife. Katherine, this is Frank Hranic."

The man stood to greet her. He was round, so much so that he had to push his chair back to get up, and when he did, his belly spilled out onto the table like a half-empty beanbag chair. Katherine recognized him. He'd been in the news when he was hired by Mayor Welge of Fall River to manage the city's convalescent care fund years earlier. Unfortunately for Hranic, a state audit had discovered that the CC fund was siphoning off money to a business in Providence, which provided phony invoices for work that was never done. She didn't recognize the round scar on his cheek, which looked like a tattoo gone wrong. A burn mark, she realized, the size of a quarter. She could still see the vague impression of a president's head.

Hranic had blamed accounting, but he suffered felony embezzlement charges along with his bookkeeper. According to Stu, Hranic had provided a statement implicating the bookkeeper in exchange for reduced charges. The bookkeeper, however, wound up on the medical examiner's table with a bellyful of crushed OxyContin. Hranic received a misdemeanor and a recommendation for thirty days of local time converted to community service for his cooperation. The audit findings put the fraudulent amount in the hundreds of thousands, but only a few thousand were recovered. And the assistant DA handling the case was none other than Clay Buchanan.

The way Stu told it, Clay had been furious when the bookkeeper died and Hranic got the huge break for nothing, but as Clay prepared to sit down with the fat man for lunch, he didn't seem furious.

"How the hell are you, Frank?" Clay said after his cursory introductions.

"Concerned," Hranic mumbled.

"About your weight? Because it's gonna kill you."

"Considering all the other things that can kill you, I'd just as soon it was food. But you didn't call me to talk about my health."

They sat. Hranic could have perched his soup bowl on his belly and eaten off it, but he stuffed his paunch back under the table.

"It's time to chat about my legal services, Frank."

"Can we talk in front of her?"

"The attorney-client privilege extends to all my staff."

"But she's just your partner's wife. Can't she be subpoenaed?"

"No. I've brought her here in her official capacity as client liaison."

Katherine almost laughed.

Clay remained serious. "First of all, if anyone ever connects you with me, you need to say that you sought my legal advice. That way, everything we do is confidential, especially where it relates to your prior criminal matter."

"Okay."

"Secondly, I'd like the balance of my fee in a lump sum now. You know the amount. I'm just accelerating the payment schedule. Let your sister know that she's going to get a bill from us for legal services. She'll write the check to our firm, as usual."

Hranic groaned.

"She still has it, right?" Clay asked.

"It's all still in an account. She shows me the statements."

"Is she distributing small amounts to you on schedule?"

"Yes, but my cash flow is shit. I need a new car."

"You can't hold money or buy expensive niceties, Frank. You can't even smell like money unless it objectively appears to be within your earning capacity, which is just about minimum wage right now thanks to you getting caught with your hand in the cookie jar. Criminal restitution remains owing. And then there's the civil judgment. They're still watching you. If you need a car, I'd say you're due for a used Toyota Corolla. Economical. Good gas mileage."

"It's been years. Can't I just get the rest from her?"

Stu darkened. "You'll eat it. Or drink it. Or gamble it. You have no self-control. I know that. Your sister knows that. That's part of the reason she won't give it all to you at once. Hell, *you* know that. Just look at yourself, you fat fuck."

"She can call it a gift. It's my money, not hers."

"And then you'll declare it on your taxes? Cast suspicion on her? Hell no. You need to practice some trickle-down economics here, my friend. Do nothing that will attract attention. Continue to draw one thousand a month and bleed it into your budget as cash to pay for groceries and gas. After five years or so you'll have it all, and you won't have blown it. That's my legal and gratuitously friendly advice."

"So you can take your full cut now, but I can't? That's what you're saying?"

"I'm not the convicted criminal, Frank. I'm just the lawyer. I provide a service for a fee." Clay patted him on one meaty shoulder. "Look, I can't legally force your sister to give you the money anyway. It doesn't exist as far as the law's concerned. If you want to put real pressure on her, you'll have to go back to our friend in Providence."

The fat man paled and squirmed, his belly jostling the table. "I'm not bringing him into it again. I paid him off." Hranic absently touched his round scar. "Besides, she's my sister. I don't want anything bad to happen to her."

"Then take your lawyer's advice. And pay me for it."

After a bit more grumbling and some small talk, Hranic hauled his bulk out of the chair and dismissed himself. Katherine waited until she heard the bell on the front door tinkle, signaling his exit. Then she looked at Clay, aghast.

He smiled and put his legs up on the chair beside her, reclining like a man who'd just had a particularly satisfying meal. "I see from your expression that you have questions," he said. "Go ahead."

"Does our firm represent Mr. Hranic as a criminal defendant?"

"In a sense."

"Because you know Stuart won't approve of it."

"You see there, this is a good example of his inflexibility. Our firm is a perfect fit for criminal defense. Always has been. Criminal law is what we did for years, for Chrissakes. Nobody knows it better than us."

"It's the principle of the thing for him," Katherine said. "But it sounds like you've already been dealing with this man."

"We've been getting regular payments from Hranic's sister for years. She has a different last name. And you're right. Stu wouldn't approve, so it's billed through me."

"Stu doesn't know?"

"Strictly speaking, I'm not doing any criminal defense work for Hranic yet. He's not charged with anything. He's done his time. I'm just helping his sister with a civil issue—how to manage money for a brother with an addictive personality."

"The money he stole."

"Let's be clear. Hranic owes money. But his sister is paying our bill."

"She's paying you off with the stolen funds she's holding for him. Is that clear enough?"

Clay grinned. "It's all in how you characterize it. She pays regularly from her personal checking account. The lump sum will be a cashier's check."

"You prosecuted Hranic. Isn't this a conflict?"

"A client can waive a conflict. No one knew his case better than me, and I knew the money was still out there; his suicidal twenty-five-year-old bookkeeper certainly didn't have it. When I went into private practice, I contacted him, and he quickly saw the wisdom of having me as an ally instead of an enemy. Sound familiar? Besides, he got a pretty sweet plea bargain."

"You asked him for a share of the dirty money."

"You're still not saying it right. His sister pays our firm fees—nine hundred and ninety-five dollars a month—for my advice. It's logged under estate planning. And, by the way, you've been accepting half of that money for the last five years. This month's check probably paid for those brand-new thigh-high leather boots I see you wearing."

Katherine blushed. "Do you like them?"

"They look right on you, and I'll bet you've wanted them for a long time, haven't you?"

"Maybe."

"And now you're getting what you wanted, correct?"

"You're sure it's not illegal to take money from a criminal? I mean, I don't necessarily agree with Stuart's ban on criminal defense, but I don't want to *do* anything illegal."

"Criminal defense lawyers get paid by criminals, Kate," Clay said. Then he waited for the simplicity of his reasoning to sink in.

Katherine retreated behind her menu to think. He made her feel like a little girl; it was hard to argue with an attorney. But the real question was: Why did she want to argue? The handsome man sitting across from her was taking control and whisking her along for what was turning out to be a thrilling ride, just as she'd always wanted Stu to do.

CHAPTER 22

Katherine walked along the waterfront with her lips pursed. It had been three days, and for the first time she thought seriously about what she was going to tell her husband about the goings-on during his absence.

"Don't overthink it," Clay had advised.

She wondered how Stu was doing. She didn't expect that he'd slain a deer and made himself venison steaks. More likely he was eating canned beans, and there were worse things than eating cheap beans. She just couldn't think of any at the moment.

The harbor was busy, with boats drifting in and out in a slow, orderly fashion, as they'd done for centuries. Tall, triangular sails scraped the sky, pulling sleek craft out into the bay, while chugging diesel engines shoved their wider burdens through the waves. Whaling photos and memorabilia hung in store windows. She noticed none of it.

Things were happening that Stu wouldn't be comfortable with, and she'd have to discuss them with him when he got back. She wasn't looking forward to it—he had a way of arguing without arguing. He calmly pointed out fact after fact, each followed by *Have you considered that?* It was annoying, effective, and annoying because it was effective. But he would miss the big picture. The drab state of their life was all the proof she needed. Stu did all the little things right, and they still weren't winning.

The beach house needed to be discussed. She wanted it so badly that she was furnishing it in her head. She had to find a way to get Stu on board and keep him from hoarding the Molson money. They'd talked about trading up before, and now they had the money. From that angle, she had a solid position.

Justifying the unexpected office expansion was Clay's problem, though she would side with her husband's partner on that, too. And Stu wouldn't approve of Hranic's sister as a proxy client. He wouldn't condone using phony associates to get clients, either. These items were touchier, although Stu couldn't complain about the results. Clay was already writing them hundred-thousand-dollar checks. He was moving forward. That was the difference between the two men. One was in motion; one was stagnant.

Then there was the little matter of the favor she'd done for Dugan. She winced. It sounded so bad out of context. But it wasn't romance. He wasn't going to fall in love with her; she could see it in his cat-that-ate-the-canary expression afterward. And she wasn't leaving Stu. Technically, it wasn't even mutual sex. Besides, it was working.

It didn't need to come up, she decided. Stu wasn't an overly jealous man, but he'd overanalyze it. The act was almost too simple for him to understand—Dugan wanted something and she had provided it. Period. Stu would drive himself nuts trying to make it more complicated than it was. Then he'd cope. He had before. He was reasonable and loyal that way. He'd forgive her. But why put him through it? There were more important things brewing. The house, for instance. A more pleasant thought. They needed to put together an offer as soon as he got back.

The waterfront restaurant was nestled between a women's apparel shop that sold nautical clothing and an exchange for used marine equipment. Katherine pushed the door open and stepped inside.

Its interior was dimly lit with paper lanterns. There were no chairs.

Instead patterned couches of different shapes were arranged around wagon-wheel-shaped coffee tables. Upscale customers sat or reclined in suits and skirts, casually taking bites of food from large communal trays. No one was in a hurry. There was no rush on the part of the staff, which dressed all in black and circulated with appetizers apparently available to all. Not a place for a quick lunch.

A young woman with her raven hair pulled back in a tight bun greeted Katherine with cool detachment.

"Reservation?"

"I'm not sure. I'm meeting someone."

"Okaaay . . ." Bun Hair gave her a shallow smile. "Is it possible this someone you are meeting has a reservation?"

Katherine's hackles rose, and she parried Bun Hair's smirk with an oversugared smile of her own. "Sorry. It might be under Hanstedt. First name is Margery. Perhaps you know her?"

The woman's face transformed, her aloof expression twisting into a cross between forced warmth and fear. "Yes, of course. Welcome. I'll seat you now."

She led Katherine toward the rear of the restaurant, making hurried small talk as though they were old friends. She selected a table near the window, apart from the rest. Semiprivate, which was good, considering the conversation Katherine intended to have.

"Would you like some wine?"

"I shouldn't."

"It's complimentary. And quite good."

Katherine shrugged her assent, and Bun Hair fled to fetch it.

When Margery entered, it was as though the First Lady had walked in. Conversations fell to a low buzz. Customers and staff alike glanced at her and then away. The braver among them waved. She nodded in return, then held her coat in the air until Bun Hair spirited it away. She didn't miss a step as a handsome young waiter put a glass of wine in her hand, and she walked straight to Katherine's table. She arrived and stood over the couch.

"Welcome to Stationbreak."

Katherine stood to greet her with one of her society hugs—friendly but formal, a light squeeze to imply familiarity and trust, but not too needy.

Margery was decked out in what Holly Plynth called "slut gear"—a black miniskirt, leather boots with heels, and a white see-through blouse with a push-up bra which served up her substantial knockers for customers to admire. She looked like a walking dessert cart without the guilt.

"Did my hostess, Sondra, greet you politely?"

"Are you working right now?"

"I own three small businesses. I'm always working."

Bun Hair's horrified look had been amusing, but it wasn't punishment enough, Katherine decided. She'd put in her own time serving people when she was young, and now it was her turn to be served well. "She could take it up a notch."

Margery nodded, making a mental note of it, and slid in next to Katherine instead of on the opposite couch.

"You look great," Margery said, observing their unwritten rule of starting all meetings with mutual compliments.

"You too. I wish I had your calves."

"So how's Stuey holding up in Alaska?"

"Don't know. No cell phone."

"Right."

"I suppose he's fending for himself."

"Or eating beans."

Just then a waiter slid a tray of barbequed clams dripping with garlic butter in front of them and a cup of white sauce with bits of red bell pepper. Margery stabbed a clam with a tiny appetizer fork and dredged the sauce bowl with it.

"How are Robert and Amy?" Katherine asked. Margery's children were nine and eleven.

"Adorable, busy, and expensive. Private elementary school is like practicing to pay for college. I also have a tedious play, poetry reading, or holiday concert to go to monthly. And the parent association wants a donation for every fund-raiser. I do it, but I make sure our name goes on all their flyers. It's good PR at least. But I don't want to bore you with mommy chatter. Let's talk about something interesting."

"Chatter is okay. I asked."

"Then I don't want to bore myself. This is big-girl time for me." She sipped her wine. "So, you called this little two-person soiree. What did you want to talk about?"

"Business and sex."

"My, my. This *is* going to be an interesting lunch. Do go on."

"I get the impression you're good at both, and I'd like to mine your expertise."

"Start digging. I'll tell you when to stop."

"All of the sudden, things are going well for me. Quite well."

"In business or sex?"

"Business. Maybe both. I'll get to that. But business first. Now, this is still confidential. And there's a non-disclosure clause, so I'm not supposed to be talking about it at all. But you know the big case I've been talking about. . . ."

"Molson. I know."

"Right. Well, it settled."

"How much?"

"A lot."

Margery twirled her hand in the air, egging her on.

Katherine looked around, then whispered. "One-point-five million to us, after the split."

Margery nodded, impressed. "Fill your 401K. Save a third for taxes."

"You sound like Stu."

"I doubt it, but if I do, he's right."

"He hasn't told me yet."

"Really? That's odd. Then how do you know?"

"Clay."

"Interesting."

"Yeah. Clay is ramping up the business."

"Smart. Leverage success."

"I know. But Stu doesn't."

"Doesn't what?"

"Know that Clay is expanding, remodeling the firm, hiring employees."

"All in a week? While Stuey's away?"

"Yeah, and Clay's asking for my help."

"If he's doing all that, he's been planning this for a while."

Katherine blinked. "Maybe so. But we've never had the capital. Now we do. And he thinks Stu will hold us back."

"Will he?"

Katherine rolled a clam around in her mouth, stalling. "Yes," she said finally. "Dammit, I feel like I'm betraying him."

"By helping his firm? No. You're doing him a favor. Small business is tough, and not everyone has the killer instinct. Stu doesn't. Clay does. It's not so different from a high school dance; you can wait all night for just the right moment, or you can get out there as soon as the music starts. Who do you think gets the dates?"

"I know. But it's complicated."

"No, it's not. Just ask yourself three simple questions: What do you want? How do you get it? Can you do that?"

"I think I know what I want."

"Do you need to be on Team Clay to get it?"

"I think so."

"Can you do that?"

"So far. But Stu's not here."

"I see. Well, in my expert opinion you can handle Stuey. When he gets home, you talk to him. Have some balls if he doesn't. Make him successful whether he wants it or not."

"Oh God, exactly! That's what I've been trying to do for years. And that's what Clay says too."

"Speaking of Clay, let's get to the sex."

Katherine's heart raced. She was well aware that Margery had hit on him at the party, and she felt a flash of something—annoyance, possibly anger. "You didn't . . ."

"No. But I did meet with him yesterday."

"Really?"

"He talked to me at Stu's party. I told him I was extremely busy, but I gave him my phone number. I made him call me. There's a trick you can use. He got in touch the day after to set up the meeting."

"That's strange. He was supposed to be going to Alaska."

"Well, I'm glad that didn't happen, because I had this little cropped jacket I was dying to try out, and I looked damn good."

"I don't think he's right for you," Katherine said abruptly. "I mean, even if you weren't married and could fool around. He's a bit intense."

"Which I find hot. Sadly, he wants me for my business. He must have another woman stashed away somewhere. Perhaps you know?"

"I don't think he does. He's concentrating on work right now. I'm even helping him get clients, if you can believe that. Did he talk to you about representing the restaurants?"

"Yes. I assume that's why you wanted to meet too. . . ."

"No. I mean, sure, we would love to represent you. But I just wanted advice."

"It's okay. I can compartmentalize. If you want to talk shop, I can put you in the business column for a few minutes. I have to warn you, though, it's dangerous to do business or sleep with your friends. If it ends badly, you risk losing the friendship."

"I'll leave it to Clay, then."

"The business or the sex part?" Margery grinned mischievously.

"That's what I wanted to ask you about. You know how you joke about fooling around sometimes? Actually, a lot of the time. I was wondering: Do you really do it?"

Margery sat back, studying Katherine, debating. Katherine had punched through the small-talk-'n'-gossip wall. Margery decided it was time for another dipped clam, and she took her time eating it. "That's very personal," she said finally. "I don't want to be the subject of rumors."

"We're friends. And we're not in business yet. Or sleeping together. Plus, I told you about the confidential settlement."

"Are you asking for advice because *you're* fooling around?"

Katherine bit her lip. Margery was direct, and smart. She was making

Katherine offer something incriminating before she spilled anything herself. "I came to you because I think I can trust you."

"I guess that tells me what I need to know. Is it Clay? I got a tension vibe when I mentioned his name."

"No. Nobody you associate with. And it's not going to be an ongoing thing. I just . . ."

"Impulsive?"

"Not particularly."

"Interesting. Go on."

"I wanted something. I saw how to get it. And, surprisingly, even to myself, I did it."

"Don't be surprised. Sex is fun. Or, at least it should be. If you get something tangible out of it, all the better."

"Do you enjoy doing 'favors' for a man?"

"If by 'favor,' you mean an oral arrangement, I think it can be a chore or a pleasure, or a bit of both. It's all in one's attitude."

And one can change her attitude, Katherine thought. "It wasn't full-on sex."

"Understood. Any details? C'mon, share at least a little of the fun."

Katherine giggled and couldn't help feeling a bit like a schoolgirl. At her age, it was a good feeling. "Huge balls," she whispered.

Margery joined her with a conspiratorial chuckle. "Really? Are we talking olives? Dried dates? Or a pair of kiwi? Maybe brown with a little fuzz . . ."

"Such imagery."

"It's the restaurateur in me. I relate to food."

"In that case, I'd say more like whole walnuts."

"Well, that *is* fun."

"But he wants to meet again, and I think he'll expect more next time. How would you handle it?"

"You already got what you want?"

"Yes."

"Do you want more?"

"Not from him."

"Then you're done. Cut it off, tell Stu, and move on."

Katherine furrowed her brow. "Tell Stu?"

"Of course. If he finds out some other way, it'll irreparably damage your marriage."

"If I tell him, it'll damage my marriage."

"You didn't actually have sex, but if you hide what you *did do* and he finds out, he'll never believe you didn't. He'll think you're minimizing. Get it?"

"So I just tell him? That's your advice?"

"Yep. Right when he gets home. The sooner it's done, the sooner it's done. And your immediate confession will make your guilt seem strong and real, even if it isn't."

"It is," Katherine said. Guilt wasn't what she was feeling at all, but saying so sounded right. Mostly, she didn't want to lose Dugan's business. And Clay would be pissed.

"Was it worth it?" Margery asked. "No judgment here. Maybe it was."

"I guess we'll see. Do you tell Richard what you do?"

Margery nodded, satisfied enough with Katherine's offering to reply this time. "We have an understanding."

"Interesting," Katherine mimicked.

"Yes, it has been."

"Don't ask, don't tell?"

"No. Ask *and* tell. That's essential. I don't even lay groundwork with someone else without communicating with Rich beforehand. He rarely objects. He likes his own freedom too much."

"Wow."

"There are a lot of available young women in the restaurant business. They like to cozy up to the male boss. Like that associate attorney flirting with Stu at your party."

"Audra? She's not a real attorney yet. More like an overgrown intern. And Stu would never do anything to get back at me. He's not vengeful."

"It's not revenge; it's just a fair trade. And giving him a free pass would get you off the hook."

"Not a chance." Katherine shook her head. Even if Stu had the guts to demand a like-kind exchange, she certainly wouldn't approve of Audra. "No. Not Stu. He would just forgive me."

"Eh, that works." Margery buried their conversation in her wine as Bun Hair drifted to a stop beside their table.

Katherine pulled out her purse, but Margery didn't budge.

"It's all taken care of," the worried-looking hostess said, manufacturing a big smile for Katherine in front of her boss. Margery coolly dismissed her, and Katherine smiled back, enjoying the thought of the trouble awaiting the girl when her boss got ahold of her later.

Katherine was amused and impressed. Margery had power. She was smart. She looked fucking fabulous. And she did what she wanted. She even did *who* she wanted. She was her own alpha.

CHAPTER 23

Margery's advice echoed in Katherine's head as she stood looking for Stu's flight on the Logan Airport arrivals board with a worried frown on her face. She still didn't know what exactly to say to her husband. Her saucy friend had issued the tell-all edict but hadn't provided delivery instructions.

Katherine decided that she would wait to disclose until she and Stu got home; that was an easy call. She could start by making him feel guilty for not telling her about Molson. That would put him in a more forgiving mood. Then she could segue into her own conduct. Taking a one-hundred-thousand-dollar advance and house shopping without him would be the starter. Her part in the revamped office charade was worse, and that bitch Audra would probably tell Stu that his wife had been there.

The Dugan thing was a bit stickier. She'd been testing speeches in her head all morning, and she still hadn't found just the right words to explain that particular client interaction.

Even if she found the right words to earn forgiveness, there was still a serious problem with telling the truth: Stu would end their representation of Dugan. No doubt. Her efforts would go for naught. Her favor would go unrewarded. She couldn't let that happen. But Margery had warned her that lies fester, and she didn't want to risk losing the man in whom she'd invested her entire adult life either, especially now that he was settling cases for millions of dollars. Unemployed women approaching forty didn't sell well in the single world.

Stu wasn't answering his cell phone, and he hadn't checked in, which wasn't like him. He typically called at every stage of a trip to review his schedule and pickup arrangements, which was annoying and comforting at the same time. Katherine stood beyond security, smiling big as the first-class passengers trickled out. Stu wouldn't be one of them on this trip. But things would be different after the Molson settlement and the Dugan contract. She waited patiently, as she had for a decade.

Katherine wondered if she should soften Stu up with some sex before telling him. She needed to redirect her energy toward her husband anyway. Her erotic adventures during his wilderness adventure had been interesting, but they were unsustainable; she couldn't continue rubbing up against Stu's partner and doing "favors" for powerful clients with her husband around. Nor could she keep ducking into the nearest phone booth like a superhero to satisfy her urges. She'd had one last session with herself the night before, imagining that her full-body pillow was Clay. *No more,* she decided. She would stop the fantasies the moment Stu appeared.

The bulk of the passengers were pouring out now. No Stu yet. She widened her smile. Any time now. She braced herself. Engaging a lawyer in a domestic debate was a challenge, but she could always use emotion. He didn't understand it well. He tried to convert it into logic and wasn't always sure of his translation. When she cried or raised her voice, he'd frown and say, "I think you're feeling upset/lonely/confused/distant/needy because of such-and-so. . . ." There was an opportunity to fill in the blank with a justification in that sort of analysis, or with contrition.

The flow of passengers had slowed. A woman with small children and too many bags was exiting. Still no Stu. *For God's sake!* Katherine checked the flight number for the tenth time. Then suddenly the hallway was empty.

She waited until crew began to emerge. She hailed a woman in a navy skirt and jacket with a gold pin in the shape of wings slightly askew on her chest.

"Are there any more passengers?"

"No. Are you waiting for a child?"

"No." Katherine smiled. A smile made people more likely to help, and the woman was going off duty. Complainers were avoided. Polite and persistent worked best. "I'm missing a husband."

"Is that good or bad?"

"A little of both."

The flight attended chuckled. "Let me get you to someone who can help."

Her charm worked like a charm. Navy Suit escorted her straight to the front of the line, where the male gate agent took over and ran Stu's name.

"He didn't board," the man said.

"In Seattle?"

"In Fairbanks."

"No. He would have called."

"I can't explain that," the agent said, decidedly less friendly than the attendant, despite the fact that he was on the clock. He returned Katherine's blank look, signaling that he'd done all he could and there were other customers waiting. He clearly wasn't happy that Navy Suit had brought her to the front of the line. Katherine's voice went up an octave, less polite, more persistent.

"Well, where is he? Can't you track him?"

"Ma'am, we can't find someone who didn't get on our plane. It's not like we lost a bag."

"No, you lost my husband."

"Maybe he lost himself."

CHAPTER 24

"Hello?" A deep voice rumbled in Stu's head.

I'm dead. And that's God. He's going to tell me that nonbelievers don't get in. Shit.

"Who the hell's in here?" the voice asked, its rich bass filling the tiny cabin.

The voice is in the cabin. Not in my head. Stu was, at first, relieved that it wasn't God, who likely wouldn't reference the devil's homeland in a simple occupation inquiry. Then an even more encouraging thought struck him. He tried to sit up. "Ivan?"

"No. But be cool. I ain't looking to cause trouble."

There was a figure in the doorway—actually, just a head peeking around the corner. Stu tried to talk again, but he could only make a sick croaking sound.

"Look, just put it down, fella," the head was saying.

At first Stu didn't know what the talking head was talking about. Then he realized that he was holding the rifle. It wasn't pointed at the head. It

was askew in his hands, as though he'd been experimenting with its ori-
entation. He let go, and the .30-06 thumped to the dirt floor.

"Are you okay, buddy?"

No. Stu looked up with pleading eyes. A full figure emerged behind
the head, and a man stood in the doorway.

"If you've got your heart set on finishing it, I'll leave you to it. But if
you need help, just say so."

Help. That is what I need! He could nod; he did nod. At least he thought
he did. But the man didn't acknowledge it; instead he darted in to grab
the rifle. Then he was gone.

Stu wondered if he'd ever been there at all. Perhaps it *was* God, and
he left when he saw who was on death's doorstep—Stuart Stark, the un-
believer. *That Pastor Richards ratted me out. I knew it!* Or else the man was
just a rifle thief. Either way, he was gone now. Stu drifted.

Then the man was back. It might have been a minute or an hour. Tough
to tell. He was pouring water into Stu's mouth.

"Swallow slowly. I don't need you chucking on me again. And here's
a cracker for starters. Damn, it stinks in here."

Stu didn't remember "chucking," and wasn't sure exactly what it was.
He allowed himself to be fed, first crackers and water, then a juice mix
and dried fruit of some sort—he couldn't really taste it. He was weak and
had to chew twenty or thirty times before he could choke it down with a
mouthful of liquid.

Then he slept.

It was difficult to tell how long he'd been out. It was night, so it had
to be somewhere between four and sixteen hours. *Or twenty-eight and forty.*
Could he have slept an entire day? Possibly. Not likely. The man crouched
beside a tidy fire, which blazed away in the pit, not too hot, not too weak.

"Ahh, finally it lives," the man said in the cheerless voice of someone
who'd been terribly inconvenienced.

Stu found he could sit up. More important, he could speak, though
his mouth felt warm and muddy, and his breath tasted like rancid milk.
"Are you the rescue pilot?" he asked, thinking it a fair and obvious question.

"Rescue? Ha!"

That doesn't sound good. The man offered no further explanation.

"Well, thank you for helping me," Stu said. "I was in pretty rough shape."

"Still are. But this talking and the sitting thing is a good sign for you. You want your gun back?"

"It's not mine. But yes."

"If you need to finish what you started, I can give it to you and leave you in peace."

"Finish what?"

"You were about to blow your own head off."

"No, I wasn't."

"Well I'm no psychologist or expert on human behavior, but yes, you were. You had the damned barrel in your mouth."

My mouth. The business end. Stu remembered it like a dream, rotating the firearm with a dull fascination until his lips were wrapped around it. "I was delirious. I didn't know what I was doing." He frowned. "What else did I do?"

The man laughed, although there was nothing funny as far as Stu could tell. "You promised me fifty grand for saving your life. From the look of your gear, you're loaded."

"Sorry, I can't honor that. The law is pretty clear about contracts made under duress. And Good Samaritan laws usually prohibit making financial demands during life-or-death situations."

"Huh. Sounds like you're recovering. You also sound like a damned lawyer."

Stu's annoyed silence confirmed it.

"Aww, crap, you're probably going to sue me for saving your ass. I've heard you guys do that."

"I won't sue you."

"Willing to put that in writing?" He gave Stu a solemn pause, then laughed. "Here, eat and drink some more."

Stu scooped a trail mix of nuts, granola, and chocolate bits from the stranger's substantial hand. He was *burly*, a word Stu found intimidating and usually reserved for men like Reggie Dugan. This man deserved the term too. He had rounded shoulders and stout legs. He even had a wide beard that squared off his face. He could have been a lumberjack or football lineman, perhaps a Harley-Davidson rider. *Or a young Santa handing out trail mix.* His clothes were well worn, but looked warm, and a bone-handled hatchet hung from his thick utility belt. The cap on his head was white fur and handmade, maybe homemade. His nose was crooked, and when he smiled, Stu saw that he was missing a tooth, which made him seem burlier than ever.

"I still feel like hell."

"You will for a few days. What have you been eating and drinking?"

"Edible grasses and water. Squirrel."

"Whatever grass it is, stop. It's obviously not as edible as you think. Squirrel's probably okay."

"I'm not planning more meals here."

"I don't know your plans."

"What's your name? I should thank you. . . ."

"Blake."

"Blake what?"

"Just Blake."

"Well, thanks, Blake. You saved my life."

"Good deed for the day."

"You're so cavalier about it. Do you go around finding dying people all the time?"

"No, I go around trapping, which is where I'm going tomorrow."

"You have a plane?"

"Nope. I got dropped in at Fur Lake. Hiked to here. I use this old place as a layover at the beginning of my rounds." He looked at the hole in the roof. "At least I did. What the hell are you doing here?"

"Floatplane. I was supposed to spend a week here. Should have been picked up days ago, but the pilot didn't come back. He might have crashed."

"Could be. That happens more up here than in the lower forty-eight, you know."

"I've heard," Stu grumbled. "But back to the issue. You can call out, right?"

"From here. No."

"Then can you take me to the nearest town?"

"You want me to pack you up in a fireman's carry and hike hundreds of miles back to civilization?"

Stu spluttered, frustrated. "Or leave me some supplies and send someone back. I have money. I can pay you for your trouble."

"You don't get it. There is no nearest town. You're way out here. There's nothing."

"And you're leaving tomorrow?"

"Right."

Stu felt his savior slipping away. It was eerily like reading the Butz appeal opinion and beginning to sense that he was losing the case prior to the punch line. The thought of enduring another day horrified him.

"You're going to leave me?"

"Unless you're going my way and I can't shake you."

"I'm overdue. Someone will come for me if I can make it another few days. I just got sick. I wasn't thinking straight. I ate a black slug."

"You need to boil those first."

"You'd really leave me? I don't have supplies."

"Well, why the hell not?" Blake grumbled. "And is that my fault?"

"There was a mix-up. I was supposed to have food and pots and pans waiting for me here at the cabin. Somebody must have cleaned it out. Please don't make me beg."

"God, no. Don't do that."

"Sorry. I'm not myself."

"And don't apologize. If you screwed up, own up to it, but don't squirm around. Be a goddamned man." Blake harrumphed and rummaged through his rather large backpack. "I'll give you what I got, but beyond trail mix and dried apples, I mostly trap and hunt. So there ain't much. My base cabin's got the basics, but that's a week's hike up the trapline from here."

Stu perked up. *A real cabin. With real food.* "I'll go with you," he said suddenly.

"You'll what?"

"I'll hike with you to the other cabin."

"You couldn't hike to the latrine right now."

"You said you weren't leaving until tomorrow."

"And you said people was coming for you."

"I don't know that for sure."

Blake looked Stu up and down. "You can't keep up in the shape you're in."

"I'll try."

"You'll have to try harder than you have been."

"I will."

The sigh that Blake emitted testified to his skepticism. "I believe a man should be able to do what he wants, so I won't stop you. But I won't stop *for* you either. You've got two days to get your strength up. You'll need it. Then I'm going."

"Great. I can't thank you enough." Stu didn't relish the idea of hiking in his condition, but Blake had done wonders in just one day. With two more, he'd be himself again. *Whether that's good enough remains to be seen.*

"Don't thank me yet. I ain't that social. We travel together and you'll probably end up hating my guts."

"How soon can I make contact with the outside world? I have important business at home that demands my attention. And my wife is probably going crazy."

"When the trappin' is done."

Stu groaned, but he didn't want to complain when Blake was willing to save his life. "Okay. How long is that? Two or three weeks?"

"Six months."

CHAPTER 25

It took two days to declare Stu officially missing, and another two to get a plane out searching for him. At least they knew where to look. Katherine turned the logistics over to Clay, who immediately flew to Fairbanks to try to help. But nothing helped. Clay went to Dugan's cabin personally in a wilderness search-and-rescue plane with a state trooper, but they found it as empty as the pilot from the tour company had reported it to be. The fireplace and bed appeared used. The trooper took pictures and sent them to Katherine. It was large and modern place with a propane stove and animal heads on the wall, as Stu had guessed, but there was not much else to see. In fact, the absence of evidence was the most striking thing about the place.

The broader search would take longer. Stu was well equipped and, according to the trooper, could be anywhere within a seven-day hike. But Katherine knew they wouldn't find her meticulous husband out hiking around. He would have been at the rendezvous point at exactly the appointed time with his bags lined up, checking the clock on his phone every few minutes.

Unless something happened.

Clay called from Fairbanks and offered to stay for the aerial search, but Katherine told him he might as well come home and leave it to the professionals. He would just be in the way, she said. Besides, she needed him in town. She could feel her world shifting. It was disorienting, and when she hung up the phone, she felt like she'd just stood up after drinking too much, or had just stepped off a merry-go-round.

Katherine arrived to pick up Clay at Logan, standing in exactly the spot she had waited for Stu. It gave her a queasy feeling, but this time the man she was waiting for appeared. She'd picked out black pants and a white blouse for herself, flattering but conservative. Comfortable shoes. It was not the time to be alluring, but she still looked good. Clay strode through security and embraced her, giving her a long, comforting hug.

"You're going to be okay," he said, his voice smooth and calm. "No matter what's happened. I promise. But you need to be ready to adjust your life. Just in case. Okay?"

"He shouldn't have gone." When she started shaking, he held her tighter.

"I know. I blame myself. I shouldn't have let him go alone, but he insisted. If I'd been there, I could have made sure . . ."

"You might be lost too."

"I doubt that." He scoffed at the idea. A bit callous but honest, too. Stu was lost, Clay wasn't.

Clay released her with a reassuring pat on the hip and turned her toward the exit. "We need to carry on," he said as he walked her out. "The search-and-rescue pros are on it, and sitting around waiting for news is the worst thing we could do. It doesn't do Stu any good and it won't do you any good. They'll call as soon as they know something."

It made sense, but she had trouble thinking of anything else. "What do you want me to do in the meantime?"

"Resist the urge to run tell everyone. That's the first thing. The cycle of worry will just keep repeating itself if you tell the story over and over. Second, go work out. Hard. And third, find something to keep you busy."

"I could do some shooting."

"Maybe. As long as you stay away from moody or artsy. Take some saleable pictures. Make it like work."

"It *is* work."

"Perfect. Then throw yourself into it. That'll be good for you no matter what happens."

Katherine took a deep breath. "What if he doesn't come back?"

"If it comes to that, we'll deal with it. 'Adjustable,' remember? Open to change."

"Got it."

"Good."

They climbed into Katherine's Corolla in short-term parking. Clay made small talk, and they tried to avoid talking about Stu. He commented that she needed a new car, and she agreed. Then they embarked on a debate about which make and model would be best, which was both a relief and sort of fun after the tension of the last few days. They settled on an Audi. Classy and practical. Katherine wondered if there was a model with a refrigerated center console, but Clay didn't want her to get something cooler than his BMW. Besides, he said, he could hook her up with a new client who had recently acquired a nice one for cheap.

"Where did you meet *this* guy?"

Clay laughed. "Larry the bondsman? He used to sit in the back of the courtroom while we asked for bail on new arrestees. The higher the bail I got on them, the more money he made when they had to go to him for a bond. Now he's a client. He takes cars as collateral. When people don't pay up, he gets them."

"Is that legitimate?"

"Yeah, and talk about your legal issues. More business for our cheap associates, eh?" He winked at her.

Katherine chuckled. Clay made it sound so easy to work the system and come out ahead. Stu, on the other hand, saw easy opportunities as illegal and immoral, or made them more complicated than they needed to be. Clay's don't-sweat-the-small-stuff approach was so refreshing that she already felt better. But she noticed that as soon as Clay stopped talking, thoughts of Stu descended upon her again like a heavy weight. He was right; she needed to keep her mind off her husband.

Clay dropped her at home but didn't come inside, and for that Katherine was both disappointed and grateful. She wanted company but appreciated the simplicity of the path forward he gave her. She called no one, went for a run, and spent as little time as possible in the house before heading to the photography studio.

The owner of the studio was Brad Bear, a tall blond man and self-made shooter with a penchant for skinny jeans. Very gay. He greeted her with a camera in one hand and a hug.

"Katherine, what a surprise. Welcome back."

She didn't mention Stu. "I'd like to log some hours. I can schedule some sittings, but if you have any overflow I'd be grateful."

"Just family portraits and early Christmas card shots."

"Perfect."

"Really?" He raised an eyebrow. "A bit pedestrian for you, especially considering . . ." He gave her a sly grin.

"What? Considering what?"

"Some recent sales."

"What do you mean?"

"Your last showing: the whaling series."

"I sold one print."

"The day of the showing, yes. But I've had a little run on your work since then."

"Why didn't you tell me?"

"Happened last week. I reconcile at the end of the month, and I was just going to call you."

"Which ones sold?"

Brad's sly grin became a full-on smile.

Katherine pouted. "Come on, tell me."

He gave a little bark of joy. "All of them!"

"What? There were nineteen left. That's crazy. I didn't authorize a re-mainders sale. Doesn't that kick in after a year?"

"I gave the standard discount for a full-series purchase, but otherwise it was a full-price sale."

"Who?"

"Archie Brooks."

"I don't know him. Did he ask to meet me?"

"No. And I didn't know him either. But his check cleared just fine."

"Did he say anything?"

"He didn't say much, but I assume he sparked to your focus on the decline and decay of the industry. Not everyone wants to see history propped up like a grinning skeleton."

"Exactly. I was just telling my friend Clay that recently."

"That's Stu's partner? The handsome one with the dark hair?"

"Right."

"Is he completely straight?"

"Oh yeah."

"You sound pretty certain."

"Certain as I can be."

"How is Stu?"

Katherine stiffened. "I'm waiting for him to come back from Alaska." She turned away in case she began to cry. She pretended to examine a backdrop, but the tears didn't come.

"Alaska?"

"He's trying to find himself."

"Well, that's a big place to look. Your total for the series after commis-sion is just under eight thousand dollars. Do you still want to do Christmas cards?"

Katherine drove home singing "Sweet, Fleet, and Upbeat" by Mod-ern Moll at the top of her lungs. She'd never sold an entire series. But the dying whale industry theme had been a fabulous idea, if she did say so herself. It touched on the theme of a failing economy, the environmental and wildlife movements, and even the fading of traditional New England culture. A full-series sale was also the sort of thing that could jump-start one's reputation, depending upon who the buyer was. He wasn't a reviewer—she knew that—but he might be a socialite or collector who would display her work. She made a mental note to research Archie Brooks. She didn't like to pester shy buyers, but it was good to know where one's work went, and a thank-you-for-your-patronage note wasn't out of order.

The whole thing was exciting and professionally satisfying in a way that regular money from commercial sittings could never be. But when she pulled into the driveway, Stu's car was there waiting for her, empty and neglected. She hit the steering wheel in frustration; she'd only been able to enjoy herself for an hour.

CHAPTER 26

The first day on the trail was the hardest. Stu gritted his teeth against the pain in his ankle and the lingering restlessness of his bowels. And, true to his word, Blake did not slow for him. Stu wasn't a hiker, and so he had no sense of time. Blake apparently refused to wear a watch. They climbed up over the ridge, out of the small mountain bowl where he'd nearly ended his life, and Stu was distressed to see another, larger mountain ahead.

Shit.

The descent was brief, and the footing treacherous—crumbled rock with no path. And he had to lift his feet every step to avoid tripping over low-growing plants. Then they were ascending again.

"How far will we go today?" Stu asked when they finally stopped to rest and munch trail mix. The sun was not at its apex, but it felt like hours had passed.

"Ten miles. Every day."

"How far have we come so far?"

"Maybe two."

The dread of starting up again ruined any enjoyment he might have gotten from their break, and then he was walking again. The landscape hardly changed, and no matter how far it seemed they'd hiked, it felt like they hadn't gone anywhere. Whenever he looked back, he could still see where they'd been for the previous hour. *I need to stop looking back,* he decided.

They veered north and, thankfully, crossed over the shoulder of the mountain instead of heading up toward the peak. The sun was descending by the time they reached a height from which they could see the valley on the far side.

"Are we stopping for the night?"

"Not here, unless we're idiots," Blake said. "The farther down we can get, the more likely we'll be below the snow line, if it comes. Another mile or two."

"I'm not sure I've got another mile or two in me."

"It's downhill," Blake said as though that settled the matter. And he was off again.

They pitched camp near the base of the mountain at the edge of an open plain, which stretched for miles in all directions and was crisscrossed with rivers and stands of trees. Blake had a tent. He also had a hatchet should they need to build a lean-to. He didn't seem concerned about cover, so Stu tried not to be either. He was just glad he had a pair of Extremes— only a small blister so far. Half of Stu's gear had been left behind in the duffel bag at the broken cabin, and he still struggled under the weight of his backpack. Blake had gone through the duffel quickly, muttering as he tossed aside hundreds of dollars' worth of Stu's clothing and equipment. He let Stu keep half of the clothes—mostly outerwear—the sleeping bag, the gun, and the medical kit, which he seemed to like very much. Stu had argued to keep *Edwin's,* despite its weight. He wasn't sure why; perhaps because he'd need it if Blake abandoned him, which seemed like a very real possibility.

"You're starting the fire," Blake said as he swept a clear area of ground free of debris for his tent.

"Why me?"

"Because that's going to be your job from now on. I figure you ain't a great hunter. You sure as hell aren't getting water for me after you picked a puddle to drink from that animals used as a toilet. By the way, if one animal takes a dump somewhere it's likely other animals sniffed its scat and pissed there too. And unless I'm mistaken, you're not much of one for putting up a shelter. Any argument, counselor?"

"Fires. Fair enough."

Blake pointed to a tree and unstrapped his homemade hatchet. The simple tool was a rough chunk of steel with a blade that had been sharpened so many times that it looked like a caveman had chipped it from obsidian. The bone handle—clearly not the first—was a thick black-and-white antler carved into a gentle forward curve. It might have been a piece of art in a souvenir shop at the Fairbanks airport, but it was a serious tool out here in the interior.

"Now strip off that bark and get some of the stuff right under it for tinder."

Stu took the hatchet and sized up the tree. The hatchet was well balanced and felt good in his hand. The perfect woodland tool. The symbol of mankind's superiority to animals. It made him feel armed, powerful, ready to take on . . .

Well, at least a tree, Stu thought.

"According to *Edwin's*, that sub-layer is the cambium," he said importantly.

"According to me, it's the stuff right under the bark. Less talk, more chop. Strip it and rip it."

Stu cocked the hatchet over his head and gave the tree a firm whack. The wedge-shaped head glanced from the bark, and the flat of the blade smacked his other wrist.

"Oww!"

Blake shook his head. "You don't hit a round tree straight-on. Can't have you choppin' your arm off."

Blake hauled himself up to demonstrate a proper chop.

"Swing at it from the side—a downward angle, then an upward angle. Two whacks is all a guy should need."

He flipped the hatchet back to Stu, who dodged instead of trying to catch the handle. When he picked it up, he swung tentatively. It took him eight chops.

Edwin's had taught Stu to make a little nest with the tinder—that much he'd absorbed. But it didn't catch readily with the flint and steel. Finally Blake held out a small cardboard box full of cigar-shaped tubes in white plastic wrappers.

Stu frowned up at the burly man and didn't take one. "Is this a joke?"

"Nope. You're struggling. I'll let you use one o' these to start your fire this one time."

"Pardon my skepticism, but with all of the bullshit manhood musk you exude, why the hell would you be shoving a box of tampons at me unless it was a bad joke?"

Blake nodded, unoffended, as though it was a perfectly reasonable question. "Because they're good for about a half dozen things that might save your miserable life."

He tore one open, fluffed up the cotton, and tucked it into Stu's cambium nest. He motioned for Stu to strike the flint and steel again. This time when Stu produced a single spark the entire nest went up as though doused with lighter fluid. The small fire that appeared from nowhere seemed a miracle to Stu, much as it must have to cave dwellers of old. Logically, it shouldn't have amazed him, but to make fire with his own hands instead of a match or some ridiculous consumer backyard barbeque version of a blowtorch felt magical.

"I did it!" he exclaimed like a Cub Scout on his first camping trip.

"There you go. Nothing girlish about that. In a pinch that cotton puff is no less manly than that rifle you're toting."

"You're saying my gun is like a big tampon?"

"Yep. It's a tool. It's whatever you need it to be. That Browning could be binoculars, a crutch, a snow shovel, even a hammer—I once had to club a wounded wolverine to death with my piece after it latched on to my leg."

"Sounds awfully violent."

"Naw. Put it out of its misery and kept me from shooting myself in the process. Those bastards are treacherous, like a small bear with something to prove."

Blake retrieved the box of tampons from Stu and held it up reverently. "You might want to start calling these babies manpons. I strained your coffee through one this morning."

Stu grimaced, but Blake kept chattering, happily extolling the virtues of the feminine hygiene product as a wilderness survival implement.

"The packaging is waterproof. And that's before you even get to how good they are for dressing a wound. They're made to absorb blood, you know."

"You don't say."

"And they're hypoallergenic. . . ."

After a dinner of dried soup reconstituted in clean water, they shared Blake's tent for the night. Stu was so tired he didn't even have the energy to feel awkward about it. Blake hung their food high in a tree away from camp so that no animals would come sniffing around while they slept, but the .30-06 slept beside them just in case, and Blake had a pistol. Before he drifted off, Stu thought he heard Blake say something about not mistaking him for a bear in the middle of the night if he got up to pee, but it might have been a dream.

Morning came early, and they were up and walking after a quick tampon-filtered cup of coffee and powdered eggs. The second day was a wash; Stu was sore all over from the prior day's hike, but he no longer felt lingering nausea, and his ankle was getting steadily better. The terrain was easier. They'd descended into the vast field, apparently heading across to another mountain. A few low hills were all that stood in their way, but the ground was alternately thin grass and boot-sucking mud, and the numerous small streams presented frequent crossing decisions. Wet feet were inevitable, and so they plunged in and waded the icy waters.

Equally foreseeable was the appearance of flying parasites as soon as

they began crossing a lowland marsh. Stu had heard about Alaskan mos-
quitoes, but another variety of insect was worse: they were smaller with a
more painful bite. Blake said they were called no-see-ums, but Stu didn't
believe him.

Blake chuckled. "Believe what you want, but this is nothing. You should
be here in spring when there are clouds of the little fuckers. They'll disappear as soon as the snow comes down or we have a hard freeze."

Blake unfolded a wide-brimmed hat with netting, reminiscent of a
beekeeper's hood, and began to put it on. Stu looked on longingly as he
swatted bugs, both real and imagined. Blake hesitated, then handed it over.

"Eh, they don't like the taste of me anyway."

"Thank you."

"Just keep walking."

And so they did, slogging through fall muck that had not yet frozen
solid. They made better time in the field, despite the soft ground, and it
was midday before they stopped at a river twenty yards wide. Blake turned
to head upstream.

"Are we there yet?" Stu joked.

"We need to keep moving. I lost a day waiting for you to stop puk-
ing."

"We're trying to go to that side, right?" Stu pointed directly across the
river.

"Yep, but there's bound to be a better crossing upstream."

"How far?"

"I dunno. A mile or two."

Stu groaned. "We're already soaked, why don't we just cross here?
Couldn't be higher than our waists. We could use the time it would take
to walk the extra mile or two to rest. Your determination to make this a
death march is garnering diminishing returns with regard to my pace."

Blake furrowed his brow. "I'm not sure exactly what you just said, but
why don't you go ahead and wade on out there. I'll watch and see how
you do."

"Why do I sense disdain and ridicule?"

"Why do you have to talk like goddamned C-3PO?"

"I don't need a lecture."

"That's just good ol' garden variety sarcasm."

"Fine. I'll head over to the other side and enjoy a much-needed respite while you go the long way around."

"Fine."

"Good." Stu started out into the river. After a few steps, he teetered on the slippery rocks.

"I'm not fishing you out," Blake advised.

"Didn't ask you to."

The water was up to his knees now. Stu looked back. Blake was pacing on the shore. Finally the big man couldn't contain himself any longer.

"Stop!"

"What?"

"Just fucking stop, okay?"

"I'm up to my thighs, and it's no problem."

"Sure. The current will run around and through your legs until it gets up to your crotch, but once it gets up into your torso, it becomes a wall of force you can't fight. Next time your foot wobbles on a rock, it will knock you down so fast your head will swim, and the rest of you too."

"Good for a laugh then. But I know how to swim."

"No. Not funny. It don't matter that these aren't rapids. If you go down and get swept up against a snag, the weight of the water will pin you and you're done."

Stu scanned the river. Logs and other woody debris dotted the downstream stretch like an obstacle course. The water did indeed feel powerful pushing on his thighs. It pressed so hard against him that it rocked him back and forth, and he wasn't even halfway yet. He watched the current pull a yellowed leaf along and then suddenly suck it down beneath a massive tangle of branches.

Am I really as fragile as a leaf floating in a small river?

"Besides," Blake called from shore, "if you get dunked and soak your pack, I'll have to spot you my only spare set of clothes, and I wore them all last week without washing them."

"All right!" Stu edged out of the middle of the river. "I'm coming back."

"Good. Crotch or lower before we cross. Let's move on. No need to test yourself here."

Stu splashed out of the water and fell in step. "What do you mean by 'test'?"

"Some men come to Alaska to get away. Some men come here to test themselves. Isn't that what you were doing? Extreme executive camping?"

"The cabin was supposed to be furnished. It shouldn't have been quite so extreme."

"Pussy camping. Same thing, only watered down."

"It was just supposed to be week in the woods to relax."

"If you wanted a week in the woods and relaxation, you would have gone to New Hampshire or Vermont, somewhere closer to home."

"What about you? You don't exactly have an Alaskan accent."

"Oregon."

"Hey, I went to school there."

"Whoop-de-fucking-doo."

"So why are you here?"

Blake kept walking and didn't answer, but Stu was feeling his oats. "Why—"

"Not your fucking business."

"No need to get agitated."

"I ain't agitated. It's just not your fucking business."

"I assume you fall in the 'getting away' category, then."

"Not. Your. Fucking. Business."

"I'll take that as a yes."

"Fuck you."

"You know, your swearing doesn't intimidate me. The dirtbags I used to send to prison swore all the time. Anyone can do it. Fuck. Fucky-fuck-fuck. Fuckity-shit-bastard-twat."

"Nobody says *twat* anymore."

"I say *twat*."

"No, you don't. You're just saying it to pretend you cuss like a regular Joe, which you don't because you aren't."

"How do you know I don't?"

"It doesn't sound right coming out of your mouth. And, by the way, if you do it over and over, it just becomes white noise anyway."

Stu smiled. "Exactly."

Blake glared at him as they walked. "I liked you better when you were pukin' too much to talk."

That night Blake left camp to lay a trap while Stu started the fire. He said it was time they ate a little meat, and Stu heartily agreed. When they woke up, they'd have something if they were lucky. Stu gathered some dry grasses and shredded them to make a tinder nest. Once he had it going, he stacked kindling in a tepee shape over it. Two bigger logs went on after orange flames were dancing over the sticks and red coals had spread along their length. He made certain there was a wide circle of bare dirt around the shallow pit he'd dug, and then he went to look for Blake.

His de facto friend was nearby, standing motionless. He seemed to be closely examining a tree.

Stu approached and whispered to him. "Are you looking for animal signs?"

"Nope. Taking a leak." Blake zipped up and turned.

"Oh. Where's the trap?"

Blake shook his head. "You're standing on it."

"Ah! Sorry."

"Forget it. I'll reset the damn thing. Wait. No, you do it. Maybe you'll learn something. Grab that snare."

"It's just a wire." Stu picked up a small circle of copper wire he'd stomped into the dirt.

"A wire *snare*. A five-inch loop of copper on a slide twist-tied to this branch. Now, hang it three inches off the ground."

"Where's the bait?"

"No bait."

"You're screwing with me."

"I screw you not."

"Then how do we get a rabbit to hop into it?"

"We don't. It's hard to change Fluffy's habits, but it's easy to figure out what they are. This is where she likes to run. So we set the trap where the rabbit lives, and she just does what she does every day, and *bam!* We got'er. That's why placement is so important, and why you should watch where the hell you step. Do you see the narrowest point in the bunny trail?"

"What trail?"

Blake bent and pointed. "Rabbit pellets there. Faint paw print there. Grass bent here. Narrow opening. Path of least resistance through the shrubs. That's a trail."

"And you just hang it in the way?"

"Yep."

"They don't sniff it?"

"I don't know. But if they do, they must not care how it smells, because they still walk right through it."

"Does it always hold?" Stu recalled his possible fish that might have gotten away. How hungry he'd been. How disappointed.

"A startled animal will flee first. When it feels the wire around its head, it will run forward. That snugs this baby right up, and wire doesn't loosen with slack." Blake glanced at the sky. "It's getting toward late evening. That's when the hoppers show. You wanna stake it out and maybe see your supper get caught?"

Stu felt a curious excitement, like a grade-school boy. "Okay. I've got a few minutes."

Blake snickered, and they set themselves up in a comfortable spot uphill and downwind. Then they sat.

Stu watched Blake, who watched the trap. The big man had, undoubtedly, watched hundreds of traps, and seen as many animals, yet his concentration was complete. He was neither eager nor bored; it was more like meditation, a perfect balance between the two that held him in a state of suspended animation.

After a few minutes Stu fidgeted. "How long?"

"Maybe an hour. More if you talk."

Stu nodded. He hadn't experienced an hour of silence for as long as he could remember. Even when researching in the office, there was traffic noise from outside, or Clay was chattering into the phone. When he'd been at the cabin, he'd been banging or stomping or vomiting most of the time. He remembered how out of place his voice had sounded after just a few minutes. Even while fishing, he'd paced and kicked dirt and thrown pebbles. Now he tried just sitting silently.

It was hard at first. Every instinct told him to impose his existence upon the world around him. *I'm here! I exist. I matter. Every boy gets a turn to speak. It's rude not to say something.* But Blake ignored him, the woods went on without him, and he finally realized that he did not matter. In the silence it was suddenly clear. The world didn't care. Blake was good at it, motionless, a tree. He didn't seem to want to exist or matter or care.

And so, for the first time in his life, Stuart Stark sat silently with another human being for an entire hour, so quiet that he could hear his own heartbeat and the breaths of his companion.

As his own silence deepened, the forest sounds grew louder. After twenty minutes he could track the whisper of the rising breeze through the treetops as it came down from the mountain. A water droplet plunked onto the soft loam twenty yards away to his right, and he heard it hit. The biggest of the trees spoke in low groans and occasional light snaps as they grew and bent under their own weight like old men with aging spines. And when the rabbit approached, Stu heard it coming.

Aside from a slightly deeper breath, Blake didn't acknowledge the animal when it came into view. Nor did Stu, and he was proud of himself for it. Scaring the hopper away would have been a rookie move. The rabbit picked its way up the trail casually, not wary like in a nature movie, not sniffing the air for danger. It was just doing what it did every day, like Blake said. The rabbit poked its head through the snare, and when it felt the wire, it charged ahead, tightening the noose around its own neck. Stu watched it struggle, caught in the trap.

Blake finally moved. He tilted his head slightly and raised one eyebrow. "Rabbit, Stu."

Stu tried not to seem eager, but he was the first one down to the snare. He stood over the rabbit, trying to appear nonchalant. "What now?"

"It's scared. Kill it."

Stu glanced back at the barrel of the .30-06 hanging over his shoulder.

Blake shook his head. "Grasp it behind the neck and by the hind legs. A quick reverse yank."

Stu took hold of the rabbit, but dropped it when it squirmed. He didn't look up—he knew Blake would be glaring. Instead he grabbed it again firmly and wrenched the neck backward. There was a light crack, and the bunny went limp. When Stu was certain it was dead, he looked up.

Blake didn't congratulate him. Instead he handed Stu his hunting knife. "You caught it, you clean it."

The blade was bright and well honed, but the handle was a worn hunk of wood, obviously a heavily used homemade replacement for the original.

Stu hesitated. "Since this is our dinner, wouldn't it be best if you did it? I don't want to screw up the meat."

"You won't."

"Do you have gloves?"

"I don't want to get my leathers all bloody."

"But my hands—"

"You can *wash* your hands." Blake pointed to a nearby stream.

The incision was made laterally around the midsection, the impossibly sharp knife sliding through fur and flesh without any sawing back and forth. Then, at Blake's insistence, Stu took hold of either side of the parted skin and pulled forward and back. The forward fur came loose more easily than Stu could have imagined, and he peeled it away from the muscle and meat with one smooth motion. It felt eerily like pulling a small dress up over its head. The haunches were tougher, but the same principle applied, and soon he had a reasonable facsimile of a meat counter display with an apron of fur hanging from each end. He severed the feet and head along with the fur using the hatchet, and when it looked more like a skinny chicken ready for roasting than a murdered mammal he felt much more comfortable.

Gutting the thing was the worst. Stu had to pull out its steaming organs, entrails, and even waste pellets with his bare hands. As the warmth of the rabbit's life poured across his palms and fingers, he had to fight the urge to gag.

Pussy move. Don't do it. Stu discovered that rinsing the carcass in the stream while he removed the guts made the process less messy. They floated away as he dug them out. Although he still had the stomach-wrenching task of ripping them free. Blake was watching him, as if waiting to see if he would chuck. But Stu kept the rising bile under control. He felt good about it; they had a week on the trail ahead of them, and he was already gutting prey while keeping his lunch down.

"Did you know you can eat the eyeballs for water?" Blake said.

And up it came.

They pressed on day after day at a pace Stu thought unreasonable for a recently ill attorney who could have stood to lose a few. And he wondered if Blake would have stopped at all had they not spotted something even Stu knew was very strange.

"What is that?" Stu said.

"New one on me," Blake grunted.

Stu squinted to see from their perch atop one of the field's small hills. Below, two narrow rivers slammed together at a right angle and, fifty yards downstream, the water poured over a wide four-foot drop. On the bank just below their merger lay a one-man mini-tractor of some sort, tilted onto its side like a neglected child's toy. It had two tracks, but no blade or bucket, and the cab was completely enclosed in an awkward square of Plexiglas.

"River restoration project?" Stu guessed.

"Don't need no restoration way out here. Everything's as natural as it gets."

"Someone building a cabin?"

"By a river with a meandering bed. Doubt it."

"What's a meandering bed?"

"The course of the river changes year to year, depending on runoff. Next year this river might be clear on the other side of the field."

"Well, whoever it is, it's someone who might be able to call home. Anyone who can get a tractor out here probably has communication with the outside world. Let's get down there."

"Fools rush in."

"We don't have to rush. We can walk."

"I'm still trying to figure out what it is."

"And the solution, it occurs to me, would be to go down there and see."

"It's not normal for me to run into someone way out here. Let alone twice. A lot of people come north so they *don't* have to run into other people."

"You thinking pot growers?"

"Don't know what I'm thinking, but when I think it, you'll be the first person I tell."

Stu held up the .30-06 to get a closer look, then remembered he was wearing a mesh hat. He pulled the netting up, put his eye to the scope, and scanned the riverbank.

Blake snorted. "Hope you're not gonna shoot, because if you hold a gun loose against your shoulder like that, the kick will leave you a bruise to remember."

"I'm just looking," Stu said. "But thanks."

"Here, let me have a gander."

Blake took the gun. Stu noticed that the big man snugged it up tight against his shoulder, and he felt a little stupid.

"What do you see?"

"A Kubota KC 250," he said without hesitation.

"Wow. How did you know that?"

"It's painted on the side." He kept his eye in the scope. "The tracks are filled in with dried mud, so it's been sittin' there a few days."

"What do you think?"

"Nice piece of equipment. Probably cost as much as a new car. Nobody would leave it out here tipped over in the mud beside an unpredictable river with winter coming. And this ain't the right place for growing weed, unless they're building a greenhouse. And there ain't been any fill or grade work done along this stretch of water that I can see."

Blake rose and handed the gun back to Stu. "Keep that handy, but point it up or down so you don't shoot me."

He strode down the hill, leaving Stu to catch up. They approached the scene cautiously. Stu noticed dark fluid leaking from the underside of the tractor. Something brightly colored littered the ground on the far side.

"This place feels bad," Blake said as they drew near.

"What do you mean?"

"Just my nose telling me something's wrong. People button up their camps and projects when fall comes. This is . . . unbuttoned."

They swung around in front of the Kubota. The scattered colors littering the ground were cloth.

"What are those, rags?" Stu asked.

"Look, the door is broken."

The Plexiglas panel that served as the entry to the cab hung askew on its hinges. The gun wouldn't be necessary, Stu thought; the cab was empty. Blake leaned inside, then he backed out, grim-faced.

"What?"

Blake jerked his thumb at the cab and stepped away. "Better see for yourself."

Stu inched forward and peeked inside. More dark fluid was smeared across the floor of the cab, though it had dried after a couple of days' exposure to the air. And a video camera was mounted on the dash. The camera was switched on but dead, its battery clearly drained. Stu wasn't sure what he was seeing, but the bad feeling Blake sensed was beginning to creep up on him, too. From the evidence at hand, it was clear the machine had been abandoned suddenly. But it wasn't until he spotted the red handprint on the seat that his heart leaped into his throat.

"Oh God . . ."

He yanked his head out and stumbled backward. Blake caught him. Stu shook him off but continued to stare at the ruined Kubota. As he did, other clues came into focus. There were long scratches on the Plexiglas door he hadn't noticed before. The devastation wrought upon the hardware store hinges was mighty; they were twisted almost beyond recognition, with one galvanized metal bolt torn completely from its guides.

"Th-there was a man inside," Stu stammered.

"There *was* . . ." Blake picked up a piece of cloth that Stu now saw was a scrap of clothing, its material not much different from that of the Great Beyond jacket he wore himself. Blake circled the Kubota, shaking his head, and finally pointed to a huge but vague imprint in a drier patch of earth. "Grizzly."

"A bear?"

"Maybe more than one."

Stu shuddered. "It broke through the safety cage?"

"It broke through a homemade door on a box full of stupid. Probably no tougher than you or me cracking open a walnut to get at the meat. My question is: Where the hell was his gun?"

Stu tentatively pushed the door wider and risked another look in the cab. There was no rifle or pistol. It was possible the driver had shot the bear and fled, but it was unlikely that it was the bear's blood inside the Kubota.

"What the hell was he doing?"

Blake joined Stu at the door and pointed. "I think the answers to all our questions might be right there." He pointed at the dash cam.

A pouch inside the cab contained spare batteries. Blake popped out the dead one and snapped a fresh one into the camera. Stu paced, watching the field, the .30-06 held at his hip. Blake stopped and turned to calmly push the barrel down toward the ground, then he hit play.

The screen was small, and the audio was tinny. They had to crowd together to watch as it played raw footage. The camera panned left and right across the field, then up and down the Y-shaped river. Stu winced as the male voice began to narrate. The camera swung to show a healthy-looking middle-aged man with a big smile. *Middle-aged*, Stu thought. *My age.* The man proudly described the modifications he'd made to his Kubota, "just as a precaution." He explained that the Plexiglas was a half-inch thick, and the roll bars were steel. The doomed hinges went unmentioned.

"Obviously not a handyman," Blake grunted. "Probably in school his whole life."

As if on cue, the narrator introduced himself as a researcher with a doctorate in environmental studies. His first name was Thomas, his last something Irish that Stu didn't want to remember. The shallow falls were an area frequented by bears, he said. The excitement in his voice when the first bear appeared was heartbreaking.

"They're here!" he cried happily. "Aren't they magnificent creatures?"

But food was thin this year, he explained. Not a lot to satisfy hungry bears fattening themselves up for hibernation. He babbled on about fat percentages in their diet, and when the big female came sniffing toward the Kubota, he greeted her, describing her investigative behavior with glee and remarking on how fantastic the footage would be. "What a stroke of luck!"

His concern began to show when she put her paws on the glass and snuffled his scent at the air hole. But it was the dramatized concern of a reality TV actor. He wasn't really scared. Not yet. Then she started pushing, and the Kubota began to rock. The shaking of the camera testified to the violence with which she was soon rattling the vehicle, but Thomas's voice didn't crack until she found the seam in the door and slid her heavy claws into it. "She's testing the door," the Irishman said. Those were his last narrative words before Stu heard the hinges squeal and snap. The remainder of the sounds Thomas made were involuntary expressions of surprise and terror. And, finally, screams.

By the time Blake switched it off, Stu found that he was sweating.

"Are we in danger here?"

"If you live among predators for long, they will eventually eat you. But even you respected nature enough to bring a gun. We'll be all right. But we should move along; at least one bear in the area has a taste for human flesh now."

"Shouldn't we find the body?"

"Naw. They ate him. Might have buried the leftovers around here, but I don't wanna arm-wrestle them for 'em."

"What about the video?"

"Might be worth something. Them reality TV shows aren't above broadcasting some poor sap's demise. They'd probably put this on one of those nature programs—*America's Most Ferocious* or some such."

Stu frowned, then cocked the camera to his ear and flung it into the river. "No, they won't."

Blake nodded respectfully.

They found Thomas's camp. To Stu's disappointment, there was no communications equipment. Blake salvaged the food, which Stu found ghoulish, but he left the money in a fat wallet they found inside the tent, along with Thomas's identification and other minor valuables. Stu wondered aloud if someone might be coming to get the Irishman; the Kubota was obviously dropped in by helicopter. Blake told him he could stay if he wanted.

"You can stay in that flimsy, expensive-looking tent right there by the feeding grounds."

They left soon after that and hiked in silence for a time. Blake still seemed intent on putting in his ten miles, despite the interruption. It was Stu who finally spoke. "Damned tragedy," he whispered reverently, as though something needed to be said.

"No one forced him to come here," Blake mumbled.

"He came to study them."

"Bears are dangerous animals. One of the few things on the planet that thinks of us as food. You plop yourself down in the middle of 'em, you're not studying; you're testing yourself. Man against fucking nature."

CHAPTER 27

It had taken two days to declare Stu missing. It took two weeks to declare the search over. And it had been two more trying months for Katherine since then. Clay explained that it could take up to seven years to declare a missing spouse legally dead, but she wasn't required to sit around waiting to settle his affairs.

"In fact, you shouldn't. It's unhealthy. Besides, you don't have seven years. You'll be in your mid-forties if you wait it out, and that's a bit old to start over."

The odds Stu was alive were almost zero. She had come to grips with that reality. The Yukon Tours pilot had even volunteered to make another trip out after the official search ended. He'd come back with nothing, and his final flight served as the last nail in hope's coffin for her.

Clay tried to take responsibility for Stu's disappearance—the trip had been his idea—and it was tempting to place blame. But Katherine pardoned him. Clay would have gone along too if they hadn't lured Dugan into a rushed meeting, and she could as easily blame herself for that. Besides, if she alienated Clay, she'd have to put her life back together entirely alone.

Katherine wandered through the house, packing up photos and emptying Stu's closets. As the spaces opened up, the rooms looked different, and, without evidence of a man in the house, she wasn't sure who she was. For two months she'd been a ghost, just drifting aimlessly, sleeping, eating, exercising, sleeping again. But that needed to end. She needed direction and purpose, an identity. Before, she'd always been Stu Stark's wife. Now she would be . . .

Whoever I want to be.

Clay's winning streak had continued during her mourning period, and she was eager to get back to the life he'd outlined for her. She craved his direct approach. It worked. He'd told her to mourn for a while—it was necessary and healthy. No big spending. No rebound man for comfort. And it had been the sort of lonely hell losing a spouse was bound to be. Cards, flowers, and backward-looking sympathizers only mired her in the loss, reminding her of it every day instead of helping her get past it.

Hello, so sorry for your tragedy; that must suck.

Clay had been supportive, calling at intervals to check in. He gave her time to grieve, but he also gave her permission to stop grieving. And, having done her time, she found herself actually growing excited to get back to life. Clay had assigned her a coming-out date, something tangible to look forward to, a specific night upon which it would be socially and emotionally acceptable to move on. And that night was tonight.

As the sun set outside, Katherine selected a burgundy dress. Not red. Too playful. But not black, either. Mourning was officially over, and the dress she wore on her first evening out would be her colorful line of demarcation.

Wine tasting at the Arbor was a job for her tallest, most uncomfortable shoes—strappy, four-inch, open-toed sandals. Margery had left an invite for *Katherine Stark and Guest* at the door. Margery understood the need to dust oneself off and get back on the horse, and a night of casually elegant company and wine would be Katherine's mount.

She missed wine. She'd laid off during the search; a depressant was just a bad idea in a time of crisis. *But now I can drink.* She was lonely, too; the compulsive masturbation had also taken a respectful hiatus, although she slept with her arms wrapped around a pillow, and sometimes her legs. *There will be real men at the party.*

But a guest?

Whoever she brought, people would talk. Clay, however, had a plan. He'd escort her to the party to "get her out of the house." Once there they'd play it cool. No flirting. They'd almost ignore each other, like at the birthday party. She'd be free to mingle, perhaps even interact with other men at a level somewhere between *friendly* and *flirty* on the flirting scale. She would be available to test the waters, but at the end of the night, her safe date would be sure she got home without prompting any gossip. It was perfect. And it was all detailed in an instructive step-by-step text she'd received from Clay that morning.

Katherine examined the fit of the burgundy dress on the sharply defined lines of her body; she'd worked out compulsively since the disappearance—another Clay commandment. The dress's padded upper gave her modest chest some shape, the midsection hugged her trim waist to form a dramatic hourglass, and her sculpted calves were visible below the hem. All very nice.

No. Not nice. Fucking fabulous.

She enjoyed using the word *fuck,* even if she was just thinking it. It was especially fun in an empty house with nobody around.

"Fuck," she said to the mirror. "Fuck, fuck, fuck."

She was flirting with herself, she realized. *Beyond flirty.* She considered touching herself again, but she wasn't sure she wanted to go to the party spent. One thing was for sure—she was definitely ready to get back to life.

CHAPTER 28

Blake was slightly less unpleasant than Stu had at first thought. After the third day, he stopped threatening to leave Stu to die whenever Stu begged for a rest stop. And by day five, Stu was no longer slowing their progress. After a week, they started making up for Stu's initial night of vomiting and first few slow days. And by the time they pushed open the door of Blake's hand-built cabin, they were right on schedule. Just in time for the snow.

Blake's cabin was not much larger than Stu's roofless shack. And although there were tin eating utensils, salt, sugar, chicken broth cubes, soap, and a few other necessities, there was no larder full of food or propane stove. Stu had to admit, the place was not so very different. But after a week in the tent, the modest cabin seemed downright luxurious. After two weeks, it felt perfectly comfortable. And after a month it was home.

The division of labor was simple. Stu split wood and kept the fire going. Blake walked the trapline.

"What do you trap?" Stu had asked on the first day.

Blake tapped his temple, then listed all his prey in a single breath. "Beaver, coyote, arctic fox, red fox, lynx, marmot, marten, mink, muskrat, otter, rabbit, red squirrel, flying squirrel, ground squirrel, woodchuck, weasel, and the occasional wolverine."

"What about bear?"

"You don't look for bear. You avoid them."

"Wolf?"

Blake nodded carefully. "Ah, yes, the wolf. I've trapped wolf before."

"Why weren't they included in your initial list? You rattled it off so assuredly that omitting them couldn't have been an oversight."

"You don't miss a thing, do you, counselor?" Blake chuckled, but he walked out without answering the question.

When Blake returned from his rounds, he threw dead animals to Stu, who earned his keep by skinning and cleaning them. Most were small, martens and minks, but the beaver were bigger, and one coyote was the size of a dog. He only ruined one pelt, a mink worth "a half day's pay" according to Blake. Stu's host swore a blue streak but immediately threw Stu another and made him try again. With Blake standing over him watching every cut and pull, Stu had gotten that one right.

For the more distant traps on the line Blake was gone overnight. He built snow caves, which Stu found fascinating. Instead of fearing the snow, Blake punched it in the gut and slept right in its heart.

"Aren't you afraid the thing will cave in and suffocate you?"

"Not if you build it right," Blake muttered.

Stu immediately had to know how it was done. *Edwin's* had a diagram, but after Blake marched Stu for a day into the hills to tend a distant trap and try it, Stu discovered that *Edwin's* was missing from his pack. He had to try to build one from memory. They slept in his third attempt that night, and it neither collapsed nor suffocated either of them.

On their way back, Blake saw three deer and pointed them out to Stu. They were distant, and Stu sighted them in with the .30-06 scope. They moved through the frosted trees with a stiff-legged walk that belied their fluid speed when running.

"We'll get one of those later," Blake promised.

When they returned from the trapline, Stu found *Edwin's* sitting in the middle of the bed with a note in Blake's spiky handwriting tucked inside that said, *I won't always be there . . . Edwin.*

They played cribbage on a worn cross section of pine log Blake had converted into a board by driving nail holes into it in two parallel spiral patterns. The pegs were red-headed and blue-headed wooden matches with their ends whittled to fit in the holes. Two of each color. They played with a tattered deck of cards with an Indian casino logo. The two of diamonds was missing, and the nine of clubs was torn so that it was always clear who had it. Several other cards were identifiable unless they were held tucked behind another card to hide their wear and tear. The quirks of the deck changed the strategy in a way that Stu found interesting, and they kept track of their wins and losses by carving notches in the wall with their knives. Blake jumped out to a large lead, but Stu learned quickly and soon was catching up.

On good days, they threw the hatchet at the woodpile, and Stu was surprised to find that the heavy head stuck nearly every time. The secret was to adjust the rotation with the distance. It took practice, but they had time. Blake carved point values into different logs in the stack so that it became a woodsman's version of darts.

Stu found that even the rapidly shortening days felt long without meetings, phone calls, clients, a commute, and a chatty wife. Blake talked much less than Katherine, both because he was a more private person and simply because he was a dude. There was a lot more time in life than he'd ever thought, and Stu fell into a ritual to keep himself busy. Early fire. Morning coffee. A trip to the latrine. One game of cribbage. Fresh meat for breakfast, or they'd mix up powdered eggs and pancakes if Blake brought nothing back from morning rounds of the nearby small traps. It was always better when they got a rabbit. Their diet was largely lean protein. While Blake was out, Stu would read one chapter of *Edwin's*. After breakfast Stu chopped wood with the full-size ax. He shoveled snow if snow needed shoveling. Then he broke the ice on the water barrel and topped it off by carrying buckets of water from the creek thirty yards away. Once a week he felled a nearby tree so it could dry out for use as firewood.

Each tree he took down also widened the clearing around the cabin. The snow was deepening, and he shoveled paths around the cabin to keep them clear, or packed them down by walking them.

One day he was shoveling paths and just kept going until he'd shoveled the entire clearing. It took three solid hours. His arms were sore and his back was tired, but it felt good to do manual labor after a decade of life behind a desk.

When Blake returned, he'd stared, amazed. "Jeezus, man, how the hell did you do that?" he muttered. "Better yet, why?"

There was infrequent conversation. Mostly about trapping or the unpredictable weather. Blake had a saying: "If you don't like the weather here, wait twenty minutes." The default discussion was whether they should play another game of cribbage; the answer was always yes, which avoided the need to find something else to discuss. Blake had stories about epic snowstorms, trapping tales, and a meticulous description of the building of the cabin, but he was comfortable with dead air, too. If he had nothing to say, he could sit for an hour without a word. One morning he took Stu out on his rounds to show him the trail of the deer they'd sighted. He pointed out tracks in the snow, broken branches, and scat. Then he put up a makeshift blind just off the path and went into meditation mode. Not to be outdone, Stu matched his silence, sitting motionless with the .30-06 cradled in his lap for most of the day. It was cold, but Stu was determined not to give up first. When the deer came, Blake simply nodded at him.

They had venison steaks for lunch. The deer was harder to skin than the smaller animals, but well worth it, and Blake was excited enough about Stu's first kill to help him field dress it. The next day, Stu built a smoker. He'd been itching to try it since he'd read chapter seven in *Edwin's* on preserving food. Then he began drying strips of venison. The key, he discovered, was to keep feeding the coals green chips, but not to allow flames to flare up, a delicate balance that he had to keep for twenty-four hours to get the meat smoked correctly. The first batch wasn't too good, but the second was so delicious that Blake declared it a worthy ingredient for a pemmican trail mix he threw together with dried berries.

Soon Stu was walking the trapline with Blake, miles every day like it was nothing. And when Blake got sick for three days, he went alone.

For the first month Stu worried about what was happening back home, each day remembering bills that were overdue or calculating client deadlines he was missing, or speculating about when Katherine might presume him dead. He fretted to himself, mostly, but eventually mentioned it aloud enough times that Blake felt it necessary to weigh in.

"Why don't you shut the hell up? There's nothing you can do about it till spring."

To his surprise, Blake's crude logic appealed to him and, as soon as he accepted it, his urban worries were buried under the Alaska snow, with the exception that he still ached knowing that Katherine was suffering.

CHAPTER 29

Clay picked her up at seven, and Katherine made sure to answer the door without her long coat in order to give him an eyeful.

"Does this look okay?"

"You look fucking great, Kate. Good work. You'll definitely impress tonight."

Her heart fluttered. There was the *F* word again. And he was still taking the liberty of calling her Kate, which she hadn't let anyone—not even Stu—do since she'd declared herself a professional photographer during college.

She grinned. "Oh? Who do I have to impress?"

"You never know." He winked. "But I'll tell you when to do so."

Stu insisted on driving Katherine's new Audi for her. They'd decided that she only needed a two-seater, and she smiled secretly as he made the little thing get up and dance, even as she suggested he slow down.

The Arbor was located in Fairhaven, across the bridge. Margery's gourmet food and wine bar was also near the water, but the feel was completely different from Stationbreak. Creeping vines hung everywhere, and a massive brick wall covered with ivy served as a backdrop for stools huddled up against huge round tables that sat eight or more people in casually elegant attire. The chandelier globes were shaped like wine bottles and wineglasses. Margery furnished high-class restaurants the way lesser women experimented with different rooms in their homes, Katherine thought.

Their names were on the list. Clay signaled for wine, and the waiter offered them several varieties. Clay chose for her. Nothing for him. Margery flitted over to greet them.

"Katherine. So good of you to come, considering."

"Considering what?" Katherine gave her a disarming smile.

"Of course. Not talking about that tonight." Margery made a lip-zipping motion. "And, Mr. Buchanan. What a surprise and a pleasure. Welcome to our humble establishment."

The place was anything but humble, and she knew it. Clay glanced about. "It's quaint," he joked.

Margery laughed. She thumped his chest with her open hand, letting it linger. "Oh, you. Let's catch up later."

Katherine felt her hackles rise, but then Margery was off greeting another guest. They moved into the bar, where she began a mental list of important people to talk to before the night was out.

"Joe!" Clay hailed an older man in an expensive suit that didn't fit; he was sitting at the bar with a glass of scotch instead of wine. He was maybe sixty, but his face was wizened and his eyes suspicious beyond their years. Clay strode to him and extended a hand.

"Joe, I'd like to introduce you to Kate. She's a local photographer."

Clay didn't use her last name, she noticed. The man Joe sized her up. She smiled and allowed it, cocking a hip for him.

"Picture taker, eh?" he said with a Rhode Island accent.

"I try."

"You gonna take my picture?" He laughed.

"I certainly could. You have a face full of character."

"She's also my new partner in the firm."

"Lawyer, too?" He seemed disappointed.

"No. Business partner."

"Good. I got no regard for lawyers. Married?"

"No."

"Even better." He smiled.

"Can I park her here with you for a minute? I need to use the rest-room."

"Sure thing." He patted the stool next to his.

Clay left. Katherine was disappointed to see him go, but she under-stood that she was on assignment. She slid her rump up onto the stool beside Joe as he ordered her a Tom Collins to replace her empty wineglass.

"Do you know Margery?" she began.

"No."

"What's your connection here? Wine lover?"

"Ha. No. Wine's a woman's drink. Clay mentioned this little party, and I had my people arrange an invitation."

"Oh. Wow. So, are you from here?"

"No. Providence. I'm here on business."

"What do you do, Joe?"

"This and that. I do some informal banking. But I guess you could say I'm mostly in transport."

"Shipping?"

"Yeah. That sort of thing. I get over here to the water to check on my investments once a month or so. But enough about that. Tell me some-thing interesting about you."

"I studied photography at UMass. I'm not just some picture taker. Sold an entire series recently."

"Educated. Good. I get tired of waitresses and pole dancers."

"Pole dancers?"

"Cheap women. They're starting to bore me."

"I'm not cheap."

"No. You don't look it. Are you from New England?"

"Grew up here."

"Local girl. Great. You like money, local girl?"

Katherine laughed. "That's a funny and very direct question."

"And that's not an answer."

"Well, they say it isn't everything."

"Yeah, they who don't have it say that."

"We do fine at the firm. And my work is selling."

"Photography, huh? I'll have to check that out."

"Do. I still have a few individual prints on display at Brad Bear's studio in Dartmouth. A man named Archie Brooks purchased my series."

"Yeah, I think I heard Dugan mention that."

"Oh! You know Reggie?"

"Yeah, I know Reggie." He laughed. "I own Reggie."

It was an odd thing to say, but Katherine didn't push it. "He's a new client at our firm."

"I heard that, too."

"How do you know him?"

"Everybody knows Reggie. But me, I fish on his boat sometimes, the *Iron Maiden.*"

"Lovely. Isn't that a medieval torture device?"

Joe laughed. "I think he named it after his ex-wife."

Clay returned as the bartender brought Katherine's drink. Joe pulled out a wad of cash and peeled off a one-hundred-dollar bill to cover it. The bartender held the money up to the light.

"Sorry, smallest I got."

Clay helped Katherine down from her stool.

"Aww, we were just getting to know each other," Joe complained.

Clay laughed politely as he led Katherine away. "Sorry, I can't loan her out tonight. She's my date."

"I guess I'll just have to get in line."

Katherine looked back as they walked away.

"What did he mean by that?"

"Nothing. It's just old-school humor."

"Are we doing business with him?"

"Maybe."

"Who is he? You know it helps if you give me a little background before you dump me on raging chauvinists."

"Joe Roff. Owns parking garages in downtown Providence and warehouses here, right on the damned waterfront. Among other things."

"Funny, I almost thought you said *whorehouses* for a moment."

"Not all success comes wrapped in a prep school uniform, Kate."

"He bought me a Tom Collins at a wine-tasting party," Katherine said, and she discreetly poured her drink into a potted plant.

"You didn't exactly come from money; don't act like you're too good for him."

The truth of the comment stung. "Where I'm from and where I am now are two very different places."

"No offense, but you need to understand that he's a big fish. Not a *New York Times*–society-page type, but self-made and does what he likes. I just hope you were charming."

"If I was any more charming, he'd have given me the hundred."

"Good."

They circulated. Clay continued to introduce her as Kate the photographic artist, which she liked. And he rebuffed Margery's advances, which she loved. He looked good doing it, too—the most handsome man in the place. There was one young waiter who might have given him a run, but the boy had a tattoo that wasn't quite right, and as soon as he opened his mouth he dropped out of the race. Smart was sexy. Dumb, not so much. She estimated that she herself was among the top three women in her age range, but Clay did not talk to the other two, and the younger twentysomethings clung to the friends they'd come with and laughed too loud. They were no threat.

Margery hooked her up with two other restaurateurs over a merlot blend. Katherine got herself invited to stop in at their joints, and laid groundwork for suggesting they acquire new wall hangings. An art dealer from Boston unfortunately did not deal in photography, but took her card and promised to pass it along. And Clay circled back to talk with Joe at the bar while she did a round of wine sampler speed dating. She was matched with the Syrah.

It was a good night. *Fucking fabulous.* By the time they walked out to her Audi, she was flying. She plopped down in the seat, closed her eyes, and let the vibration of the engine run through her.

"Well, there's only one thing that could make this night better," she said, letting eight glasses of wine do the talking for her. She giggled. *Whoops, flirting stage three.*

Clay grinned. "Let me guess: midnight gelato with dark chocolate drizzle at To Die For?"

"Not what I was thinking. But yes!"

She laughed all the way home. During the trip, she parodied an imaginary conversation between Margery and Joe Roff. Clay was so attentive that he missed her turn. Then she realized they weren't going to her house. The shoreline road was familiar, but she hadn't driven it in the Audi or with Clay, and certainly not at eighty miles per hour. It was exhilarating. When they pulled up, her heart was beating *one hundred* miles per hour.

"Care to give me the tour," Clay said, and he held up a key that she immediately recognized.

Her heart skipped a beat. "Where did you get that?"

"Good news. They accepted your offer."

"What offer?"

"I knew what you could pay. I filled out the paperwork for you."

"You forged my signature?"

"You're welcome."

"I was waiting to make sure everything came together."

"You were being a pussy. Come on." He got out of the car, shut his door, and ran around to open hers.

Clay led her straight to the living room, where they stood in front of the wall of windows. She couldn't wait any longer. She kissed him. He kissed her back, and she lost herself in his mouth, her hands clutching at his lats. After eight wines and months of waiting, she found she had no patience. She reached down. *He's not ready yet.* It wasn't a problem, but she was mildly surprised. Dugan had been ready from the moment he'd touched her, probably before.

Clay took the hint and peeled her burgundy dress up to her neck so that she stood like a ballerina with her hands in the air in her bra and thong. But he left the dress tangled around her arms and head. Then he pushed her face-first over the couch. She was able to breath, but couldn't move her arms or see, feeling both trapped and exposed. Unable to see, her other senses were heightened. She smelled her own perfume on the dress, felt the room's cool air on her bare body.

Clay pressed himself up against her, his mouth at her ear. *He's still not ready?*

"What did you do with Dugan, Kate?" he whispered.

She hesitated. "What do you mean?" she said through the dress.

"I know something happened. Tell me about it. And don't lie."

Katherine hesitated. "Am I in trouble?"

"Not unless you lie."

"You want to hear what I did with another man while you and I are . . . ?"

Clay twisted her dress tighter around her wrists. "Tell me."

"I don't know, I—"

"Tell me!" he barked, and he slapped her exposed butt so hard she was certain it left a red handprint.

"A-a-a favor," she stammered. "An *oral* favor."

And then, finally, Clay Buchanan was ready.

CHAPTER 30

The caribou herd chose the easy path through the snow, and it was there that the alpha gray waited for them. The trap was laid where they were most likely to go. *No different than setting a snare on a rabbit trail,* Stu thought. The rest of the pack was scattered through the woods, waiting for their leader to ambush the herd.

Stu crouched uphill and downwind from them, motionless, as he had been for an hour. The snow fell lightly but steadily enough that it dusted over his tracks and coated him with a white crust that made him look like the hunched, snow-crowned shrubs all around him. None of the animals that were locked in the struggle for sustenance and life in the theater of the wild below knew he was there. And though he carried the Browning, he was just a spectator today, an audience of one, the only human who would ever witness this particular drama.

He couldn't help wondering if *his* caribou was among the herd. He couldn't remember its features—he'd been new to the sight of the great animals, and it had been hard to distinguish between them. These, too, had all looked alike at first, but he'd been coming here for a month, and now they were as distinct as though they'd sat in his Criminal Law II class with him all semester. *More so.*

Thirteen males strutted arrogantly through the group, their massive antlers held high. Yet despite their bravado, they were careful to stay safely within the loose exterior border of the herd. There was a small group of females. *Cows, not does,* Blake had told him. They clumped together, the healthiest-looking beasts of the bunch. One other kept trying to nose her way in, but they kept their circle tight and their rumps toward her. The rest congregated loosely, scooping snow away with their hollowed hooves to get to rare and precious winter lichen. The eldest male had lost weight over the fall, and the female with the notched white bib had been moving slowly lately—possibly sick. The wolves would try to take one of the herd, and Stu laid odds on these two as the likeliest victims.

As Stu watched, the herd stirred, one of them suddenly aware that something was amiss. Nostrils flared and heads rose. They began to move up the trampled path toward the shallow snow in the nearby small clearing, where it would be easiest to run. *A mistake.* The walk became a trot, and when they reached the open space, the alpha gray showed himself. The caribou turned as one, as though joined at the shoulders by invisible ropes, the ripple of their doomed vector echoing through the herd like a virus.

The alpha gray closed the gap with an amazing burst of speed, but he didn't land in the midst of them. Instead he floated at the herd's edge, watching, waiting, shepherding. They ran, then turned, and ran again, each animal determined not to be *the one* today. Then it happened.

The herd veered to its right down a trail between the trees, and the excluded female who'd wanted so badly to join the cows veered left. She was not weak or particularly old. In fact, she looked to be in good condition. She simply made a bad choice.

Without the herd around, the wolves closed on her quickly. A second wolf was waiting on the trail, and it leaped to tear at her flesh as she passed. It did not need to take her down, but simply to confuse her, to throw her off her stride. When she stumbled into a deeper snowdrift, a third wolf bounded from the woods and threw itself against her. She spun in the snow and faced her antagonists, panting. The wolves slunk around her, feeling her out, careful to avoid her sharp hooves and small antlers. There was a quick feint, and when she twisted to protect her flank, the alpha surged forward and clamped his jaws onto her exposed neck. It was intimate, a joining of teeth and flesh and blood, their furred bodies pressed together in an embrace as she weakened and then faltered. The weight of two more wolves brought her down, and it was over quickly.

Stu watched the conclusion through the scope of the Browning. He put the crosshairs on the carcass. He could take a caribou himself, he thought. Or even a wolf. He didn't; he wasn't the hunter today. *But I could.*

Two weeks later Stu carved a cribbage notch in the wall, moving to within one win of Blake.

"You're a lucky bastard," Blake grumbled.

"My father told me that we make our own luck."

"Make our own odds, maybe, but luck still has a hand in things, and she can be a real bitch."

"You know, you're fabulous company, but it's about time I got back to my wife. The snow has melted to below the second row of logs on the wood-pile."

"I know."

"How soon can we go? And don't give me a bunch of shit. I haven't asked for a week."

"Yeah, you've been a good boy. I'm thinking I'll head out in another two or three weeks."

"Can't we accelerate that timeline?"

"You still can't talk like a regular guy, can you, esquire?"

"Okay, let's get the fuck out of here, shall we?"

Blake laughed. It was a hearty laugh, not malicious, and he considered Stu with sympathetic eyes. Then he walked to a log in the wall and peeled off a strip of wood. A hollow had been carved in the log behind it.

Blake pulled out a bottle of Johnny Drum bourbon that was tucked inside and flashed it at Stu with a grin.

"I been saving this."

"You've been saving a bottle of cheap whiskey?"

"Oh no. This is the good stuff. You must be thinking of the green label. This is *black* label, aged more than four years. Almost twenty bucks a bottle."

Blake was poor, of course. Stu cursed himself silently for being insensitive. The man's stripped-down life didn't afford him luxuries, and he was offering Stu the best he had. Stu saw that he was fighting off a hurt expression.

"Oh! Wow. I've never had the black. May I?"

Blake grinned. "Hell yeah! Let's break out some dirty glasses."

Blake retrieved tin cups, the bottoms of which were burnt black from doing time over the fire. He filled them both with whiskey. Stu didn't want to guess the equivalent in shots. Then Blake settled himself on the log bench and passed Stu a cup.

"Thing is, you can get out of here sooner than three weeks."

"Really? When do you think?"

"Tomorrow morning."

"What?"

Blake took a long swig. "When I found you, you couldn't boil water without a microwave. But you can take care of yourself now. You don't need me. You can walk the fifty miles to Fur Lake, as we call it. That's an easy five-day hike for you. The shape you're in these days, you'll knock that out no problem. And you have the best damned clothing of any amateur woodsman I ever met. A floatplane checks the lake once a week for trappers coming out, starting about now. It'll take you to Fairbanks in trade for a pelt or three."

"I can't take your furs."

"Sure you can. You did your part. I'll send what you need along with you. Although the pilot would probably take your credit card, too." Blake knocked back another slug and shivered like he was starting to feel it. "But I got a question for you before you go."

"Shoot."

"Did it make you feel like a big man putting guys in jail?"

"What?"

"Did you enjoy it?"

"No. I mean, I don't know. It was my job."

"Driving a truck is a job. Doing people's taxes is a job. Trying to put a man in prison is a battle. Man against fucking man."

"I didn't look at it that way."

"Huh. Well, you got fired. So maybe you should have."

Stu took a long drink, choking it down. "They put themselves in prison. Made their own luck. It's a parade of dirtbags. After a while I didn't even remember a lot of their names. I was just a cog in the machine. A highly educated cog, I suppose. But it's like processing widgets."

"Naw. A man's not a widget. You challenge him like that, it's personal."

"Not for me."

"Maybe not for you, but maybe it is for them."

"How would you know?"

Blake shrugged. "Just how it seems to me."

"My turn."

"My turn what?"

"For a question. You had a question. I've got a question."

Blake snorted. "What is this, truth or dare?"

"No dare. This trip was my goddamned dare." Stu laughed and drank.

"Go on then. Out with it."

"You know I've got a wife, right?"

"You've mentioned it. Every day."

"Were you ever married?"

"You know what they say. You don't lose your wife in Alaska, just your turn."

"That's crude."

"And funny. And true."

"It doesn't answer my question."

Blake suddenly found his bourbon interesting. He swished it around with his finger, drank, then swished again. "I had a wife. But not up here."

"You split up?"

"Yeah. It was a totally fucked-up thing."

"You don't have to talk about it if you don't want to."

"She wanted to go back to school. . . ."

The fire crackled between them, and Blake stared into it.

"She was classified as a mature student, you know? Which means she was about the same age as her women's studies professor. Only thing was, this prof was a guy. A guy! Teaching feminist stuff! What kind of guy does that? Anyway, she came home talking about all kinds of historical oppression of women, which is apparently still going on, mind you; we men just don't see it. She started treating me like I been an asshole my whole life just because I'm a fella."

"And this killed the marriage?"

"No. I was okay with that. I listened to her big new words. I told her it was great and I hoped she felt empowered and shit. I really wanted her to be educated. Who wouldn't want a smart wife, right?"

"So what happened?"

"She got empowered, all right. Trouble was, I was still me. We had always fit so well together, but suddenly we didn't match up anymore, it seemed. I went to one of those college tea-and-fucking-crumpets parties at the campus once, and I could tell she was embarrassed by me. She had me shake her guy-teaching-chick-stuff professor's hand. She actually made me shake that little bastard's hand. He asked me what I did, and when I told him I was doing my welder's apprenticeship, he says, 'Oh, so you work with your hands,' like the trades were some punishment for people who couldn't go to college. And when I complained about him after we got home, she takes his side. Said I was reading things into what he said. I should have seen it coming then."

"People grow apart. At times my wife and I have been—"

"She grew apart all right. He filled her head with feminist shit. He asked her if she was being subjugated by her man. He made me out to be a Neanderthal, told her how she needed to be her own woman, get independent, think for herself, try new things. Then her legs grew right apart."

"Oh." Stu kept his mouth in his cup, trying to think of something else to say, but nothing seemed right.

Blake spat in the fire and waited for the sizzle to subside. "He was the same as any other caveman, you know. He just wanted to mount up. Had a different pitch, is all. She didn't understand that. Still doesn't. Guess she wasn't as smart as she thought she was."

"So you confronted her?"

"I confronted *him*. He's the one who did it. I went to his goddamned office, just like she was doing. He offered to shake my hand again. Can you believe that? He wanted to talk it out. He talked a lot. A lot like you, actually. Only in circles. Always ducking the issue. I was, like, 'Did you stick your dick in my wife or not?'"

"That's fairly direct."

"I know, right? But he keeps yapping about her evolving and making her own choices, like that's going to postpone the inevitable." Blake paused for a sip. "When I finally hit him, he went straight down. He was weak. Hundred and forty pounds soakin' wet, I'd guess. Soft. Desk jockey. A real man wouldn't have crumpled like that. My public defender said I was in worse trouble just because he was such a pussy."

"They call it an eggshell victim."

"Whatever. It would have been just a misdemeanor, but I guess I broke his nose."

"Making it a felony."

"Right. I don't know why that's a big deal. I've broke my nose. I think it looks better."

Blake drank. Stu sipped too, letting the story settle.

"That can't be the only reason you came to Alaska," Stu said.

"The prof's college had a lot of pull in town. I would have just pled out, but the prosecutor told my public pretender 'no deals.'"

"It still can't be more than a couple of months in the local jail with no weapon involved."

There was silence. The crackling of the fire took over the room.

Stu looked up. They rarely made eye contact when they talked. As with dogs, it felt too much like a challenge. Or else kind of gay. But Stu looked now, and he saw that Blake's eyes were damp. At first Stu thought it must be from his fiery drink or stray smoke. But then Blake's voice cracked.

"It got worse."

"Worse at home with your wife?"

"Yeah."

"What happened?"

"I hit her, too."

Stu sat back, stunned. "Oh."

"In front of our little girl."

"Ohhh."

"Mary was going on and on about what I had done to the fuckin' woman studier, saying it just 'validated' everything professor pussy had said. Can you believe that? After she started it all, she was blaming me! Then she said I wasn't as good a father as he would be, either." Blake took a breath. "And I just got so mad that I went ahead and proved her right."

Stu didn't comment. He'd prosecuted men like Blake before. Dozens. They beat their wives. They went to jail. Some got out and did it again and went to jail again. Others just faded away. Some went to Alaska, apparently.

"You think I'm a piece of shit," Blake mumbled.

"No," Stu lied. He could think of nothing else to say.

"It's okay. Everyone does, even me. It happened while I was out on bail for the busted nose thing."

"How long ago?"

"Six years."

"You could go back now, clean this up."

"I can't undo it. I was everything bad the guy said about me come true."

"People forgive."

"Prosecutors don't, do they? The warrants for my arrest are still sitting there in the DA's computer, along with a count of bail jumping now. I'm nothing to them but another dirtbag in the parade, right?"

Stu winced. "They listen to reason and the law. Your charges are pretty stale. They'll make a deal now if you return voluntarily and haven't been in any trouble in the ensuing six years."

"I been clean. I been a ghost."

"I could help you."

Blake looked up at him for the first time in the conversation, for the first time Stu could remember. "You told me you don't work with criminals. I think your words were: 'Thank God, I don't have to represent those pukes.'"

"I've shared a room with you all winter. You're not a puke. You obviously have a bit of an anger problem, but we could get some counseling or therapy as part of your sentence to offset jail time."

"I don't have a mental problem."

"Acting out physically is deviant behavior for dealing with relationship frustrations. It's a symptom of several diagnoses in the *Diagnostic and Statistical Manual of Mental Disorders*."

"I think it's more normal to punch someone."

"Oh yeah? Well, I don't punch people."

"You ever had your woman cheat on you?"

"My wife? No."

"Don't need to be your wife to know how it feels. From the way you limited your answer to your wife, it sounds like you had a girlfriend do it to you."

Stu frowned. "Maybe, but we were in our twenties. People don't own each other at that age. It was just dating. She was free to do what she wanted." He looked at his cup. He could see the bottom. It was probably a good time to stop drinking and shut up, he thought. Instead he held it out for more.

Blake poured. "I'll bet when you were a twentysomething yuppie type, you didn't think she was free to do *who* she wanted."

"Thanks for your middle-aged blue-collar perspective."

"You don't have to tell me."

"No. You told me. I'll tell you." Stu drank. The relatively cheap whiskey was going down more smoothly now. "Okay, it *was* my wife."

"Oh."

"But it was before Katherine and I were married. She had this old boy-friend from back in college. He was the guy who got her into photography."

"Art guy. Shit."

"She and I had been dating for about a year, but still living at separate apartments. One weekend she got busy, and I didn't see her for a couple of days. Then this cardboard box shows up on my porch. I had no idea what it was. So I open it up, and right on top is a photo of Katherine in college. She's wearing a UMass sweatshirt, posing in some sort of studio. There's a stack of these pictures, sort of in chronological order. The next shot is her with her sweatshirt off, bra and jeans. Then no bra and jeans. Then less."

"Birthday suit?"

"Yeah, toward the bottom. They were mostly classy and mostly from college. Mostly. But the last one . . ."

"Your girl doing him a favor," Blake guessed.

"A what?"

Blake made a crude motion with his hand and mouth.

Stu winced. It would have been rude and offensive if he hadn't been exactly right.

Blake continued. "From that previous weekend, those days you didn't see her."

"Yeah."

"What did she have to say about her little portfolio?"

"Nothing."

"You make her burn 'em in front of you?"

"No. I didn't even show them to her."

"What the hell did you do?"

"I packed them up and put them on her porch so she'd think he left them for her. She doesn't know I ever saw them."

"Jesus! You're kidding."

"Nope."

"What did she say about the guy?"

"She said he was 'passing through town' and looked her up. She said they met for lunch, but he got jealous when she told him that she was seeing me."

"I take it she told him that after the cocksicle photo op."

Stu cringed again. "I guess so."

"And he left you a present to show you who the real man was."

"Apparently."

"Did you go find this asshead?"

"No. He didn't owe me anything. She was the one who impliedly promised herself to me, then made this choice."

"So you told her she was a cheatin' bitch and she begged you to take her back?"

"Not exactly."

"How not?"

"We didn't get into it."

"Did she admit she favored him?"

"I didn't ask."

"But you knew."

"So why ask?"

"To let her know she can't walk all over you."

"She doesn't walk all over me. The problem took care of itself, drove itself right out of town. Why perpetuate the conflict?"

"Are you kidding? You are such a pussy!"

"I'm not a pussy. I've faced down murderers and rapists. You said so yourself."

"Another man does your girl, rubs your nose in it, and not only can't you confront him about it, you can't even face *her*."

"Well, then, what does the great relationship therapist in the stupid fur hat suggest I do?" Stu was mad. His anger and the bourbon allowed the words to tumble out before he could stop them. "Hit her?"

Blake went silent, and for a moment Stu thought that the big man was going to take a swing at *him*. The bearded welder took a deep breath and flexed his large fingers in and out of fists to calm himself, something it looked like he'd been practicing for years. In the end he spoke in a measured voice. "You and I both handled our shit like shit. But I admitted I'd do mine over differently. And you should too."

"I'm pretty confident my handling of my shit was superior."

"Slightly better than terrible is still bad. At least I stood up for myself. Grow a pair, for Christ's sake."

"I've got a successful marriage. My wife is devoted to me. *Res ipsa loquitur.*"

Blake chuckled.

"What's funny?"

"The lawyer stuff you spew. What the hell does that even mean?" His chuckles turned to machine-gun laughter, and he had trouble stopping it.

"It means, 'The thing speaks for itself.'"

"What thing?"

"I don't know. The successful marriage thing nullifies the photo thing."

Blake was still laughing. He slapped Stu on the back and downed the last of his third cup of whiskey.

"You have a messed-up view of the world, brother. There are insults in life that you can't reason away. You can fight, you can forgive, but you can't just absorb them. It's a poison that lodges in your manhood and permanently shrinks your balls."

"Colorful. But life's not about the size of your balls."

"Maybe not in the courtroom, counselor, but when two bucks go head-to-head in the field, yes, it is."

CHAPTER 31

Stu woke early with a headache and a smile. He started a fire for them
and took his trip to the latrine. Packing five days' worth of supplies, a pile
of marten pelts, and his few remaining belongings into the Great Beyond
pack took less than half an hour, then he and Blake sat down for one last
game of cribbage. Stu pegged past his host with a three-card run and a
"go" in the last hand to win, which brought them to even.

"A-fucking-mazing," Blake grumbled.

They ate deer sausage and buckwheat pancakes, then Stu chopped his
wood for the day and checked the water barrel. It was the first day that
there wasn't a layer of ice on top.

"Guess it's time," he said.

Blake stood in the cabin door, looking uncomfortable. "Guess so."

Stu retrieved his pack.

Blake caught him by the shoulder. "Hey, all that stuff we said last night.
Can we just forget that?"

"Sure."

"I'm sorry I called your wife a cheating bitch. I'm sure she's very loyal now."

Stu nodded. "She is."

"And hey, take the hand ax. I've still got the full-size." He handed Stu the homemade antler-handled hatchet. Then he pulled one more small fur from his own pack. "Take this, too, if you want."

"What is it?"

"Deerskin."

"A bag?"

"A hat."

"Oh, like yours."

"Well, yeah. It's the only kind I know how to make."

"You made me a hat?" Stu took it and turned it over in his hands. He recognized the coarse fur. "This is from the deer I shot."

"Sorry. I made it before you called mine 'stupid.' If you don't want it, no big deal. It's not a Valentine's gift or nothing'."

"I'm touched."

"Aww, shut up. Just take the damn hat or don't. I don't care one way or the other."

"Thank you." Stu knew what he had to do. He slid the hat over his head and pulled it down around his ears. "Tell me one thing," Stu said.

"How you look?"

"I know how I look. Tell me why you don't trap wolves."

Blake put a pine needle toothpick in his mouth and slid it around with his tongue for a bit. "Most animals I trap know the game," he said finally. "They run and hide and you try to catch them. But not wolves. They still think they're an apex predator. Their pack has an alpha male that thinks he's apex-apex. He shows his dominance by being tough, and he's the only one who breeds with the female. He takes challenges head on. It's a simple system, one I can understand and respect.

"I used to trap them until I caught this big black alpha. A proud animal all rippled with muscle. I found scars from all his victories under that valuable fur when I skinned him. Defeat wasn't the problem for this guy. He would have been ready for that. He would have faced it, looked it right in the eye, and accepted it, even if it meant his life. But he couldn't stare down a hidden, spring-loaded alloy metal contraption that clamped onto his leg. After it grabbed him, he just limped around it, confused, until he died. When I found him, there was a big circle of red, like a bloody snow angel. The sad thing wasn't that he lost; it was that he didn't understand how to fight."

It took Stu three days to hike back to the grizzly research site. He immediately saw that the camp had been cleared. Someone had come and recovered Thomas's belongings. *A grieving colleague blaming him- or herself and probably wondering if the bear ate the camera, too.* The only thing left was the bloodstained Kubota. The tractor had been pushed upright, but it still sat at the river's edge like a huge red gravestone. Whoever had found Thomas hadn't had the means to airlift it away, or hadn't wanted to. The river gurgled like a baby, the sun was warm on his skin, and it was hard to imagine the sudden violence that had erupted there.

Stu swore he hadn't lingered, but he might have. Time got away from him sometimes in the wilderness now; he no longer felt the need to check his phone for the time every few minutes—nor could he, because it was long dead. And he found himself just standing beside the water, listening, seeing, feeling. He felt uneasy, then he saw the bear appear at the tree line about one hundred yards away. It stood and sniffed, then dropped to all fours and started in his direction.

Shit!

There was no mistaking its intention. It didn't hesitate or amble his way like a curious woodland creature, but came straight at him, low and steady like the massive predator it was. It had a large hump on its back—a grizzly.

Thomas's grizzly.

Stu actually felt his balls tighten and crawl up into his lower belly.

It's just doing what bears do, he thought ridiculously. *Nothing personal.*

But it *wasn't* just doing what bears did. It had decided to expand its palate and consider Thomas food. It had decided to respect Stu no more than a fish. *Fuck you humans,* it was saying.

The nearest trees in the opposite direction were hundreds of yards away, and *Edwin's* had been quite clear that trying to outrun a bear was like trying to outrun an NFL lineman—they looked big and slow, but they were faster than any normal human being. Stu groaned. There was only one place to hide. He edged back and stepped into the Kubota. It hadn't saved Thomas, but it could save him. The thick Plexiglas would hold if he could just secure the door. He was able to wrestle it into place, and jamming the wedge-shaped hatchet into the crack near the broken hinge seemed a promising idea. But if the bear got through, there would be little time to shoot, and if it didn't die instantly, it might not matter. Besides, the son of a bitch was challenging him.

I'm not going to be dragged out of this cage.

Stu kicked the door back open and stepped out. He shed his pack and walked into the river, setting his feet shoulder-width apart and snugging the .30-06 to his shoulder. The bear was galloping toward him now, like a horse. Fifty yards, then forty. Stu cocked the rifle and flipped off the safety. The scope was of no use against the charging animal. He aimed down the barrel. The gun's report echoed across the field. The bear kept coming. It was in the river, plowing water. Stu stood his ground and fired again. The bear stood midstream and uttered a low growl. They stared at each other.

"Come on!" Stu shouted.

He fired once more, ten yards away, a clear shot at the middle of the bear's chest. The bullet hit with a meaty slap, and the huge animal went to all fours, injured but still coming.

Stu decided he was dead. Another short charge through the water, and the grizzly would tear him limb from limb.

Like Thomas.

But the spring runoff was heavy, and when the bear reached midstream, the water crept above its legs into its torso. It faltered, and on its first misstep the strong current took ahold of it. The weakening grizzly tumbled and was swept downstream. Shot three times and dying, the bear surrendered to the river.

Stu watched it float away. *I won!* He felt a surge of adrenaline unlike any he'd ever felt before. It was a simple sensation—the primordial thrill of continuing to live. He stood victorious at the river's edge, and his balls resumed their customary position outside of his body.

CHAPTER 32

The bush pilot at Fur Lake was a pro with a four-seat Maule and a flight plan. *Unlike that idiot Ivan, who's about to get one hell of a suing.* He took Stu on in exchange for the furs Blake had given him, asked him to unload his weapon per company policy, stowed his gear, and welcomed him aboard his clean, well-maintained aircraft. It even had a professional logo painted on the side: BEST BUSH.

Stu curled up in his seat. He was tired from his five-day hike, but it was a good tired, the sort a guy might feel after a healthy workout, and a cushioned upright seat felt luxurious. He smiled big and relaxed as the buzzing engine lifted them up out of Fur Lake; it was the most comfortable place he'd slept in months.

He woke up over Fairbanks.

The landing lake used by Best Bush was the same lake used by Yukon Air Tours, and the pilot agreed to taxi over to the Yukon dock and drop Stu off.

He would confront Ivan, Stu had decided. It was best to catch witnesses unaware, before they knew a lawsuit was brewing. They were more likely to apologize and admit fault. Stu considered several theories of liability as they made their landing, and he quickly scribbled a list of questions designed to pin down Ivan's explanation. If he were lucky, he would be able to plug in his cell phone and record the conversation.

Stu climbed out onto the dock with his pack and Ivan's .30-06, and he gave his competent pilot a teary-eyed thank-you, which puzzled the man greatly because Stu had hardly spoken a word to him the entire trip.

Then he was walking up the hill into the forest of creepy Old Man Winter faces. Ivan must have heard the plane taxi to the dock, because the wood-carving pot pilot was out of the house and walking down the hill toward him. Stu waved and Ivan waved back, obviously not recognizing him. Stu realized he looked different—thirty pounds lighter with long hair and a beard. He smirked.

I look like one of his carvings in a stupid fur cap.

"Hey, dude, can I help you?" Ivan called out.

"Hello, Ivan. We need to talk."

Ivan stopped in his tracks. "Whoa!"

Stu wasn't sure what Ivan was going to do—he looked like he was going to throw up. He just stared at Stu for a time, thinking, or at least trying to. Stu looked at his list of questions and took a deep breath, willing himself to sound reasonable despite his anger.

"Ivan, you understand that you were supposed to come and get me last fall, correct?"

"You're alive."

"Yes. I am. Thank you. But you were supposed to come back to get me, right?" Stu didn't wait for Ivan to process what was happening. Instead he tried to lure him into admitting fault by minimizing Ivan's negligence, a technique he'd learned working with the cops. "Maybe you just mixed up the days. Totally understandable. Is that what happened?"

"I went back. You weren't there. I thought you were dead."

"You have a flight log we can look at to see when you went, don't you?

"I can fix this."

"I'm sure you can, but we need to figure out what happened first. Do you mind if we go inside where I can plug in my phone?"

"Uh, yeah. Sure." But Ivan didn't move. Instead he glanced around as if looking for someone.

Unnerved, Stu did too, but there wasn't anyone for miles, as far as he could tell. The distant sound of the receding Best Bush plane and the chirp of a chickadee were all he heard. It was just the two of them.

"After you," Stu said.

"Okay. Can I have my gun back?"

Stu had completely forgotten about the Browning .30-06. He'd grown accustomed to having it hang on his shoulder like an extra limb. He shrugged it off and handed it over.

Ivan took the rifle and backed away up the hill two steps. He gave Stu a pained expression. "I'm sorry, dude," he said.

"It's okay. I'm fine. We just have to get some of the details straight." *And once we do,* Stu thought, *I'm going to ruin you.*

Ivan raised the gun and pointed it directly at Stu's chest. "No, I mean it. I'm really sorry about this."

Stu's heart leaped into his throat. He raised his hands defensively and tried to keep his voice calm. "Don't panic. It's okay. I forgive you for leaving me at that crappy cabin."

"Cabin?" Ivan licked his lips, confused and exasperated.

"We don't need to talk right now if it's not a good time. Things worked out. I'll just go."

Ivan glanced about again. He cocked the gun and flipped off the safety. "Things did *not* work out. Jeezus! They most certainly did not! You're *supposed* to be dead."

"Don't pull that trigger. You can't take it back if you pull that trigger."

"Sorry, dude," Ivan said again, and he pulled the trigger.

The gun's hammer made a quiet click as it fell on the empty chamber. Time stood still for a moment as they stared at each other, each of them surprised. Then Ivan turned and ran toward the house.

Other guns! Stu remembered that Ivan had four more rifles and two pistols in the closet just inside the back door, undoubtedly as loaded as Ivan had wrongly assumed the Browning would be. Stu glanced around. There was no safe place to run on the property and no neighbor for miles. If he fled, the obviously unstable pilot could simply grab another gun and hunt him down.

There was no time to debate it. Ivan already had a five-step lead on him. Stu yanked Blake's bone-handled hatchet from his belt and hurled it at Ivan's back.

It was a good throw. Not perfect. A bit low. But good enough. Ivan took three more steps up the hill before the heavy blade turned over and sank into his left buttock with a meaty *thunk*. He cried out and went down.

"Ahh, God!" Ivan groaned

Stu ran to him, kicking the empty rifle away for no better reason than that it had just scared the shit out of him. He flipped Ivan over, his skinning knife in his hand, though he didn't remember drawing it.

But the pot-smoking pilot was no longer a threat. He clutched his buttocks and writhed. The hatchet had fallen into the dirt. Stu grabbed it and threw it clear.

"Why?" Stu shook him. "Why did you just try to kill me?" Saying it aloud made it real and frightening.

"My ass." Ivan was moaning now.

"Damn right, it's your ass! Attempted murder, pal. Fifteen years in prison. Why the hell did you do that?" Stu held the knife up. His pulse raced. His breaths came hard and fast. He was so hyped up, he felt as though, if Ivan tried anything, he might lose it and stab him in his goddamned face.

Ivan raised one shaking hand as if to ward him off. It was covered with blood—not spattered, but painted solid so that it looked like he was wearing a red glove. Stu looked down. Ivan's jeans were stained dark around his thigh. A small pulse of blood spurted into the dirt through the gash in the denim. The hand ax had hit an artery, he realized. Ivan was bleeding out.

"Hey! Hey, don't die on me. . . ."

But Ivan's eyes were glazing over more than usual. Stu recognized the symptom; it was straight from *Edwin's. Shock.*

"Aww, shit!"

He tore Ivan's belt loose and yanked down his pants. The blood was flowing, but the wound spanned Ivan's cheek and the thick flesh of his upper thigh. There was no way to apply pressure. Stu couldn't tie a tourniquet around a butt cheek. He took Ivan's face in his hands. Ivan was conscious, but fading.

"Keep talking, Ivan. I'll get you help. Why did you try to shoot me?"

Ivan spoke with great effort. "I was just supposed to leave you there. No offense. I don't even know you."

Stu stood, horrified, and backed against a carved tree. "You left me out there on purpose?"

Ivan's breathing grew shallow and rapid. He clutched at Stu's pant leg, but Stu kicked his hand away in disgust, and it fell to the ground, twitching.

Ivan wheezed, his voice weakening. "You said you'd help. . . ."

Stu recognized a dying animal. He'd seen them all winter. "Sorry, dude."

CHAPTER 33

It felt different killing a man. Stu thought it would feel more tragic than killing the bear. But the bear was the nobler creature. It came at him head-on. No deception. No pretense. It didn't try to trap him or trick him. It simply challenged Stu to a straight-up fight for supremacy, for life. *Well fought, bear!* he might have said, whereas he wanted to spit on the sneaky son of a bitch on the ground at his feet.

The *explanation* for killing a man, however, would be decidedly more complicated than for a wild animal. Stu wondered what he might say.

I came back to confront the pilot who left me in the woods with shelter and plenty of gear. I was angry because I was an incompetent camper who ruined my cabin and almost starved myself. I hit my victim from behind with a hatchet while he was running away because he pointed a gun at me that I knew to be unloaded. Then I pulled down his pants and let him bleed to death. That about sums it up.

Stu gave his summation standing over Ivan's body, then smacked himself in the forehead. It sounded terrible. It *was* terrible. If someone had dropped such damning facts on his desk when he'd been a prosecutor, he would have charged himself. *Murder two, at least.* Twenty years. Ten with a good plea bargain.

He glanced at the lake, then at the house. He'd seen enough police reports to know that suspects made hundreds of mistakes at the scenes of their crimes. If he thought of fifty of them, he'd be doing well. He already had Ivan's DNA on his clothes. But he had one advantage. He was dead. Like Blake, he was a ghost. Or, at least, nobody knew he was alive.

The first item on the agenda was to get away from the body. He wouldn't hide it—that would be an entirely new crime. There was no posing the scene as an accident. That never worked; forensics were too good these days. *And how does a guy accidentally hit himself in the ass with a hatchet?* He had to get somewhere and think, and as little as he wanted to go into the house, it was the only immediate choice.

The back door was open. There was nothing of interest in the kitchen. The living room offered little more. The smell of marijuana was overpowering as soon as he opened the bedroom door. *Big surprise.* He wanted badly to call Katherine. *But not from here.* Nor was it a good idea to charge his cell phone. It could be traced as soon as it was turned on. In fact, he was lucky its battery was as dead as the man lying out in the creepy forest of carved trees with an extra hole in his butt.

Stu shivered. That man had tried to kill him. Not just today, but also six months ago. He'd clearly said Stu was "supposed to be dead." Stu wondered why. Was he protecting a stash and thought Stu was DEA instead of ex-DA? He was dumb enough, Stu supposed.

Stu wore his gloves as he walked through the house. The more time he spent here, the more danger there was he'd get caught at the scene or leave evidence. He had to make it quick. The computer was on, but he didn't dare touch it. Use of the computer after the time of death would be noticed, and anything he was interested in searching for would likely hint at his identity.

The Browning would have to be disposed of. It was possible Ivan had told Search and Rescue he'd loaned the rifle to Stu. The lake would serve that purpose, somewhere away from Ivan's property. He couldn't take Ivan's car, either, obviously; nothing was easier to trace. Stu kicked a carved wood bear, frustrated.

In the end the only thing he took was a wad of eight one-hundred-dollar bills he found in the bedside table beside several bags of weed. It would spare him using his credit card before he absolutely needed to. Cash, especially drug money, was one thing an investigator wouldn't know was missing unless the owner said so, and Ivan certainly wouldn't be saying so.

Stu hiked three miles before hurling the Browning into the lake, then another three before trying to thumb a ride into town. The hitchhiking was good in Alaska. The first truck stopped, and he rode in the backseat of the extended cab with Blake's deerskin cap pulled down, pretending to sleep so the driver wouldn't chat with him.

At the airport he registered himself at a kiosk under his middle name, Paul. He listed Stuart as his surname. Then he paid in cash. His Massachusetts driver's license contained both names in only a slightly different order, and it got him past security after a short breath-holding moment in front of the guard's podium. He was on the plane almost before his heart rate returned to normal.

Ivan's words haunted him. The dead pilot had said he was "supposed to" abandon Stu in the Alaska interior. Stu analyzed the words from every angle and concluded that, unless Ivan had been hearing imaginary voices—which was a distinct possibility—another person was involved. Thus, it was possible somebody else wanted Stu dead. *Another reason not to reveal myself yet.* He immediately wondered if Clay was in danger too. His partner had also been slated to come on the trip. *Or Katherine.* If someone had it in for him, she might be a target. When he got to Seattle, he'd be brave enough to go online and peek at his e-mail accounts to confirm that the two of them were okay. Until he got out of Fairbanks, however, he wouldn't log on to anything, and the cell phone would remain as dead as he was supposed to be.

Katherine was alive. A moment on a pay-by-the-minute computer terminal at the Seattle airport revealed recent pretentious e-mails between her and her friends—someone was furnishing a beach house. He had only a half an hour, so he didn't linger. She was fine.

He needed to check on Clay, too. Stu plugged in his cell phone, but the account had been discontinued, and so the thing was now little more than an expensive clock. He used the terminal to tap into the law firm's computer system. The front page had been changed. There was a new professional photo of their building and, oddly, a second phone number for a Providence office. It also had a memorial photo of Stu and a short obituary. Exactly as he'd predicted, everyone thought he was dead. He couldn't help reading it.

> *New Bedford resident Stuart Stark recently went missing in Alaska and is presumed to have passed on. He was forty. A good lawyer, Stu devoted his life to serving his clients. He is survived by his wife, Kate. He will be missed.*

That was it. Stu puzzled over it. It was odd to see his life summed up in a paragraph. He thought he'd done more, but it was disturbingly accurate; he'd apparently devoted his life to people who paid him to deal with their problems, and he was survived by a woman who was now called Kate. *Survived* was a bizarre word. It sounded like they'd both been lost in Alaska and only she had made it out. And he never called her Kate. No one did.

Stu took a chance and punched the firm password into the log-in box. The photo of the building disappeared, and document lists came up as the screen morphed from scenic to functional. He was in. Motions were getting filed and billings were being logged. The firm was still up and running, which meant Clay was okay too. That was good. Stu had the urge to call him. Or Katherine. The yearning to tell someone he was alive was strong. *But not smart.* He hadn't analyzed things thoroughly enough yet. There was more investigation to do, and neither Clay nor Katherine was known for discretion; either one might blab to other people as soon as they hung up the phone. But if he saw them in person, Stu thought, he could impress upon them the seriousness of his predicament. Contact with those he loved and trusted was going to have to wait.

Just then a message box popped up.

Who is this?

Someone else was in the system, possibly Clay himself. Stu's common sense told him to get out, but he was typing before he could stop himself; the longing for contact was suddenly overpowering, and he really needed a friend.

Who is THIS?

His message popped up below the first like a visual echo. There was a time lag, during which he regretted answering, and Stu half hoped that the person at the other end would simply shut it down, thinking him an interloper. But then a reply appeared.

This is associate attorney Audra Goodwin.

CHAPTER 34

Katherine directed the men installing the Viking stove, yelping and waving her arms when they began to drag it across the inlaid wood floor. *Idiots!* A coordinating Sub-Zero refrigerator was due on Tuesday. She was satisfied; they were the best she could get without jumping to something exotic. Holly had a Viking and swore by it.

The house had just closed, and she was already starting to furnish the place and sleep in the master suite. She'd been reluctant to close the deal at first, but Clay had encouraged her. When she'd fussed about it, he'd smirked, written her another check for a hundred grand from the firm's account, and told her to shut the hell up.

"We're flush," he said. "Start acting like it."

He was already spending Joe Roff's money—another likely score. The guy hadn't been just bragging when he'd scoffed at Reginald Dugan. Roff could run tens of thousands of dollars through the firm in his first two months as a client, Clay said. The retainer alone would be fifty grand. He'd also purchased all Katherine's remaining prints from Brad Bear's studio at full price before leaving town, which covered a Sub-Zero quite nicely. His patronage, along with the purchase by the still-mysterious Archie Brooks, had prompted Brad to ask for another series. Katherine was thinking of doing something similar to the declining whaling industry theme, maybe shots of decaying textile buildings. A spring jaunt around New England for a few days would be just the thing for her, she thought. Bed-and-breakfasts at night, wine and antiquing at quaint shops by day, all of it bookended by shooting sessions to catch the morning and evening light. Perhaps Clay could sneak away with her. She would ask him when he arrived in half an hour, she decided. It would be about the time the incompetent stove installers were due to leave.

She had the workmen done and shooed out by the time Clay rang the programmable doorbell, and she answered the door in pocketless jeans and a new bodysuit—casual, but sharp, something a woman living on the beach might lounge in on her deck.

He still had his shirt and tie on, though the suit jacket was absent. *No fitted shirt,* she noticed. He'd been putting on a little weight since they'd kicked the firm into high gear. She still had to resist hugging him.

"Enjoying yourself?" he said.

"It's not furnished yet, but the kitchen appliances are being installed, and I bought the model couch in the living room."

"Good memories?"

She grinned. "It's already been broken in."

"Twice," he reminded her with a smirk.

Katherine blinked. She and Clay had only done it once. He could only mean Dugan. "I meant you and me."

"Of course." He gave her a swat on the butt and walked past her. "We should talk business."

"Okay."

"I'm putting together more deals, and things are happening quickly, but we haven't really defined your role going forward."

"My role?"

"Well, you're a partner for purposes of past and pending accounts, but you're not a lawyer."

"Right." Katherine felt a rising panic. She was suddenly certain he was about to tell her that she wasn't part of the firm going forward. Once the Molson money was distributed and the other small cases were wrapped up, he'd have no need for her. Without an income stream, she'd be broke in a million-dollar home.

"We need a new job for you," he said.

Katherine breathed a sigh of relief. "Of course. I'm absolutely willing to work."

"Glad to hear it."

"I'll do whatever it takes. My photographs have been selling."

Clay evaluated her, cocking his head and thinking aloud. "You present as sophisticated and professional. You also know a lot of the locals."

"And I throw marvelous parties."

"Maybe the head of PR. Or personal assistant. I've mentioned the term *client liaison*. Any of those titles strike you?"

"Personal assistant sounds too much like a secretary."

"So I'm guessing no on that one."

"What would the head of PR do?"

"Promote the firm. Make me look good. You always advocated for Stu."

"I can do that."

"Help me find associate attorneys."

"Sure."

"And bring in clients. That's the most important."

"Already proved my worth there, haven't I?"

"Indeed." He paused. "I can't justify a full fifty percent of profits, but I can give you a generous salary or commission. You'll be taken care of."

Katherine didn't like the sound of it, but she put on a happy face. "Do we need a contract?" she said cheerily.

"Don't worry. We can work it out."

"Shall we spit on our hands and shake?"

"Funny. Keep it up. Speaking of clients, Joe is coming to town."

"Yeah. So?"

"We're close to signing him. We should entertain him while he's here."

"Take him to Brandi's. He seems the type."

Brandi's was an underground strip club at the north end of New Bedford in a converted bank building. Both Stu and Clay had prosecuted cases out of the joint—DUIs, assaults, possession of controlled substances. The manager, a tall guy people called Dinky, had been sent away for hiring underage girls to work the bar, and occasionally the customers. He was replaced by a small guy who took his nickname and sold ecstasy and Oxy at the old drive-up teller window through its vacuum-tube-canister delivery system.

"He asked about you," Clay said. "He thinks you're 'classy.'"

"I *am* classy."

"You're also the new head of PR, and we need to PR him."

"What do you suggest?"

"He won't talk business in public. We'll have him here. This beach house is where we'll impress clients away from the office. I can't entertain at my bachelor condo."

"The house isn't furnished yet."

"So put out some folding chairs. Or rent furniture if you have to. Just have it ready. Appetizers and alcohol, too. And I'd like you to have a certain feel about you."

"What kind of feel?"

"I dunno. Professionally alluring. Business sexy."

Katherine gave Clay a hard look. "You'd like that, or *he* would?"

"Look, we agreed that we'd do what we had to do to get where we wanted to be. I'm doing my part. This is your part. It's the job you wanted, right?"

Katherine understood. It was a negotiation. Everything was. Life was. "If I do this, I want you to spend a few days driving around New England with me while I work on my new photo series."

Clay considered her counterproposal. Finally he nodded. "All right. Sure. I would love to spend a few days driving around New England with you."

CHAPTER 35

Audry's follow-up message was curt and professional.

If you are not Clay Buchanan or Kaylee McIntire, you are not an authorized user of this site. I am setting up a trace now.

She was bluffing. There was no trace.

No, you're not, Stu wrote.

The response was immediate, informal, and completely without capitalization: *who is this? clay? don't b an ahole.*

Stu debated. His fingers hung over the keys, then stroked them. *I'm your drinking buddy.* There was virtual silence. He typed again. *Three coats of varnish can protect a floor, but not a lace tablecloth.*

wtf? no . . .

Yes.

i need more.

Stu thought hard. He couldn't say anything that identified him; the messages would be stored if Audry didn't delete them. *You've dated men older than me, the bitchy woman never said happy birthday, and your boss's karma is off.*

omg! nfw!!!!!!!!!!!!

I have no idea what you just said.

god, that does sound like you

It is.

i don't think so, but . . .

Your interview with the firm was less than five minutes.

if this is clay, i'm quitting in less than five minutes.

The gate agent was calling Stu's flight over the intercom and had been for several minutes, he realized. He had to go.

It's easier to prove in person, he typed. *Can you pick me up at Logan to-night? At car rental. Nine o' clock???*

i don't know

I'll just hope then.

no promises

PS very important—tell no one.

The gate agent announced last call for passengers boarding Stu's flight. He had to go. He typed a final message.

I trust you, Audry. I have to.

Then he ran for the gate.

The euphoria of human connection evaporated quickly, and Stu regretted the entire exchange by the time he settled into his seat.

Audry?

Contacting Katherine would have made sense. Clay would have made sense. But Audry? She was a part-time research assistant. He hardly knew her. She was probably on the phone right now with her BFD, Stu thought, or whatever the hell women called their friends.

I'm so weak.

He cursed himself. He'd resolved to remain anonymous until he snuck off the West Coast. And he'd vowed to fully investigate before he revealed himself. That was the plan. Then he'd outed himself to the very first person to ask who he was. *To be fair, she was the third person,* he thought, *if I count the ticket agent and security at the Fairbanks airport.* Regardless, he was spicing himself the same flavor of dumb as every fleeing defendant he'd prosecuted for years. He'd given Audry only dubious reasons to believe him, less reason to pick him up, and no reason to keep his secret. It was maybe the stupidest, most impulsive thing he'd ever done—next to falling through a roof, wading a chest-deep river, or throwing a hatchet at a stoned pilot's ass.

She won't be there, he thought. *But the police might. Or a killer.*

He had not yet puzzled out who besides Ivan might want him dead or where the culprit might be; he hadn't had the chance while sweating his way on and off planes. Hadn't wanted to either. Too awful. Too personal. But things were less immediate now that the crime scenes were in his rear-view mirror. Now he could study the facts and inferences to be derived therefrom. He needed to. He was out of Alaska, the most likely home of his suspect. He would soon be in New England, the only other possibility.

He spent the first hour recalling and reviewing what he knew about Ivan. The guy lived alone, he was a pilot, he ran a crummy little business, he smoked and very likely sold pot, and he had guns. Those were the basics. But he had no way to profit from Stu's death. No animosity. No clear motive. He was not a leader type. He was a better candidate to be a henchman, hireling, or lackey with someone else pulling the strings. Money was the simplest motive, and Ivan *did* have his credit card number, Stu realized. Ivan could have been working for an organized credit card fraud gang in Fairbanks. Such gangs were common and sometimes violent. They collected active card numbers in any way possible and could have run up a tab in the months Stu was gone. Stu considered it. They wouldn't have needed to kill him. *Possible, but not compelling.*

It was also possible Ivan had simply forgotten him. Gotten stoned. Mixed up the days. Something. Perhaps he hadn't come back because he was scared Stu would sue—which was absolutely true. Much more plausible, but didn't explain his cryptic comments: *I was* supposed *to leave you there.*

A flight attendant in a sharp blue vest and short blond hair arrived to offer Stu a pack of nuts in a blue foil pouch. She had a long straight nose and smooth skin, and gave him a polite smile. After a half year living with Blake and scrounging for every morsel, he had two immediate reactions. He wanted to thank her profusely for the food, and he wanted to hug her, acts that were emotionally unrelated. He thanked her, but without the hug, instead giving her his best smile. In return, she gave him a look of distaste, making it clear her smile had been polite *only*. Then he remembered his unruly hair and beard. *Not pretty.* Equally offensive were his ratty jeans stained with rabbit blood, which hung limp and baggy around his thinned waist, and his shirt with yellowed armpits.

She quickly moved on and left him to his unpleasant theories about murderous Alaskan conspirators. More sinister was the thought that someone from his prosecution past had known Stu's plans and had been in cahoots with Ivan. Perhaps a defendant Stu had put away. Unlikely, but the theory was viable. Stu decided to make a list of the more sinister defendants he'd sent away and their approximate release dates. He called back his squeamish attendant and requested a paper and pen. Then he promptly fell asleep.

The descent into Logan woke him. Stu had the bizarre sensation that his entire trip had been a dream, and he had the urge to ask the fat woman spilling into his seat what month it was. But his worn backpack, which was stuffed under the seat as near to him as possible like a security blanket, shattered the illusion.

He had no luggage aside from the pack, which he slid onto his back instinctively before exiting, like a suit of armor. Then he pulled the deerskin cap over his head. *No chance anyone will recognize me,* he thought. *Although my Unabomber look might draw security's attention.*

Stu strode past the car rental desks without giving them a glance. Anyone watching for him would expect him to stop and scan the desks as soon as he saw them. Instead he went directly to an exit and walked outside, where he waited on the sidewalk for five minutes. When he could stand it no longer, he went to another door and reentered, surveying the room from the other direction.

She was there.

Audry.

The middle-aged novice associate attorney stood in front of the Avis counter, checking her phone for messages. She wore tapered jeans tucked into brown leather boots and a billowy navy blouse with a low-cut cowl neck. A russet-colored belt defined her waist. The outfit looked like it had been thrown together, but somehow it was also fashionable—innocuous and pleasant at once.

Stu took a deep breath and stared straight ahead. He walked by without looking at her.

"Parking," he said as he passed without breaking stride.

She didn't look up from her phone and didn't follow him.

Dammit.

He'd have to contact her more directly, Stu thought. But when he reached the door, he saw her glance about and begin walking his direction. She'd pretended not to hear him and delayed following so that no one watching would think she was with him. *Smart,* Stu thought, and he exited.

Stu walked slowly, allowing her to follow, and didn't stop until he was in the parking garage with no direct line of sight from the terminal. He watched for her and spotted a man in a black coat. The man turned down his aisle. *He's following me!* The man pulled out an object, and the beep of a nearby Honda Pilot sent Stu into a crouch, ready to flee. It took a moment for him to realize the object the man held was his key fob. The man climbed in, casting Stu a wary glance of his own, and drove off.

I'm jumpy, Stu thought, but then he'd just killed someone, and someone had tried to do the same to him. Couldn't be too hard on himself for being a bit paranoid.

Audry appeared and, with a deep breath, he presented himself for her inspection. She kept an understandable distance at first.

"Hello, Audry," he said. Hearing his voice would help, he hoped.

She took a few more steps forward, then gasped and hurried to him, mouth agape and eyes wide.

"Oh my God. It *is* you!" She gave him a huge, unexpected hug. It was a firm, clinging embrace, like that of someone who thought they'd lost a dear friend. When she finally let go, she looked him up and down. "Wow. You look great and like shit at the same time."

"Thank you for coming."

"I can't believe this. Holy crap! Pardon me if I freak out a little. What happened? Did you walk out of the wilderness? You must have been snowed in all winter, right?"

"Sort of."

"How come nobody knows? I've been wondering the whole way to Boston. I almost called my BFF, but you seemed so serious about not telling anyone."

"Let's talk in the car."

"Where are we going?"

"Home."

They found her Subaru, a practical blue thing with all-wheel drive and reasonable gas mileage. Stu offered to drive. Audry told him not to be stupid and to get in, which he did without further protest. She shot him a warning look when they came to the gate, and so he knew better than to offer to pay, but he kept track of the cost, knowing that she was buried in student loans, both hers and her daughter's.

"You know that people think you're dead, right?" Audry began.

"Yeah, somebody already filled me in on that."

"Things have happened."

"I figured they would."

"Stu, you've been gone almost six months. Even your wife thinks you didn't make it."

"I have some things to fix. I get that."

"So why aren't you telling anyone?"

"The Yukon Tours pilot left me out there. Until I do some investigating, I don't want anyone to know." He omitted any talk of Ivan or murder plots.

"Deep undercover, eh? Are we going to sue said pilot?"

Stu looked out the window, avoiding her eyes. "I don't think he's worth suing at this point."

She accepted it, and him.

He didn't learn much asking her questions. She knew less about his wife than Stu thought she would. Audry was working more hours for Clay, it turned out, but she still only saw him a couple of times per week, and he didn't discuss Katherine. Nor did Katherine come to the firm often—only a few times. Stu wondered if Clay had bought out Katherine's inherited interest in the firm so that she could move on. She wasn't a lawyer, after all. Audry said the name Stark hadn't been removed from the letterhead yet.

They didn't talk clients. There would be time for that later. And Stu spent the remainder of the trip from Boston to New Bedford being peppered with excited questions and recounting wilderness survival stories. It was relaxing, he found, and sort of fun. Her eyes lit up when he described his encounter with the grizzly.

"Not only did you survive six months in the arctic, but you shot a freakin' grizzly? Man, I should have given you more credit."

"More than what?"

"More than before. You've done some amazing things."

"I did what I had to do. I'm not proud of it all."

"If I shot a bear that was trying to eat me, I'd make it into a rug."

"Or maybe a stupid hat."

"No! Is that a bearskin hat?"

"Deer actually. It's part of my look-like-shit look."

"Oh yeah, I said that. Sorry. You really could use a haircut and a shave though."

"You also said I looked great."

"Yeah, that too."

"What did you mean?"

"Hmmm." She looked him over, recklessly ignoring the road. "You've obviously trimmed down, and you don't look so soft anymore."

"Soft?"

"Desk job. You had soft hands. Now you have calluses, strength, some color in your cheeks. And the way you carry yourself has evolved."

"How's that?"

"I dunno. Alert. Upright. Not slouching around like a dog trying to avoid getting whacked with a newspaper. More like, if I were a bear, I'd think twice before eating you."

CHAPTER 36

When they pulled up to Stu's house at eight p.m., he felt an overwhelming sensation that he didn't belong. Something had changed. About him. About the house. Nothing he could put his finger on. A new planter on the porch? A garden hose off its hook? Maybe his beard.

"You okay?" Audry asked.

"I haven't practiced what I'm going to say to Katherine."

"You don't need practice, you dork. Just hug her and be you."

"All right. I'm going in."

"Will you wave once you're safely settled?"

"Like a grade-school kid?"

"Humor me. I'm a parent."

"Okay, sure."

"Don't get into a long make-out session and forget me." She smiled.

"I won't forget you."

Stu thanked her again and went around to the sliding glass back door. The lights were on upstairs. His keys had been a casualty when he'd abandoned half his gear at the small cabin, but he knew how to lift the sliding door off its track and move it aside.

The living room was dark, and he stumbled into the couch before he decided to switch on the light. He blinked. The furniture had been moved. In fact, it wasn't the same furniture.

"What the hell?"

He felt a presence and looked up. A small boy of perhaps five years stood on the stairs, staring at him. Stu didn't recognize him.

"Who are you?" the boy said.

"I'm Stuart," Stu said stupidly. "I live here. Who are you?"

"I'm Johnny. I live here."

Stu was stumped for a moment. Then the foreign furniture and the presence of the boy came together to make sense.

"Well, this is a funny situation, Johnny. Where is the woman who lived here before you?"

"She went to the beach."

"The beach?" It took him a moment. *Ahh, the beach house from the e-mails.*

Just then a man appeared with a baseball bat—a nice one from the look of it. Stu could almost read the name of the Red Sox player who'd signed it. The man grabbed the boy and shoved him up the stairs.

"What's going on?" a female voice called down.

"Get back upstairs, hon! And call the cops! A transient has wandered into our house!"

The man was scared. Stu could see it. A rabbit. To him, Stu was a predator that had wandered into his hutch. But trapped animals were dangerous, especially when protecting their young. A badger that wasn't quite dead had torn the sleeve of Stu's coat to ribbons a month earlier. He'd had to duct-tape it back together, and was lucky he didn't have to do the same to his arm.

The man advanced, cocking the bat behind his head. He caught a ceramic lamp on the backswing, disintegrating it with a loud *crash*. It was clear the man had no idea who Stu was, and Stu didn't enlighten him. Given that Stu still did not know what the hell was going on, and he was now adding breaking and entering to his criminal résumé, the idea of revealing himself to a complete stranger seemed worse than ever.

"Sorry, wrong house," Stu said. He walked calmly toward the door but didn't turn his back, and he remained ready to bolt. A man in his own house could pound an intruder to pulp with a bat and no jury would ever convict him, even if the intruder were fleeing.

Once outside, Stu ran to the Subaru and slid into the passenger seat. Audry stared at him expectantly.

"Go," he said.

"What happened?"

"New owners. It's probably better if they don't get your license plate."

"Oh. Jeez." She started the car.

Stu buckled in. "They were, however, nice enough to tell me where Katherine is. Do you have Internet access on your phone?"

A quick search for *beach house* in Katherine's e-mail account revealed an address, and he punched it into the phone's GPS.

The drive was short, and soon they were pulling up to another home, only this one was on the South Dartmouth waterfront and had an expensive stamped-concrete driveway. Audry turned off the headlights, and they sat in the darkness of the moonless night.

"She couldn't afford this," Stu said.

But the e-mails clearly said she'd bought the house, and they'd provided the address. Katherine had even gabbed at length about how she was furnishing the place. But it didn't feel right. Stu had never believed in karma, but if he had, he would have said this place felt more wrong than the stranger-occupied home he'd just been chased out of.

Which leaves me nowhere, he realized. And he suddenly felt as homeless as he looked.

Audry waited while he just sat and stared.

"This is the place, right?" she said finally.

"The black Cadillac in the driveway isn't hers. She drives an old Corolla."

"It has a garage. Or maybe she upgraded the car, too."

"I'm just a little gun-shy after the baseball bat incident, okay?"

"Then peek in a window."

"The windows all face the water."

"Go around."

"Trespassing."

"God, don't be such a lawyer." Audry threw off her seat belt and got out of the car.

She was around the corner and headed for the back of the house before Stu could get out of the car.

"Wait up. . . ."

He caught up to her as she was shinnying up the lattice to the deck.

"Are you crazy?" he whispered. "Someone will see you."

Audry whispered back. "The lights are on inside. We can see in, but the glare will keep anyone from seeing out."

Then she was on the deck. Stu rolled his eyes and climbed up after her. When he pulled himself onto his belly on the composite decking, she was frozen in a crouch in front of two all-glass French doors. A single overhead light inside illuminated the sparse bedroom, and Stu followed Audry's gaze like a fellow moth staring into a flame.

Katherine was nude. Spectacularly nude. She stood in the center of the room, her clothes puddled on the floor. Stu's heart leaped into his throat.

"Wow," Audry whispered, "she's in great shape."

Stu had the sudden urge to pound on the glass, to go to her, to take her in his arms and have her right then. Probably on the floor. But something stopped him—the same feeling of not-rightness he'd felt in the driveway.

In his moment of hesitation, the door to the bedroom opened and Clay walked in.

He was dressed. Well dressed. Tie and slacks with expensive leather shoes. He smiled, and Katherine returned his smile with a nod. She didn't hide her naked body.

Audry laid a hand on Stu's shoulder. "Oh God, Stu, I'm so sorry. I didn't know."

Stu steeled himself for their embrace. But Clay didn't take Katherine in his arms or begin to undress himself. Instead he simply inspected her. She allowed it, turning to present her body from several angles. Then Clay was directing her. After the brief examination, he gave her a firm swat on the rump and pointed to the bed. Katherine didn't protest. Instead she walked to it, leaned over, and put her hands on the mattress. It was carnal, animal—arousing, even. Again, Stu felt the urge to get in there and claim her. But he had to process things first.

Audry tugged on Stu's sleeve. "Stu, let's go. You don't want to see this."

Stu shook her off. "It's okay. She thinks I'm dead. She's lonely. I get it."

I can deal with this, Stu told himself. He'd spent six months eating rabbit and drinking boiled water. *I killed a freakin' bear.* He could handle this, he thought. He even felt the familiar old instinct to forgive. *Once I get things sorted out, it's all going to be okay.*

Then another man walked into the room. *What the hell?*

He was about sixty and wore a thin robe. No shoes. No socks. No pants. He looked at Clay, who nodded toward Katherine.

Stu recognized him at once. Joseph Roff. The police called him Big Fish, because he ran a crew in New Bedford and had a penchant for fishing. He'd never been prosecuted in Bristol County, but he routinely posted bail for several local frequent fliers—smugglers, small-scale loan sharks, Oxy peddlers, and the like—his crew, his "school of small fry." Roff managed his interests through intermediaries and lived in Providence, which put him beyond the reach of the county. New Bedford cops didn't have the resources to launch an extended investigation into organized crime that would require a multijurisdictional sting. And Roff's little fish lurked below the level of offenses that the Feds cared about. So no federal prosecution either.

Clay took a seat in Stu's favorite recliner and made no move to stop Roff from walking to where Katherine stood bent over the bed without a stitch of clothing on. Stu knew that whatever Joseph Roff had his fingers into was dirty and, as he watched, the known criminal slid them right between the cheeks of his wife's fabulous ass.

CHAPTER 37

"No flipping way! Shut! Up! Are you kidding me?" Audry was animated. She ran through a series of almost-swear-words, occasionally repeating herself. And the way she was flailing with her arms, Stu worried about her driving.

"We need to calm down," he said.

Audry took a deep breath. "You mean *I* need to calm down, right? Look at you. You're analyzing this, thinking it all through, like you do. Amazing. You should be more freaked out than I am."

Stu put his hand on the wheel and eased her back into the proper lane of travel. "I don't think that's possible, but believe me, I'm plenty surprised and perplexed."

"Perplexed? I'd think you'd be insanely jealous and furious. I don't get it; the average man would have gone nuts trying to stop that."

Stu frowned. He'd considered stopping it. In fact, he'd felt like throwing a deck chair through the window. But if someone was trying to kill him, and if that someone was tied to a man like Roff, revealing himself might have put Katherine and Clay in immediate danger.

Whereas getting screwed isn't inherently dangerous.

"I had a good reason." It sounded lame. Audry was questioning his masculinity. What kind of man didn't stop another man from doing his wife? His fiery associate probably thought he was the same pussy he'd been when he'd left. *And maybe I am.* He couldn't let it lie. "I haven't told you everything," Stu said. "This isn't the most shocking thing that's happened in the last twenty-four hours."

"Really? Wow!"

"But it could be related."

"This I gotta hear."

"No. It's time to cut you out. It's obviously dangerous, and it was selfish of me to involve you in the first place. I was . . . lonely."

"Bullshit. Tell me. You can't stay at my place unless you let me in on what's going on."

Stu hesitated. "I wasn't expecting to stay with you."

"Where else can you go?"

"Motel?"

"Noble but stupid. I have a guest room. But you have to tell me what's going on."

Stu had ideas. Theories. He realized that he wanted to talk them through. He *needed* to talk them through with someone else before he could believe them. Otherwise, they felt like invalidated little puffs of crazy drifting through his brain.

"I killed a man," he said suddenly, throwing himself off the confession cliff, knowing that telling her about Ivan's death forced him to tell her everything.

"You said it was a bear."

"I did that, too."

Audry gave him a sideways glance. "Should I be calling the police?"

"Probably."

"Great."

"He tried to kill me first. Don't worry. I'm not a danger to anyone."

But he was a danger. He could feel the capacity for mortal combat in him. It was like a new superpower—he could kill. He'd killed things all winter long. *Only to survive,* Stu told himself.

"Now I definitely have to hear the rest."

"You're not scared?"

"This is maybe the most intense thing I've ever gotten sucked into. Hell yes, I'm scared! But I wouldn't miss this for the world." She was sweating, but she was also smiling. "So tell me, who did you kill?"

Audry's apartment was spotless. Stu was a bit surprised, given how busy she was. He'd thought dishes would be stacked in the sink, the kitchen table piled with mail, grocery coupons, and bar review materials, maybe a yoga mat in front of a big-screen TV, unboxed workout DVDs, and an unreturned romantic comedy rental scattered about. He'd thought wrong.

She offered him a seat on her stylish but inexpensive-looking couch, then grabbed a computer tablet.

"Okay, where do we start our analysis?"

"I think I'm most comfortable treating this like a case. Then again, the man who acts as his own attorney has a fool for a client."

"What does that even mean?"

"It means it's hard to be objective when the case is about yourself."

"Then I'll be your attorney."

"You have one year of experience. No offense."

"Zero years as an actual attorney, if you're going to get technical on me. And you're wasting time. What do we know?" She fired up the tablet, fingers tapping like frenetic raindrops on the touch screen. "I'll make a list of facts and theories."

"Well, for starters we know Ivan tried to kill me. No doubt. Pointed the gun at me and pulled the trigger. He ran when it didn't fire."

"Then you hit him with the ax?"

"Hatchet."

"Jeez," she mumbled under her breath. "What did he say, exactly?"

"He apologized. And he said I should be dead."

"Doesn't mean he planned it. He could have meant he *assumed* you were dead, and he panicked when you appeared, because he'd blown the pickup and knew he was in serious trouble. Plus, you said he seemed high."

"Agreed. But when I said things had worked out because I was alive, he disagreed with me. He said things *hadn't* worked out."

"As though leaving you was a plan that failed."

"Right."

"Better, but still not conclusive."

"He also said, 'Sorry, dude, I don't even know you.'"

"He actually said *dude* before he tried to shoot you?"

"Yeah."

"What a tool. Go on."

"The fact that he didn't know me or steal anything from me means he had no personal motive."

"Promising. . . ."

"He seemed surprised that there was a cabin. And here's the really creepy part: he said, 'I was *supposed* to leave you there.'"

"Those were his words?"

"Verbatim."

"You're sure? You've been through a lot here."

"I'm sure. In fact, I'll never forget them."

She tapped, then stared at what she wrote, thinking. "Somebody put him up to it. There's no other reasonable interpretation."

"That's what I think."

"I think it too." She started a new paragraph. "Okay, what next?"

Stu took a deep breath, but he couldn't say it, so Audry did.

"The, um, gangster in your wife's bedroom is a bit of a red flag."

"True. You can write down that a known criminal is blackmailing Katherine and my partner."

Audry typed, then cocked her head. "Or not."

"What do you mean?"

Audry gave him a sympathetic look. "I mean that we should consider all possible explanations."

"That *is* the possible explanation." Stu frowned. He didn't like where Audry was going.

"It's just that . . . they didn't *look* blackmailed."

"Yeah? And how would you describe the blackmailed look?"

"I dunno. Not-okay-with-it, maybe?"

"You think my wife looked okay with . . . with that?"

"Hey, it's just an observation. Woman's perspective, maybe. Just a feeling I got."

"I don't do karma, remember?"

"Got it. But, for what it's worth . . ."

"It's worth very little."

"Fair enough. I'm typing *worth very little* next to it in our notes."

"Look, if I hadn't feared for Katherine's safety, I would have gone right in there."

"I'm sure you would have."

"He could have had a gun."

"Can't imagine where he'd have hidden it."

Stu stood. "I need a long hot shower. Where's the bathroom?"

The shower had a frilly white curtain and was littered with seven bottles of different types of shampoo, conditioner, and body wash, most of them pink and half full. The bar of soap was the size and shape of a potato chip. He used green-tea-scented liquid soap on his body and chose nourishing coconut milk shampoo that promised to "volumize" his hair. The first time he rinsed, the water was brown. He shampooed four times with different products before it ran clear. There was a razor, also pink.

Stu emerged forty minutes later wrapped in a towel with a rough goatee and his long hair swept back with sculpting cream to keep it out of his eyes. He looked vaguely like a middle-aged surfer.

Audry put down her tablet. "Wow. Look at you." And she did look, shamelessly.

"Have you got any clothes that would fit me that aren't pink?"

"I think so. Want me to burn those?"

She sent him back into the bathroom with a UConn T-shirt and purple sweatpants that said SASSY across the butt. Audry giggled when he walked out, but assured him that he looked lovely.

They argued about calling the police, then switched sides and argued again to be sure they hadn't missed anything. In the end Audry reluctantly agreed that Stu's biggest advantage was that he didn't exist. He could investigate with impunity as long as he was a ghost. As soon as the police stepped in, any suspects would scatter or circle the wagons. But Audry made Stu promise that he would turn things over to them as soon as possible.

"In the meantime you should sleep," she said. "You look exhausted." She opened the door to her daughter's smallish former bedroom, which was home to a fluffy cat named Sasha. The room was as ridiculously tidy as the front room and, again, pink. The single bed was tiny—and the most comfortable-looking sleeping accommodations Stu had ever seen.

"Rest up," Audry said, laying a hand on his shoulder. "Tomorrow we go to work."

CHAPTER 38

Katherine lounged on the brass bed, a heavy four-poster that sat solidly on the slightly tilted wide-plank floor of the historic Willimantic Inn's uppermost room. The huge 1700s house had also been a tavern in its heyday, and then a home for unwed girls during the downturn of the textile industry. A Kennedy had once slept in the very bed upon which she was stretched out like a yawning cat. Rich in history, the inn sat on ten acres of land in southwestern Windham County with easy access to Thread City, as historic Willimantic had been known when the American Thread Company, ATC, had been located there. ATC had been one of the largest producers of thread in the world at the time and the first factory ever to use electric lighting. There were still mill buildings on the river, which Katherine had spent hours shooting the evening before. Afterward she'd gone for a run, then purchased an armoire, which the Afterlife Antiques dealer promised he'd rush ship to New Bedford so that she'd have it waiting for her when she got home.

Home.

The beach house was beginning to feel less empty, and she thought she'd be ready to tackle it again after her little vacation. Moving had been a difficult and trying experience. She'd labeled more than one hundred boxes, and the movers she'd hired had failed to show up. She'd had to completely rearrange her schedule and call another company. She'd left the old appliances at the William Street house and gotten rid of most of the old furnishings, and she'd had to spend weeks shopping for new furniture. It was hard work, and when she was done, it would take another week of decorating and styling before she could throw a party to show the place off.

The photo trip had been a brilliant idea. She hadn't realized how exhausted she was from managing the move and buying things—and from the residual stress of her husband's disappearance, of course. It was the best vacation she'd had in a long time. It helped that Clay was in a good mood.

He sat at the room's antique desk in his underwear. Katherine noticed that the bikini style was starting to look a bit small on him; the flesh of his belly was creeping over the waistband. They'd eaten well at some fabulous restaurants over the last few months. And he'd been too busy at the office to work out, he'd said. Whatever the case, it looked like it was time for him to make the jump from bikinis to briefs or boxers.

"I'd like Margery to cater our housewarming party," Katherine said.

"Sounds great. I'll invite our star clients."

"I'd hoped our personal gatherings wouldn't always have to include the big two. Maybe some new blood? The chair of the arts commission, maybe. Or the operations manager at Acushnet—his sister went to UMass with me."

"You need to keep in mind who's buttering your biscuit, darlin'."

"I'm quite aware of that."

"Good. Then it's settled." He smiled. When she pouted, he walked to the bed and took her head in his hands. "Look, you're a social dynamo, but you need me to harness that energy, to point it toward the real money. Would you like some live music at your party?"

"Ooh, that sounds fabulous. A string quartet. Music students from UMass play for an hourly rate. And I'll invite the department chair. That's perfect."

"See. You're a networking genius. And maybe he'd like to stay for the private after-party."

"Puh-leez, he's seventy."

"Then he'll be even more grateful."

"You're wicked." She playfully swung a pillow, which he caught and wrenched out of her hand. "But you're not serious, are you?"

Clay held her by the wrist, smirking. "No. We can't get his business. The university already has lawyers." He gave her a firm buffet in the head with the pillow, then threw it on the nearby love seat and sat down beside her. "Besides, we're doing fine. It's funny, I'd almost lost hope that life could be this good. Guess it took a tragedy to make me realize it. He was a good guy, Stu. But you have to admit, he was holding us back. Both of us."

Katherine nodded, but frowned. "I don't want to think about that right now. He's in the past. Have you thought about our future?"

"Of course. Our next step is to buy the Bluestone Building."

Katherine smiled, but it wasn't what she meant. "Together?"

"As partners. A couple hundred down and we can split the mortgage. Fifty-fifty or seventy-five–twenty-five—whatever you're comfortable with. We'll write off the interest. Imagine: no rent. It'll be heaven."

"I'd rather have a summer place. All my friends have second homes."

"You just got a house on the water."

"But an apartment in the city would be exquisite. Manhattan, or even Boston."

"Someday. Let's stop paying rent first."

"Do we have a couple hundred?"

"We have a banker named Joe to front us the cash, and a financier named Molson who is going to pay it all off in about a month."

"And what about *our* future?" Katherine ran a hand over his thigh so that there could be no mistaking her meaning this time.

A look of annoyance flashed across Clay's face, a dark shadow that came and went as though the sun had briefly ducked behind a cloud. He swatted her rump. "You just enjoy the trip, partner, and I promise life will keep getting more interesting."

CHAPTER 39

"Here's a list of follow-up I've done so far this morning," Audry said.

Stu looked up with his mouth full of Cheerios. She sat across from him with her computer tablet. She'd been up for hours, researching, and had let him sleep until ten. She turned the tablet toward him. Her list was a page long. It was Internet research on Roff.

Joseph Roff was sixty-three years old. His name had originally been Koph, but he'd changed it—Audry noted the reason as "unknown." He had four sons, a daughter, and a deceased wife. A state business license showed that he lived in Providence, but he owned properties in New Bedford through a limited liability corporation called New England Imports, of which he was president and sole board member. Audry's list indicated that NE Imports showed up in searches for Bolt Construction three times and twice with Reggie Dugan. *Interesting.* Roff had also acquired an interest in a bankrupt Thai restaurant in New Bedford called the Poor Siamese, which was odd. The man had made the news only twice, but once it was in connection with an embezzler named Hranic, with whom Stu was familiar. In the article, it noted that Hranic had previously worked for NE Imports.

Stu skimmed the rest of Audry's list and raised an eyebrow. At the bottom was the name Sophia Baron.

He pointed. "Sophia Baron? What's this about?"

"You mentioned that Clay had dated a woman who whacked out and quit law school. I found her."

"I doubt I used the term *whacked out*, and I didn't know we were looking for her."

"You said to cast a broad net. Those were your words."

"I meant cast it at Roff. The criminal."

"We don't know who the criminal is. Besides, I have this nagging thing."

"Thing?"

"A feeling."

Stu rolled his eyes. Audry acted on feelings more than he was comfortable with. But he was curious about Sophia. She was, after all, the most beautiful classmate he'd ever had. "Fine. You have an e-mail or phone number for her?"

"Better. She's in Manhattan right now."

"That's four hours away. We can't waste that much time just to talk to one of Clay's ex-girlfriends about . . . What are we even talking to her about?"

"She'll meet us halfway."

"You already contacted her?"

"That's why I'm wasting your time."

"Why? What did you tell her?"

"That I'm investigating a matter involving Clay Buchanan. And she was very eager to help."

They met Sophia Baron in New Haven at the local park. There was a gazebo with a table. Audry brought a cappuccino for her. She was waiting on the bench and accepted the coffee gratefully, sipping while hiding behind the Grande-size cup. Stu marveled again at how beautiful she was, a woman approaching forty with grace and elegance, her only noticeable imperfections being troubled frown lines and the repeated tucking of her hair behind her ear, even when it was already tucked.

"Hello, Stu," Sophia said quietly. "Your partner said you'd be here. Thank you for coming."

"Of course," Stu said, confused. He took her hand to shake it. "You remember me?"

"Oh yes. Everyone always said you were a nice guy, and people's hearts don't change, not deep down." She shook her head. "I should have dated someone like you."

Stu could feel her discomfort and need to talk. He gently placed his other hand on top of hers and patted it, something he would never have had the courage to do in law school. To his surprise, she smiled gratefully and added her other hand so that their four hands formed a mutually reassuring pile on the table between them.

Audry kept the discussion moving. "Sophia didn't want to go into detail with a stranger over the phone."

"This is extremely personal," Sophia said.

Stu nodded. "We appreciate whatever help you're willing to give us." He was still unsure what sort of help she *could* give them.

"Audry promised that what I tell you won't end up in a lawsuit. I won't testify."

"Correct," Audry assured her. "We're just gathering background on Clayton Buchanan. Any prior character evidence we uncover wouldn't be admissible in any event."

"Character evidence?" Stu said.

"He did something bad, didn't he?" Sophia's comment was more statement than question.

"We don't know," Stu said.

Sophia tucked her hair. "I know."

"Go ahead, Sophia," Audry urged.

Sophia took a deep breath. She looked across the grass—not at Stu, not at Audry, but at some point in the distance.

"We met when he arrived at law school. He seemed confident. I was too, I thought. A good match. A power couple, you know. He was good-looking. I was modeling. Both future lawyers. We did the normal stuff at first; we met up for coffee with mutual friends, tried to run into each other at the same parties. He didn't seem to need to study like I did, and so I assumed he was brilliant."

No, Stu thought. *Just allergic to work.*

"When we began to hang out alone, I was ready to take it further, but he waited a while, which surprised me. Then one night he started asking me about other boyfriends I'd had and what sort of things I'd done with them. Sexual things. It was playful, and he told me it didn't bother him. In fact, he wanted to hear, so I told him about something I'd done with my college boyfriend. A thing in the library. Clay got really excited, and we did it for the first time. I didn't think much of it. It was a little naughty, and I just thought he was open-minded, not jealous. Those are good things, right?

"But every time after that he wanted to know more about what I'd done and with who. And how. And where. Whenever we had sex, he'd ask me to talk about guys I'd been with. When I'd tell him, he'd encourage me to say how much I liked doing it with other men. After a while I'd described every sex act with everyone I'd ever dated. I even started to make some up; it was what got him going. That was our routine.

"Then one day he asked if he could tie me up. I was actually relieved to do something besides talk about other men, and the first time we did, it was actually kind of fun. He just tied my hands and used a blindfold. Normal stuff."

Normal? Stu fought to keep his expression neutral, but having Sophia Baron explain to him that she liked having sex blindfolded was not in any way normal for him. In fact, it was an unreachable fantasy. And she trusted him, which made Stu feel guilty just hearing it, like a dirty little boy peeking at his beautiful babysitter after promising to turn his back while she changed into her swimsuit. Telling the story was uncomfortable for her, he thought, and it wasn't fair for him to imagine it out of prurient curiosity. He tried to will himself clinical as she spoke.

"It became a thing," she continued, her purging creating its own momentum now. "He called our bondage sessions 'private parties.' He'd blindfold me, gag my mouth, then tie me to the bed on my stomach and put headphones on me. He made sure I was comfortable, and he played my favorite songs. I actually thought it was kind of sweet. Then there was the sex, usually after drinking. One night we did it four or five times, or so I thought."

"What do you mean by you *thought*?" Audry said gently.

"The blindfold slipped. I could see a sliver of the room, and there was Clay, my supposed boyfriend, sitting in a chair next to the bed."

Stu waited for her to go on.

"He was fully clothed," she added.

"And what happened?" Stu asked.

"He wasn't behind me," Sophia said.

"I don't understand."

". . . someone else was," Audry finished for her.

"Several someones, I think," Sophia said.

"Oh," Stu whispered, sucking in a breath, "my God."

Sophia tucked her hair again and blinked away a tear. "The crazy thing is, I would have been willing to try things for him if he'd asked, if he'd loved me."

"Really?" Stu said, unable to stop the curious boy in himself.

"It's true," Audry cut in. "We girls will do all kinds of kinky stuff if we trust a guy one hundred percent."

"I still don't even know who the other men were," Sophia said. "Except one—this fat jerk who hung around Clay and wrote his Con Law term paper for him."

Stu immediately knew who she was talking about. Tom Franken. A classmate. Loudmouth. Drinker. Smart, and ready to let you know it. But Stu was surprised Tom would help Clay cheat.

"Whenever this guy was around me that semester, he made crude puns about sex. I had no idea what he meant until the night I discovered that our 'private parties' had *not* been private. Then I understood why he'd written Clay's paper for him."

"Clay pimped you out," Audry concluded.

Stu grimaced. "Did you report him?"

"I couldn't." Sophia tucked her hair yet again. "I had orgasms."

"I'm sorry, what?"

"At the time, I thought I was having sex with Clay, my boyfriend. You understand? My body reacted to what those men did to me; he secretly took videos of them giving me orgasms. Before that, he had recorded me talking about how much I liked having sex with other men. How could I convince the police it wasn't consensual if Clay had those to show them?"

Stu shook his head. "Jeezus. He preemptively created his own exculpatory evidence."

"I quit school. I couldn't walk down the hall without wondering who—"

"I understand," Stu said. He wanted to comfort her, to reach out and hold her hand again, but she was busy tucking her hair with it.

"I gave up a career as an attorney."

"You're in New York?"

"Yes. I'm on my feet now. Good job. But relationships have been tough."

"Not married?"

"I've had some trust issues with men."

"Right."

"You don't have to say any more," Audry offered. "I think we have what we need."

"Okay," Sophia said. "Thank you for listening. I've never told anyone." She sat silent for a moment, visibly decompressing, then she gave a weak smile. "I saw you on *America's Unsolved*, you know. I told my roommate, 'Hey, I know that guy.'"

Stu nodded. "You've trusted me with something deeply personal, Sophia. Now I have to trust you."

"All right."

"I sort of went off the grid since that TV stuff happened."

"You got fired. I know. I'm sorry. I shouldn't have brought it up. I'm so stupid. . . ."

"No, no. You're fine. Everyone heard about that. But this meeting is a secret. In fact, *I'm* a secret. I'm in hiding."

"And you're investigating Clay?"

"Right."

"Did he threaten to kill you, too?"

CHAPTER 40

"Threatening to kill is only one step removed from attempting to kill," Audry said from her couch.

Stu spoke over his shoulder as he punished stir-fry with an angry spatula. "Clay never threatened me. Can we be absolutely sure Sophia is credible? She does seem a bit messed up."

"As you would expect. But she has a good soul. I could feel it. Besides, she was one hundred percent right about Clay's sexual fetish. It's exactly what we saw him do last night. He's a watcher."

"What is that supposed to mean? He's some sort of voyeur?"

"No, a watcher. He gets off on watching other men take his woman."

"You think he tried to have me killed so he could watch Katherine have sex with someone besides himself? He could have just put a friggin' ladder up to our bedroom window."

"Lust and jealousy are traditional and powerful motives for homicide, aren't they, Mr. Prosecutor?"

"Conceded. But he's obviously not an overly jealous person if he wants to see other men with his women."

"Au contraire. The jealousy is what makes the fetish so compelling. It drives the watcher's urge to take the woman himself, to win her back, to mark his territory. It's competition at the most base level. He probably had to have Sophia talk about other men to get it up."

"And now he's dragged Katherine into it."

"Unless she's just . . . into it."

"Thanks for that thought."

"I'm just sayin'."

"You talk like a teenager, you know that?"

"Because I have a teenager."

"And how do you know all this fetish stuff anyway?"

"Internet porn."

"Oh."

Stu sprinkled a few forgotten seasonings that he'd discovered in the back of Audry's cupboard across the frying pan, and he flipped the pan's contents in the air a couple of times.

"Thanks for cooking dinner, by the way," Audry said. "I'm starving."

"I'm not surprised, judging from your fridge and cupboards."

"I'm not much of a cook. My daughter, Molly, was queen of the kitchen by the time she was fifteen. I brought home a lot of weekday salad-'n'-pizza deals from Gino's, like a typical law student, only a decade older. But look at you. You're spoiling me."

"I don't mind. I've always found it fun to cook for someone else."

Audry cocked her head. "I'm curious, Stu. Why don't you have kids?"

"Where did that come from?"

"It just surprises me. You seem the type. Nice. Responsible. Ten times the dad material of most men. You seem like a waste of a perfectly good father figure."

"We just decided we didn't want them."

"Whose idea was that?"

"Ours. We discussed it."

"Yeah, but one partner is always more anti-kid than the other."

"She wasn't anti-kid. She just wasn't, I dunno, pro-kid."

"So it was her, and you lost the debate."

"Nobody lost. We compromised. We had a dog for a while."

"But kids are everything. They're the reason we're all here and the only real path to immortality; part of you goes on. You don't get that with a dog."

"You have a cat, I'd point out."

"I'm in withdrawal. Sasha's a substitute kid, like methadone. When she goes, I'll move down to a fish. Or relapse."

"You mean have another baby?"

"At thirtysomething? It could happen."

"You'll need a man."

"Nah. Just sperm. And you can get that just about anywhere."

Stu wasn't sure exactly where to take the subject from there, so he changed it. "What else can you find out about Roff? That guy's a *real* criminal."

Audry screwed up her eyebrows, thinking. "He's also a prospective client, although I'm guessing he's on board at this point and we should have a new file on him. So at the office I'll be in a position to ask all the business-related questions about him I like."

"I can't ask you to feed me information about a client who didn't hire me. You could be disciplined by the bar."

"I can't get disbarred for learning information myself. I'll only tell you things if they're matters of grave importance."

"Funny," Stu said. "I don't want Clay noticing you poking around, either."

"He's gone for three days. Got a text this morning. And he's had me working a lot more lately. I go in after hours all the time." Audry gave him a smile. "It's sweet of you to worry, but I'm a grown-up."

"You're wearing penguin pajamas with slipper feet."

"With a guest here I can't very well walk around in just a T-shirt and panties like I usually do, now can I?"

Stu's heart skipped a beat, and he returned his attention to the stir-fry. "I still don't believe Clay would try to kill me. He was a prosecutor. I've known him since law school."

"You *didn't* know him in law school, remember? And he's the one who sent you to Alaska."

"But he would have been there too if it hadn't been for the meeting Dugan called at the last minute." Stu stopped stirring suddenly and turned to Audry. "Oh shit. It was Dugan's cabin I was supposed to go to."

"And the pot pilot dropped you somewhere else?"

"Yep."

"Did Dugan know the pilot?"

"Probably. My driver knew who Dugan was. We'll need to check into it."

"If Dugan is our bad guy, that could mean Clay is just your pervy partner having weird sex with your wife."

"Lovely."

"That's a step up from a friend trying to kill you."

"Actually, I might be able to live with weird sex at this point. They both think I'm dead, after all."

"Okay, then, let's talk about Reginald Dugan."

Audry threw a sweatshirt over her pajamas to drive them to the office. At nine thirty p.m. no one would be there, and she had a key card to get in. Stu wore pants and a shirt she'd bought him at a men's store with cash on the way to meet Sophia. He kept track of the money Audry spent so he could pay her back, adding it to the parking fee at Logan, gas to and from Boston, a box of Cheerios, and milk. The flat-front jeans, fitted button-down with rolled-up sleeves, and brown deck shoes she'd picked out for him were a far cry from the billowy work shirts and boxy slacks he'd worn the last time he'd walked into the Bluestone Building.

At least the gaudy sign still has my name on it.

Audry led him into the lobby, where he turned circles, marveling at the polished marble and Katherine's framed prints on the walls.

"Wow."

"Wait until you see the office."

"How did Clay pay for the firm's share of this? I know damn well that cheapskate Sitzman didn't fund all this renovation."

"Molson."

"Molson couldn't cover this and a house on the water."

"It covered a lot. It's three million in fees."

Stu stopped in his tracks. "No, it's not."

"Yes, it is." She cocked an eyebrow, daring him to disagree.

He stood and thought for a time. A long time. Bad thoughts. "Maybe that explains some things. But I'm surprised that much money has come through so quickly."

"It hasn't. They're borrowing against the anticipated settlement."

"Banks don't loan on settlements."

"I don't think they're using a traditional bank."

"Can you get me into the financials?"

"No."

"Sorry I asked. That's not fair."

"I meant that I can only log you in to the system. I don't have access to the books. But you might. You're still a partner. You're not even legally dead yet. That can take seven years. If the passwords haven't been changed . . ."

Audry logged in. Stu tried to access the financial records. He was in luck; the passwords were the same.

Why change them for a dead man? he thought. *Especially if you're lazy and sloppy.*

He confirmed the Molson terms. One-third contingent fee. Three million, just as Audry had said. Then he spent two hours reading the financials for Dugan and Roff. He wasn't sure what he was seeing at first, but money was coming in and going out at an alarming rate in Dugan's account. Hours were being billed to case names, but there were no case files yet to match. A portion of that money was then being pumped back into Dugan's client trust account. Roff's was set up the same way, with an initial deposit of fifty grand as a retainer, but no corresponding legal work.

"Jeezus."

"Good stuff?"

"Bad stuff. I'm just not sure what it all means yet."

Stu took a break to dig through Clay's desk for additional records. Some lawyers still kept hard copies that left no electronic trace. Instead he found the nearly empty bottle of Booker's bourbon and a .357 Magnum.

"Hello. . . ."

Audry leaned over the desk, curious. "What?"

Stu held up the pistol for her to see. It was a short-barreled gun with a long curved hammer that jutted from the back like a thumb hitching a ride, and it was so heavy he couldn't tell if it was loaded without holding it at an awkward angle and peering into the cylinder.

"Holy crap!" Audry yelped.

"His new clients must make him nervous. Does he carry this when he meets with them?"

"I have no idea." She stared at the pistol, eyes wide. "We're not taking that with us, are we?"

Stu inspected it, thinking. It was indeed fully loaded. "No," he said finally.

"Whew! Well, that certainly got my blood pumping." Audry let out a nervous chuckle. "We should head home and go to bed. We can play detective again in the morning."

She was right, Stu decided. She was usually right, despite her odd reliance on feelings and karma or, perhaps, because of it. He needed a break from thinking in order to relax or vent or laugh, to simply let go somehow.

"Okay. You got a beer at your place, drinking buddy?"

The drive to Audry's place was short; she lived near the office. Stu changed into the SASSY purple sweatpants Audry had given him to sleep in and ducked into the bathroom to brush his teeth.

"Your turn!" he called through Audry's closed bedroom door when he was finished.

Then Audry's door opened, and she walked out.

Stu stared. He didn't mean to, but couldn't help himself. The pajamas were gone. Her white T-shirt was snug, but it was also long and fell to the top of her thighs. Two completely bare thirtysomething legs stuck out from beneath it. She had delicate feet, Stu noticed. No bra. Obviously no bra. No glasses, either. And she was staring back at him. *Perhaps because she's having trouble seeing?* Stu told himself.

"What's up?" he said stupidly.

"This has been exciting, Stu. And dangerous, like you said."

"You okay?"

"I'm a big girl." She walked past him to a low cupboard and bent to rummage inside. Her shirt pulled up. Panties. Thong. Stu politely looked away.

She returned with a can of beer. Just one. She opened it and took a sip, then handed it to him. He drank. It was cheap, warm, and tasted fantastic. He handed it back.

"You know," Audry said, "after people share a dangerous experience, they are much more inclined to want to fool around. There are studies on this, including one that showed a significantly increased likelihood of action between new couples after they'd crossed a rope bridge over a chasm together."

Stu felt himself stirring in her loaner sweatpants, but there was no way to adjust them without drawing attention to it. She was close, maddeningly close, and he had to fight his own instincts. "I don't want to take advantage of your hospitality."

"I told you, Stu, I'm a big girl. I invited you to my place, and now I'm standing here in my underwear. Who's taking advantage?"

She sipped from the can, then stepped to him and kissed him, letting the beer pour out through her lips and into his mouth. He drank in both, the kiss and the cheap beer. They swirled together and tasted like youth. Audry grabbed the tie on his sweatpants and led him down the darkened hall.

Audry's bedroom was her living room's evil alter ego. Laundry was stacked on the bed, bar review materials were piled haphazardly on a desk, and all of the boxes, exercise gear, and pairs of shoes that might have otherwise cluttered the common areas of the apartment were stacked in the open closet, which could not be shut because its contents were spilling out like a rockslide.

Audry swept the laundry from the bed, pulled off her shirt, and wriggled out of her panties, all with a beer in one hand. She drained it, tossed it toward a wicker garbage can, then fell back on the bed and pulled Stu down on top of her.

He wondered if he'd know what to do. He'd had the same routine for a decade. It had proved reliable, though, and so he kissed her on the mouth while he used his fingers down below. To his great relief, it worked. Audry arrived quickly. Very quickly. Shaking the bed. Then she exhaled heavily, like a balloon letting out all of its air.

"Whew! Sorry, I've been thinking about this since last night." She didn't wait for a reply, but simply reached down to undress him.

He was definitely ready. Stu laid his cheek against hers and nuzzled her neck as he entered her and began to gently rock his hips back and forth. He finished as quickly as she had.

"Thank you," he whispered in her ear.

"You're done?"

"Sorry, I haven't touched a woman in six months," he said sheepishly. "Longer than that, frankly."

Audry rolled out from under him and propped herself up on her elbows, smiling, as comfortable nude as she had been in slipper pajamas.

"That's right! You've been fasting." She cocked an eyebrow. "So did you take care of it yourself out there in the wilderness?"

"There wasn't really enough privacy for that."

"Wow. You must be seriously pent up."

"Given my abbreviated performance just now, apparently so."

"And so very polite for a guy who has such an obvious and pressing issue."

"What do you mean by pressing issue?"

She pointed. "You're already ready to go again."

Stu glanced down at himself. He was. Audry was still talking. He was unaccustomed to chatter in bed. He'd always thought it would be distracting. It wasn't. It was interesting and, coming from Audry, oddly endearing.

"I think I know what you need after six months in the wild," she said.

"Yeah? What do I need?"

"What every red-blooded male needs once in a while."

She flicked on the bedside lamp and rose to her hands and knees. He couldn't politely avert his eyes this time; she put her bare hindquarters on display, and the sudden light illuminated everything.

Stu stared, mesmerized. *Definitely not routine.*

She began to wave her hips back and forth. "Go ahead, it's natural, it's . . ."

Instinct.

Audry looked back over her shoulder at him. "Come on, Stu, man up."

CHAPTER 41

Stu awoke to find Audry inches away, already wide-eyed and smiling at him through her glasses. She mussed his hair playfully, and then crinkled her brow.

"Apologies for being so intimate so suddenly. I know you've only had one serious relationship, but I've dated quite a bit over the years."

Stu's first impulse was, surprisingly, jealousy; he wanted to be the only male who mated with her. He fought it down. "You mean I'm not your first?" he joked instead.

She laughed. "I have enough experience to know that you're a good guy."

"It's funny, and I'm sure this sounds strange coming from me, but the karma just felt right."

Audry cocked her head, curious. "Stuart Stark, that's not very analytical."

"Don't you agree?" He was suddenly nervous. *What if she didn't?*

Audry spoke with great sincerity and looked him directly in the eyes.

"I think it felt so right that we're ready to take the next step." She paused and took a deep breath. "Stu, I'd like to make waffles with you."

Breakfast brought the return of reality and discussion of the disaster in which Stu found his life. It might have been a depressing shift, but he felt a primal drive to resolve his problems now, and Audry continued to dot the conversation with knowing grins and I-can't-believe-we-just-did-that looks coupled with random, fascinated commentary on their sex.

"And this morning it was pointing straight at me, like a divining rod."

"Maybe I like you a lot."

"And maybe it's just the six-month thing. But, Stu, I want you to know that if this was just for fun, or just to find a human connection after crossing a metaphorical rope bridge together, that's okay. You have a life to sort out, and I understand that."

Practically speaking, Stu knew she was right. She was always right, although not in the annoying way most lawyers were. "Understood. First things first. Sort my life. Call you when this is all over."

"Don't make promises. Let's just enjoy some waffles together." She tossed one on his plate and poured a syrup smiley face on it. "Did you resolve any of your bigger issues after last night?"

"I think you shook some things loose, yes."

"I meant, did you put anything together from our trip to the office, silly? Do you have a cohesive theory yet?"

"Even better," Stu said. "I have a plan."

Stu stood on the porch of a modest one-and-a-half-story beige home with a recently built and still unpainted dormer that didn't match the roofline and looked like it had been added by an amateur handyman.

Rusty Baker answered the door in a white T-shirt and work pants covered with wallboard dust. He was strong, and his bulging shirt could hardly contain him. The retired detective had lifted weights like a fiend when Stu knew him, and he was stronger at sixty-five than he had been at fifty-five.

He was also the most trustworthy man Stu had ever met. It would be a delicate conversation. Rusty wouldn't do anything illegal, even for a friend. After the thirty-year struggle of enforcing the law while avoiding daily ethical pitfalls, doing the right thing was anchored deep in the man's bones.

"Hello, Rusty," Stu said.

Rusty stared for a moment; then his eyebrows arched high above his bushy moustache.

"Holy God! You're supposed to be dead."

"That's what the last guy said. And I need to keep it that way. Can I come in?"

Stu's next visit was to the Great Beyond, where he found his favorite clerk. The khaki-covered teenager looked up from the cash register, staring. He remembered Stu's face but, fortunately, not his name.

"Hey, bro! How was your trip to Alaska?"

"Well, I survived. And I wanted to thank you. The equipment you recommended was a real lifesaver."

"No problem."

"I'm in a bit of a hurry today, though. Can you find me these items?" Stu handed him a list.

The young clerk raised an eyebrow and nodded. "Totally, dude. We can start with hatchets. Right this way. . . ."

It was difficult to read Katherine's e-mails, but fascinating. Piecing together a person's life from snippets of messages was harder than he'd thought it might be, especially when she preferred the phone and texting, mediums to which he didn't have access. His wife had grown tight with Margery Hanstedt, it seemed; there were numerous banal messages between them about who in town was doing what and going to be where on which night. There were also many e-mails about the beach house. And Katherine had apparently sold an entire photo series, which seemed impressive. But there was one thing Stu had learned about e-mail in his time at the prosecutor's office: there was always one that mattered. In Katherine's case, it was written six months after he'd gone missing. To Margery.

M, I so love your life, and I think I could have my own version of it now. I don't think the thirteen-year mistake was my fault. When I chose, it was a good decision. He had it at first. But despite all my work, somehow he lost it.

Stu read it again, parsing the grammar and syntax until he was certain. There was no alternative interpretation—*I'm the thirteen-year mistake.* It was jarring—painful, even; his wife had loved a life she thought he'd give her, but not him. He had to admit that she was right, though. Whatever that life was supposed to have been, somewhere along the line he'd lost it.

Most recently, Katherine's e-mails concerned taking a few days' vacation, though it was unclear what she was taking a vacation from, because she didn't work. Stu stiffened. According to Audry, Clay was gone too.

They're together.

He waited for this to hurt as well, but strangely it didn't. He'd already seen his wife frolicking naked with a man who was the opposite of everything he'd ever stood for. It had been dramatically framed for him in the picture window of the beach house. *Like a photograph.* This time, instead of injured, he felt provoked. The Stu who absorbed insults was dead, and having another male marking in his territory wasn't a new emotional wrecking ball; it was simply motivation.

Days later Stu sent Audry to Brad Bear's studio to sniff around. She insisted that she help, and it seemed a safe chore. Besides, Brad would recognize him.

Afterward she showed Stu how to create a reasonable facsimile of University of Oregon letterhead on her home printer. It didn't need to be perfect. If its lack of authenticity survived more than a casual read, it would serve its purpose.

There were two important phone calls to make, and Stu made the first from a courtesy phone at a bowling alley. For the second, he waited another day and delivered it from a prepaid cell phone Audry had purchased for him with cash. The first call was to the law offices of Buchanan, Stark, where he left a message with Kaylee, the young-sounding receptionist. The second was to an investigative reporter with *America's Unsolved*.

Sylvia Molson's home was located in the north end of New Bedford. Stu's wheelchair-bound client lived in a nine-hundred-square-foot single-level ranch-style house she rented near Brooklawn Park. Its happy yellow paint was peeling, and the ramp up to the front door was a makeshift plywood affair. *She hasn't gotten the bulk of her money yet.*

Sylvia answered the door herself. *No caregiver.* She recognized Stu immediately, wheeled out, and hugged him until he couldn't lean over her chair any longer. He tried to immediately focus on the settlement, but she was less interested in her money than his well-being. *That's just how she rolls,* Stu thought, and he couldn't help but love her for it.

Stu hustled her inside before anyone could see them together.

"They found you!" she said, wheeling into her kitchen to boil water for tea.

"I sort of found myself."

She nodded. "That happened to me after my accident. I didn't really understand my life until it was changed so dramatically that I was forced to reexamine it. Chamomile?"

"Thank you, but I'm in too much of a hurry."

"You always were. You should try yoga. I'm practicing it again, you know."

"I didn't know that."

"I don't do as many poses, obviously, but I'm much better at the ones I still do. It's about focus. Clarity."

"Speaking of clarity, I need to explain something to you."

They spoke. There was lying involved, but it was for a good cause. Sylvia nodded, neither excited nor outraged, but simply processing. And by the end, she was the one reassuring him.

"Don't tell anyone you saw me. Not ever," Stu reminded her for the third time as he walked outside and back down her ramp. "And call Roger Rodan today. He'll know what to do."

"Be safe," Sylvia said.

Stu gave her a wry smile. "Oh, I'm done being safe."

CHAPTER 42

Stu took one last look up and down the Pope's Island dock and then threw a leg over the port gunwale of the *Iron Maiden*.

The boat was an older Hatteras, thirty-some feet in length. Stu didn't know much about boats, but he'd learned a bit during the case. The vessel had been expensive in its time, one of Bolt Construction's assets and a write-off. Aging now, it was probably still worth nearly a hundred grand. Stu had seen photos many years ago, and they were still seared into his memory, but they'd shown him nothing. And the boat had been admittedly "clean," according to Marsha Blynn, Stu's own expert witness at trial, which hadn't helped him establish corpus delicti. She allowed that it was still possible that Butz's confession was true. There'd been no blood at the house, and so the idea that he'd dismembered the body on board the vessel was somewhat believable. But Rusty Baker had privately sworn the forensics guys would have found something if Butz had cut Marti with a reciprocating saw in the boat; it was too messy not to leave spatter that an amateur cleaning would miss.

Butz had probably struggled carrying and cutting up the corpse, which was no easy thing. Dead carcasses were limp and heavy. Stu had hauled a fully dressed-out deer only a few miles and had been sore the next day. Afterward Blake had laughed and suggested he build a litter next time. And Marti Butz had been a good-size woman. Stu had memorized her vital statistics for trial. Indeed, he'd been over the details a thousand times.

But never while standing here.

Stu leaned against the *Iron Maiden*'s transom, imagining how Butz might manage a five-foot-six, one-hundred-and-seventy-eight-pound woman. Stu had always said it was difficult to think like a killer when one wasn't a killer. *But now that I am a killer, how would I manage it?* When he and Blake had dressed out their deer, they'd done it away from the cabin, just as Marti would have been taken out of Buzzards Bay. Butz would have stored her body in the cabin for the trip, of course. The cutting was then done at sea. The only place to work on a heavy corpse without the risk of getting blood on carpet, upholstery, or wood was in the open stern. Stu turned in a circle.

Unless . . .

When he'd gutted his first rabbit, Stu had stood beside a gurgling stream and held the carcass in the water. The blood had washed away even while he was cutting. It was cold as hell on the hands, but everything came out clean, and the entrails washed away to be recycled into the natural environment.

Stu peeked over the stern of the *Iron Maiden*. There was a platform that ran the entire width of the boat and sat only inches above the water. It was just wide enough to lay a body across. *Like a litter.* There was even a little door that swung open for access. *Swim platform? Do they call it that on a fishing boat?* Stu's heart raced as he pictured it: Butz crouching there with Marti's body lying essentially on the water, her blood washing away in the waves as he worked. It seemed obvious now. *Why not then?* Stu puzzled over it for a moment before it hit him. *The platform wasn't in the photos.* He was certain. The years hadn't dimmed the images in his head; the boat had been flat-backed, its name uninterrupted across the stern. Stu took a closer look at the platform. It partially covered the letter *I*. It was also brighter white than the boat, newer. The difference in shade was subtle, but it didn't quite match. *This platform is a replacement!* Stu realized. The platform that Butz had used to cut up his wife had been missing when the police searched and photographed the boat. *He'd removed it. . . .*

"Hello?"

The voice startled Stu, but he forced himself not to spin around too quickly. He didn't want to seem as nervous as he was. He looked up through his dangling hair and smiled. The young man wore a polo shirt with a logo. *A marina staffer.* Stu breathed a sigh of relief. It could have been worse, much worse. The man was young, maybe twenty. Stu had known that visiting the boat was a risk. *This guy could remember me.* But, with the goatee and his long hair, Stu looked very different from the clean-cut attorney he used to be. *Besides, it's been worth the risk.*

"Hello," Stu replied as pleasantly as possible. Then he tucked his face into his chest again and pretended to fuss with the platform.

"Need anything, sir?" It was a test. One of the staffer's duties was to watch the docks for thieves, and he didn't know Stu.

"This darn platform is loose," Stu said. "Almost killed myself stepping in. You'd think, being a construction company, we'd keep our equipment in better repair, but we've got lazy asses at Bolt just like anyone. Last employee to take her out obviously didn't stop to fix this when he brought her back in."

"Need any tools?"

"Naw. I've tightened it best I can. I'm just gonna tell Reggie Dugan. He can get it fixed if it needs anything more."

"Okay, then. Have a good day, sir."

Stu smiled to himself. "Thanks. Already am."

CHAPTER 43

Katherine knew something was wrong when Clay didn't return her calls for three days. The first time she left an upbeat message. *One day is fine,* she thought. *He'll be catching up at work.*

Two days was more suspicious, but excusable, and she left a message with a curious tone.

Three days confused her. *I'm not some first date you don't call back,* she texted. He'd held her hand during their trip, and they'd talked about the future, at least the future of their business partnership. She cursed herself for pushing him for a deeper commitment to their personal relationship. A successful partnership and intermittent physical intimacy were enough for now, she decided. She left a message expressing mild concern.

When he didn't call her back on the fourth day, she left no message and drove straight to the office.

She found reception empty. Kaylee was gone, her computer turned off, the day's mail still piled on her sleek desk. And it was only three o'clock. Katherine grabbed the mail and smacked the button for the elevator.

The ride up was smooth, but she was rattled to a stop when she reached the top. The squeaky doors opened onto a quiet hallway. Empty cubicles. None of the temporary or fake associates were working. No paralegals or secretaries. As she made her way to Clay's large office in the rear, Katherine tried to remember if it was a holiday. Without Stu and his regimented calendar, she sometimes lost track of the days.

Clay was at his desk, his back to the door. When she entered, he spun in his high-backed brown leather chair and leaped up, grabbing for his desk drawer. When he saw it was her, he relaxed and sat back down.

"Come in. Don't bother knocking or anything."

"I phoned ahead. No answer."

"I've been busy."

His tone was dismissive, and Katherine did not like it. She noticed that the glass in his hand was filled with amber-colored liquid.

"You're drinking," she said. "That's new."

"Special occasion."

"Big news?" She smiled hopefully.

"You could say that."

"I'd be happy to hear it."

"Really? Would you be happy to hear that the fucking police called me?"

Escalating tone. Ominous. Dangerous. He swiveled his chair back and forth like a pacing animal. Katherine eased into the chair across the desk from him, still clutching the mail. She chose her words carefully.

"As your partner, I share your successes *and* your challenges. I'm here to listen."

Clay rearranged himself in the chair. He looked at her, suspicious, then frowned. And, finally, he spoke.

"Seems an old friend of mine has accused me of something that happened over a decade ago during law school."

"What is it?"

"It doesn't matter. The allegation alone is bad enough."

"Who?"

"This fat fuck named Tom Franken."

"Why would he accuse you of something that long ago?"

"Some detective contacted him about this thing. So now he's trying to save his own ass by accusing me. The officer made him give a statement saying I was responsible. Typical cop trick."

"It's not true, right?"

Clay gave her a brow-lowered glare. "Right. Tom had problems in his wild youth, back when I knew him. It doesn't surprise me that he has problems now that he's a big-boy attorney. But he should know better than to cross me."

"What do we do?"

"Nothing? Deny? Wait and see?" Clay took a drink. "If anything more happens, I'll have to get my own attorney. The problem should be too old for anything to come of it, but I don't remember the statute of limitations in Oregon for a class whatever-the-hell felony."

Katherine looked around for something to occupy her while Clay brooded and the silence settled. She began to sort the letters from her lap, separating the junk and business mail atop Clay's desk, while Clay tapped his temple with an irritated finger.

After several uncomfortable moments, it was clear Clay had more to say.

"What is it?" Katherine asked. "There's something else. I can tell you're still upset."

"You know the pilot who dropped off Stu in Alaska?"

"Yes."

"Someone killed him with an ax."

"My God."

"Yeah. Ivan was one of Dugan's guys. Someone left the message about it with reception, but they didn't leave a name. I don't like it."

Katherine held up a letter from the University of Oregon.

"Open it," Clay commanded.

She did. It identified Clay. There was language about plagiarism and cheating and revoking his degree. It cited the confession from Tom Franken. At the bottom it was cc'd to the Massachusetts Bar Association. She stopped reading.

"I think you'd better look at this one."

She handed it to him, and he read, his eyes growing wider as they scanned the page. Suddenly he began slapping the letter against the desk as though he could beat it into submission.

Katherine watched anxiously. "I hope it's not serious. Is it?"

"I don't know! Can the Massachusetts Bar act on old bullshit accusations? Do they need a conviction of some sort? Can any of this even be brought up after ten years? I don't know! That's the kind of crap Stu was good at."

"How can I help?"

"You can't! I don't need you! I need your husband."

Katherine pushed the rest of the mail away, wanting nothing to do with it, but Clay eyed the stack.

"Anything else?" he asked in a low growl.

"Bulk mail. Except this." She pointed to a letter with a name above the return address. "Roger Rodan?"

"Sounds familiar." Clay leaned out and plucked it from the desk, then sliced it open with a silver letter opener and began to read.

Katherine watched his face change. It was an unpleasant process, like watching a handsome Hollywood actor turn into a snarling werewolf. He put his drink on the desk and rose from the chair.

"Are you kidding me? No! Is this a joke?"

"What?"

Clay didn't answer. Instead he repeatedly jammed the letter opener into the antique desk she'd picked out for him to celebrate the remodel. "No! No! No!"

Katherine didn't dare speak.

Clay took a deep breath then leveled a malignant stare at her over the top of the quivering opener, which jutted from the wooden desktop. "Sylvia Molson is contesting our fee, just like Stu said."

"What does that mean? Will this delay getting the money?"

"No! This won't delay the money! If Stu was right, this means the money's not coming at all!"

Katherine stared, trying to process the information. "Stu's usually right," she whispered. "You didn't tell me that he—"

"It doesn't matter what I told you! We owe Joe Roff hundreds of thousands of dollars that aren't coming."

"Oh God. I just bought the house."

"This isn't about your house, you stupid bitch! He is going to burn quarters into my goddamned face!"

Katherine's mind reeled, and the words she had to say were painful. "I could sell it."

"We can't sell this office we remodeled. We're renting it!"

Katherine felt a rising panic. "I'll talk to Joe. He likes me. I'll do whatever I need to do, like you said."

Clay took a deep breath and flopped down in the chair. For a moment he just stared at the ceiling, then he coughed up a sardonic chuckle. "Kate, Kate, Kate," he said. "You don't get it. Joe and Reggie thought it would be funny to fuck a prosecutor's wife; that was part of the agreement to advance us the money. But make no mistake: to men who can have nineteen-year-old strippers whenever they want, your middle-aged ass isn't worth three hundred thousand dollars."

CHAPTER 44

Audry stood in the doorway, regarding Stu through her bug-eye glasses. She wore a skirt with heels and a white blouse. No pajamas this time— she had a habit of throwing them on as soon as the sun went down, like a kid eager for a bedtime story. No T-shirt and panties, either. She looked like a lawyer again.

"So you're just going to leave town? Run away? That's the plan?"

"Yes," Stu lied. He found it hard to lie after so many years of seeking the truth. *I'll have to practice that,* he thought. "I've done the analysis. I can't take on an organized crime boss and his entire crew. If they want me gone, they'll get me. Worse, they'll go after people I care about, including you. It's better that they think I'm dead."

"And I can't take any of the brilliant research I've done to the police."

"Not a word."

"So you're cutting me out."

"I'm protecting you."

"I'm a big girl, remember?"

Stu smiled and tried not to stare. "You certainly are. But career crim-inals are like wild animals. They do what they do, and if you get tangled up with them, they'll do it to you. I'm already tangled. You're not."

"What about Clay?"

"I have a feeling his life is about to get very tangled. That's all you need to know."

"You tease!" Audry shook her head then softened her tone. "And Kath-erine?"

"I don't know. I haven't been able to think through all the facts and make the necessary conclusions on that one yet."

"You think too much. How do you feel?"

Stu hesitated. He'd been so busy gathering information and seeking answers that he hadn't decided how he felt. It was like a safety mecha-nism—focusing on logical solutions kept him from wanting to punch somebody in the nose.

"Angry," he said finally. The answer surprised him.

It surprised Audry, too, but she nodded. "Okay, then. Go with that."

Stu gathered his things. He found *Edwin's* in the bottom of his pack, tattered and torn. He flipped a few pages then realized he didn't need it anymore. He gave it a nostalgic pat and dropped it in the recycling bin.

When he was ready to leave, Audry hugged him. She was a whole-body hugger and squeezed like she meant it.

"This has been the best job ever," she said into his shoulder.

"You know that's a really odd thing to say, given the circumstances, right?"

"You know what I mean. This is what it's all about. I'm helping a hu-man being fix his life, not reviewing some boring precautionary contract provision for a proposed business venture. Not writing a will, just in case. You're real. And totally *not* boring."

"I'm not?"

"Nope." She finally released him from her clinch. "I've never dated someone who killed a man. Or a bear."

"Both were self-defense."

"I know."

Stu was sad when she let go. It was the closest he'd felt to a person in . . . He couldn't remember how long.

"This is for you." He handed her a thumb drive.

"What is it?"

"A list of our legitimate clients. You'll also find a signed letter of introduction for you, backdated to when I was alive. If Clay doesn't retain them for any reason, this will send them your way."

"My own law firm?"

"It's a start."

"Are you going to tell me where you're going?"

"No."

Stu turned to go. Then he paused. It felt wrong that his last word to Audry might be *no*. He was already being less than chivalrous, disappearing after sharing an intimate night. *And waffles.* Especially after a trip across a metaphorical rope bridge together. He looked back over his shoulder. Though it was dangerous to promise, it had to be okay to hope.

"But I hear Oregon is nice."

CHAPTER 45

Katherine took a long look out at Buzzards Bay from her half-furnished living room. It was a lonely view. A very nice home with no company had a way of feeling very empty. Clay had promised to call her as soon as his meeting with Roff was over. He hadn't, and it was getting late. It could mean a lot of things, none of them good.

They were criminals, Roff and Dugan. Hranic, too. She understood that now. They were the type of people her husband had prosecuted. It had been easier to switch sides than she'd thought. The line between law and outlaw was as thin as the line between Stu and Clay.

The doorbell rang with a ridiculously solemn bong that echoed about the room. Her heart skipped a beat. Clay was supposed to call, not drop by. What if it was Roff or Dugan? Or both? They burned quarters into the faces of people who owed them. Just when she was about to become the hottest middle-aged woman at the gym. She banished the thought—it was too ugly. But then she recalled that Raymond Butz worked for Dugan. Butz's wife had been made to disappear completely. Like Stu.

Oh no . . . .

Katherine took the phone with her to answer the bell, although she wasn't sure who she'd call if she needed help.

CHAPTER 46

Stu was curious to see how he would feel when he saw her. Over the previous six months he'd examined his marital situation from every angle. The disturbing facts he'd discovered upon his return added another layer of analysis, but none of it answered his most basic question about his wife. For that, he had to see her one more time.

And so he'd rung the bell and then ducked behind Katherine's perfect new row of boxwood hedges like a kid playing doorbell ditch. He peered at her through the branches, standing motionless and invisible in the brush, listening, watching, trying his best to get a sense of her karma as she stood in the doorway, staring into the night, skittish and wary. To his surprise, it took only a moment to answer his question. And the answer was *no*.

Seeing her brought none of the relief or joy he'd promised himself while in the wilderness. Instead he felt a gap. There had always been a distance between them, he realized. But he hadn't given it the weight it deserved, because it was an intangible thing, a space, a feeling, and he'd never trusted his feelings. He consulted them now, though, and found he no longer had the urge to go to her. She'd never been the right mate for him, and now she'd weakened, given up the struggle and taken the easy path, where the traps were laid. His instincts told him to walk away. It wasn't anger, exactly. It simply was not love.

He would leave Katherine to her photographs and her new friends, he decided. Audry had weaseled the name of her art patron out of Brad Bear. *Archie Brooks.* Archie was a regular in the criminal courts. Stu remembered him. He was loosely associated with Roff's crew. His purchase of her series had been orchestrated by Clay to create the illusion of success—Katherine was a sucker for flattery. Her whaling series was stacked somewhere in a waterfront warehouse, decaying right alongside the industry it portrayed.

Stu felt no guilt. They wouldn't kill her; she didn't know enough, and they could take their house back if she owed them money. They might screw her again, he supposed.

But getting screwed isn't inherently dangerous.

The money she had would run out, and soon she'd have to fend for herself. But she hadn't come from money, Stu thought, and so she should know how to survive without it. Besides, she was an excellent hostess. Perhaps Margery would give her a job in one of her restaurants.

CHAPTER 47

Stu waited inside the New England Imports warehouse. It was a large but innocuous structure—as he'd expected an organized crime figure's building might be—with a corrugated blue metal roof, two big white garage doors, and a man-door. It sat at the dark end of the wharf on the New Bedford side of the bridge, wedged between similar dockside monoliths that were equally lifeless. Old fishing nets hung on the outside below the rusted metal NE IMPORTS sign, giving the building a neglected look. *Like one of Katherine's photos.*

The single huge storage area was nearly empty—no bales of marijuana, chopped cars, or crates of tommy guns. Just a sloop nestled in a maintenance cradle, and boat parts stacked on shelves along the walls. Every sound echoed around the open space, giving it a ghostly feel. The building's interior office was a small cubical built against the wall on one side. Thin partitions made up its other three walls, and it jutted out into the massive room like a perfectly square tumor. Stu crouched in its shadow.

He found he preferred crouching over sitting. It kept him alert, and he'd been doing it for more than an hour, motionless, and listening to the creaks and groans of the wood walls and metal roof. The unmistakable skitter of a rat caught his ear. Just one. In the rafters somewhere above. But it wasn't his prey tonight. He kept his head cocked toward the exterior door. He'd hear it open. He'd also hear any human footsteps on the concrete and know the exact distance to the shoes that produced them as they approached. Stu closed his eyes and just listened. He was comfortable waiting, patient and calmer than he had any right to be.

The rasp and click of the bolt on the man-door alerted him. There was an effort to turn the knob slowly, quietly, but it didn't matter. Stu heard it as clearly as if someone had knocked. He didn't move, but simply opened his eyes, watching from the shadows and listening. The footsteps were coming. One pair.

Good.

He'd left a single torchiere lamp lit inside the office, on the other side of the thin wall. The remainder of the warehouse was dark. It would lend his visitor a false sense of security to approach in darkness, Stu thought, and the light in the office would draw him like a moth.

A shadow approached. Stu heard the footsteps and quick nervous breaths. Still, he didn't move. Instead he watched from his hiding place as a human silhouette walked right past him and peeked into the open office.

In the darkness, Clay Buchanan didn't see the wire loop that encircled the upper portion of the door. As Stu had estimated, his partner was just over six feet tall, and his head fit neatly through it. Stu raised the old wooden oar he'd found leaning against the wall and slapped it against the concrete with an impressive *bang*. Clay leaped forward like a spooked rabbit, and the snare tightened around his neck.

The wire line on the back of the snare was twisted over the doorframe with just enough slack that Clay could turn in place but couldn't take more than one step in any direction. He spun and yanked, jamming one finger up between his neck and the wire, but he was unable to pry it loose.

Stu stepped from the shadows.

"Don't struggle. It'll just get tighter. And be careful not to lose your footing or you'll hang yourself."

Clay turned and stared. It took a moment before he could speak. "Stu?" He wheezed.

"Hi." Stu pushed past him and walked behind the desk, where he sat on the chair. "Having a bad week?"

"What the hell's going on?" Clay's throat was constricted so that he sounded a bit like he'd inhaled helium.

"I thought it was obvious. I'm back from my adventure."

Stu could see Clay's mind churning. *An animal in a trap is still dangerous,* he reminded himself.

"Thank God, it's you. I thought I was dead."

"Funny, that's what everyone keeps saying about *me*."

"I don't know what you think, buddy," Clay said, "but I can help you figure it out."

"I think you had an idiot pilot leave me out in the wilderness to die so you could collect the full Molson settlement. And I think you're laundering money for midlevel organized crime figures."

Clay had to think for a moment. But his response was still impressively quick. "No. It was them, not me," he said. "I had no idea they were going to leave you out there. My God."

"Oh? You didn't know Dugan was a crook when you brought him to the firm? I don't find that credible."

Clay licked his lips. "They had their hooks in me way back when we were prosecutors. I was drinking, spending, gambling. I owed them."

If you live among predators for long, they will eventually eat you.

Clay continued talking, fast and high-pitched. "They had dirt on me, man, even then. It killed my career."

It was Stu's turn to think. "You gave their crew low bail and plea bargains when you were a DA, didn't you?"

"Yes."

"Jeezus. And Malloy figured it out and asked you to quit voluntarily to avoid the scandal."

"Dugan approached me again this year. He said he wanted to do business, legitimate business. I didn't know they were still after you for Butz."

"Whoa, whoa, whoa! What?"

"I figured it out later, after you were gone."

"Talk. Now."

"Butz is one of Dugan's men. He knocked his wife around one night, and she threatened to go to the cops with everything she knew about their crew. That's why they killed her. Not because of some craft store bill."

Stu's head spun. It made sense. The three-hundred-dollar financial motive had always been weak. *Was I wrong all these years?* He hadn't ever seriously considered how the murderer *felt* about him. He'd just been doing his job, after all. He hadn't even used the man's first name, because *Ray* made Butz sound like someone's wisecracking uncle at the barbeque grill, while calling him simply *defendant* during trial was an effective prosecutor technique to depersonalize him to the jury. *Like a widget.*

Accused men take that shit personally, Blake had said. And Stu had pursued Butz despite a historic lack of evidence. He groaned. It was a plausible explanation—he'd unwittingly pissed off a member of the local mob.

Clay gave him a sympathetic look. "Are you ready to cut me down?"

"It's a simple matter of untwisting the wire."

Clay looked up and, after deciphering the trap's elementary setup, released himself. He stepped out of the office, and Stu rose to follow him.

Stu found himself standing face-to-face with his partner in the huge empty space of the warehouse. Dim light from the office lamp leaked out, casting an oblong halo around them, illuminating them like two boxers in a ring.

"You had me scared there, Stuey," Clay said.

"I had to test you."

"Did I pass?"

"So far."

"Great. Now we can take care of this mess. Have you called the police yet?"

"Nope. Came to see you first."

"Then who else knows you're alive?"

"No one." The lie came more easily than it had with Audry.

"Not Katherine?"

"Just you."

"Thank God." Clay nodded, then reached inside his new and very expensive-looking jacket.

Stu felt many emotions when his partner pulled out the .357. Strangely, disappointment was the foremost.

Clay leveled the gun at him. "I'm sorry, buddy."

Stu wondered momentarily why people apologized before killing other human beings. Then Clay pulled the trigger.

The dry *click* echoed in the empty warehouse. Clay tried again, then stared at the gun as though it had magically transformed into a pigeon.

"It's dangerous to keep a loaded gun in your desk drawer," Stu said. "I did my homework, Clay. Did you? No? You never do."

"Wait! I didn't mean—"

"To kill me? I wasn't sure before, but I am now, beyond a reasonable doubt. It was you. They might have gone along with it, maybe even welcomed it, but you put the hit on me. You initiated this."

Clay brooded, then smirked. "So what are you gonna do, Stuey, go to the police? You've got no proof. This doesn't come back to me. The only witness is dead."

"I know. Perfect crime, eh? If we were in court, you'd be right, for a change. But we're not."

Stu reached inside his own tattered coat and removed the shiny new hatchet he'd purchased at the Great Beyond.

Clay's dark eyes went wide. He dropped the empty gun with a heavy *clunk* and put his hands up. "Wait a minute. You can't—"

"It looks like we're at a bit of an impasse here. I don't really have a choice. You called me a pussy in front of everyone. You tried to kill me. Then you took my woman. What kind of man would I be if I let those insults stand?"

"I don't know what you mean."

"Did you stick your dick in my wife, or didn't you?"

"I thought you were dead!"

"I'm sure you did."

"This isn't you, Stuart. You're a rational, reasonable, law-abiding guy."

"I'm not the same goddamned guy."

"But you're not a killer."

"I killed a bear."

"You did?"

"And a pilot."

"Ivan—"

"I see you knew him." Stu thumbed the blade on the hatchet. "Do you know how to field dress a deer? I do."

"Don't! They'll catch you."

"How? I'm dead. Besides, I have a feeling your new friends will handle the cleanup. They won't leave a mess in their warehouse. I'm guessing they'll take you for a little trip on the *Iron Maiden*."

Clay's eyes darkened again. "Fine. You try to kill me. But know this: you're not man enough to take me without an unfair advantage." He pointed at the hatchet.

Stu frowned. Even in the end, his manhood was being challenged. He could kill his rival, but it wasn't enough. He needed to defeat him in a head-on fight. No tricks. No traps. No tools. Just claws and teeth. *Like wolves.* Stu turned and hurled the hatchet into a nearby post. Clay stared, his eyebrows arching.

And then Stu was on him.

They slammed together with their arms outstretched, snarling in the pale light of the torchiere lamp. Then they went to the ground, struggling, groping for throats and kneeing groins. Without any formal training, it was grunting, sweaty work. Clay gouged one of Stu's eyes so that he couldn't see out of it, and Stu bent Clay's little finger until it folded backward with a muffled *snap*.

It was also exhausting and, after wrestling desperately for minutes that seemed like hours, Stu began to sense Clay getting tired. Stu's shovel-hardened shoulders flexed, and his sturdy hiking legs found leverage. He forced Clay back and, inexorably, began to impose his will, shoving his partner up against a post where he might be able to pound his head against the rough wood.

Then suddenly they separated.

It was a move born of desperation; Clay knew he was losing. He was out of shape. *Soft.* He kicked free and scrambled to his feet, pulling him-self up on the post, where the hatchet hung waiting. Clay yanked it free and raised it over his head, his pinky dangling at a grotesque angle.

Stu glanced about, but the only thing within reach was the unloaded pistol. He scooped it up and held it out like a cross to ward off evil. Un-fortunately, he'd made certain it was unloaded; he'd even poured several layers of super glue over the firing pin to help ensure it would be useless to Clay. He hadn't considered that he might have to use it himself. He turned the piece over in his hand, his heart still hammering in his chest from the battle he'd finally faced head-on, and lost.

Hammering . . .

Clay coughed up a laugh. "This is classic," he said, panting. "We're law-yers. We're hired guns. But you're out of bullets, buddy. You're shootin' blanks. You're an empty gun, Stu. And I've had you pegged since—"

The .357 struck Clay in the side of the head so hard that he rocked backward and had to pinwheel his arms in the air for balance. Stu grabbed him by the shirt and broke his nose with the butt of the pistol on his next blow.

The hatchet came down, but Clay was unsteady and Stu ducked in-side the swing, twisting so that the blade struck him behind the shoulder instead of in the head. He felt it bite and carve a chunk of his flesh from his scapula, but the gambit had been worth the price. Clay's wild attack brought him close and exposed his throat. Stu didn't hesitate; he clamped his teeth onto Clay's neck, crushing his windpipe and tearing his flesh, bathing both their chests in blood.

Stu clung to his partner, pinning his arms with a bear hug to prevent further hatchet mischief while Clay fought for air. His own injured shoul-der screamed, but he'd known pain and survived it for months; he could damn well brave it for a few more seconds now.

There was an awkward silence between them as they stood in the bloody embrace. It felt odd hugging. Clay struggled to get loose, but Stu found he was the stronger animal. He felt Clay weakening. And then, finally, the struggle ceased. Stu held on for a moment longer to ensure it was over, then let Clay fall to the ground, limp, and stood over his carcass.

EPILOGUE

The courtroom in Eugene, Oregon, was nearly empty; just a few pro se defendants in street clothes waiting to enter pleas to minor charges.

The judge squinted at Stu. "You've indicated that you're from Portland, Mr."—he checked the pleadings—"Stuart."

"Yes," Stu lied; he'd gotten better at it. "And I studied at U of O right here in town. Go, Ducks."

"Fine. What's your business down here in Lane County?"

"I have an affidavit from my client's former wife," Stu reported, cutting through the preliminaries; the tired-looking judge was near the end of his workday and obviously eager to move things along. "The case is almost seven years old, and she's agreed that the no-contact order can be dropped."

"What about the other victim, the professor with the broken nose?"

A young assistant district attorney in tan slacks and navy sport coat cut in. "That witness couldn't be located."

Stu continued. "He was removed by the university for misconduct with multiple female students, which was the motive for my client's admittedly inexcusable assault here." He nudged Blake, who stood beside him freshly shaved and wearing a collared shirt Stu had loaned him.

"I know I shouldn't have hit him," Blake said on cue. "I was mad. And I'm sorry."

The judge nodded and turned back to Stu. "Anything to add, counsel?"

"The man standing before you screwed up a long time ago. He's come back to Oregon for a second chance." When the judge didn't blink, Stu added one last comment. "He also saved my life."

The judge's eyebrows arched slightly, the most emotion he'd shown in the hour Stu had been waiting for Blake's case to be called. "And you haven't seen your daughter for seven years, sir?"

"No, sir," Blake said.

"Your honor," Stu said, "I've arranged to have her waiting outside the door. They can be reunited right now if you sign that order."

Five minutes later, in the hallway outside, Stu stepped away to give Blake private time with his daughter. He pulled out a prepaid cell phone. There were two missed calls.

The first was from his favorite Massachusetts attorney, who had just passed the bar. He smiled. The message was an answer to his cross-country invitation to visit Oregon for a week to celebrate. An enthusiastic *Yes!*

Good karma.

The second call also had a Massachusetts area code, but no message. Stu called that number back.

"Rusty. You called?"

"Something's happened to your partner. No one has seen him for a week, and the PD is searching warehouses owned by some serious assholes. Doesn't sound good. I thought you should know."

Stu waited an appropriate amount of time to appear surprised. "So now we've both disappeared?"

"Yep. Tell me it's not related, pal."

"I can't. All the more reason for me to stay dead. Thanks for keeping your ear to the ground for me."

"Sure. And those vultures from *America's Unsolved* are back. They're all over Malloy about Clay's connection to this Roff guy out of Providence. Apparently, they got a tip about exchanges of favors while Clay was still at the DA's office."

"Really? I'm curious."

"They've made a public disclosure request for all documents related to plea bargains and bail amounts given to Roff's known associates for the last twelve years. Malloy is scrambling to distance himself, but he either admits he knew and looks like he covered it up by letting Clay quietly resign, or he says he didn't know and comes across as ignorant of corruption in his own office. It's a potential election-loser for him either way. Now Malloy will have to go after Roff. In the meantime, *America's Unsolved* is ruining his career."

"Crazy stuff, man."

"Yeah. Glad I'm off the job these days; there's a lot of shit going down here all of a sudden. By the way, they found the original exterior platform from the transom of the *Iron Maiden* stored in one of those warehouses."

"The *Iron Maiden*? Whoa, that takes me back. But that boat didn't have a platform as far as I remember."

"Apparently, it did. I heard they took it to the lab."

"What does that mean?"

"You're the one who told me they just need a scintilla of corroborative evidence to refile the case. Hell, you had to tell me what the word *scintilla* meant."

"Huh. Well, Malloy will have to try that one without me this time. And that's too bad about Clay."

"You don't sound sad."

Stu detected a hint of suspicion in the retired officer's voice. The man was wise and still a detective at heart.

"I'm sad that he chose his friends poorly. Sounds like he messed with the wrong guy. Do they have any evidence to identify a suspect?"

"Nah. Clay is just flat-out missing. Could be a no-body homicide."

"Yeah, those are tough."